1 SUN

Saddle and Bound

Valentina Iania

Copyright © 2024 by Valentina Iania

The moral right of the author has been asserted.

All characters and events in this publication are fictitious. Any resemblance to real persons, living or dead, is purely coincidental.

All rights reserved.
No part of this publication may be reproduced, stored in a retrieval system, or transmitted in any form or by any means, electronic, mechanical, photocopying, recording, or otherwise, without the prior written permission of the author, except in the case of brief quotations embodied in critical reviews and certain other non-commercial uses permitted by copyright law.

Cover design by Lino Tricarico (Dalkanwolf)

About the author

Valentina Iania is an author of small-town, cowboy, and spicy romance, making her debut with *Saddle and Bound*, the first book in the *Sunrise Ranch* series. In addition to her small-town romances, Valentina is currently working on a diverse range of series, including sports, college, dark, and millionaire romance. No matter the genre, her stories are filled with intense chemistry, strong characters, and thrilling, sexy journeys.

Valentina's shared love of books began on her Bookstagram platform, where she connected with fellow readers before pursuing her lifelong dream of writing. You can connect with her on Instagram (@valentinaianiaauthor) and TikTok, where she shares her latest updates and writing adventures.

With many more series in the works, Valentina invites you to join her as she continues to craft captivating stories that will keep you turning the pages.

About the book

Saddle and Bound is the first book in the *Sunrise Ranch* series. While it can be enjoyed as a standalone, I highly recommend reading the entire *Sunrise Ranch* series to fully experience the world and its characters. This series will be part of a larger collection of interconnected series, featuring characters from *Sunrise Ranch* in their own stories. Additionally, there will be special themed books for events like Halloween, the holidays, Valentine's Day, and more, allowing you to dive deeper into the world with each release.

Rosie
The rules were simple... keep love out of the picture, get through the summer as quickly as possible, and return to my life.
But then I met Alex. The arrogant, sexy cowboy with a smile that could melt any woman... and it turns out, I'm no exception.
When I leave my city life behind to spend the summer at Sunrise Ranch, I expect to find peace, quiet... maybe a little time to relax. What I get instead is Alex. He's arrogant, stubborn, and determined to push all my buttons. And trust me, he does.
We're constantly at odds with each other: fighting, teasing, challenging each other like it's some sort of game. He's the most annoying person I've ever met. His worst trait? He's damn hot.

I'm definitely not his type. And I'm not interested. But the more we argue, the harder it becomes to ignore what's building between us.

I'm only here temporarily, and I have my reasons for keeping my distance — very far away from him.

Alex
Staying focused on my work has never been an issue. Until she showed up.

Rosie is damn out of place with her fancy outfits. And she's so damn tempting.

I can't stop thinking of all the ways I could make her lose her mind.

I can't stop thinking about her, period.

She drives me wild. In every possible way. Every sharp remark, every little challenge we throw at each other, only makes me crave more.

I want her closer. With me. Beneath me.

I try to keep my distance, but the more I do, the more I want her. Her lips. Her fire. Her heart.

I want it all.

Tropes
- Enemies to lovers
- Opposites attract
- Forced proximity
- Secret heart
- Slow burn
- Wild cowboy/ City girl
- He teach her

This book is for me, as I've decided to follow my dreams, and for all those who haven't done it yet. Do it! It doesn't matter where you are in life…find the time and the courage to make your dreams come true, believe in yourself, and think about yourself.

Chapter 1

Rosie

"Service announcement: a pair of red panties has been found. The owner can go to the console to retrieve it."

I listen absentmindedly from my lounger under the sun. My groggy brain takes a few seconds to process the announcement. A few more seconds to realize I could be the owner... but you know that annoying sixth sense that tells you something, only for your reason to step in and warn you about your own paranoia? Well, my reason convinces me that I'm just being paranoid.

But still... that nagging feeling refuses to let me relax.

"Rosie, I think these are definitely yours," Lexy announces, just as irritating as my inner voice. As always, she gives voice to her thoughts without thinking.

I open my eyes to find Lexy standing in front of me, holding up a pair of red lace panties, her mischievous grin making my blood rush to my cheeks. I can't quite process the absurdity of the situation. "What are they doing there?" I stammer, trying to maintain some composure.

"I got them from the DJ at the console," Lexy explains, chuckling. "He said they were found on the path leading to the stables. Seems like your style."

I hear a male laugh behind me and turn around abruptly. Alex, the ranch's riding instructor, approaches with an amused expression. "Ah, so that's where it ended up," he says, looking at me with a sly smile. "I found them while checking on the horses and took them to the console."

I feel like I'm about to explode with a mix of embarrassment and anger. "Yes, it's mine," I reply curtly, trying to sound neutral. "Thanks for finding them."

Alex raises an eyebrow, still amused. "Are you sure they're yours?" he asks, holding the panties just out of my reach.

"Alex, stop being childish," Valentina intervenes, trying to suppress a laugh. "Give Rosie her panties."

Finally, Alex hands them to me with a theatrical flourish, and I snatch them from his hand, stuffing them into my bag with as much dignity as I can muster. Lexy keeps laughing, while I do my best to avoid Alex's piercing gaze.

"How funny," I mutter, though my tone is anything but amused.

"You know, Rosie," Alex says, his voice relaxed in that way that drives me crazy, "you could loosen up a little. We're not in Los Angeles here. No one's judging you."

I look at him, biting back the sharp response I'm dying to give. "Thanks for the advice," I reply with a tight smile. "But I think I know how to relax."

Alex grins again, tilting his head slightly. "We'll see," he says simply, before walking away, leaving me with a mix of embarrassment and frustration.

Chapter 2

Rosie

One day before

After nearly 24 hours of travel, with intercontinental flights and multiple layovers, I feel as though I've crossed not just an ocean, but an entire universe. Los Angeles feels like a distant memory as my dad's car winds along the twisting road leading to Sunrise Ranch, nestled on the outskirts of a small town in southern Italy.

My eyes, heavy with jet lag, scan the landscape outside the window: rolling hills, centuries-old olive groves, hay bales, and golden wheat fields stretching as far as the eye can see. It's a world completely different from the skyscrapers and constant traffic I'm used to. Occasionally, my dad's red Fiat passes people on horseback, tractors, and the typical Ape motorcycles on the road.

It feels like I've not only changed world... but also era. Everything seems so absurd and strange...

I absentmindedly run a hand through my hair, trying to tame the red locks that the journey has tousled. I try not to think about how disastrous I must look. The anxiety, which I tried to suppress during the long flight, now returns with force. Three months. Three whole months in this remote village. How will I survive? My job at the marketing agency, my routine, my life... everything put on hold for my father's wedding. Thankfully, I managed to take a little time off from work, using up some vacation days I'd accumulated but never taken, along with a bit of remote work. At least my career is safe, for now.

"We're almost there," Dad announces, his voice betraying a mixture of fatigue and excitement. "Val and Lexy can't wait to finally meet you in person."

I nod, trying to appear casual and happy while struggling to smooth out the wrinkles in my crumpled suit. I suddenly feel out of place dressed like this. I hadn't even considered that my office attire and sky-high heels might make me feel even more self-conscious. Usually, I like to dress well. I like being impeccable and elegant. I don't mind other types of clothing... but I simply never find myself in situations that call for more casual attire. What I do dislike is feeling sticky, not having perfectly styled hair, and not having flawless makeup.

"How much longer?" I ask, my voice hoarse from fatigue.

"Just about ten minutes," Dad replies. "You'll see, the ranch is beautiful. You'll like it."

I sigh, resting my head against the window. The humid heat of southern Italy seeps into the car despite the air conditioning, making me long for California's dry climate.

When the car finally stops in front of an imposing gate with the words **SUNRISE RANCH**, I realize we've arrived.

We pass through the impressive wrought-iron gate, and as the car proceeds along the driveway lined with towering pines and firs, I can't help but look around, trying to absorb every detail. The trees flanking the entrance open up, revealing a breathtaking landscape that leaves me speechless.

To our right, a vast olive grove extends as far as the eye can see, the silver leaves of the olive trees dancing in the light breeze. To the left, I glimpse a lush orchard, branches laden with ripe peaches and golden apricots. The air is infused with their sweet scent, mixed with the pungent aroma of wild rosemary.

Further ahead, I spot an enclosure where several horses graze peacefully. Their sleek coats shine under the sun, and the sound of their occasional neighs breaks the silence of the countryside.

As the car advances, I notice several wooden cabins scattered across the property. Some are hidden among holm oak groves, others overlook small, thriving vegetable gardens.

Each structure seems to have its own unique character, inviting exploration.

In the distance, a field of hay bales creates a golden expanse stretching to the horizon. Spots of vivid red dot the field on the sides—wild poppies, I imagine—adding splashes of color to the landscape.

As we approach the end of the driveway, I finally see it: the main house. It's a limestone farmhouse, imposing yet welcoming, with olive-green shutters and a red-tiled roof. A veranda shaded by a pergola of flowering wisteria extends along the facade, promising a cool retreat from hot summer days.

The car stops in front of the house, and for a moment, I remain motionless, overwhelmed by the beauty surrounding me. Sunrise Ranch is more than I could have ever imagined: a corner of paradise that leaves me speechless. At this moment, overwhelmed by everything around me, I forget all that was bothering and annoying me earlier.

A group of young people is waiting for us in the garden. Two girls run toward us.

"Robert! Rosie! You're finally here!"

The shorter of the two is a bundle of energy, with long, wavy light brown hair and bright hazel eyes. The other is her exact opposite: tall and with a rebellious air accentuated by piercings and tattoos.

I get out of the car, stumbling on my heels. "Nice to meet you," I say, trying to smile despite my nervousness.

"We're so happy you're here!" exclaims the one with long, wavy hair—she must be Valentina. I'm immediately swept into a hug and receive two kisses on the cheeks. The other girl does the same, but with less energy. Lexy... if I remember correctly.

"How was the trip?" someone asks.

I'm about to answer when a male voice makes me turn abruptly.

"Hey, princess, careful not to break an ankle!"

I find myself standing face-to-face with a man who looks like he's walked straight out of a forbidden fantasy.

He's tall, broad-shouldered, and muscular, with long brown hair that falls in unruly waves, framing a face almost too handsome to belong to reality. That crooked smile he's wearing, equal parts maddening and devastatingly sexy, hits me like a bolt of lightning.

His deep brown eyes, sharp and unashamedly confident, are framed by lashes so thick they might as well be illegal. A light dusting of scruff shadows his strong jawline, adding a rugged edge to a face that's already doing far too much damage to my self-control.

He's dressed in a snug, well-worn tank top that clings to every ridge of his sculpted torso, leaving absolutely nothing to the imagination. His broad chest commands attention, and the way his body narrows to a lean, powerful waist is downright scandalous. Paired with faded, low-slung jeans and mud-caked boots, he exudes an effortless, rugged charm that feels both untamed and dangerously attractive.

Pull yourself together, Rosie, I scold myself fiercely.

I fight to look away, but the heat climbing my face betrays me. My thoughts are spiraling wildly, every nerve in my body seeming to betray my better judgment.

Why on earth is my mind entertaining such inappropriate thoughts about a total stranger, one who already feels like an absolute pain? *It's probably just the exhaustion from traveling,* I tell myself. But even as I try to rein in my thoughts, I can feel my irritation brewing.

I don't even know his name yet, but somehow, I already know one thing for sure, I'm going to argue with him, and I'm going to enjoy every second of it.

"Excuse me?" I reply, feeling irritation rising.

"I'm Alex," he introduces himself, ignoring my tone. "If you want to survive here, I suggest you leave those stilts in your suitcase."

Before I can respond, another guy intervenes.

"Don't mind him. Alex doesn't know how to behave. I'm Chris, Val's boyfriend. Welcome!"

I smile weakly, grateful for the interruption. In the following minutes, I'm overwhelmed by a sea of names and faces. Fran, Diego, Aurora... all so welcoming, so different from the anonymous crowd I'm used to. After the energy of the group of young people, Maria, my father's future wife, welcomes me with her usual kindness and hyperactivity that reminds me of her older daughter, Valentina, or Val, as they apparently call her.

"Come, I'll show you your room, you must be tired," says Val, taking me by the arm after all the introductions... which will take me a lifetime to remember.

As we head toward the house, I find myself standing next to Alex, who's almost blocking the entrance. Val says something to him, but I don't hear a word because I'm too distracted.

He shifts slightly, but not enough to avoid brushing against me as I try to follow Val.

"Hey, Rosie," he says softly, so close I can almost feel his warm breath on my skin. What I do feel very clearly, though, is the way he says my name, irritatingly sexy in a way that makes it hard for me to breathe properly. "Are you sure you don't want to go for a horseback ride? It might help you relax. That is, if you can ride, of course."

I also catch the scent of him, and despite his worn clothes, he doesn't smell bad. In fact... I discover, with some horror, that I actually like the way he smells.

Leather and pine.

Of course, I can't seem to come up with a response. I just shoot him the most cowboycidal look I can manage.

Damn it... what's wrong with you, Rosie? You're not that kind of girl!

Despite my mental scolding and my irritation at Alex fucking cowboy, I can't help but notice how the setting sun lights up his hair, casting an almost... *no, Rosie, focus!*

I enter the house while wondering how I'll survive this summer. The feeling from before returns, and I can't help but think that this earthly paradise and that annoying guy with muddy boots have just disrupted my perfectly organized world.

Summer has just begun, and with it, a new adventure that I'm not yet ready to face. I'm not the adventurous type. I'm the type who needs routine and to keep everything under control. Yet, somewhere deep inside me... I like this place. Somewhere inside me, I feel electrified, intrigued, curious... all emotions that I'm not used to feeling and that I probably don't even know how to truly recognize... so I take all these thoughts and lock them away neatly in a corner in the antechamber of my brain. It's easier to feel irritation than to ask too many complicated questions.

My room is small but cozy, with a large window overlooking the fields. I hear the chirping of birds and the rustle of wind through the trees. But above all, I hear the incessant song of cicadas. *Careful not to break an ankle*, I mutter to myself, finally taking off my heels and massaging my sore feet.

Who does he think he is? I can't believe I ever thought he was attractive.

It might help you relax. That is, if you can ride, of course

Ugh. So irritating. So smug. So obnoxious.

I decide not to waste another thought on him, but I promise myself that next time, I'll have a sharp comeback ready.

It's going to be a hellish few months.

I close my eyes and let the exhaustion take over.

Alex

I step back, but I can't resist taking one last glance at Rosie. My heart nearly skipped a beat when she got out of the car. Who would have guessed Robert had such a sexy daughter?

Seriously, this girl doesn't even seem real. With that cascade of red waves, those big brown eyes, her little upturned nose dusted with freckles, and those full lips... lips I'd better not think about.

But trying not to think about her lips, my mind goes straight to her body.

Damn! What made her think it was a good idea to dress like that on a ranch? That ass wrapped in that tight skirt is mouthwatering. And that white blouse? I could pop those buttons off in a second.

Damn it! I almost disgust myself.

Since when do I think about colleagues' daughters like this? And since when do fancy girls turn me on? Damn, it pisses me off! She's so out of place here with her trendy clothes and refined manners. The contrast with the rustic ranch environment is obvious, and I couldn't help but crack that joke. The annoyed look she gave me was... damn exciting!

Wait... why am I moving away? I make another stupid decision and place myself near the front door, knowing Rosie will pass by soon. I don't know what's come over me with this redhead.

I don't know why, but there's an odd pleasure in teasing her... even though I don't even know her.

"Are you already embarrassing our guest?" Val asks, stopping me and walking up with an amused smile and raised eyebrow. Rosie is trailing behind her, of course... in those ridiculous shoes.

"Just a little harmless fun," I reply, raising my hands in surrender, but mentally plotting to drive her crazy.

Drive her crazy?! Now that thought's taking me down a dangerous path... no, best not to think about that. She's definitely not my type. And I'm pretty sure I'm not hers. Not even close. And I still can't figure out why my mind keeps wandering about this redhead I don't even know. I've literally just seen her.

Valentina shakes her head, laughing. "Alex, sometimes you're really just a big kid."

I turn to look at Rosie, flash a grin, and wink at her. The fiery look she gives me is intense. I'm really getting under her skin... and I like it.

Rosie's trying hard to look relaxed, but I notice the tension in her eyes. Her movements are stiff, and she's scanning the place, almost like she's trying to figure out where she is and how to fit in.

A sly smile creeps up on my lips as I realize I really do enjoy poking at Rosie, getting under her skin a little. It's a way to shake her out of her stiff, perfectionist attitude. There's something irresistibly fun about watching her try to keep control while I work to push her out of her comfort zone.

This is going to be one hell of a summer...

For professional reasons, I can't help but analyze every little gesture and movement. And this little princess isn't being honest. The short, clipped answers and forced smiles tell me she's hiding something, maybe a side of herself she doesn't want to show. It's like there's an internal battle going on between the Rosie who's used to LA and the one she could discover here, in this remote ranch. I wonder what she's trying to protect and why she seems so determined to keep control.

My musings could be entirely wrong, though, because I'm totally distracted by that damn redhead walking past just now, way too close, Because, being the massive dickhead that I am, I didn't give her enough space. And I've got to figure out how to not show everyone the damn erection I'm sporting right now.

Especially with Robert, her dad, not too far away.

As I try to mentally scold myself and compose myself... my voice just slips out on its own. Well done, brain-mouth coordination!

"Hey, Rosie," I say, stepping closer with a sly grin. "You sure you don't want to take a ride? It might help you relax a bit... that is, if you know how to ride."

She shoots me a deadly glare, but I see a spark of challenge in her eyes.

Perfect.

Exactly what I was hoping for. There's something thrilling about going toe-to-toe with someone so stubborn. Now I really need to get out of sight and do something about this... situation.

The day ends without further incident, but Rosie continues to occupy my thoughts. There's something about her that challenges me, provokes me, and definitely excites me WAY too much. One thing's for sure, though: this summer is not going to be boring.

Chapter 3

Alex

Today

The early afternoon sun beats strongly on my back as I walk towards the training corral. The familiar smell of earth, horse sweat, and leather envelops me, awakening my senses. This is my domain, the place where my passion transforms into art.

I carefully observe Tornado, the young thoroughbred I'm training this week. His bright eyes and attentive ears tell me he's ready for the session. I enter the corral with fluid and confident movements, immediately establishing my presence. Tornado looks at me, curious but cautious.

I begin the warm-up routine, guiding the horse with vocal commands and subtle gestures. Every movement, every command is the result of years of experience and a deep understanding of equine psychology. I feel Tornado's energy flowing through the lead rope, like a silent conversation between us.

As I work, I'm aware of every muscle of the horse, of every change in his posture. This is what I love about my job: the delicate dance between man and animal, the trust that builds slowly, the satisfaction of seeing a horse grow and learn under my guidance.

The ranch pulses with life around me: the rhythm of hooves on packed earth, the distant neighing of other horses, the rustle of wind through the pines. This is my world, where I truly feel alive.

Meanwhile, I can't get the image of Rosie out of my head. So out of place, so arrogant in her attempt to maintain control. It amuses me, in a way. And, of all things, I can't stop thinking about her in a bikini... truly illegal. This morning she wore a blue bikini that fit her perfectly. It wasn't too revealing... it was simple. But that girl is a walking bombshell without even trying.

As if I need more fuel for my fantasies...

Since Rosie arrived at the ranch, I've had almost more erections than in the last year. I've lost count of how many times I've jerked off thinking about her.

This is seriously annoying.

I need to get her out of my head... but she's damn near everywhere! This morning, I even found her underwear. Apparently, she doesn't even know how to hang laundry. I found them on the path, for crying out loud. She's definitely used to some high-tech apartment dryer, like the princess she is. And those panties were damn delicious, and I was really tempted to keep them... but when I went to the beach and saw Rosie looking so sexy, the challenge and irritation pulled me right back in.

As I adjust the saddle on one of the horses, I hear a movement behind me and turn. Rosie is walking towards me, with an expression that exudes determination and, perhaps, a bit of anger. She's wearing one of her damn blouses and a fluttering skirt. God... this woman is trying to kill me!

"Hey, cowboy," she says with a sharp tone. "I thought I'd find some peace and quiet here, but apparently that's not possible."

I raise an eyebrow. "Oh, sorry if my work is disturbing you," I reply, with a note of sarcasm in my voice. "Can I help you in any way?"

"You can stop acting superior," she retorts, crossing her arms over her chest. "I'm not here to be made fun of."

Fuck. My brain can only process how those tits lift and the fact that she just said "made."

I swallow and try to remember how to speak.

"Making fun of you? Princess, I'm just getting started," I say with a smirk, deliberately letting my eyes roam over her. I have to try not to focus too much on those tits, damn it. They're just perfect. Not too big, not too small. Exactly the way I like them. "But if you can't handle a little teasing, maybe you should head back to the city where things are... softer."

She stares at me for a moment, her eyes flashing with anger and challenge. "I'm not here to entertain you, Alex. I'm here for my father's wedding, and I have a million things to do."

I smile, leaning against the corral fence. "You know, Rosie, maybe you should learn to relax a bit. You're not in the city anymore. Life is different here."

"I don't need your advice," she snaps back, raising her chin. "I know very well how to manage my time."

I look at her, amused by her stubbornness. "Really? Because so far you just seem like a stressed-out city girl on vacation."

Rosie grits her teeth, her face flushed with anger. "Maybe I'm just totally irritated by you."

I smile even more. "Well, I'm glad to take up so much space in your thoughts."

If only you knew how much space you take up in mine...

She doesn't respond, turning abruptly and walking away with determined steps. I watch her go, head high and taking long strides. How she manages to walk these dirt paths in those high heels is a mystery.

"Hey princess... I think the mud is ruining your fashion show. Are boots or hiking shoes not cool enough for you?"

She turns but doesn't deign to give me a response. She makes a rude gesture and resumes walking.

"Those gestures don't suit a little princess," I shout back. I see her walk even faster.

Have I mentioned how much I enjoy making Rosie Thorne angry?

Chapter 4

Alex

Chris: Hey Alex, you got something to tell us?
Diego: Maybe about some red panties? 😏
Fran: You must've really liked those panties to pull a stunt like that 😂
Alex: You're all hilarious. What are you, twelve?
Chris: Admit it, you're enjoying this way too much
Diego: Or maybe you're just trying to get her attention... in your own way. 😏
Alex: You guys seriously need hobbies. I've got nothing to admit, and Rosie's none of your business.
Fran: We'll see tonight then. This is gonna be good. 😂

As I mount my horse and head toward the corral, my thoughts inevitably drift back to Rosie. Truth is, I haven't stopped thinking about her since I last saw her, just a few hours ago.

Who am I kidding? I was thinking about her even before she stormed in here, all fired up.

I've been wandering around the ranch more than usual, making up excuses just to catch a glimpse of her. Took the horse on a longer route, went searching for an extra bucket... pathetic.

I seriously need to stop. Why the hell is she on my mind every damn second?

I enjoy needling her, pulling out that side of her she's so desperate to keep hidden. I like the way she tilts her chin up and challenges me. I like those irritated, sexy-as-hell looks she throws my way. Damn it... focusing on work has never been this hard.

Pulling the reins as I reach the corral, I can't help but think back to when she came here. She came to give me a piece of her mind. I'm sure of it. She wasn't here for peace and quiet. She was looking for me.

That thought gives me more satisfaction than it should, but I try to push it away. I need to stop thinking about Rosie. Damn it, even her name excites me in ways it shouldn't.

The sun starts to set, painting the sky with warm colors as I finish settling the horses for the night. This is the part of the day I like best, when everything quiets down, and I can reflect on what's happened.

But tonight, I'd rather not reflect on anything. Especially not Rosie.

Doesn't matter, though. Whether I want to or not, I can't get that damn city princess out of my head.

Rosie Thorne is the most infuriating woman I've ever met. And the most dangerously tempting.

Tonight is our guys' night, a weekly tradition we've always had. Most of the time, we gather at the Rusty Spur, the ranch saloon, to drink, joke around, and catch up on the latest news. The name of the saloon is a historical gem from our friendship. Long before Chris and Val founded the ranch and bought this land, when we were just young men, we used to pull pranks in an old, abandoned building we had nicknamed the Rusty Spur. When Chris bought the land and expanded, building the saloon... it just felt like the perfect name. Now, many years later, it's still our meeting place, still a spot where we pull pranks, and still a place that makes us happy. And now, it's also a gathering spot for the men from the nearby ranches.

When I arrive, Chris, Diego, and Fran are already seated at our usual table with beers in hand. Everyone except Chris. He doesn't drink, he's health-conscious and takes his training and fitness too seriously. The rest of us are still in shape, but we don't mind the occasional beer or drink. Especially the beer from the Rusty Spur, which is the best I've ever tasted and is supplied directly by Rustler's Brew.

The sound of laughter and music fills the air, creating an atmosphere of camaraderie and relaxation. The bar is made of wood. There are double doors at the entrance, with the second door serving an aesthetic purpose. It's beautiful, in classic Wild West style. The style blends with the typical mountain cabin vibe, with a few (fake) bulls and deer heads mounted on the walls. There are some cowboy-style details and seating that resembles tents. There's a mechanical bull in the corner. We've had fantastic challenges with Val, Lexy and Rory on it. Those three are crazy... they know how to play and are the most fun girls I've ever met. It's no surprise that Chris fell head over heels in love with Val practically as soon as he met her. He's always loved her, and finally, he found the courage to tell her. He's always been the type to dream of settling down, of building a family... but Val gave him more than he ever imagined. They're inseparable, a perfect match in every way, and I couldn't be happier for them.

A soft rock band is playing. There's always live music. Each day of the week has something scheduled. We mainly alternate between Rock and Country.

Chris, with his long, curly hair tied back in a man bun, raises his hand in greeting. "Hey, brother, got announcements to make here too?" His striking eyes study me, their sparkle betraying his amusement. He's laughing, but I can tell those sharp eyes are trying to read what's going on in my head. He knows me better than anyone else, and all the guys are well aware that this isn't like me. Normally, I'm much more reserved, taking my time to warm up to strangers. With my friends, though, I'm different—I laugh, I joke, I play pranks. But that's because they're my brothers.

Diego, who looks exactly like Travis Fimmel in that iconic billboard ad—the one where he lounges with long, golden hair, smoldering eyes, and an infuriatingly perfect smirk (and yes, *exactly* like that)—shakes his head, letting his blonde hair sway as he flashes a mischievous grin. The resemblance irritates him to no end, which, of course, means that we—being the stellar friends that we are—have made it our mission to tease him about it constantly. Ever since Rory pointed it out, we haven't let him forget it, and it's become one of our favorite running jokes.

"You're such a bastard, you know that?" he says, his grin widening despite himself.

Fran, the most reserved of us all, with his reddish hair and sharp green eyes, chuckles quietly under his breath. "Alright then, spill it. We want all the juicy details."

I sit down, taking a beer and taking a long sip. "Well, I knew they were Rosie's. I found them while checking on the horses this morning and thought it would be fun to stir up a bit of trouble... I don't know what they were doing there. There was a lot of wind last night, they probably blew away from the laundry."

Diego laughs, giving me a pat on the back. "You're terrible. But I have to admit, it was a masterstroke."

"She didn't find it as funny... we know you, but you can't behave that way with the guests," adds Chris, with a smile that could melt anyone. I don't know how serious he is in his reprimand. After all, I don't have bad intentions, but you can't really joke with everyone. However, despite her fiery attitude, I don't think Rosie is the kind of girl you can't joke with.

Fran nods, with a mischievous smile. "So, what did she say afterward? Did she get angry?"

"She was more embarrassed than anything," I respond, remembering her flushed face... "but then she defended herself well." I admit. I want to give credit to her. She's not a lamb, and that's something I like. And despite my attitude, I don't want to seriously make fun of her. But it infuriates me that she makes me lose control. This has never happened to me before. She's been here for such a short time, and she's already thrown me completely off balance. I can't get her out of my head, I can't stop being angry, and I can't keep my mouth shut. That part, I don't explain to my friends. The explanation I gave them seems to be enough for now. I don't like lying to them, but... what am I supposed to say? That I don't even know what's happening to me anymore?!

I know nothing will ever come of this. She's completely off-limits. I need to get that through my head, loud and clear. I just have to stop thinking about her.

We spend the evening joking and telling stories, as we always do. The friendship I have with these guys is the most precious thing I have, and knowing they're always there to tease me and support me is reassuring. As the night progresses, our group continues to laugh and joke, enjoying our guys' night. The connection I have with these guys is unique, they're my family. I know I can count on them for anything, and this gives me a great sense of security.

The bar continues to fill up, but we remain in our little world, sharing old stories and new laughter. Occasionally, someone throws a joke about Rosie, and everyone bursts out laughing. "Really, Alex, you should be more careful," says Chris, his eyes sparkling with amusement. "We wouldn't want her to decide to wage war on you."

"Hey, I'm always ready for a challenge," I respond with a sly smile.

Fran smiles, raising his glass. "To us. And to our guys' nights."

We all clink our glasses together, feeling the warmth of the friendship that binds us.

Chapter 5

Rosie

Lexy created the "Wild Chicks" group
Lexy added Rosie
Val: Welcome to the club, Rosie! Ready for the craziest night of your life? 😂
Aurora: We can't wait to get to know you better! 😉
Rosie: Thank you! What do you have in mind?
Lexy: A bit of wine, lots of gossip, and tons of laughter. 😊
Val: And maybe even some embarrassing secrets to share. 🙄
Aurora: Like, who has a crush on who and who has the worst taste in men. 😆
Rosie: Sounds interesting! I definitely need a distraction.

I'm still fuming over Alex's announcement about my red panties. Every time I replay the scene in my mind, with that smug, mischievous grin of his, my face heats up—half with embarrassment, half with rage. I can't believe I actually wasted more than a passing thought on how sexy he looked. It must have been exhaustion because now all I find him is utterly infuriating!

I solemnly swear I will not think about Alex fucking cowboy in the shower again.

I solemnly swear I will not think about Alex fucking cowboy in the shower again.
I solemnly swear I will not think about Alex fucking cowboy in the shower again.

Despite my mental rants... this is the mantra I'm muttering to myself barely ten minutes later.
And you know what?
I'm even angrier at that damn cowboy!
I'm getting ready for the evening with Vale, Lexy and Aurora. When I arrive, they are already comfortably seated with glasses of wine in hand, laughing and chatting.
Aurora, Chris's younger sister, is his complete opposite: straight blonde hair, gray eyes, and the elegant, regal poise of a ballerina. She's younger than us, but the age difference hardly shows... the girls seem to have formed a very close-knit group. She's sitting in a position that looks anything but comfortable. She's checking her phone, but as soon as she notices my entrance, she greets me with a smile.
"Rosie, finally!" exclaims Vale, getting up to greet me with a warm hug. "Come, sit down and relax. This evening is all for us."
Lexy hands me a glass of wine. "Welcome to our secret haven. Here we can talk about anything and anyone without censorship."
Aurora smiles conspiratorially. "And by 'anyone' we mean just about anyone. Even certain guys who work at the ranch and pull stupid pranks."
I laugh, finally relaxing a bit. "Thank you so much, girls. I really needed this evening."

Lexy raises her glass for a toast. "To Rosie, our new friend, and to girl nights without filters!"

We all clink our glasses and the atmosphere immediately becomes lighter.

"So," Vale begins with a sly smile, "Rosie, tell us a little about yourself. We're curious to know how you're settling in here."

I smile, trying to relax. "Well, it's been a big change coming here. I'm still a bit out of my element, but I'm getting used to it. And you're all helping me a lot."

Aurora nods enthusiastically. "And don't worry, it will just take a little time. Then it will all feel natural."

Lexy looks at me with a mischievous smile. "By the way, Rosie, how was your first close encounter with the 'prankster' side of the ranch?"

I sigh, laughing a bit. "Oh, you mean the red underwear prank? It really caught me off guard."

Vale shakes her head, laughing. "Alex has always been a bit of a prankster, but don't worry, we'll get our revenge."

Aurora nods with a knowing smile. "Exactly. We've got a long list of little pranks in the works, and we can definitely add this one to it. But I have to admit, Alex doesn't usually act like this with strangers." She glances at Val, who raises an eyebrow, then adds, "With us, he's playful and relaxed... but he's my adoptive brother. I know him well, and he takes time to open up to new people." She shoots me a pointed look, her smile almost too knowing. "I'd say you've gotten under his skin."

I return her smile but shake my head. "I doubt that," I murmur. These new revelations catch me off guard. I hadn't expected Alex to be Rory and Chris's adoptive brother, nor do I fully believe he's as guarded as Rory describes. But what do I know? I barely know him, right? And yet, hearing these pieces of his life only leaves me with more questions than answers.

Why was he adopted? What happened to him? What's his story?

If Rory's right, there's so much more to Alex than meets the eye.

I decide not to ask. The girls, I'm sure, would be more than happy to fill in the gaps. Judging by their sly smiles, they're already entertaining ideas about something more between Alex and me. But I don't want to pry into something so personal, and I certainly don't want to discover anything that might tether that cowboy more firmly to this place. He's already taken up a permanent spot in my head—and, apparently, in my panties—and I've barely scratched the surface of knowing him.

I take a long sip of wine, willing myself to think about anything else.

We continue chatting and laughing, sharing more ridiculous stories. Then Val leans in, looking like she's about to spill something juicy. "Remember that time you accidentally texted your 'crush' to the wrong group, Lex?"

Rory laugh, already knowing where this is going. "Oh, you mean the time she sent all the juicy details about her date to the study group?"

Lexy bursts out laughing. "Exactly! I thought I was texting Vale. Instead, I texted *everyone* in the study group! They got all the details on my date... and the 'crush of the moment.' It was mortifying."

Aurora is laughing so hard she's holding her stomach.

"No way! How did they react?" I ask, feeling bad for her.

Lexy just shakes her head. "Oh, I became the topic of conversation for weeks. I'll never make that mistake again."

I chuckle, already feeling more at ease. These girls laugh, joke around, and don't take themselves too seriously. Maybe I really could relax a little with them. Suddenly, I realize how tense and perfectionistic I always am. And just as suddenly, I realize these are the exact kind of comments an annoying cowboy might throw my way.

I feel a wave of irritation building and down the rest of my wine. The wine, by the way, is excellent. The girls mentioned that they produce it at the ranch and that harvest season is one of their favorite times—they have a blast helping out with the grape picking. Val and Lexy love cooking with their mom, and Rory joins them when she's here.

The whole thing almost moves me... I love this cozy, family atmosphere and the bond Val and Lexy share with their mom. I can't help but feel a little sad, though, thinking about how I never had that.

"These stories are priceless. I don't feel so embarrassed anymore."

Lexy raises her glass. "Here's to girls' night! No knights in shining armor, just wine, laughter, and embarrassing moments."

Aurora nods, grinning. "And maybe a few more stories to add to our collection."

Vale looks at Aurora with a teasing smile. "Oh, remember when you were *totally* in love with Chris's friend?"

Aurora's face turns pink, and she quickly glances at the floor. "Uh, I... I didn't..."

Lexy bursts out laughing. "Oh, don't try to deny it! We all knew. How many times did we catch you spying on his training sessions?"

Aurora groans, hiding her face in her hands. "I was just... curious! And, okay, maybe a little obsessed."

Vale smirks. "A little? You practically had a shrine to him. And the things you'd say when you tried to talk to him... I still can't believe you asked him if he liked your... 'fashionable' new boots."

Aurora shakes her head in embarrassment, laughing. "I was so awkward! He never took me seriously."

She pauses for a moment, clearly thinking it over, then sighs and looks up at us with a defensive smile. "Okay, fine. I was 14, alright? I was just a kid back then. I had no clue what I was doing!"

Lexy bursts out laughing. "Aww, poor little Rory. But hey, I'm pretty sure you weren't the only one who had an awkward crush at that age."

Aurora rolls her eyes but can't help smiling. "I guess... but still. That's not something I want anyone remembering about me."

Vale grins mischievously. "Well, lucky for you, we *never* forget. Those moments are forever etched in our memories."

Chapter 6

Rosie

Group Chat: Wild Chicks]
Lexy: Hey Rosie, have you thought about how to get revenge on Alex for the panties prank? 😏
Vale: Oh yes! We absolutely need to come up with something epic!
Aurora: How about hiding all his boots? 👢
Rosie: Hmm, not bad. But I want something more... embarrassing 😈
Lexy: Ooh, I like how you think! Let me think...
Vale: Girls, wait! I've got a brilliant idea! 🤩
Rosie: Really? Tell us!
Vale: What if we...

While I read Vale's message, an even better idea pops into my mind.

Rosie: Vale, your idea is fantastic, but wait... I just thought of something even more diabolical 😈
Lexy: Shoot, Rosie! Don't keep us in suspense!
Rosie: Okay, here's the plan. I'll need your help...
Lexy: Rosie, you're an evil genius! 😈 I can't wait to see Alex's face!
Vale: This will teach him not to play stupid pranks!
Rosie: Girls, are you sure he won't get really angry? You know him better than I do...
Aurora: Trust us, Rosie. Alex can take it. Besides, he asked for it!
Vale: Exactly. Don't worry, everything will be fine.

Rosie: Okay, if you say so. Shall we meet in an hour to put the plan into action?
Lexy: You bet! 🤠
Vale: I'll be on time! 👍
Aurora: I can't wait! This is going to be epic! 😂

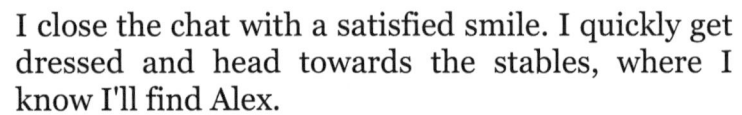

I close the chat with a satisfied smile. I quickly get dressed and head towards the stables, where I know I'll find Alex.

I find him brushing a horse, his back turned to me. I pause for a moment to admire the view: the muscles in his arms flex as he works, and his hair is slightly tousled by the wind. His worn, dark brown cowboy hat hangs from his shoulders. Broad shoulders that could span a mile. God. For a moment, I almost regret what I'm about to do. Almost.

I listen to that little voice inside me, which seems to know better than I do, and ladies and gentlemen, Rosalie Thorne is about to pull off the bluff of the century.

"Hey, cowboy," I call out, trying to maintain a neutral tone.

Alex turns around, a smile forming on his face when he sees me.

If it was already hard to focus on anything but his physical appearance when he was turned away, now, with him facing me, those intense eyes and that infuriating expression — almost like he's genuinely pleased to see me... to annoy me, of course — it's even worse.

If I'm starting to find that look sexy, I clearly need to get my head checked because something's seriously wrong.

"Look who's here. The city princess deigns to visit the stables?"

Fortunately, when he opens his mouth, everything becomes clearer, and irritation takes the lead again. I seriously need to have a word with the Rosie who's all hot and bothered by this damn cowboy because, clearly, my mantras aren't doing a thing.

I ignore the provocation and approach, feigning interest in the horse. "I thought maybe you could teach me something about horseback riding. You know, since I'll be here for a while."

Alex raises an eyebrow, clearly surprised by my request. "Really? I thought you preferred to stay away from all this."

I shrug, trying to appear nonchalant. "Well, I decided to give this place a chance. Unless you're not up to the challenge of teaching..."

I see a spark in his eyes. The challenge has been issued, and I know he can't resist. "Oh, I'm more than up for it, princess. Get ready for the lesson of your life." He says it with that usual arrogant grin, and I have to resist the urge to tell him exactly where he can shove it.

He won't be laughing for much longer.

He rolls up his plaid shirt sleeves, revealing his forearms.

I've never found forearms sexy in my life, but I swear on the universe, I could faint at the sight of his.

How he manages to wear a shirt in this heat... it's a mystery. Maybe it's to protect himself from the dust.

As Alex begins to explain the basics of horseback riding, I glance at my watch. The girls should be in position in a few minutes. My heart beats fast with anticipation.

"So, first we need to choose the right horse for you," says Alex, leading me towards the stalls. "How about..."

At that moment, a loud metallic noise resonates from the other side of the stable. Alex turns sharply.

"What the hell...?" he mutters, heading towards the source of the noise.

It's the signal I've been waiting for. With a quick movement, I grab the water bucket I had previously hidden and dump it completely over Alex.

His cry of surprise echoes through the stable, immediately followed by the laughter of the girls who come out of their hiding spots, smartphones in hand to capture the moment.

Alex turns around slowly, completely soaked, his hair sticking to his face. For a moment, I fear I've gone too far. Then, to my relief, I see a smile forming on his lips.

"Well, princess", he says, shaking his head like a wet dog and spraying me with water, "I have to admit I didn't see that coming. You got me." The girls applaud and laugh.

"Consider this your warning, cowboy."

Alex approaches, a dangerous glint in his eyes. His wet shirt clings to his body, outlining every muscle. I swallow, trying to maintain focus. "Oh, don't think this ends here," he says, his voice low and full of challenge. He moves closer until we're only inches apart. I can feel the heat of his body despite his wet clothes. "This is war, Rosie. And I assure you, you have no idea what's coming."

His intense gaze almost makes me forget how to breathe. I lift my chin, refusing to back down. "All talk, cowboy," I reply, my voice huskier than I'd like. "We'll see who has the last laugh."

"Oh, you can bet on it," Alex murmurs, so close I can feel his breath on my skin. For a moment, the world around us seems to disappear. Then, suddenly, he steps away with a smirk. "Better go change. But remember, princess: revenge is a dish best served cold."

As I watch him walk away, I feel a shiver run down my spine, and I'm not sure if it's from excitement or the challenge. Maybe both. "Wow," Lexy whispers in my ear. "If the sparks between you two were real, we'd have just witnessed a fire." I shake my head, trying to dissipate the tension. "Don't be silly. It's just... competition."

But as we leave the stable, amid laughter and jokes, I can't help but think that maybe, just maybe, this stay at the ranch will be much more dangerous and exciting than I had imagined.

The rest of the day passes in a whirlwind of activity. Between the preparations for Dad's wedding and the work I can manage remotely, I barely have time to think about the prank I pulled on Alex. Barely.

Somehow, that damn cowboy always finds his way into my head, and at one point, the silence in my room while I worked was so deafening I could practically hear my thoughts about him screaming at me.

And that's how I gave in to my weakness once again and found myself touching myself, thinking about him without even realizing it.

Damn it.

Damn it.

Damn it.

I swear this is a first for me.

At the ripe age of 29, I've never had any serious relationships. I never wanted to tie myself down to anyone. After what happened with my parents, it always seemed infinitely sad to get close to someone just to lose them. I saw the devastation in my father after my mother died.

I haven't had many casual flings either. I'm not a virgin, don't get me wrong, but I've never had an especially active sex life. I never really felt the need, and I never thought much about it.

I've always had other priorities.

Priorities I still have now. So why the hell is this happening now, and with him?

I need to forget about his existence. His forearms, his messy hair, his penetrating eyes, his broad shoulders, his rough and seductive voice... damn it, here we go again!

By evening, I decide to distract myself elsewhere. I head downstairs to where the hustle and bustle of everyone usually is and find Dad and Maria preparing dinner. We usually eat together, as a family. I volunteer to set the table, heading into the dining room while Dad and Maria stay in the kitchen.

As I focus on my task, I sense a presence behind me. My instincts already tell me who it might be. I feel the familiar tingling, and then I smell that unmistakable scent of leather and pine.

I turn and find myself face-to-face with Alex, who's wearing a clean, dry shirt, sleeves rolled up. I fight every urge to look down at his forearms. There's enough space between us, but suddenly it feels like there's none at all.

"Hey, princess," he says with that familiar arrogant smile I resist the impulse to shove right back up his ass. "Did you have fun today?"

He steps closer.

I raise an eyebrow, trying to seem unaffected. "Oh, yeah. It was... refreshing."

Alex laughs, a low, dangerous sound that sends chills down my spine. I don't think I've ever heard a laugh sexier than that.

Great. As if I needed more material... What the hell is he doing? He's getting dangerously close. I instinctively take a step back but bump into a chair. He reaches out to steady me, then leans in with the other hand. Now he's definitely too close.

His arm is practically pressed against mine. Then he pulls back.

He was grabbing napkins and silverware.

Nonchalantly and impassively, he starts helping me set the table.

Like he hasn't just thrown me into complete disarray. Again.

"Well, well. You know, I was thinking... since you're so interested in horseback riding, how about a private lesson tomorrow morning? At dawn?"

I look at him suspiciously. "At dawn? Are you serious?"

He walks around the table, continuing to set it on the other side.

"Dead serious," he responds, a glint in his eye. "Unless you're scared, of course."

What a son of a...

"Scared? Me?" I shake my head, knowing I'm falling right into his trap but unable to pull back. "I'll be there."

"Perfect," Alex says, moving closer again. His scent invades my nostrils, and I can swear there's something illegal in it. "Can't wait." He winks at me, and I hate when he does that. It's so irritating and damn sexy. I already feel my panties getting wet.

I hate him. I hate him, I hate him.

With one last enigmatic smile, he walks away, leaving me stunned. What the hell just happened?

Later, during dinner, I can't help but glance at Alex. He's laughing and joking with the others, but every now and then our eyes meet, and I feel a jolt run through me.

[Group Chat: Wild Chicks]
Rosie: Girls, I need advice. Alex invited me to a "private lesson" tomorrow at dawn. What should I expect?
Lexy: Ooh, interesting! 😏 Be careful, it could be his revenge.
Aurora: Or it could just be an excuse to be alone with you... 😌
Vale: Knowing Alex, probably both. Prepare for anything!
Rosie: Thanks, this makes me feel SO MUCH better 🙄
Lexy: Come on, it'll be fun! And if things go south, we're here for you 💪
Vale: Exactly! Team Rosie in full force! 🎉
Aurora: Just remember to wear something comfortable. And maybe bring a change of clothes...

I close the chat, not entirely reassured. As I prepare for bed, my mind can't help but wander to what tomorrow morning might bring. But I'd be lying if I said that's the only thing keeping me awake tonight.

I can't believe how I react when that damn cowboy is around. And I certainly can't believe how much he still affects me even when he's not here. I need to get a grip. By now, the jet lag should be long gone, so... it'll probably pass.

I tell myself it's just exhaustion. Of all the people in the world, I can't be feeling this way about him.

He's already irritating enough—I can't let myself find him too attractive.

But still, my mind drifts back to the days until I leave. Too many left. But once I'm out of here... I'll leave this whole mess behind. I just need to survive it and try to focus on something else.

Finally, I manage to fall asleep, slipping into a whirlwind of disjointed dreams, full of galloping horses and those damn, piercing eyes.

When the alarm goes off at 5:30, I've already been up for a while. The rooster keeps waking me up every morning... but always at a different time. Seriously? I miss the soundproofed walls of my apartment. I never realized I hated roosters so much. I'm not particularly a heavy sleeper... but I like to wake up calmly, at my own pace, and especially with peace and quiet.

I get up with a mix of excitement and nervousness.

I dress carefully, opting for comfortable jeans and a light shirt (kindly provided by Val. I absolutely must go shopping, mental note). As suggested by Aurora, I put a change of clothes in a backpack, along with a water bottle and some snacks.

When I arrive at the stables, the sky is just beginning to lighten. Alex is already there, leaning against a fence, looking far too awake for this hour of the morning. I can't help but notice him. He's standing there, all confident and in control of his body. He's wearing worn jeans that I don't understand how they can be so sexy. And don't get me started on how that t-shirt fits him! Better not. Better not linger on his lean and defined physique.

"Good morning, princess," he greets me with a smile. "Ready for your lesson?"

"Born ready," I reply, trying to appear more confident than I feel.

Alex nods, then turns towards the stalls. "Good. Today we'll be riding Storm."

I follow his gaze and see a magnificent black stallion looking at us with intelligent eyes.

"He's... beautiful," I whisper, approaching cautiously.

"He is," Alex confirms, with a note of pride in his voice. "And he's also one of the most difficult horses to ride on the ranch."

I look at him alarmed. "What? But I thought this was a beginner's lesson!"

Alex smiles, a smile that makes me want to hit him and kiss him at the same time. "Oh, it is. But you didn't specify what kind of beginner you wanted to be."

As he starts to saddle Storm, I have to struggle particularly with two things:

1. Not staring with too much adoration at every muscle that flexes with his every movement.
2. Not punching him in the face.

Chapter 7

Alex

I can't help but smile as I get Storm ready for the lesson.

Rosie caught me off guard, I'll admit. That bucket of water? Brilliant. And the look on her face when she did it? Priceless.

When I first saw her walk into the stables, my heart skipped a beat. For the second time, she came looking for me of her own accord. Well, if we're keeping score, it's two to infinity. Considering the countless times my feet have taken me to find her somewhere around the ranch, unbidden.

I knew she was up to something when she showed up here. She's not as good at lying as she thinks. Especially when she gave herself away, trying to brush off my teasing. But I played along, too eager to resist. I certainly didn't expect her to have planned something like that.

The city princess has more guts than I thought. And damn it... I'd convinced myself my obsession with her was just a passing fantasy. I thought it was nothing more than a stupid crush because of her fancy, maddeningly perfect clothes—and how damn good she looks in them. But then I saw her in simple jeans and a blouse, and holy hell! I've never seen anyone more irresistible. Especially when her eyes sparkle with that defiant challenge.

Those jeans fit her perfectly. Her ass is the most tempting thing I've ever seen.

Staying up all night to finish work early? Worth it. Yeah... because clearly, I'm supposed to be working right now.

But with Rosie Thorne around, that's impossible.

I take a little longer than necessary to saddle the horse, trying to deal with the painfully obvious hard-on I've got going on. Last night was bad enough—rushing out after helping her set the table. It took every ounce of self-control I had to act casual, pretending I wasn't burning inside and wanting to turn her around and take her right there on the table, consequences be damned. I had to escape to hide the evidence.

God, I'm pathetic.

I bolted to my room and jerked off to thoughts of her. Her lush red lips, fiery hair, that perfect ass, and that sharp tongue I'd love to silence in the most sinful ways. The scent of roses lingering around her.

Once wasn't nearly enough.

Neither was twice.

By the time I showed up for dinner, I was drained from three rounds back-to-back. I tried to focus on every possible topic the others brought up, desperate to avoid thinking about Rosie and risking another escape.

But... ignoring her? That's just impossible.

I shake my head, trying to focus on the task at hand. I can't afford to be distracted, not with Storm. This stallion is as unpredictable as a

summer storm, just as his name suggests. But he's also the perfect horse to test Rosie... and moreover, I'm particularly attached to him. He's a very important horse to me... and I don't know why, but I want Rosie's first experience to be with him. All this sentimentality seems absurd, especially considering the fact that I don't even know her. But that's how it is. I feel strange things related to her, and among these oddities is the fact that I absolutely want her first time to be on my favorite horse. I acknowledge it, act on it, and decide to ignore it. Right now, I have absolutely no intention of psychoanalyzing my absurd behaviors.
As I finish saddling Storm, I hear Rosie's footsteps approaching. I turn around and, for a moment, I'm breathless. The dawn light illuminates her from behind, creating a halo around her red hair. I'm not used to seeing her so casual, but I'm starting to think she would look good in anything. Or that she would look really good without anything on. I try to forget that last thought too. She looks... comfortable. As if she belonged in this place.
"So, cowboy," Rosie says, approaching Storm cautiously but without fear. "Where do we start?"
My smile widens. "First of all, you need to let him know who's in charge. Approach slowly, maintain eye contact."
"Good," I say, approaching. "Now, gently stroke his muzzle."
Rosie reaches out, hesitating only for a second before touching Storm. The horse visibly calms under her touch.

I watch as Rosie follows my instructions. Her posture is stiff, but her movements are fluid. Storm snorts, shaking his mane, but doesn't move. Is it normal to be jealous of a horse? Because right now, all I can feel is a deep, irrational jealousy toward my own damn horse. The way Rosie's looking at him, the soft affection in her eyes, the gentle touch of her hand—I want all of it directed at me.

I'm losing my mind.

I have to stop thinking about her.

I try to shove all these completely inappropriate thoughts into some distant, far-off corner of my mind. Swallowing hard, I focus on giving her an appraisal.

"You have a natural talent," I comment, surprised and impressed.

Rosie looks at me with a triumphant smile. This is the first time she's smiled at me like that, and I immediately want more. It's the most beautiful, radiant smile I've ever seen. It warms my heart, my soul, and makes me feel a thousand indescribable things I've never felt before.

Now I'm really losing it with these thoughts. I have to stop—seriously. A fleeting attraction? Sure, I can begrudgingly and painfully admit it's not so fleeting anymore. But these thoughts? No way. They're dangerously close to something deeper, something raw and unfamiliar that I don't dare even name. The idea alone feels like stepping into quicksand. I clear my throat, but even so, when I try to speak, my voice comes out low and rough, betraying every effort to stay composed.

"Let's see how you do in the saddle." And before helping her mount, I do another inexplicable thing. I put my cowboy hat on her head. At first, she seems really confused. So am I... especially when images of her wearing only my hat start popping into my head, and I have to force myself to cover those thoughts with something gruesome or disgusting.

But by now, it's clear there's nothing I can do about the erections Rosie keeps giving me.

"Complete package," I tell her... trying to divert attention, and I wink at her, in the way I know irritates her but that she might secretly like a little. She surprises me too... because she rewards me with a smile. I think it's the first real smile I've seen her make since she arrived here. It's different from the smile she gave me before. That one had already felt like the most beautiful, satisfying smile in the world, both to my eyes and my stupid heart. But that one was triumphant. It was a smile of victory.

This one, though, is for me. It's all for me.

Damn, I swear the whole world just stopped spinning. This smile, soft and shy, it's entirely mine. It's the most beautiful smile I've ever seen, and hell, I can't get enough of it. I want more. Endless more.

"I like it," she says simply.

Damn it... this is my downfall.

I should've known that Rosalie Thorne would be nothing but trouble.

I help her mount, trying to ignore the electric shock I feel when my hands touch her waist. Once in the saddle, Rosie looks a bit uncertain, but determined.

"Okay, princess," I say, taking Storm's reins. "Hold on tight. Let's go for a ride."

I guide Storm out of the corral and towards the fields. The sun is fully rising now, painting the sky pink and gold. Rosie looks around in wonder, and for a moment I forget to breathe. She's... beautiful.

"So," Rosie says, bringing me back to reality. "This is your big revenge? A dawn ride?"

I laugh. "Oh no, princess. This is just the beginning."

With a fluid movement, I jump into the saddle behind her. Rosie startles, surprised by my sudden closeness.

Did I already mention I'm an idiot who makes stupid decisions? Because if I haven't, let me just put that out there again.

If she flinches, barely noticeable, my reaction isn't anywhere near as subtle. I don't know if she realizes it, but my heart picks up speed, my breath catches, and I forget how to inhale properly. My palms start to sweat, and when I finally manage to suck in some air, it carries the faintest hint of roses.

That scent... it's so intoxicating, so perfectly elegant, it feels like it was made just for her.

I have to know what it is. I need to find out, so I can turn it into my own personal addiction.

But for now, all I can do is pretend I'm indifferent, like I'm a completely normal human being.

Thank God she's got her back to me right now and can't see my face.

Unfortunately, that means I have a perfect, breathtaking view of her ass. So damned perfect that I have to focus every ounce of willpower not to accidentally brush against her, considering how hard I am right now. Harder than stone, and there's no saving me.

"What are you doing?" she asks, her voice a bit higher than usual.

"Teaching you how to ride," I respond, my chest pressed against her back. "Unless you're afraid of being this close to me."

I feel Rosie stiffen, then deliberately relax. "Afraid? Of you? In your dreams, cowboy."

I smile, even though she can't see me. "Good. Then, hold on tight."

With a slight kick of my heels, I urge Storm into a gallop. Rosie lets out a small cry of surprise, then starts laughing. The sound of her laughter, mixed with the noise of Storm's hooves, creates a melody that makes me wish to never stop.

As we gallop across the fields, with the dawn surrounding us and Rosie in my arms, I realize that this "revenge" might not have gone exactly as I had planned. But somehow, I can't bring myself to be sorry about it.

Chapter 8

Alex

The sun hangs high as we return to the stables, its warmth a stark contrast to the cool morning air we left behind. I steal a glance at Rosie, noticing a newfound radiance in her eyes that she's trying desperately to conceal.

"Well, princess," I say, dismounting Tempest with practiced ease, "ready to admit that horseback riding isn't the torture you imagined?"

Rosie struggles slightly as she dismounts, pointedly ignoring my offered hand. Her eyes flash with defiance as she retorts, "Don't flatter yourself, cowboy. I'd still take a good book over this equine misadventure any day."

"Is that so?" I can't help but smirk. "And here I thought I caught you smiling out there in the fields."

"Must have been a heat-induced hallucination," she quips, but I don't miss the ghost of a smile tugging at her lips.

As we make our way towards the main house, we spot Valentina and Chris emerging, their fingers intertwined. They're lost in hushed conversation, their eyes speaking volumes of unspoken affection.

"Hey, you two!" Chris calls out, reluctantly breaking his reverie with Val. "How'd the lesson go?"

I grin mischievously. "Our princess here claims it was an absolute nightmare."

Rosie's glare could melt steel. "Don't put words in my mouth, Alex."

Valentina laughs, exchanging a knowing look with Chris. The love radiating between them is almost palpable, and I notice Rosie shifting uncomfortably beside me, clearing her throat.

"So," Valentina says, redirecting her attention to us, "we're throwing a barbecue tonight. You'll join us, right?"

"Wouldn't miss it," I respond without hesitation. I turn to Rosie, eyebrow raised in silent question.

She sighs dramatically, but I catch a glimmer of interest in her eyes. "I suppose some decent food might help me forget the aches and pains I'll be nursing tomorrow."

Our growling stomachs remind us of our original breakfast mission, and we bid the lovebirds farewell.

As we walk, I can't help but reflect on Val and Chris's fairytale romance. I remember the night Chris confided his proposal plans to me, Diego, and Fran over beers on the porch. The mixture of nerves and elation in his voice, the dreamy look in his eyes – it was a moment of pure, unfiltered joy that I'll never forget.

Rosie's voice pulls me from my reverie. "They seem genuinely happy together," she muses, a hint of wistfulness coloring her tone.

"They are," I confirm, my voice softening. "They've built this ranch and their life together from the ground up. Their wedding next year? It'll be the event of the season."

Rosie nods, her eyes distant, lost in thought. For a moment, I find myself wondering about her past—about potential heartbreaks or missed connections. Does she have someone waiting for her back home? The thought sends an unexpected pang through my chest. I shake my head, trying to banish the dangerous path my mind is wandering down.

Rosie is temporary, I remind myself sternly. A fleeting presence in my world, here today and gone tomorrow. And me? I'm just the irritating cowboy who gets under her skin, the one who makes her eyes flash with annoyance and her cheeks flush with anger. I'm not the type to settle down, never have been. So why does my heart race every time she looks at me? Why do I find myself searching for excuses to be near her?

And yet... There's something about her that draws me in, like a moth to a flame. The way she challenges me, the rare moments when her guard drops and I catch a glimpse of vulnerability beneath her prickly exterior. It's intoxicating and terrifying all at once.

I can't allow myself to think of Rosie in that way. It's a recipe for disaster. But as I watch her, bathed in the golden morning light, I can't help but wonder: what if?

"So, princess," I say, desperate to lighten the mood and my own conflicted thoughts, "ready for tonight's shindig? I hope you packed something suitable. We wouldn't want your designer duds getting barbecue sauce on them."

Rosie gives me a sharp look, but there's a smile playing on her lips. "Don't worry about me, cowboy. I know how to dress for any occasion."

"Hmm... yet it seemed the opposite to me," I reply with a grin.

Rosie gives me one of her killer looks... and I feel that the planets have resumed their ordinary motion. I enjoy bantering with Rosie, but I need to keep in mind what my place is.

I don't give her time to respond, even though I notice she's preparing for war. Before she can decide to say anything to me, I distance myself.

Chapter 9

Rosie

[Group Chat: Wild Chicks]
Lexy: BBQ SOS! 🧯 Just realized I'm clueless about starting a fire! Who's coming to my rescue?? 🔥💀
Vale: Oh, Lexy, sweetie, that's what we keep Chris around for. He's our grill master, remember? 😂
Rosie: Girls... I've never actually been to a barbecue...
Aurora: Chill, ladies! It's just a cookout... though with Alex around, someone might end up getting burned 😏
Lexy: Ooh, Aurora! Are you talking about Rosie or that crush you've been nursing forever? 👀
Rosie: Hey! I don't get hot and bothered over anyone, especially not that infuriating cowboy!
Vale: You sure about that, Rosie? Because I could've sworn I saw sparks flying this morning... 😉
Rosie: Hilarious. Can we please change the subject?
Lexy: Not a chance!
Lexy: And... Rory, spill the beans about which of your brother's friends makes you weak in the knees! 🍦
Aurora: I don't!!! I have no idea what you're on about! 😳
Vale: Oh, come off it! We've all seen you making eyes at him since... FOREVER!!!
Aurora: Would you drop it already? That ship has sailed.
Vale: Something went down, little Rory... and we're going to get to the bottom of it!

Lexy: You bet! And Rosie, don't think you're off the hook. We want all the juicy details about your "lesson" with Alex!
Rosie: There's nothing to tell! Shouldn't we be focusing on the barbecue anyway?

I close the chat with a sigh, a mix of amusement and frustration. These girls are incredible, but sometimes they make me feel like I'm back in high school. Still, I'm glad they're acting this way... I was already panicking about the barbecue, but in the end, their playful jabs lighten the mood. I adore them as if I've known them forever. And then there's Alex... I shake my head, trying to focus on the work in front of me.

My laptop sits open on the makeshift desk I've set up in my room at the ranch. Files of documents, presentations, and spreadsheets stare back at me, reminding me of all the looming deadlines. Working remotely has never been this challenging. I rub my eyes, feeling the fatigue building up. Los Angeles seems like a distant memory, yet the pressures of my life there continue to chase me. Deadlines, client calls, reports to complete... everything seems so insignificant here, surrounded by the wild beauty of the ranch.

I smile to myself, thinking about how I felt this morning. It was unexpectedly nice... except for the company, of course! That damn irritating cowboy with that smile that makes me want to hit him and kis... What am I thinking?? I must be exhausted, clearly! It's definitely the jet lag and the 5:30 AM wake-up call. But... I find myself thinking again about our dawn ride, the way his arms encircled me...

"Focus, Rosie," I mutter to myself, turning back to stare at the screen.

But it's hard. My gaze keeps wandering to the window, to the green fields and distant hills. I'm starting to understand why Dad fell in love with this place. There's a peace here, a sense of belonging I've never felt in Los Angeles.

I think about all the people I've met in these few days. Vale and Chris, so in love and welcoming. Val with her contagious energy, her big smiles, and constant hugs... you can see she's happy, and I'm not used to such overwhelming people like her... it still feels strange to see her so lively and receive all these hugs. I smile to myself... she's so small and energetic, she's just like Tinkerbell! And then... Lexy with her loose tongue. Aurora and her sweet shyness. Diego, Fran, and all the others... they seem like such a beautiful family.

And then there's Dad. I see him happier than he's ever been. He wants me to move here, I know. He's never asked me explicitly, but I see it in his eyes every time he looks at me. He wants me to be part of this new life he's built.

But how could I? My career, my life... everything is in Los Angeles. This small town in southern Italy is a completely different world. And yet...

I sigh again, looking at the clock. The barbecue will start in a few hours, and I haven't done anything productive yet. I force myself back to work, trying to ignore the little voice in my head that keeps wondering what Alex will think of what I'll wear tonight... Good grief! What will I wear? All my outfits are very formal... and I only have sky-high heels.

And there I go, distracted again. Will I ever get through this mountain of work? And why does my life suddenly seem so dull and gray? What is this enormous weight I feel? I shake my head, trying to rid myself of these confused thoughts. I force myself back to work, but every word I write seems empty, meaningless. It's as if this brief stay at the ranch has called into question everything I believed in.

After another half hour of frustrated attempts to concentrate, I shut the laptop with a sharp gesture. There's no point in continuing like this. Maybe a walk will clear my head.

I leave my room and head outside. The fresh, fragrant air hits me immediately, making me feel more alive than I have in months. I walk aimlessly, letting my thoughts wander freely.

I think about my life in Los Angeles. My elegant but cold apartment. The long hours at the office, the business dinners, the glossy parties. Everything seemed so important, so crucial. But now? Now it all seems so... empty.

And then I think about these few days at the ranch. The laughter shared with the girls. Chris's kindness and Vale's contagious energy. The peace I felt riding at dawn. And yes, even Alex's provocations.

I stop abruptly, realizing where my feet have taken me. I'm at the stables. And, as if fate wanted to mock me, here's Alex coming out at that very moment.

"Hey, princess," he greets me with that irritating smile of his. "Lost your way?"

I roll my eyes, but I can't hold back a smile. "No, cowboy. I was just... exploring."

Alex looks at me for a moment, as if trying to read me. Then, to my surprise, his smile softens. "You seem thoughtful. Everything okay?"

For a moment, I'm tempted to open up, to share all my worries and doubts. But I hold back. "I'm fine," I answer instead. "Just a bit stressed about work."

Alex nods, but he doesn't seem convinced. "You know," he says after a moment, "sometimes the best thing to do when you're stressed is to completely distract yourself. How about giving me a hand with the horses?"

I look at him, surprised. "Me? But I know nothing about horses."

"Exactly," he replies with a grin. "So you'll have to focus completely on what you're doing, with no room for other thoughts."

I hesitate for a moment, then nod. "Okay, why not?"

As I follow Alex into the stables, I feel a strange inner conflict. I'm still troubled by all my thoughts, but... surely I imagined it, or I'm going crazy, or I need to make this thing disappear from my head before it even manifests because what I felt when Alex caught sight of me... seemed very similar to relief. It's surely because I'm going crazy. I'm definitely tired. That damn rooster keeps me from sleeping, and I've been working too much lately. Yes, that's definitely it.

But then it all disappears. My inner conflicts no longer exist. Los Angeles, fatigue, lack of sleep no longer exist.

As I start learning how to brush a horse, I feel the weight on my chest lighten a bit.

Alex makes no comments about how out of place I am in my fuchsia heels.

Chapter 10

Rosie

With a deep breath, I make my entrance to the barbecue evening. Nervousness makes my hands tremble slightly as I adjust my flowing green dress, the most country-like thing I managed to find in my city wardrobe. My high heels sink slightly into the soft ground, making me wobble for a moment.

The scene before me is a whirlwind of colors, sounds, and scents that momentarily takes my breath away. My father is at the barbecue, focused on the smoking grill, wearing a chef's apron and a relaxed smile I haven't seen on him in years. Next to him is Maria, his future wife, radiant in her floral dress, her blonde hair shimmering in the sunset light. She's helping with food preparation, moving with grace and confidence. I vaguely remember that Maria works at the ranch preparing jams from the local harvest, and the way she moves in the kitchen betrays her passion for food. I make a mental note... I should familiarize myself with my future stepmother... maybe offer to help her with the harvest or in preparing jams or the wonderful desserts she makes... but I'm hopeless in the kitchen. Now that I'm an adult, I don't have time to learn. When I was a child, my mother died before she could teach me. And my father was too busy with work to cook... he only did it on weekends.

The sound of a guitar draws my attention, distracting me from this wandering of thoughts. Lexy is playing country music, her melodious voice rising in the evening air. She's wearing a black fringed skirt and a beige top, her bare feet tapping the rhythm on the ground. Next to her, Val dances with abandon, her blue dress swaying with every movement. She's barefoot too, and her face is lit up with a contagious smile. Aurora is sipping a cocktail (a Spritz perhaps?! It's orange so I think so).

The ranch boys are gathered in a corner, laughing and joking among themselves. They're all barefoot, as if it were the most natural thing in the world. I watch them as they engage in friendly wrestling, their bodies moving with a strength and agility that betrays years of physical work.

Suddenly, I feel a gaze on me. I turn and meet Alex's eyes. The cowboy is watching me with an intensity that makes me blush. It's irritating how sexy he is, with his worn jeans and unbuttoned shirt revealing a hint of tanned chest. I try to look away, but I find myself irresistibly drawn to him.

Alex approaches with his usual crooked smile. "Welcome to the party, princess," he tells me, his gaze running along my body. "Nice dress. Although..." He leans towards me, whispering in my ear: "Maybe you should take those shoes off if you don't want to end up with your nose in the dirt."

I feel a shiver run down my spine at the sound of his voice so close. I straighten up, trying to maintain my composure. "I'm fine like this, thank you," I reply in a tone I hope sounds confident.

Alex raises his hands in surrender, but his smile widens. "Suit yourself, princess. But don't say I didn't warn you."

As Alex walks away to join the other guys, I stand still for a moment, trying to calm my racing heart. I look around, observing the scene of happiness and simplicity surrounding me. For an instant, I feel out of place with my fashionable dress and high heels. But then my father sees me and nods, his face lighting up with joy.

With a sigh, I head towards him, deciding that perhaps, just for tonight, I can allow myself to let go a little. After all, what's wrong with taking off your shoes and feeling the grass under your feet, at least once? I think about it... but I still don't do it. It's hard to let go when you're used to following rules and being perfect.

I approach my father, feeling the heat of the barbecue on my skin. "Hi, honey," he greets me with a warm smile. "You look beautiful tonight."

"Thanks, Dad," I reply, suddenly feeling shy. Maria turns to me, her face radiant.

"Rosie! It's so good to see you," she exclaims, wrapping me in a hug that smells of herbs and wood smoke. "I hope you're hungry, we've prepared a real feast!"

I look at the plates full of food, feeling my stomach growl. "It all looks delicious," I admit.

"Go get yourself something to drink," Dad encourages me. "And maybe you could take those shoes off. You look a bit... unstable." I blush, aware of how out of place I must look. With a sigh of defeat, I bend down to unfasten my heels. The cool grass under my bare feet is a surprisingly pleasant sensation.

I head towards the drinks table, trying to ignore the curious glances from the other guests. I grab a glass of what I think is Spritz and look around, suddenly feeling alone in the midst of all these people.

"Hey, city girl!" Val's cheerful voice makes me jump. She approaches dancing, her eyes shining with joy. "Finally got rid of those death traps! Come on, dance with us!"

Before I can protest, she grabs my hand and drags me towards the group that's dancing. Country music fills the air, and I find myself swaying awkwardly, trying to follow the rhythm.

"Relax!" Val shouts over the music. "Let yourself go!"

I close my eyes for a moment, trying to let go of my inhibitions. Slowly, I begin to feel the rhythm flow through me. My movements become looser, more natural.

When I reopen my eyes, I meet Alex's gaze. He's dancing too, his movements fluid and confident. He smiles at me, a different smile from usual, sweeter, almost admiring.

For a moment, I forget everything. I forget my job in Los Angeles, my worries, my feeling of not belonging. In this moment, I'm just a girl dancing under the stars, surrounded by laughter and music.

The evening flies by quickly with dancing, chatting, and delicious food. I find myself laughing at Chris's jokes, discussing horseback riding with Fran, singing (off-key) along with Lexy.

As the night progresses, I find myself sitting on a hay bale, somewhat apart from the party. I observe the scene in front of me: my father dancing sweetly with Maria, Val and Chris exchanging loving glances, the ranch boys telling stories around the fire.

"Deep in thought, princess?" Alex's voice startles me. He sits next to me, offering me a bottle of beer.

His shirt is unbuttoned more than it was at the start of the barbecue, revealing just enough to set my imagination on fire. His hair is deliciously tousled, as if the breeze—or perhaps his own hands—had a hand in the chaos. He looks wild, effortless, and utterly captivating.

I swallow hard, trying to steady the storm inside me and focus on the question he just asked. But it's impossible when every inch of him pulls at something deep and uncontrollable within me.

"A bit," I admit, accepting the beer. "It's all so... different."

"Good different or bad different?" he asks, his tone surprisingly serious. I think about it for a moment. "I don't know," I answer honestly. "But maybe... maybe it's not so bad."

Alex smiles, a genuine smile this time, without a trace of sarcasm. "You know, princess, maybe there's hope for you after all."

He doesn't say it in an irritating way—there's a teasing lilt to his voice. He's trying to distract me, to make me laugh, and it's working.

I look at him, feeling something stir inside me. For the first time, I see beyond the facade of the arrogant cowboy. I see a kind, strong man, with a depth I hadn't noticed before.

"Maybe," I whisper, more to myself than to him.

We sit in silence, looking at the stars and listening to the music in the distance. And for the first time since I arrived at the ranch, I truly feel at home.

Then Alex asks me to dance with him...

Chapter 11

Alex

I lean against the fence, observing the party in full swing. The barbecue smoke rises lazily into the evening sky, and the smell of grilled meat mingles with that of hay and warm earth. It's a perfect evening, one of those I love the most. There's something special about summer evenings at the ranch, something that makes me feel alive and free.

Robert is at the barbecue wearing a relaxed smile I haven't seen in a long time. I barely remember the man he was when we hired him at the ranch... perfect in his work but always a bit distant, sad or empty... or stressed. Something that reminds me of his daughter. Since he met Maria, he's changed. He's happier, more serene. I see them together, and I realize how much he deserves this happiness. Maria is perfect for him: radiant in her floral dress, with blonde hair that shines in the sunset light. I've always admired her: a sunny and positive person... like her daughters. It's no wonder Val captured the heart of the hard-to-please Chris! Maria's passion for cooking is evident, and I see it in Val and Lexy too. They love to cook and have a lot of fun doing it together. It's an art, a way of taking care of the people they love... definitely adorable... I wish I possessed this skill.

The sound of Lexy's guitar fills the air, distracting me from my thoughts, and her melodious voice rises above the murmur of people. She's wearing a black fringed skirt and a beige top, her bare feet tapping the rhythm on the ground. Next to her, Val dances with abandon, her blue dress swaying with every movement. She's barefoot too, and her face is lit up with a contagious smile. Those two make me laugh with their inexhaustible energy. I see Chris looking at Val with loving eyes, and I can't help but smile. Those two are made for each other.

I approach the guys who are laughing and joking. They're all barefoot, because it's wonderful, natural, therapeutic... and simply our way. And I invite them to do what we always do: we challenge each other in a friendly wrestling match made of acrobatics and fights. We love training together, challenging each other, and showing off who's stronger. Our bodies moving with strength and agility. This is our life, simple but full. I take advantage of Chris being obviously distracted by admiring Val... and I take him down. I love playing with them; they're my brothers.

And then I see her. Rosie.

My gaze stops on her as she makes her entrance into the courtyard. She's wearing a flowy green dress and high heels that sink slightly into the soft ground. I see her falter for a moment, and a smile escapes me. She can't help but be elegant, even here at the ranch. I don't even know if she knows what "simple lifestyle" means... I don't know anything about her, to be honest. Except for some fatherly and probably highly biased comments that Robert has let slip... I know absolutely nothing. Even though the girls already seem to adore her and I... I can't stop thinking about her.

But no... I must be delirious; it must surely be that damn Irish beer that Diego has been supplying us with since his three-year stay in Ireland. Red and alcoholic... just the way we all like it! The girls like it too... if Val, Lexy, and Aurora can be called that... I've never seen girls more similar to us in my life... they're definitely fantastic!

Rosie's presence is magnetic, and I can't help but observe her as she looks around, a bit nervous. Her eyes wander over the scene in front of her: her father at the barbecue, Maria helping him, Lexy and Val dancing and singing, and then her eyes meet mine.

I forget everything else. I walk towards her and smile. "Welcome to the party, princess," I say, letting my gaze run along her body. "Nice dress. Although..." I lean towards her, whispering in her ear: "Maybe you should take off those shoes if you don't want to end up face-first in the dirt."

I feel a shiver run down my spine at the sound of my own voice so close to her. She straightens up, trying to maintain her composure. "I'm fine like this, thank you," she responds with a confident tone, but I can see the slight blush on her cheeks.

I raise my hands in surrender, my smile widening. "As you wish, princess. But don't say I didn't warn you." As I walk away to join the other guys, I can't help but cast one last glance in her direction. There's something about Rosie that intrigues me, something that makes me want to know her better. Yet, I also notice a tension in her, something she can't completely hide. I worry. What's troubling her? Why can't she let go?

I think back to when I saw her this afternoon—she looked so lost.

An absurd, irrational urge took hold of me: the need to help her, to take care of her. When I asked if she wanted to lend me a hand, I fully expected one of her fiery glares and a sharp *go to hell*. But instead, she looked at me with those big, impossibly expressive eyes, and to my surprise, she agreed.

I showed her how to brush the horses, and we settled into a quiet, comforting rhythm. We worked side by side, and I watched as Rosie slowly began to relax, her tension melting away.

I wish I knew what was weighing on her. I wish she'd let me in.

I continue to observe the evening unfold, between laughter and dances. Rosie approaches her father and Maria, and I see how loved she is. Robert nods to her, his face lit up with joy. I see her blush and then, with a sigh of defeat, she takes off her heels. I smile to myself, knowing I was right.

I lose myself in the music, letting myself be carried away by the rhythm. The evening passes quickly, and I find myself laughing and joking with the guys, telling stories around the fire. And then I see Rosie, a bit apart from the party. There's something in her eyes that worries me, a sadness hidden behind that forced smile. I realize that I care about her more than I'd like to admit.

I approach, but Val's cheerful voice inviting her to dance makes me smile. Val always manages to make everyone feel welcome. I watch Rosie as she lets herself be dragged towards the dancing group. She closes her eyes for a moment, and when she reopens them, I see a new light in her eyes.

As the night progresses, I find myself sitting next to her on a hay bale, where she has retreated by herself. I offer her a bottle of beer, and I see surprise in her eyes. "Thoughtful, princess?" I ask, my tone more serious than I expected.

"A little," she admits, accepting the beer. "It's all so... different."

"Good different or bad different?" I ask, curious to know what she really thinks.

She thinks for a moment. "I don't know," she answers honestly. "But maybe... maybe it's not so bad."

I smile, a genuine smile this time, without a trace of sarcasm. "You know, princess, maybe there's hope for you after all."

I look at her, seeing something move inside her. For the first time, I see beyond the facade of the city girl. I see a kind, strong woman, with a depth I hadn't noticed before. But I also see her tension, her difficulty in letting go completely. There's something holding her back, and this worries me.

"Maybe," she whispers, more to herself than to me. We sit in silence, looking at the stars and listening to the music in the distance. It's a comforting silence, and I delude myself that maybe she might like it here and that she could feel at home. I don't know why this thought crosses my mind, and I don't even know why a little later I let myself be guided by impulse and ask her to dance with me.

I hold out my hand, feeling my heart hammer in my chest when Rosie accepts it. Her slender fingers intertwine with mine, soft against my calloused skin. I guide her towards the improvised dance floor, my eyes caught by the movement of her bare feet on the grass. Every step seems like a dance in itself, light and graceful.

Her green dress flutters around her legs with every movement, revealing glimpses of skin that leave me breathless. Her hair, usually impeccable, is now moved by the evening breeze, some rebellious strands caressing her face. She's no longer the perfectly composed city girl - she's wild, free, beautiful.

I gently place my hand on her waist, feeling an electric spark run through me at the contact. Her skin is warm under the light fabric of the dress, and I have to resist the urge to pull her even closer. Our bodies move closer, and we begin to move slowly to the rhythm of the music, every movement charged with unexpressed tension.

Rosie's scent envelops me. Her eyes, illuminated by the flickering light of the lanterns, shine with a light I've never seen before. There's mischief in that look, a spark of adventure that makes me want to discover every secret she hides.

And it's absurd, another thought that flashes through my head: that here, a bit distant from the others, under the stars and surrounded by nature, we look like a magical painting. I swear I'm not a poetry reader or an art lover, and where this sudden romanticism came from, I have no idea. I hope Chris isn't contagious.

For a while, though, I decide to enjoy it because it makes me feel... serene, at peace, in my place.

But then I realize that Rosie won't stay. She'll return to her life in the city, and I... maybe I'll be more hurt than I'll ever admit even to myself.

I shouldn't be involved in this story, I shouldn't feel this way. Yet, here I am, worried about her and more attached than I should be. How did I end up in this situation?

I'm Alex, the cowboy who always has everything under control.

But with Rosie, everything seems different, complicated. And I can't help but wonder what will happen when she leaves.

So... my big mouth does what it always does when I feel a bit uncertain.

"Who would have thought the city princess could move like this," I murmur in her ear, my voice husky. I feel her shiver at my touch, at the warmth of my breath on her skin.

Rosie looks up, a mischievous smile on her lips. "There are many things you don't know about me, cowboy," she responds, her voice low and seductive. Her hands, initially timid on my back, now move with more confidence, fingers tracing patterns on my shirt. She's going to be the death of me.

If she had even the faintest idea of the things I want to do to her, she wouldn't be standing this close. Hell, she'd probably run off, disgusted.

If she knew how badly I crave her, how completely she's undone me... Damn it, I've never been this reckless—not even as a teenager. And yet, here I am, barely holding myself together, all because of her.

We continue dancing, our bodies getting closer. Every movement is a promise, every touch a spark that threatens to ignite us. The tension between us grows, almost palpable, charging the air with electricity.

After a few songs, we stop for another beer. And another. And another one. The alcohol flows in our veins, dissolving the last barriers. Rosie laughs more freely now, her head thrown back, her neck exposed in a way that makes me want to...

"You know what would be really crazy?" she suddenly says, interrupting my thoughts. Her eyes shine with a dangerous, exciting light.

"What?" I ask, already ready to follow her into any adventure.

"Let's go for a swim in the lake!"

I laugh, incredulous and excited at the same time. "Are you serious?"

"Absolutely," she responds, grabbing my hand and dragging me away from the party.

We run towards the lake, laughing and stumbling along the path. The damp grass under our feet, the low branches brushing us as we pass. We arrive at the shore, panting and euphoric, adrenaline rushing through our veins.

Without hesitation, Rosie dives into the water with a cry of joy, the water rising around her like a silver veil.

The moonlight caresses every curve of her body. I'm left breathless, unable to look away. I follow her, diving in next to her. The cool water envelops us, a stark contrast to the heat of our skin. We swim, joking and splashing each other. Rosie laughs, a free and contagious sound that echoes on the surface of the lake.

As we swim, our bodies brush against each other under the water. Every accidental contact sends electric shocks through my body. Rosie's wet dress clings to her like a second skin, revealing curves that leave me breathless. It's a struggle to keep my eyes anywhere but on the delicate curve of her breasts, perfectly framed by the clinging fabric of her soaked dress. The cool water has left her nipples visibly hardened, and the gentle bounce of her chest with each movement is becoming harder and harder to ignore.

The way the dress molds to her, leaving little to the imagination, is utterly distracting. My self-control is hanging by a thread, every shift and sway drawing my attention like a magnet. I know I shouldn't look, but resisting feels like an impossible feat. She's utterly alluring, and it's driving me to the brink.

We move closer, drawn to each other like magnets. Our hands brush under the water, and I feel a jolt run through my body. We're so close now that I can count the water droplets on her eyelashes, see the desire in her eyes.

Rosie moves even closer. I can feel her heart beating wildly, or maybe it's mine. Her hands wander over my chest, light as feathers. My breathing becomes heavy.

My hands find her waist, pulling her even closer. Our faces are inches apart, our breaths mingling. The air between us is charged with tension, with unexpressed desire.

For a moment, time seems to stand still. We're on the edge of something dangerous, exciting. My eyes lower to her lips, wet and inviting. Rosie bites her lower lip, an innocent gesture that sends waves of heat through my body.

"Hey, princess," I tease her, splashing water in her face. 'I thought city girls couldn't swim.'

Rosie gives me a challenging look. "Oh, really?" With a quick movement, she pushes me underwater.

I resurface, coughing and laughing. "Now you're in trouble!"

A water battle begins, both of us determined to win. We chase each other in the lake, laughing and shouting like children. The alcohol in our veins makes everything more fun, more intense.

At one point, I grab her by the waist, trying to submerge her. But Rosie is surprisingly strong. She wriggles, turning towards me. Suddenly, we're face to face, our bodies pressed against each other.

For a moment, we stay like this, panting and surprised. I can see every detail of her face: the water droplets on her eyelashes, the slight blush on her cheeks, her lips slightly parted.

"I got you," I whisper, my voice huskier than I'd like.

"Are you sure?" she responds, a mischievous smile curving her lips.

There's a tension in the air, an electricity that has nothing to do with our usual rivalry. For a moment, I wonder what would happen if I leaned a little closer, if...

But then Rosie splashes water in my eyes and frees herself from my grip, swimming away laughing.

"You'll have to do better than that, cowboy!" she shouts over her shoulder.

I shake my head, emerging from my trance... I need to clear my thoughts.

What was I thinking? This is Rosie, the city princess, a girl I've only known for a few days. Yet, as I chase her in the lake, I can't help but smile.

Chapter 12

Rosie

The rooster's crow abruptly tears me from sleep. I grunt, fumbling for the pillow to cover my ears. Who on earth decided roosters were a good alarm clock? My phone vibrates insistently on the nightstand, adding to the morning concert. I reach out to grab it, blinking sleepily as I try to focus on the screen. It's the girls' WhatsApp group, and it's exploding with messages.

Val: Good morning, princess! Slept well after your moonlit swim? 🌊💦
Lexy: I bet she dreamed about a certain cowboy all night! 😏 A
Aurora: Or maybe she didn't need to dream about him... maybe they spent the night together 😏
Me: Ha ha, very funny. You know there's nothing between Alex and me.
Val: Sure, sure. And I'm allergic to horses.
Lexy: Speaking of longing looks... Aurora, don't you think it's time to talk about a certain cowboy you couldn't stop staring at last night?
Aurora: I don't know what you're talking about... 😳
Aurora: I wasn't... I wasn't staring!
Lexy: Of course... you were just admiring the scenery. A very muscular, jean-clad scenery, I imagine 😏
Val: Our little prairie flower is blooming! 🌸

Aurora: I hate you all. 😑
Val: You love us and you know it!
Me: Speaking of love... Val, you and Chris were so sickeningly sweet last night I nearly got diabetes just watching you.
Lexy: 🤢🤢🤢
Val: What? We were perfectly normal!
Aurora: If by "normal" you mean looking at each other like you're the last glass of water in the desert, then yes, totally normal.
Val: Oh, stop it! We're just... happy.
Lexy: We know, honey. And it's beautiful to see you like that. Even if it's a bit nauseating.

I smile as I read the messages, feeling a warmth spread in my chest.
I also feel something else... which feels very much like a throbbing hangover.
Congratulations, Rosie... only you can get drunk on beer at a family barbecue... and have a hangover too.
I try to get up... there's no point in trying to sleep anymore.
I bump into the nightstand... obviously I can't see anything in the dark, but I already know the light will bother me.
I slowly raise the shutter, looking out the window where I can see the ranch slowly waking up. In the distance, I spot a familiar figure moving among the horses.
Alex.

My heart skips a little, firstly because it's... well, Alex.

Secondly, thinking back to yesterday.

I shake my head, trying to dispel these dangerous thoughts.

What am I doing? This isn't my world, it's not my life. I can't afford to get involved, especially not with Alex.

Alex.

His name evokes a storm of conflicting emotions within me. On one hand, there's this undeniable physical attraction. Those deep, intense eyes that seem to look straight into my soul. That long, wild hair that gives him a rebellious, untamed air. His crooked smile, that body sculpted... he's undeniably attractive, in a rugged, primordial way that makes my knees weak.

There's something so... authentic about him, so far from the refined and polished men of the city.

He's like a force of nature, wild and free like the horses he adores. And then there's that sweet and caring side I glimpsed last night during our dance under the stars. The way he held me in his arms, strong but gentle, as if I were something precious.

But on the other hand, there's everything else. His arrogant attitude, that constant teasing, making me feel out of place. His conviction that I'm just a "city princess" incapable of adapting to this life.

And maybe he's right, isn't he? This isn't my real life. I'm here only temporarily.

No, I can't afford to complicate things. It's better to keep my distance, to return to our "enemies" relationship. It's simpler that way. Safer. Even if a part of me craves that contact, that connection I felt last night, I must be rational.

I decide that from today on, I'll go back to treating Alex like the arrogant cowboy he is.

No more moments of weakness, no more moonlit dances or night swims.

I have to remind myself why I'm here: to help my father and then return to my life in the city.

With this new determination, I prepare to face the day. It doesn't matter how attractive Alex is or how alive this ranch life makes me feel. I must stay focused on my goal. As I get dressed, I cast one last glance out the window. Alex is still there, working with the horses. His movements are fluid and confident, in perfect harmony with the animals. For a moment, my heart races. His long hair waves in the wind, and even from this distance, I can see the concentration in his eyes. There's a wild grace in him that takes my breath away. Then I grit my teeth and look away.

He's just an arrogant cowboy, I mutter to myself. *And you're just passing through. Don't forget that, Rosie.*

But as I leave my room, ready to face another day at the ranch, I can't help but feel a twinge of regret. I firmly ignore that little voice inside me that rebels against this decision, that whispers to me that maybe I'm making a mistake.

I go down the stairs, trying to focus on the familiar sounds of the farm waking up. The scent of freshly brewed coffee welcomes me in the kitchen, where I find my father and Maria chatting quietly. "Good morning, honey," my father greets me with a smile. "Did you sleep well?"

I nod, trying to look as fit as possible even though I actually feel a bit like a corpse.

"Yes, thanks. The rooster was an... interesting wake-up call."

Maria laughs. "You get used to it, believe me. Soon you won't even hear it anymore."

I sit at the table, gratefully accepting the cup of coffee Maria hands me. As I sip the hot drink, I try to plan my day. I need to do some shopping (I need more practical clothes and I can't keep dipping into Val's seemingly inexhaustible wardrobe), I need to focus on work, on the accounts, on anything that keeps me busy and away from...

"Hey, princess. Ready for another day of hard work?" Alex's voice makes me start. I turn to find him leaning against the doorframe, with that usual crooked smile of his. His hair is tied in a messy ponytail, and there's a smudge of dirt on his cheek. He looks so... at ease, so in his element. For a moment, I forget my resolution. Then I recover and raise an eyebrow.

"Always ready, cowboy. Don't underestimate me."

His smile widens. "Don't always feel attacked, princess."

There's a spark in his eyes that makes me tremble internally. But I maintain my neutral expression, reminding myself of my decision.

Enemies.

We're enemies.

"Well," I say, standing up. "I'd better get to work then." I walk past him, deliberately ignoring his scent of leather and pine.

I can't afford to be distracted.

I can't afford to forget who I am and why I'm here.

But as I walk away, I feel his gaze on me. And I can't help but wonder if I'm really doing the right thing.

Chapter 13

Alex

My phone vibrates insistently on the nightstand. I grab it, sighing when I see it's the 'Cowboy Stallions 🐎🍆' WhatsApp group of the guys.

Chris: Hey cowboy, how's your princess after the midnight swim? 🏊🤠
Diego: I bet you kept her "warm" all night, huh? 😏🔥
Fran: Guys, don't make him blush! Our tough Alex has a soft heart after all!
Me: Go to hell, idiots. Nothing happened.
Chris: Sure, and I'm the king of England. We saw you, champ. Diego: Speaking of longing looks... Fran, tell us about how you were drooling over Aurora last night.
Fran: Fuck off, Diego. Don't talk bullshit.
Chris: Hey, that's my sister you're talking about. Watch where you put your eyes, Fran.
Fran: Relax, Chris. I didn't do anything wrong.
Me: You're a bunch of teenagers. Get back to work, idiots.
Diego: Yes, boss. Can't wait to see how you "work" with the princess today 😏

I toss the phone on the bed, running a hand through my hair. The guys can be real assholes sometimes, but they're right about one thing: I can't get Rosie out of my head.

I get up and move to the window, looking out at the ranch fields. The sun is just rising, painting the sky pink and gold. Usually, this view fills me with peace, but today I feel restless.

Rosie.

Her name evokes a storm of conflicting emotions within me. That night swim, the dance under the stars... I can't stop thinking about it. The way her body fit perfectly against mine, her scent, her smile...

What you were about to do...

But then I stop myself. What am I doing?

I barely know her. I don't even know if she's single, for heaven's sake!

And even if she were, what would change? She belongs to a completely different world from mine. I realize that, despite the time we've spent together, I know practically nothing about her. About her life in Los Angeles, her dreams, her fears.

Is she really happy there? Sometimes she seems so tense, so out of place here at the ranch. But then there are moments when I see her relax, when I see a glimmer in her eyes that makes me think that...

I have to stop this, damn it!

I don't even know what kind of life she leads in Los Angeles.

Is she one of those city girls who spend their time in expensive restaurants and exclusive clubs?

And then there's the most important issue: she'll go back to Los Angeles. This isn't her life, it's not her world.

And me? I'm tied to this ranch, to this land. It's all I've ever known, all I've ever wanted.

I sigh, resting my forehead against the cold window glass. Why am I tormenting myself like this? Rosie is just a temporary complication in my life. Soon she'll be gone, and everything will go back to normal.

Yet, as I prepare to face another day at the ranch, I can't help but feel a twinge of... something. Regret? Desire? I don't know.

What I do know is that I need to focus on my work, on my duties. I can't afford distractions, especially not in the form of a city princess with eyes that seem to hide a thousand secrets.

As I leave my room, I vow to keep my distance. To treat her like I would any other guest at the ranch.

It's better this way, I tell myself. For both of us.

But as I head towards the stables, I can't help but glance towards the window of her room. And for a moment, just for a moment, I think I see her big brown eyes looking back at me.

I shake my head, trying to free myself of thoughts about Rosie and focus on work. But it's easier said than done.

After finishing the first work shift, I enter the kitchen to grab a coffee. And there I see her. Rosie is sitting at the table with her father and Maria.

She looks... uneasy. And that makes me uneasy too. I don't like seeing her like this.

"Hey, princess. Ready for another day of hard work?" I ask, trying to maintain my usual teasing tone.

She looks up when I enter, and for a moment, I expect to see... what? A smile? A glimmer in her eyes? Instead, her gaze is almost... guarded.

I see her start slightly, then quickly compose herself. She raises an eyebrow and responds, "Always ready, cowboy. Don't underestimate me."

Her tone is defiant, but there's something in her eyes... a kind of distance that wasn't there last night. Did what happened at the bonfire mean something to her? And should I care?

"Don't always feel attacked, princess," I reply with a smile, but inside I feel a strange unease.

I see her stand up, passing by me. "Well," she says. "I'd better get to work then."

As she walks away, I can't help but catch her scent, notice how her body moves with grace even in this rustic environment. This brief exchange has reignited in me the desire to provoke her, to push her beyond that composed facade she seems to have rebuilt. But at the same time, I realize how little I really know her. I don't know what she thinks about what happened between us, I don't know if she's happy here or if she can't wait to get back to her life in Los Angeles.

And suddenly, I find myself wanting to know. To truly know her, beyond this stupid rivalry we've built.

But instead of asking questions, of trying to understand, I find myself staring at the door she left through, torn between the desire to follow her and the desire to keep my distance.

Why do I care so much? And what am I supposed to do with these feelings I can't control?

Chapter 14

Alex

With my head still full of thoughts about Rosie, I head to the ranch gym. It's well-equipped and has everything we might need. We all enjoy working out, so building it seemed like a good investment. The gym is simple, nothing fancy, but a bit more modern than the classic style of the rest of the ranch. The walls are painted in a soft gray, with a few wooden accents to tie in the rustic theme. One of the main walls is lined with large mirrors, while another features shelves holding weights, resistance bands, and other workout tools. In one corner, there's a cardio area with treadmills, stationary bikes, and an elliptical machine. On the opposite side, there are strength-training machines and a bench for weightlifting. At the center, there's an open space with mats for bodyweight exercises or stretching. There's also a dedicated dance space for Rory. She's an extraordinary dancer, and when she's home from college, she uses the gym to refine her routines. Her movements are so graceful, it's impossible not to be in awe of her talent. I'm incredibly proud of her—not just for her dancing but for the person she is. Rory is also an exceptional student, my brilliant adopted little sister. She's achieved so much already, including earning a scholarship to Halton University, one of the country's oldest and most prestigious institutions. She's truly made us all proud.

Val and Lexy, on the other hand, are full of energy and always up for adventure. They love trying out every sport—those two are unstoppable. If there's a challenge to take on, you can count on them to dive right in without hesitation.

There are also locker rooms and showers, divided for men and women, since the girls enjoy using the space to work out too.

When I enter, I see the guys are already there. Chris is lifting weights, muscles tense under the strain. Diego is on the pull-up bar, while Fran is jumping rope.

"Hey, Romeo!" Diego greets me, coming down from the bar. "We thought you'd got lost in your love story."

I roll my eyes. "Very funny. Are you ready to be humiliated or what?"

Chris grins, putting down the weights. "Oh, someone's in a fighting mood today. Trouble in paradise with the princess?"

"Shut that mouth before I shut it for you," I retort, but without real malice. This constant joking between us is comforting, familiar.

"Ooh, someone's touchy," Fran laughs. "Come on, champ, let's see what you've got."

We start with pull-ups. It's a silent but intense competition, each of us trying to outdo the others. I feel my muscles burn, but I push beyond the pain.

"Fifteen... sixteen... seventeen..." Diego counts. "Come on, Alex, I think Rosie could beat this record!"

The mention of Rosie makes me lose concentration for a second, and I almost lose my grip. I recover quickly, but not fast enough for the guys not to notice.

"Oh oh, looks like we've touched a nerve," Chris grins.

"Fuck off," I grunt, dropping to the ground. I did twenty pull-ups, more than all of them, but I don't feel satisfied.

We move on to weights. As I lift the bar, I feel the familiar burn in my muscles. I focus on that sensation, trying to chase away thoughts of Rosie.

"Hey, Alex," Diego says between sets. "I bet you're thinking about how to impress your princess with these muscles, huh?"

"Yeah, right," I snort. "Why don't you think about how to impress your mystery girl instead?"

Diego almost drops the weight he's lifting, and the other guys burst out laughing.

"Hit and sunk!" Chris exclaims.

"I don't know what you're talking about," Diego mutters, but the blush on his cheeks betrays him.

"Oh, come on," Fran chimes in, "we know there's something going on..."

Diego tries to keep a serious expression, but then he bursts out laughing too. "At least I don't spend my nights taking moonlit swims."

All eyes turn back to me, and I feel the heat rising to my face. "Oh, shut up and get back to training," I grunt, lifting a heavier weight to distract them.

We continue like this for an hour, alternating exercises and jokes. It's exhausting, but somehow cathartic. Every push, every lift seems to take away a bit of my frustration and confusion.

In the end, we're all sweaty and panting, lying on the gym floor.

"Damn, Alex," Chris pants. "You were a beast today. What did you have for breakfast?"

I shrug, staring at the ceiling. "Nothing special."

"Mhm," Diego murmurs. "Nothing to do with a certain city girl, right?"

I feel anger bubbling up again. "How many times do I have to tell you? There's nothing between me and Rosie."

"Sure, sure," Fran says, sitting up. "That's why you can't stop thinking about her?"

I get up abruptly, feeling the need to move, to do something. "You don't know what you're talking about."

Chris gets up too, putting a hand on my shoulder. "Hey, man. We know it's complicated. But maybe... maybe you should talk to her instead of trying to ignore what you feel."

I look at him, surprised by his seriousness. For a moment, I'm tempted to open up, to share all my worries and doubts.

But then I shake my head. "There's nothing to talk about. She'll be leaving soon, and everything will go back to normal."

The guys exchange a look I can't interpret.

"If you say so, man," Diego says, but he doesn't sound convinced.

As we leave the gym, I feel the weight of their gazes on me. As we walk towards the showers, the silence between us is charged with unspoken tension. I know the guys want to say something, but they're holding back their words, perhaps for fear of pushing me too far.

Finally, it's Chris who breaks the silence. "You know, Alex," he says cautiously, "there's nothing wrong with admitting you like someone."

I sigh heavily. "It's not that simple, Chris."

"And why not?" Diego chimes in. "She's pretty, you're... well, you. What's complicated about it?"

I stop, running a hand through my sweat-damp hair. "It's complicated because she doesn't belong to this world. She's here only temporarily. She has a whole life waiting for her in Los Angeles. And I don't know what the hell is going through my head. I don't even know her, damn it. She's just a pretty girl... I don't know why you're all getting so worked up," I burst out. I feel a bit stupid for saying she's just a pretty girl... I know she's much more than that. And I don't even know why I know that, considering I don't know her.

Am I going crazy?

Fran pats me on the shoulder. "You have time... you can decide whether to use it and try to figure out if there's something between you or just have fun. Why are you tormenting yourself like this?! And Alex, remember that her father lives here.

She's alone on the other side of the world... maybe she'll decide to stay."

His words hit me harder than I'd like to admit. A part of me, a part I'm desperately trying to ignore, clings to that hope.

"We don't know," I finally say. "We don't really know her. I don't even know if she's happy there, if she has someone waiting for her... and then... what about the rest of her family?"

I don't know what to be more uneasy about. I can't bear to think that she might have a boyfriend in America... this thought definitely bothers me.

And even the last thing I blurted out worries me. Is she alone? I hadn't thought about the fact that Robert had told us his first wife had died many years ago. Suddenly, I'd like to talk to Rosie. Understand what's going on in her head... what she's had to face...

"And why don't you ask her?" Chris suggests. "Instead of making assumptions, why don't you try to really get to know her?"

I remain silent for a moment, reflecting on his words. He's right, I know. But the idea of having such conversations terrifies me. It's all a mess. I'm not used to these things. I don't even know what "these things" are. I can't ask a person out of the blue to tell me the secrets of their soul if I don't trust myself.

"I don't know if I can," I finally admit, my voice barely more than a whisper.

Diego puts an arm around my shoulders. "Hey, you don't have to do it alone. We're here for you, man. If you want, we can organize something. An evening all together, no pressure. So you can get to know her better without feeling embarrassed."

The idea isn't bad, I have to admit. Maybe, in a group context, I could relax enough to really talk to Rosie.

I think back to the night of the barbecue. To her... she seemed so nervous and out of place. To her letting go when Val offered her a lifeline. To her then withdrawing and seeming... melancholic?

And then to us...

Us...

"Maybe," I say slowly. "It could work." I don't know if this slips out of my mouth out of pure selfishness, because I'd like to have her back like that evening, or because I feel relieved at the prospect of spending time with her and having more opportunities to talk without necessarily resorting to a date right away.

A date that would be awkward. I wouldn't know what to say, what to do, how to behave.

The guys smile, clearly satisfied with having made progress.

"Great!" Fran exclaims. "And maybe we can invite your mystery girl too, eh Diego?"

Diego looks panicked. "There's no mystery girl."

Chapter 15

Rosie

I stare at my laptop screen, the figures and graphs dancing before my eyes without making any sense. I sigh heavily, running a hand through my hair. It's useless. I can't concentrate. My mind keeps wandering, going back to the night of the barbecue, the swim in the lake, the dance with Alex...

Alex. Why can't I get him out of my head? *He's just an arrogant cowboy*, I repeat to myself for the umpteenth time. Yet, the memory of his smile, the warmth of his body against mine as we danced, makes my heart race.

I abruptly close the laptop. It's clear I won't accomplish anything productive today. I stand up from the chair, feeling restless and nervous. I need air, to move, to do something to distract myself from these confused thoughts.

As if sensing my discomfort, I hear a knock at the door. "Come in," I say, trying to hide my agitation.

Maria enters, her face lit up by her usual warm smile. "Hey, honey. How about joining us girls for some ranch work? We're going to pick fruit and then make jams and pies."

For a moment, I hesitate. The idea of getting my hands dirty with manual labor makes me feel a bit uncomfortable. But then I think of the alternative: staying here staring at the computer screen and tormenting myself with thoughts about Alex.

"You know what? That sounds like a great idea," I respond, surprising myself.

Maria claps her hands, excited. "Fantastic! Val has already prepared some more suitable clothes for you. Come on, let's get you changed!"

I follow Maria to Val's room, where I find denim overalls, a bright red top, a pair of worn but comfortable boots, and a cowgirl hat. I look at myself in the mirror after changing and barely recognize myself. I look... different. More relaxed, perhaps. Less "city princess" and more... well, ranch girl. I almost wish Alex could see me... *damn it, Rosie, can't you go five minutes without thinking about him!*

"Wow, Rosie!" Lexy exclaims when she sees me. "You look like a real cowgirl!"

"Careful," Val adds with a smirk. "You might turn a certain cowboy's head..."

I feel my cheeks flush. "I don't know what you're talking about," I mutter, but my heart races at the thought of Alex. He'd probably tease me. Or make one of his comments.

We head out to the orchard, the warm sun on our skin and the air fragrant with ripe fruit. Maria guides us among the trees, showing us which fruits are ready to be picked.

"Okay girls, let's make a bet," Aurora exclaims with a mischievous grin. "Whoever picks the least has to... um... wash Alex's jeep!"

"Oh my," I giggle, "that's practically an archaeological expedition!"

Val raises an eyebrow. "Why, have you inspected it up close, Rosie?"

I feel my cheeks blaze. "N-no, it's just that... you can see it's dirty, can't you?"

"Mhmm," Lexy murmurs with a smirk, "sure, sure..."

Maria intervenes, saving me from embarrassment. "Come on, girls, don't torment poor Rosie. Focus on the fruit!"

As we pick, Val starts humming a terribly off-key country song.

"Hey Val," I interrupt, laughing, "maybe you should leave the singing to Lexy. We wouldn't want the fruit to run away from the tree!"

"Ha-ha, very funny," Val replies, throwing an apple at me that I barely dodge. "At least I don't dance like I have two left feet!"

"Hey!" I protest. "I danced... decently the other night!"

"Oh yes," Aurora chimes in with a smirk, "especially when you were in the arms of a certain cowboy..."

"Aurora!" I exclaim, feeling my face go up in flames.

Maria laughs softly. "Leave her alone, Aurora. I remember how I was when I met Rosie's father..."

"Oh no," I groan, covering my face with my hands. "You're way off... there's nothing between us! And please, no embarrassing stories about Dad!"

They all burst out laughing, and I'm surprised to find myself joining in, feeling strangely light.

Chapter 16

Alex

I can't get Rosie out of my head. All day, I've been watching her move around the ranch in those damn overalls that look incredibly good on her. Her hair tucked under her cowgirl hat, with a few rebellious strands caressing her face... it's a breathtaking sight.

I see her laughing with the other girls while picking fruit, her face illuminated by the sun and a joy I've never seen in her before. She seems so at ease, so... right here. As if she belongs in this place.

I find myself searching for her wherever I go. When I'm in the stables, I catch myself looking towards the orchard. When I'm working on the fences, my eyes wander to the house, hoping to see her come out. It's a constant and dangerous distraction.

And the situation is definitely getting worse. I can't focus on work; I'm risking making stupid mistakes. This morning, I almost left the calf pen gate open, all because I saw her pass by with a basket of apples and couldn't take my eyes off her.

I think about the evening the guys want to organize, the opportunity to get closer to Rosie. But now I realize it's a terrible idea. I can't afford to get any closer. I can't risk falling even deeper into... whatever this is.

No, I have to go back to being the annoying cowboy. I need to keep my distance, protect myself. Protect her. Because I know that in the end, she'll leave, return to her life in Los Angeles, and I'll be left here with a broken heart.

But how can I annoy her? How can I push her away when all I want is to draw her to me?

I see her heading towards the stables, and I know this is my chance. I take a deep breath, trying to summon that part of me that knows how to provoke her, how to make her angry.

"Hey, princess!" I call out as she approaches. "I see you're trying to blend in. Too bad your five-hundred-dollar-a-liter perfume gives you away."

What I don't admit is how much I'm obsessed with her fragrance. How desperately I want to bury my face in her hair, trail my nose along her neck, and breathe her in, losing myself in her essence forever. I don't tell anyone that her perfume fills every breath I take or that I'd peeked into her room when she'd left the door open—just to find out what she wears. I'd seen it on her dresser: small, delicate, elegant, and pink. I couldn't have imagined anything else. Miss Dior feels like it was made for her.

I see her face contort into a grimace of irritation. "Oh, really? At least I don't smell like I've bathed in a mud puddle."

"Touché," I reply with a smirk. "But at least I know how to tell a cow from a bull. Or do you need Google for that?"

Her eyes flash with anger. "I don't need Google to figure out that you're an idiot, Alex."

I'm an idiot. And this... this really hurts. It hurts to hear what she thinks of me, even if she's saying it in a moment of irritation. But it's just another reminder that someone like Rosie could never see anything good in someone like me. And I'm the idiot who's obsessed with her, the one who's bound to end up with a broken heart.

What stings even more is the look of disappointment in her eyes.

Well, Rosie, if you thought there was something different about me, you were wrong. There's nothing good here, and the sooner you realize that, the better it'll be for both of us.

I throw back a theatrical remark, but it's all a mask. The truth is, I just want to disappear.

"Ouch, that hurts," I say, bringing a hand to my chest in feigned pain. "Almost as much as it must hurt to walk in those heels in the fields. Oh wait, you've finally abandoned them?"

"You know what, Alex?" she finally says, her voice sharp as a razor. "At least I have a life beyond this ranch. What will you do when you're too old to play cowboy? Tell stories to the cattle?"

Her jab hits me harder than I'd like to admit. "Better to tell stories to the cattle than live an empty life in a big city, right?"

"Empty?" she hisses. "At least my life has a future, Alex. What do you have beyond this land and a few horses?"

Her words wound me deeply, but I try not to show it. "I have freedom, Rosie. Something you'll never know the meaning of, trapped in your golden cage."

I see a flash of pain in her eyes, quickly replaced by anger. "You know what? You're right. I'm not a cowgirl, and I don't want to be one. I prefer my 'golden cage' to a life wasted playing tough guy with cows!"

With these words, she turns and leaves, leaving me with a mixture of bitter satisfaction and deep regret. I got what I wanted: I pushed her away. But the pain in her eyes, the hurt in her voice... it makes me feel like I've made a terrible mistake.

I watch her walk away, her determined stride betraying her anger. A part of me wants to run after her, but I remain motionless, paralyzed by the inner conflict that's consuming me.

I run a hand over my face, suddenly feeling exhausted. What am I doing? Why am I so attracted to a girl I barely know and who belongs to a completely different world from mine? It's as if we're two planets in different orbits, destined to brush past each other but never truly meet.

I think back to the moments we've shared: the night swim, dancing under the stars, even our bickering. There's a spark between us, undeniable and powerful. But is it enough to bridge the chasm that separates us?

"Hey, cowboy," a familiar voice calls from behind me. I turn to see Chris standing there, his brow slightly furrowed, concern etched into his rugged features. His hands are stuffed into his jeans pockets, but his posture is loose, casual—like he's trying not to push too hard. "I saw everything. You alright?"

My brother steps closer, placing a firm hand on my shoulder. His piercing eyes, a striking mix of amber and green, lock onto mine, reading me the way he always does—like I'm an open book. A wave of gratitude swells in my chest. Chris has always been my anchor, the one person who can see through the layers of bullshit I try to wrap myself in.

And for once, I don't bother pretending. I let out a heavy sigh, rubbing the back of my neck. "I don't know, Chris. Everything just feels... complicated."

Chris nods slowly, his face softening as he gives my shoulder a reassuring squeeze. "What's the real problem?" he asks, his tone steady but probing, his voice as calm as a still lake.

What's the real problem? Hell, I wish I knew.

One moment, I'm burning up with desire, scanning every corner of the ranch just for a glimpse of Rosie, craving the way her presence lights up the air around her. Every move she makes, every subtle shift, seems designed to set my blood on fire. But then, just as quickly, I'm furious—at her, at myself—because I can't stand how completely she's taken over my thoughts. She's everywhere, and no matter how hard I try, I can't push her out of my head. It's maddening, this tug-of-war between wanting her so badly it aches and resenting her for making me feel this way.Chris waits patiently, but I can feel his eyes on me, tracking every flicker of emotion that crosses my face.

"It's a good question, bro," I mutter finally, the words heavy on my tongue. Because what else can I say? I'm as lost as he is.

Chris nudges me gently toward the low stone wall nearby, his hand briefly pressing against my back. "C'mon, sit," he says, his tone light but firm. He hops up to sit beside me, boots scuffing the dusty surface, and I follow suit, our shoulders almost touching. It's like when we were kids, sitting on the barn roof, hashing out life's problems over cans of soda.

"Listen," he begins, resting his forearms on his thighs, his hands dangling loosely between his knees. He glances at me sideways, a smirk tugging at the corner of his mouth. "I think this girl's got you more twisted up than a barbed wire fence. And you know what? That's not a bad thing. I've never seen you lose your cool over anyone."

I scoff, shaking my head, but before I can argue, Chris raises a hand, cutting me off with a playful look that says, *Don't even try it.*

"Bro," he says, his voice dropping an octave, more serious now, "I know letting people in scares the hell out of you. It's been that way since... you know. I've seen it. I've seen you. So don't waste your breath denying it." His gaze softens as he nudges me lightly with his elbow. "Maybe you're losing your head over her. Or maybe," he adds, his smirk returning, "you just need to get laid. Either way, live a little."

I huff out a laugh despite myself, shaking my head at his audacity.

"If you want to joke around with her, do it. If you want to flirt, try it. See where it goes. But don't do this, man." He gestures at me with a small wave of his hand, like he's trying to encompass the mess I'm in. "Don't sabotage everything before it even has the chance to be something."

His words hit me like a one-two punch. He's always known how to cut through my defenses, and this time is no different. Chris has this way of balancing tough love with genuine care, and it's why I've always trusted him with the things I can't say to anyone else.

I swallow hard, my throat tight, and stare down at my boots, scuffing the dirt beneath them. "Thanks," I say finally, my voice low but full of meaning. It's not much, but I know he gets it. He always does.

Chris smiles, clapping me on the shoulder before standing and stretching with a groan. "We're family, bro. We're all here for you. But if you ever need just me, you know where to find me."

He tosses me a wink, the teasing glint back in his eyes as he heads off toward the barn. I watch him go, a small smile tugging at my lips. Chris always knows how to leave me feeling seen, and for that, I'm endlessly grateful.

As Chris walks away, I find myself staring at the spot where Rosie disappeared. With a deep breath, I head towards the stables. I have work to do, and for now, it's better to focus on that. The familiarity of daily tasks comforts me, anchors me to the reality of the ranch that has always been my life.

I feel like a complete idiot. Maybe I should apologize to Rosie... although from her response, she doesn't seem to have a high opinion of me and what I do.

And how did you expect her to respond?

I practically asked her to insult me... and I ruined a moment when she seemed serene and relaxed.

All because of my stupidity. Because of my absurd convictions. Because of fear.

And as the day progresses, the weight of the words I exchanged with Rosie weighs more heavily on me. Thinking back to our conversation, I realize that this time I might have really crossed the line. It wasn't our usual playful banter; there was venom in our words, an intention to hurt that had never been there before.

I stop, leaning against the fence. What came over me? Our relationship has always been made up of jokes and provocations; it's my way of being. But before... before it was different.

What if I had lost her before I even really had her? If I had ruined everything before giving us a real chance?

I sigh heavily, running a hand through my hair. I can't deny that there's something between us, an attraction, a spark that goes beyond our differences. But perhaps it's precisely the fear of this attraction that pushed me to behave this way.

I think back to the words we exchanged.

At least I have a life beyond this ranch.

Golden cage.

We hurt each other, touching each other's most sensitive points.

But why? Why do I feel the need to push her away like this? Is it really just because we're too different, or is there something else?

I can't deny that since that damn first time I saw her, Rosie Thorne hasn't left my mind.

I just hope my stupid heart isn't involved too.

In any case... I need to find a way to apologize to Rosie.

And there you have it, ladies and gentlemen, another thing I'm not good at.

Did I mention I'm a disaster?!

Chapter 17

Rosie

I walk away from Alex with long strides, feeling tears threatening to fall. I won't give him the satisfaction of seeing me cry. Not for him. Not for an arrogant cowboy I've known for just a few days.

Yet, his words have hurt me more deeply than I'd like to admit.

Better to tell stories to the cattle than live an empty life in a big city.

Empty? My life isn't empty. It can't be. I have a successful job, friends, a rising career. How dare he judge me like that?

But an annoying little voice in my head whispers: *What if he's right?*

I shake my head, trying to banish that thought.

No, he can't be right. He doesn't even know me, he knows nothing about me or my life in Los Angeles.

I stop near the orchard, leaning against a tree and taking a deep breath. The air fragrant with ripe apples helps calm me a bit, but the whirlwind of emotions inside me doesn't subside.

I think back to the words I said to him.

I prefer my 'golden cage' to a life wasted playing tough guy with cows!

I grimace at the memory. I was cruel, I know. I didn't really mean what I said. But he had hurt me and I... I wanted to hurt him back.

But why? Why did his words hit me so hard? Why do I care so much about what a stubborn cowboy, whom I've known for barely a few weeks, thinks?

The truth is that Alex has occupied my thoughts since I first saw him.

"Stop it, Rosie," I scold myself out loud. "He's just a cowboy. An irritating, arrogant cowboy and... and..."

And one who makes me feel alive like I haven't felt in years. Who makes me question everything I thought I knew about myself and my life.

The memory of our dance under the stars, of the night swim in the lake, makes my heart race. There was something in those moments, a connection that went beyond our differences and our bickering. A spontaneity that I've never had. A feeling of freedom...

Bare feet on the grass. Wet, messy hair in the lake. The way you felt in his arms...

But then I think of his words today, the venom in his voice, and I feel a pang of pain in my chest. Maybe I was wrong. Maybe I saw something that wasn't there. Maybe Alex is really just an arrogant cowboy who can't wait to get rid of the city princess.

Yet, I can't shake off the feeling that there's more to it. That behind that tough facade lies something deeper, something that irresistibly attracts me.

I run a hand over my face, frustrated.

What's happening to me? I came here to help my father, not to lose my mind over a cowboy.

This isn't me. I don't lose control. I always have my day planned. I've got a five-year plan to stick to. And I sure as hell can't lose my mind over Alex.

No matter what I think... you already did it. Have I mentioned how much I hate that little voice in my head? It makes assumptions about me, but it doesn't know a thing. I *cannot* lose my mind over Alex fucking cowboy!

Okay, fine, he's sexy. But there are a lot of sexy people.

And did I mention how much he irritates me? He's always so careless, so damn annoying, living in the moment, not caring about his appearance...

Not that he needs to.

Damn inner voice!

I have a life in Los Angeles, a career, a future...

But as I look around this ranch, I find myself wondering if those plans are really what I want. If the life I've built in LA is truly as fulfilling as I've always believed.

I sigh deeply. I don't have any answers, just a pile of confused questions and conflicting feelings. The only thing I'm sure of is that Alex, in some way, has managed to shake me to the core, making me question everything.

And I don't know if I should hate him or thank him for it.I continue to walk aimlessly around the ranch, trying to sort out my thoughts. The sun is setting, casting long shadows on the ground and tinting everything with a warm golden glow. It's beautiful, I have to admit. So different from the Los Angeles sunsets, obscured by smog and skyscrapers.

I stop near the horse corral, watching them graze peacefully. There's a peace here that I've never experienced in the city. A simplicity that, I must admit, has its charm.

"Damn it, Alex," I mutter to myself. "Why do you have to make everything so complicated?"

Because that's what he's done.

He's complicated everything.

Before meeting him, my life was orderly, predictable.

I knew exactly who I was and what I wanted. Or at least, I thought I did.

But now? Now I'm not so sure anymore.

I lean against the fence, letting the rough wood slightly scratch my hands. It's a real, tangible sensation, so different from my aseptic life in Los Angeles.

"What are you doing here, Rosie?" I ask myself out loud. "What are you really looking for?"

Fucking cowboy!

Irritating, frustrating, charming Alex. With his sarcastic comments and his smile that makes my knees weak. With his passion for this land and this lifestyle that I can't fully understand, but that intrigues me more and more.

I realize that, despite our arguments, despite the harsh words we've exchanged, a part of me can't wait to see him again. To exchange more banter, to feel that spark of electricity again when our eyes meet.

"You're crazy," I tell myself, shaking my head. "Completely crazy."

But maybe a little madness is exactly what I need. Maybe it's time to stop being the perfect and controlled Rosie that everyone expects me to be. Maybe it's time to let go a little, to see where this strange adventure takes me.

As I walk towards the house, my phone vibrates frantically. I pull it out and see a flurry of notifications from the "Cowgirl Bootcamp 🤠 👢" group chat. I roll my eyes, but I can't hold back a smile.

Val has renamed the group

Lexy: 🚨 RED ALERT GIRLS! 🚨

Val: What? Did you break a nail feeding the horses? 💅

Aurora: Or worse... did you run out of self-tanner? 😱

Lexy: 🙄 Ha-ha, you're hilarious. No, BOMBSHELL news! The guys have organized an evening!

Me: An evening? Like... with people and things?

Val: No, Rosie, with cows and hay 🐄 Of course with people! Aurora: Wait... WHICH guys exactly? 👀

Lexy: Our favorite cowboys, of course! 🤠

Me: Define "favorite" 😒

Val: Oh, don't be difficult, Rosie! We all know you can't wait to dance with a CERTAIN cowboy 🐓

Me: That "certain cowboy" can go take a hike 😤

Aurora: Uh oh... trouble in paradise? Spill the beans, Rosie!

Me: Let's just say Mr. Shiny Boots decided to be a jerk today

Lexy: Oh no! What did he do?

Me: Nothing important. Just the usual arrogant and unbearable Alex

Val: Wait a minute... I have an idea! 💡

Aurora: Uh oh, Val has an idea. Should we be worried?

Val: Let's make those cowboys eat dust! Tomorrow night we'll be so sexy they won't know what hit them!

Lexy: I like how you think, sister! Operation "Cowgirl Revenge" is officially underway! 🔥

Aurora: I'm in! Rosie?

Me: ...I don't know, girls. I don't think that...

Val: Come on, Rosie! Don't you want to see Alex's face when he sees you?

Lexy: Think about how jaw-dropped he'll be! 😲

Aurora: And maybe he'll realize how much of an idiot he's been!

Me: ...Ok, I'm in. Let's show these cowboys what city girls are capable of!

Val: YEEHAW! 👑 Prepare your sexiest outfits, girls!

Lexy: Shiny boots and short skirts, here we come! 👢👗

Aurora: Let the Cowgirl Revenge begin! 🔥

I put the phone back in my pocket, a mix of nervousness and excitement growing inside me. Maybe this evening will be the perfect opportunity to put Alex in his place. And if I happen to have a little fun in the process... well, all the better!

As I approach the house, I feel the girls' energy infecting me. The sadness and confusion I felt after the spat with Alex are fading, replaced by a new determination.

Enough with the games, enough with the childish bickering. It's time to change the game.

A mischievous smile forms on my lips as I think about tomorrow night. Alex won't know what hit him. I intend to flirt seriously, to show him exactly what I'm made of. No more helpless city princess, it's time he sees the real Rosie.

And all those worries about who I am, what I'm doing here, about my future? I push them into a corner of my mind. Now is not the time to think about it. Now is the time to have fun, to let go, to be bold.

I enter my room with a determined step, feeling charged and ready for action. I open the closet enthusiastically, but... my smile falters. In front of me, I see only my usual office clothes, elegant suits and silk blouses. Nothing suitable for an evening at the ranch, let alone for seducing a stubborn cowboy.

"Damn it," I mutter, running a hand through my hair. How can I transform into a sexy cowgirl with a Wall Street wardrobe?

I grab the phone, an idea forming in my mind. If there's anyone who can help me in this mission, it's my new friends.

Me: SOS girls! 🆘 I need a sexy cowgirl outfit ASAP! My wardrobe is a disaster 😱

The response is immediate and enthusiastic.

Lexy: Fear not, Rosie! Operation "Cowgirl Transformation" is underway! 🤠

Val: I already have the perfect outfit in mind! 👗

Aurora: And I have the perfect boots to complete the look! 👢

I smile, feeling a new wave of excitement. With the girls' help, I'll be ready to conquer the ranch - and a certain cowboy - in no time.

Me: Girls, you're the best! 💚 Operation "Ranch Conquest" can begin!

I close the phone, feeling more confident than ever. Tomorrow night will be a night to remember, and I can't wait to see Alex's face when he sees me. Let him prepare, because Rosie the cowgirl is about to make her debut!
I lie down on the bed, a satisfied smile on my lips as I imagine tomorrow evening. Excitement runs through my veins, mixing with a determination I haven't felt in a long time.
My phone vibrates again. It's Val.

Val: Hey Rosie, tomorrow at my place; pre-evening preparation with all of us. We'll make you a true rodeo queen! 👗🐎

I smile even more. The idea of getting ready with the girls fills me with joy. It's something I haven't done in... well, too long.

Me: I'll be there! Can't wait! 😊 But... how about we also go shopping? I need to upgrade my wardrobe.

I close my eyes, letting the anticipation for tomorrow envelop me. For the first time since I arrived at the ranch, I feel truly excited about something. It's no longer just a matter of work or duty to my father. It's something just for me.

For a moment, I think about my life in the city. My job, my friends, the routine I left behind. It all seems so far away now, almost as if it belonged to another person.

I shake my head, chasing away those thoughts. It's not the time to think about the past or the future. Now I just want to focus on the present, on this new Rosie that's emerging here at the ranch.

I pick up my phone. I open the gallery and scroll through the photos until I find the one I was looking for: a selfie I took with the girls today, all smiling and a bit dirty after a day of work at the ranch.

I look at my face in that photo and see something different. My eyes shine with a light I haven't seen in a long time. My cheeks are flushed, but not from makeup.

I look... happy. Truly happy.

With a smile, I set that photo as my phone background.

It's a reminder of who I'm becoming here, of this new Rosie that's emerging.

Tomorrow night will be just the beginning, I tell myself.

The beginning of what, I don't know yet. But I can't wait to find out.

And if along the way I happen to make a certain stubborn cowboy lose his mind... well, all the better.

Chapter 18

Alex

I didn't see Rosie at dinner yesterday, and I haven't seen her all day today. She's skipped every meal—or maybe she's had them somewhere else, with someone else.

It's all I can think about.

I should be focusing on the horses' training schedules. This afternoon, Cherry—a new mare we're adding to the competition roster—needs her first round of athletic prep. But instead, my thoughts keep circling back to Rosalie Thorne.

Is she avoiding me?

The idea cuts deep, sharper than I'd like to admit.

Last night, we were all at the table. I tried to sound casual when I asked if we should wait for Rosie. Robert shrugged it off, said she was probably tired from the day's work and didn't want to disturb her if she was resting.

This morning, I went for coffee at 8:30—the time the princess usually graces us with her presence for breakfast. But she wasn't there. Rosie is nothing if not predictable, and her absence was a red flag I couldn't ignore. For the second time, I wondered: is she avoiding me?

I spent more time wandering the ranch than I should have, circling places I had no reason to be. I should've stayed in the pens, assessing the training of the five veteran horses. But no matter where I went, there was no sign of her.

Lunch came and went. She wasn't there either. The girls were gone too, which made it easier to deflect attention when I asked about them. Maria said they were out somewhere—maybe in Elm Hollow, the little town closest to the ranch. She didn't specify if Rosie was with them, and I didn't push it.

The last thing I need is more smirks and raised eyebrows from the guys. They're already relentless, tossing out teasing remarks every time I so much as glance around or ask a question.

How irritating.

The sun is setting now, casting long shadows across the ranch. I've done my best to focus on my work, but no matter how hard I try, my thoughts keep drifting back to that fiery-haired princess. I haven't seen Rosie all day, and it's souring my mood more than I care to admit.

Preparations for the evening are in full swing.

The air is charged with excitement and a bit of nervousness, at least on my part.

Chris is arranging the wood for the bonfire on the beach, while Diego and Fran are carrying cases of beer and the sangria Maria prepared. The smell of freshly baked pizza wafts through the air, making my mouth water... even though my stomach is in knots and I don't think I could eat a thing.

I didn't even have lunch today. I showed up for lunch just to see Rosie... but since she wasn't there, I excused myself, saying I wasn't hungry and that I'd get back to work. Which is totally strange for me... I love eating and I'm always ravenous. With all the energy I burn during the day...

Could I be coming down with something?

"Hey, Alex!" Diego calls out to me, his voice carrying easily across the yard. "My cousin Jake and his friends will be here soon. They said they're bringing tequila, too!"

Jake's a bull rider, just like Diego. They train together often, and you can tell they're tight. There's always a bit of competition between them —they're two of the best, after all—but it's the kind that drives them forward. Friendly, if not a little fiery.

Thanks to the two of them, bull riding has taken off around here. Before they hit the circuits, it wasn't a big deal in these parts. Now, more and more guys are getting into it. Between our ranch and Jake's, we're building something that's starting to feel pretty substantial.

Jake's family ranch is near Sunrise Ranch, so he's around a lot.

I nod, forcing what I hope passes for enthusiasm. Truth is, the thought of having more people here sets me on edge.

Especially knowing Rosie will be here.

She will, right?

Rosie.

Just her name is enough to make my stomach clench.

Maybe I really am coming down with something.

After our last squabble, I don't know what to expect. Part of me wants to apologize, another part wants to provoke her again. And a part, a part that I'm desperately trying to ignore, just wants to take her in my arms and...

"Earth to Alex!" Chris's voice pulls me back. He's standing in front of me, grinning.

"You alright, buddy?"

"Yeah, yeah," I mumble, running a hand through my hair as I grab a log for the bonfire. "Just... thoughtful."

Chris claps me on the shoulder. "Relax. It's going to be a great night."

I nod again, forcing myself to focus as I help him stack wood. The physical task steadies me a bit, though the knot in my stomach doesn't ease.

The sky turns a vibrant orange and pink, the first stars peeking through. The bonfire crackles cheerfully, casting dancing shadows on the sand.

All around me, the others are laughing and joking, their energy buzzing with excitement. And yet, all I can think about is whether Rosie will show up.

And if she does... what the hell I'm going to say to her.

Chapter 19

Alex

Jake and his friends arrive, bringing with them a wave of laughter and energy. Jake's sister, Mia, is with them, along with a couple of her friends. The atmosphere immediately becomes more lively.

Chris takes his guitar and starts strumming a few chords. His husky voice rises in the evening air, singing an old country song we all know.

It's at that moment that I see them arrive.

The girls make their entrance on the beach, and for a moment, time seems to stand still. They're all beautiful, dressed to impress. But my gaze immediately finds Rosie, and the rest of the world fades away. I vaguely hear Diego choking on something... but it seems so distant.

Rosie is wearing a pair of denim shorts that look incredible on her, showing off her muscular legs. A top that accentuates her chest in a way that makes heads turn, and over it, a plaid shirt tied just below her chest, in perfect country style. And then... my eyes stop at her feet. She's wearing a pair of shiny, perfect cowboy boots.

My heart skips a beat. Or maybe ten.

Rosie's hair tumbles over her shoulders in loose waves, framing her face. Her lips curve in a small, teasing smile as our eyes lock. There's mischief there, a daring challenge that ignites something primal in me.

She's not the city princess I first met. Tonight, she's a queen, and damn if she doesn't know it.

I can't help the way my chest tightens. My pulse thunders as she crosses the sand toward us, her hips swaying like a melody I can't ignore. She knows I'm watching. Hell, the entire beach probably knows I'm watching.

I swallow hard, trying to maintain my usual composure as Rosie and the other girls approach the bonfire. The chatter around me seems muffled, as if I were underwater. All I can clearly perceive is her.

"Hey, cowboy," Rosie greets me with a smile that could light up the entire ranch. There's a confidence in her voice I've never heard before. Her stance is relaxed, and it's the sexiest thing I've ever seen. The knot of her shirt hugs her chest, and I'm practically drooling.

"Hey, princess," I reply, surprised I can string together a coherent sentence. "Or should I say cowgirl?"

She throws me one of her smoldering looks, and all I want to do is whisk her away and make her mine.

Whose idea was it to spend an evening together like this? How did I think it was a good one?

"How about just calling me Rosie?"

Before I can answer, Fran steps in, handing Rosie a bottle of beer. "Welcome, ladies! You're all stunning tonight."

Rosie accepts the beer with a smile, her eyes never leaving mine as she takes a sip. The way her full, red lips wrap around the neck of the bottle makes my throat go dry.

My thoughts turn filthy, unbidden, and I curse under my breath.

Right now, I'd give anything to feel those lips wrapped around me, to taste her, to lose myself in her entirely.

"So, Alex," she says, stepping a little closer. Her intoxicating scent fills the air, that fragrance that has become my obsession. "Ready to show a city girl how to have fun on a ranch?"

Her tone is playful, but there's an edge of challenge in her words that reignites something inside me. Our usual game of teasing, but with a new intensity.

I'm glad to see Rosie isn't holding a grudge for how stupid I acted before. This is our unspoken truce, our way of apologizing and making peace.

"Always ready, princess," I reply, finding a bit of my swagger. "But are you sure you can keep up?"

She raises an eyebrow, a smirk tugging at her lips. "Oh, I think you might be the one who needs to keep up, cowboy."

The electricity between us is palpable, so much so that I wonder if others can feel it. But before I can say anything else, Chris starts playing a more upbeat song and the girls drag Rosie towards the improvised dance area.

I watch her as she moves to the rhythm of the music, her hips swaying hypnotically. I can't take my eyes off her, and I realize I'm not the only one. I see Jake and his friends watching her admiringly, and I feel a pang of... jealousy?

"Dude," Fran's voice brings me back to reality. "If you don't do something soon, someone else will."

Chris stopped playing some time ago, and the music has been replaced by a pair of Bluetooth speakers. I still haven't made my move. I feel frozen, my gaze anchored to Rosie, who's utterly magnetic. I find myself staring at her, unable to look away. The way she moves, confident and seductive, makes my throat dry. I watch as the guys drift toward the dance floor, but I remain stuck in place, weighed down by a foreign, unwelcome feeling that's been gnawing at me ever since I noticed the way their eyes lingered on the girls. On Rosie.

I can't stop watching her. Then I see Jake edging closer, too close to Rosie's direction, and the jealousy burns hotter inside me. I can't bear to see her laughing at his jokes, moving with grace to the rhythm of the music. They start talking, and their conversation flows easily, her laughter bright and unrestrained. It cuts deeper when I think about how I can barely string together a normal conversation with her.

Every now and then, Rosie casts a glance in my direction, and I wish I could look away. But I can't.

Fran strolls over, handing me a beer. "Man, you look like you're about to explode," he says with a smirk.

I take the bottle and drink deeply. "Don't know what you're talking about," I mutter.

Fran raises an eyebrow. "You'd make a terrible poker player. Why don't you just go over there and get your girl?"

"She's not my girl," I reply automatically, but the words sound hollow, even to me.

Just then, the music shifts. A slow, sultry country ballad fills the air. I see Jake moving closer to Rosie, his hands sliding to her hips.

That's it.

Taking a deep breath, I finish my beer and stride toward the dance floor. Rosie spots me as I approach, her eyes locking onto mine. Her gaze could set the entire ranch ablaze. She arches an eyebrow, then turns her back to me, returning her attention to Jake.

"Mind if I cut in?" I ask, my voice coming out sharper and more forceful than I intended. Great. Apparently, I've decided to embrace my inner caveman. Did I mention how infuriating Rosalie Thorne can be?

Jake nods, clapping me on the shoulder before stepping back. "Sure thing," he says, leaving Rosie and me a little space.

Rosie takes a step closer, invading my personal space. Her scent, sweet, delicate, elegant, makes my head spin. Her expression is stormy, her eyes blazing.

"Can't mind your own business, can you, cowboy?" she snaps.

Without waiting for a reply, she pivots and heads toward the center of the dance floor, throwing me a challenging glance over her shoulder. I follow her like a man possessed, drawn in by her magnetic energy.

Then, on impulse, I reach out, gently grabbing her arm and pulling her back toward me. My grip is firm but careful—not enough to hurt her, but enough to stop her in her tracks.

"Starting to like cowboys, are we, princess?" I emphasize the word *princess,* knowing full well how much she hates it. And yet, for the briefest moment earlier, when I saw her laughing with Jake, I felt a flicker of something raw. Now, though? Now, I can't help but savor the thrill of making her mad.

I pull her closer, her face now inches from mine. Her eyes meet mine in a fiery stare-down.

Our bodies are closer than they need to be. I can feel the heat of her skin, smell the delicate fragrance of her hair. It's intoxicating. One hand rests on her shoulder, the other slides to her waist, holding her steady. I catch a flicker of something in her—a slight startle, a blink, a swallow—before she finds her voice again.

"Jealous, cowboy?" she taunts, putting the same biting emphasis on *cowboy.*

I start to fire back a sharp retort, but instead, my grip on her waist tightens slightly, betraying me. Her brow arches, her defiant expression sending a thrill through me that's impossible to ignore.

"How about a dance?" I murmur, my voice so low I can barely hear it myself. My lips are close to her ear, brushing lightly against the delicate curve of cartilage. She doesn't pull away. Instead, I squeeze her waist again, my hand moving in an unconscious caress, mesmerized by her.

The music shifts again, the melody turning slower, more sensual. Rosie begins to move, her acceptance of my invitation silent but unmistakable. Every movement is deliberate, graceful, and maddeningly alluring. Her hips sway to the rhythm, her eyes never leaving mine.

Our hands brush against each other, and a jolt of electricity shoots down my spine.

We dance, our bodies close but never too much, caught in a delicate game of attraction and resistance. I fight against the impulse, the urgent need, to cling to her, to press myself against her, leaving not the slightest gap between us.

"Not bad, princess," I comment, striving to keep my tone detached. But my voice betrays me—it's pure adoration.

Rosie smiles, a flash of challenge sparking in her eyes. "Oh, you haven't seen anything yet, cowboy."

She turns, her back just inches from my chest. I can feel the warmth radiating from her body, see the curve of her neck. I want to sink my lips, my teeth, into it. My eyes trace the perfect curve of her hips, and I can't help but imagine touching her, squeezing, spanking her.

The urge to touch her, to punish her for every infuriating second of tonight, is almost unbearable.

"You're a very insolent princess," I murmur, my lips brushing against her ear again, my hands steady on her hips.

She turns back to face me, her freckles up close and her eyes searing into mine. "Maybe," she whispers, "but who says I like being good?"

The tension between us is thick, the air electric.

"Oh, you're far from good," I breathe. "You deserve a punishment." The words slip out before I can stop them. I barely know what I'm saying anymore. My focus is entirely on keeping my hands where they are—and failing miserably.

She leans in slightly, her voice dripping with satisfaction. "I doubt anyone could give me one, cowboy."

Her challenge lights a fire in me, but I can't speak, completely captivated by her. I tighten my grip on her hips, lost in the moment.

We keep dancing, each movement a duel, each glance an unspoken promise.

Around us, the party continues, but it feels like we're alone in a world of stolen glances, fleeting touches, and unsaid words.

As the song ends, Rosie pulls away slightly, her lips curving into a sly smile.

"Thanks for the dance, cowboy," she says, her voice a perfect blend of sweetness and provocation.

Before I can reply, she turns and walks toward her friends, leaving me behind with my heart racing and a thousand questions spinning in my head.

And that's when I realize: the city princess just got her revenge.

Chapter 20

Rosie

I race up the stairs, my heart pounding wildly in my chest. I don't know if it's from the frantic sprint at the end of the party or... No. I can't even think about that.

I reach my room and slam the door shut behind me, leaning against it. The cold wood barely helps me catch my breath.

"Damn it, damn it, damn it!" I mutter under my breath, running a shaky hand through my hair, trying to push away the thoughts threatening to consume me.

What the hell happened out there? I was supposed to be in control, to keep him on edge. This was supposed to be my revenge, my chance to drive him mad. And instead... instead, I was one step away from throwing myself into his arms. Like a love-struck girl with her heart racing out of control.

With an exasperated sigh, I push off the door and start pacing the room, my bare feet brushing against the rough carpet. I can't calm down. Inside me, it's a storm—anger, frustration, desire.

Alex.

That damned, arrogant, insufferably sexy cowboy. How is it possible that he affects me like this? With that cocky grin, his swaggering, self-assured confidence that makes me want to slap him and kiss him at the same time... and those arms—strong, capable, holding me in a way that had my whole body screaming for more.

"Stop it, Rosie!" I snap aloud, shaking my head like I could physically rid myself of those thoughts. But it doesn't work. I *can't* stop thinking about him. I can't stop imagining him in all the ways that make my pulse race.

I stop in front of the mirror above the dresser. For a moment, I don't recognize the woman staring back at me. Messy hair, flushed cheeks, eyes shining with a light that both confuses and terrifies me. I've never seen myself like this before.

"What the hell is happening to you?" I whisper to my reflection, my voice tinged with desperation.

I collapse onto the bed, staring up at the ceiling, and for a moment, it feels like I can't breathe. Logic says I should be furious with myself. I should be angry for losing control, for giving into this twisted desire. But instead, here I am, smiling like an idiot. *Why the hell am I smiling?*

I think about the way he looked at me. The way he held me. The heat radiating off his body when we were too close—*much* too close—and how, even then, I didn't want to pull away.

You're a very insolent princess.
You deserve to be punished.

The memory of his words hits me like a lightning bolt, making me burn all over again.

God, how much I wanted him then. How much I still want him. To be taken, held, punished—in every possible way. To feel his hands on every inch of my body, marking me, claiming me.

"It's just physical attraction," I tell myself, though my voice rings hollow even to my own ears. "Nothing more."

But even as I say it, I twist and turn in the bed, desperate for any kind of release, the need for him gnawing at me.

It's more than desire. It's more than a game. It's something that's *consuming* me, filling every part of me until I can't think of anything else.

Damn cowboy.

"It's only temporary," I murmur, burying my face under the pillow. "Soon, I'll go back to my normal life."

But the need doesn't fade. It *never* fades. Even after I touch myself, desperately seeking relief in every way I know, imagining that it's his fingers instead of mine, nothing is enough.

"You're in trouble, Rosie," I whisper into the darkness of my room. "Serious trouble."

I toss and turn, unable to sleep. My thoughts keep spiraling, always circling back to Alex. Just when I'm about to give up and surrender to a sleepless night, my phone buzzes on the nightstand.

My heart leaps as I grab it. A message from an unknown number lights up the screen:

Unknown: Hey, Princess. Hope you're resting up—morning chores start early. ;)

I can't help the smile that tugs at my lips. That teasing, cocky tone... it could only be him—Alex.

But how the hell did he get my number? And why is he texting me in the middle of the night?
I type back quickly:

Me: How did you get my number, cowboy? And what do you mean by that?

His reply comes almost immediately. I stare at the screen, rereading his message:

Cowboy: I have my ways, Princess. Glad to see you're curious. I've got some fun challenges lined up for you. ;)

The thrill of his words sends a wave of excitement through me, mixed with something darker. Something dangerous. I bite my lip, fighting the urge to smile.

Me: Oh, really? And what makes you think I'm interested in your challenges?

His response comes back quickly:

Cowboy: Let's call it a talent for reading people.
Me: All right, Mr. Know-It-All. What's this big challenge you've got in mind?
Cowboy: Tomorrow, just some basic ranch work. I'm sure you'll manage.
Cowboy: Then, how about a camping trip this weekend? Just you, me, nature, and the stars. Let's see if the city princess is up for the challenge. ;)

A shiver runs down my spine—part excitement, part panic. Camping? With Alex? Just the two of us?

Me: Interesting, cowboy. I'll think about it.

I try to sound nonchalant, even as my heart pounds against my ribs.

Cowboy: Do that. And in the meantime, dream of wide-open prairies and bonfires under the stars. Goodnight, Princess.
Me: Goodnight, Cowboy.

I set the phone back on the nightstand, my mind racing, the smile still on my face.
A camping trip with Alex... The thought excites me and terrifies me in equal measure.
Camping. Alone. With Alex.
The panic starts to set in as I stare at the ceiling in the dark. I've never been camping before. What do you even bring? How do you pitch a tent? What if there are snakes? Or worse... bears?
Wait... what's worse, a bear or a snake?
I toss and turn, my mind spinning. I can't let him know I've never camped in my life—he'd tease me for weeks. But how am I supposed to hide my total lack of experience?
And then there's the matter of being alone.
Me. And Alex.
I can barely resist him when there are other people around.

The thought makes my pulse race.

Will my desire for him outweigh my desire to kill him?

I groan, running a hand down my face in frustration. How did I even end up in this situation?

This summer was supposed to be simple—helping with a wedding, trying not to hate every minute of it not getting lost in the desert with an irritatingly attractive cowboy.

"You're crazy, Rosie," I murmur into the darkness. "Completely crazy."

I toss and turn, unable to settle down.

How am I supposed to survive this camping trip?

More importantly, how am I supposed to survive Alex?

With those thoughts swirling in my head, I close my eyes, knowing sleep will be a rare luxury tonight.

Chapter 21

Rosie

A persistent knocking at the door abruptly tears me from sleep. I blink in confusion, trying to orient myself in the dimness of the room. What time is it?

"Mmh... coming," I mumble, my voice thick with sleep.

I drag myself out of bed, stumbling slightly as I reach the door. I'm still half asleep and my brain hasn't started functioning properly yet.

Without thinking, I grab the handle and open the door.

"Yes?" I ask, rubbing my eyes.

It's at that moment that I realize two things simultaneously: first, it's Alex standing in front of me, already fully dressed and awake. Second, I'm still in my pajamas. Not just any pajamas, but the fine silk ones I treated myself to before leaving - a camisole and short shorts that leave little to the imagination.

Alex's eyes visibly widen, quickly scanning my body before returning to my face. I feel the heat rising to my cheeks as the realization of what's happening hits me like a bucket of cold water.

"Good morning, princess," Alex says, an amused smirk curving his lips. "I see you're... ready for the day."

I desperately try to cover myself by crossing my arms over my chest, but I know it's too late.

"Alex! What... what are you doing here?"

"It's milking time," he replies, clearly trying to hold back a laugh. "I warned you last night, remember?"

Oh God. The milking. The message. I thought he was joking!

"I... I didn't think you were serious," I stammer, trying to close the door.

But Alex blocks it with his foot. "Oh, I was very serious," he says, his tone now more determined but still with a trace of amusement in his eyes.

"The cows don't wait, not even for a silk-clad princess."

With one last look that makes me feel as if I'm naked, he turns and walks away down the hallway.

I close the door and lean against it, my heart racing. This is absolutely not how I had imagined starting the day.

I rush to the closet, my mind whirling between embarrassment and an unexpected spark of excitement. Alex's look... there was something in his eyes...

I shake my head, trying to focus. I don't have time for these thoughts now.

I have cows to milk, for heaven's sake!

I take one last look in the mirror... my hair is a mess, but it will have to do.

I open the door, ready to face whatever this day has in store for me.

Chapter 22

Alex

I can't get the image of Rosie in that damn silk pajama out of my head. I try to focus on milking, but my mind keeps going back to that moment in front of her door.

My mind is a terrible place right now.

I need a distraction, and fast. The tightness in my jeans has been unbearable for a while now... Thank God Rosie didn't catch a glimpse of the situation earlier. But now, I have to deal with this before she gets here..

I certainly didn't expect to find her so... exposed. The tank top was so thin that I didn't have to imagine anything, the short pants showing off those toned legs. And the silk... God, that silk sliding over her body like a caress.

"Focus, idiot," I mutter to myself, trying to concentrate on the cow in front of me.

But it's useless. I keep seeing the way her messy hair framed her face, that sleepy and confused expression that made her even more adorable. And then, when she realized the situation, the blush that rose to her cheeks...

I sigh, running a hand over my face.

I can't afford to develop feelings for her.

My brain won't quit. I can't stop imagining what it would feel like to run my hands over that soft, bare skin, tracing the curve of her hips, pulling her closer until there's no space left between us. Her breath hitching under my touch. Her body trembling.

Would her skin taste as sweet as her perfume smells?

"Damn it, Alex!" I exclaim out loud, startling the cow.

I apologize to the animal, stroking its side to calm it down. I need to regain control of myself.

Last night, she had me wrapped around her little finger. The way she moved—confident, sensual, fiery—it was impossible to look away. She knew exactly what she was doing, too. And then to realize it was all part of her revenge? That stung.

But it didn't matter. I couldn't stop watching her.

Even after the dance, when she ignored me completely, keeping to the girls. Even when we all gathered around the fire and roasted marshmallows, she wouldn't look my way. I sat across from her like a lovesick fool, still hypnotized.

And then she disappeared.

Back in my room, I did what I've done every night since she got here—let out some of that pent-up frustration, thinking about her. But it wasn't enough. Not even close.

Damn city princess. She's scrambled my brain, and instead of trying to sort myself out, I keep looking for more excuses to be near her.

She's a drug, and I'm hooked.

That's why I sent those messages. I was a little buzzed, sure, but I won't blame the whiskey for this one. It just gave me the nerve to say what I wanted without overthinking it.

Rory handed over her number without hesitation, grinning like a cat who caught the mouse.

When Rosie answered, I felt like I'd won the lottery. We texted for a while, and yeah, I was vague about this morning's chores. A little mischief never hurt anyone, right? But inviting her on the camping trip... That was a gamble.

Just the two of us, alone in the middle of nowhere.

What the hell was I thinking?

But the thought of being with her out there, away from everything, has me counting the hours until the weekend.

I'm still lost in my thoughts when I see her walking toward me. My pulse skips.

If I thought the silk pajamas were bad, this... this is pure torture.

Rosie approaches with an uncertain step, wearing overalls that look incredibly good on her. They're short, and the straps hug her curves in an almost indecent way. But it's her face that strikes me the most. She's done two little braids, giving her such an innocent and adorable air that contrasts absurdly with her natural sensuality.

"Good morning again," she says, a slight blush still on her cheeks.

I swallow hard. "'Morning" I manage to say, desperately trying not to stare at her for too long.

I turn towards the cow, trying to focus on the task ahead of us. "So, princess, ready for your first milking lesson?"

Rosie comes closer, the smell of her vanilla shampoo mixing with that of hay and animals. It's a combination that shouldn't be so seductive, yet it is.

"More than ready," she responds with a determined smile. "Where do we start?"

I try to maintain a professional tone as I explain the procedure, but it's difficult when all I can think about is how easy it would be to slide those straps down her shoulders...

"Alex?" Rosie's voice brings me back to reality. "Are you okay? You seem... distracted."

"I'm fine," I respond too quickly. "Now, let's see how you do with milking."

I guide her through the steps, trying to focus on the task and not on how close she is, on how her hands brush against mine as I show her the correct technique.

Rosie tries hard, but it's clear she's never done anything like this before. I should be amused by her clumsy attempts, should tease her as I normally would. But all I can think about is how adorable her concentrated expression is, how much I want to kiss that frustrated pout from her lips.

"Come on, princess," I say, trying to sound playful and not as desperate as I feel. "Don't tell me a simple cow is too much for you."

Rosie gives me a challenging look that makes my knees weak. "Never underestimate me, cowboy. I'll show you."

And as I watch her determined to master this new skill, I realize I'm in trouble. Serious trouble.

Because it's not just physical attraction. It's something more, something dangerous and unfamiliar, yet decidedly and unmistakably clear. And the thought of camping on the weekend, of having her all to myself under the stars...

I watch Rosie, her tongue sticking out slightly between her lips with effort. It's such an innocent gesture, yet it makes me have thoughts that are anything but pure.

"There, like that," I guide her, placing my hands on hers to show her the correct movement. The contact sends an electric shock through my entire body.

Rosie looks up, her eyes meeting mine. For a moment, time seems to stand still. We're so close that I can count the freckles on her nose, feel her light breath on my skin.

"I... I think I got it," she says softly, without moving away though.

I clear my throat, trying to regain control. Trying to push away the lingering thoughts of the ambiguous gestures we just shared. "Good, then... try on your own."

I step back, suddenly feeling cold without her body close to mine. I watch her as she resumes milking, this time with more confidence.

"I did it!" she exclaims after a few minutes, a radiant smile on her face. "Look, Alex! I really did it!"

Her enthusiasm is contagious and I find myself smiling too. "Well done princess, maybe there's hope for you after all."

Rosie gives me a light punch on the shoulder, leaving a milk stain on my shirt. "Oops," she says, not looking sorry at all.

"Oh, you want to play it like that?" I respond, dipping my fingers in the milk bucket and splashing her lightly.

Rosie jumps, looking at me with wide eyes. For a moment I fear I've gone too far, but then I see a flash of mischief in her eyes.

"You..." she starts, but doesn't finish the sentence.

She takes a handful of milk from the bucket and splashes it on my chest, leaving a white trail on my shirt.

Her laughter is full of joy, yet there's something different in the air, something more subtle and intense. "Now you've really done it," I say in a low voice, my eyes shining with an unspoken promise. Without thinking too much, I take some milk again and splash her neck.

The liquid slides down her smooth skin, creating an almost hypnotic contrast with her complexion.

She looks up and, for a moment, we're alone in this universe made of glances and sighs. Her eyes meet mine, and the world seems to stop. There's a spark in that look, something dark and inviting, and I know she feels it too. The game has taken a turn that neither of us had foreseen, but now we're trapped, and neither of us wants to get out.

Her chest rises in a deep breath, and I can clearly see the effect all this is having on her. Her heartbeat accelerates, visible in the way her throat contracts, as if trying to control the wave of sensations coursing through her body. But there's no control, not anymore.

Without a word, her gaze lowers to the milk dripping down her skin, then slowly rises back to me, and that slow and deliberate gesture hits me like a shock. I feel an irresistible urge to move closer, but I hold back. The tension building between us is almost unbearable, as if every second we're walking on a very thin wire.

Her lips part again, and I wish she would say something, but at the same time I don't want to break the silence.

She raises a hand and, with a slow and almost uncertain gesture, touches her neck where the milk has left a shiny trail. Her fingers move lightly, tracing the path of the liquid on her skin, and I'm completely hypnotized by that gesture. I bite the inside of my cheek to keep from doing something rash, like moving closer and taking her place, letting my hands explore that smooth, warm skin.

"Rosie," I murmur, her name coming out like a prayer from my lips.

I see her eyes lower to my lips, her breath becoming quicker. I'm about to do something stupid, I know it. I'm about to ruin everything. But right now, with Rosie in front of me, covered in milk and more beautiful than ever, I can't think of anything else but how much I want to kiss her.

I lean slightly forward, my heart racing in my chest...

I lean towards Rosie, the world around us seeming to vanish. I can feel her breath mingling with mine, I see her eyelids lower slightly in anticipation...

"Hey, Alex! Are you done with the milking? We need help with... oh!"

Diego's voice makes us startle, abruptly separating us. I turn to see my friend standing at the barn door, his eyes moving from me to Rosie with obvious surprise.

"Am I... interrupting something?" he asks, a smirk forming on his lips.

"No!" Rosie and I respond in unison, perhaps too quickly to be convincing.

But even if we had been the most convincing people in the world... well, the scene was unequivocal.

Diego raises an eyebrow, his gaze lingering on our milk-soaked clothes. "Sure, and I suppose the milk bath is a new milking technique I don't know about?"

I feel my cheeks warm with embarrassment.

"There was a... small accident," I mutter, running a hand through my damp hair.

Rosie nods vigorously beside me but doesn't say a word. Diego looks at us for a long moment, clearly unconvinced. Then he shrugs. "If you say so. Anyway, when you're done... um, cleaning up, we need help with the horses."

"I'll be right there," I respond, trying to sound as normal as possible.

Diego nods and turns to leave, but not before giving us one last amused look. Then with a laugh he disappears, leaving us alone again.

Silence falls in the barn, loaded with unresolved tension and unspoken words. I glance at Rosie, who is staring intently at the floor.

"I... maybe we should go change," I say finally, my voice slightly hoarse.

Rosie nods, finally looking up. There's something in her eyes - confusion, desire, maybe a little fear - that makes me want to take her in my arms and never let her go.

Instead, I take a step back. "I'll see you... I'll see you later?"

"Yes," she responds softly. "Later."

I watch her walk away, my heart still racing in my chest. What just happened, or what was about to happen...

Chapter 23

Alex

'Cowboy Stallions 🐎🥛'

Diego: RED ALERT! 🚨 I just caught Alex and Rosie splashed with milk! 🥛💦
Chris: WHAT?! Details, now! 👀
Fran: @Diego dude... I think you might be a bit confused about what you saw... aren't you old enough to have had the talk?! 🎉
Diego: idiot I mean exactly what I said. They were milking
Fran: I don't want to repeat myself...
Me: Guys, it's not what you think...
Diego: Oh yes it is! There was more sexual tension in that barn than in a porn movie! 🔥🐮
Me: I hate you all. 😑
Chris: wtf?? Do I need to remind you that I'm your boss and that all of this violates every possible hygiene code? Get rid of that milk and don't make me take disciplinary action!
Me: sorry boss... it was kind of an accident
Chris: I'll turn a blind eye this time... if you tell us all about this "accident"
Fran: Alex, just remember one thing for the camping trip: butter makes great lubricant! 🧈😏
Me: ... I'm blocking all of you. 🙍
Diego: Aww, our little Alex is growing up! 👶➡️🤠

Alex: Goodbye. ✌️

Diego: DON'T YOU DARE LEAVE THIS CHAT! We need all the juicy details!

Me: ... I hate you all. Deeply. 😑

I close the chat with an exasperated sigh, tossing the phone onto the bed. The guys will never stop teasing me about this. As if the situation with Rosie wasn't complicated enough already.

I make a mental note to apologize to Chris... I know I haven't maintained a professional attitude and I need to get back in line. I've never behaved like this before and I've always been very serious at work...

What the hell is that little redhead doing to me?

"Little redhead"

Have I started using nicknames now?

Princess...

Shit!

Apparently, I've been using nicknames for a while...

Have I mentioned that I'm screwed?

I run a hand through my hair, still damp with milk, thinking back to what happened in the barn. We were so close... for a moment I really thought I was going to kiss her. And, damn it, I wanted to. I wanted it more than anything else.

With a grunt, I head towards the bathroom. I need a shower and to clear my head. As the cold water runs over me, I try to focus on the work ahead. The horses need to be taken care of, there are fences to repair, a thousand other things to do.

But my thoughts keep going back to Rosie. To the weekend camping trip. To how it will be to have her all to myself under the stars.

"Focus, idiot," I mutter to myself, turning off the water. I can't afford distractions, not with all the work that needs to be done at the ranch.

I get dressed quickly, my mind still a whirlwind of confused thoughts about Rosie. Damn it, I really don't know anything about her. What's going through her head? Is she just playing with me? Is there someone else in her life?

And what if it's all in my head? If this... thing, whatever it is, was just one-sided?

I shake my head, trying to free myself from these thoughts. I have work to do, I can't afford to be so distracted.

I go down the stairs, determined to get to work and not think about Rosie for at least five minutes. But fate, apparently, has other plans.

As soon as I set foot in the entrance, I see her. And she's not alone.

A tall guy, with perfectly combed hair and a toothpaste commercial smile, is standing next to her. Before I can even process the scene, Rosie jumps into his arms with a cry of joy.

My stomach painfully contracts as I watch the guy hug her and spin her in a pirouette worthy of a romantic movie. Rosie laughs, a sound of pure happiness that hurts my chest.

For a moment, I stand still, unable to move or look away. All my doubts and insecurities seem to materialize before my eyes in this perfect scene.

Of course Rosie has someone. Someone from her world, someone who can offer her much more than a simple country cowboy.

I suddenly feel stupid for even thinking there could be something between us. The memory of our almost-kiss in the barn now seems like a bad joke.

I swallow hard, trying to compose myself. I need to get out of here before they notice me. Before Rosie sees how pathetic and disappointed I am.

I can't bear this scene. I can't stay here a second longer. But just as I'm about to turn and flee, Rosie looks up and our eyes meet. For an instant, I see something in her gaze - surprise? Embarrassment? - but then her face lights up in a smile.

"Alex!" she calls out. "Come here, there's someone I want you to meet!"

I feel bile rising in my throat. The idea of approaching, of shaking hands with that perfect guy, of having to smile and make conversation... it's more than I can bear right now.

"I have things to do," I grunt, my voice hoarse and sharp even to my own ears.

Without waiting for an answer, I turn and walk away with long strides. I need to get out, to get as far away as possible from this happy little picture, from Rosie, from everything.

I leave the house almost running, ignoring Rosie's confused and perhaps hurt look. I can't think about it now. I can't think about anything.

I head towards the fences, determined to lose myself in physical work. Maybe, if I push myself hard enough, I'll be able to erase the image of Rosie in that other guy's arms.

But as I grab the tools and start working furiously, I know it won't be that easy. Because that happy laugh, that radiant smile... they keep echoing in my mind, a painful reminder of what I can never have.

I work on the fences for hours, pushing my body to the limit. The sun beats down hard on my back, but I barely notice it. I'm too focused on hammering, sawing, nailing - anything to keep my mind occupied.

But no matter how hard I work, I can't get rid of the dull ache in my chest. The image of Rosie hugging that guy keeps haunting me.

"Hey, cowboy!" A familiar voice makes me jump. I turn to see Chris approaching, a concerned expression on his face.

"Chris," I mutter, wiping sweat from my forehead. "What are you doing here?"

He shrugs. "Diego told me you seemed a bit down. Thought I'd come check on you."

I shake my head. "I'm fine. I don't need a babysitter."

Chris studies me for a long moment, then sighs. "You know, buddy, we might be idiots sometimes, but we know when one of us is hurting."

His words hit me harder than I'd like to admit. I look away, focusing on the fence.

"I don't know what you're talking about, but I would have come to find you anyway. I owe you an apology for my behavior. It won't happen again," I mutter, continuing to work.

But Chris doesn't leave. Instead, he comes closer, leaning on the fence next to me. "Alex," he says in an unusually serious tone, "you don't have to tell me anything if you don't want to. But I'm here if you need to talk. And I don't need your apologies... I know how you work and how good you are at your job. Everyone lets their guard down sometimes... you're my brother, I'm not going to make a fuss about this."

His gentle tone almost makes me crumble. For a moment, I'm tempted to tell him everything. But I can't. I'm not ready to admit out loud what I feel for Rosie.

"I appreciate you coming," I say finally, my voice a bit hoarse. "But I'm fine, really. I just... have a lot of work to do."

Chris nods slowly, clearly unconvinced. "Alright," he says. "Then... let's get to it."

He grabs some tools and starts working with me. We proceed in silence, but he doesn't leave me alone. A comforting silence... it's nice not having to talk to someone to be understood.

After a while, Chris pats me on the shoulder. "Hey, what do you say we all go to the Rusty Spur tonight? It might do you good to distract yourself a bit."

I hesitate for a moment. The idea of having to pretend to be cheerful and carefree doesn't appeal to me. But maybe Chris is right. Maybe I need a distraction.

"Okay," I finally accept. "I'll be there."

Chris smiles. "Great! See you later then. And Alex... whatever's worrying you, it'll be alright. You'll see."

As I watch him walk away, I feel a mix of gratitude and frustration. My friends are there for me, I know. But how can I explain to them something I don't even fully understand myself?

I return to work, trying not to think about Rosie, the mysterious guy, or what I feel. For now, I focus on the present. On the wood under my hands, on the sun on my skin, on the work to be done.

The rest... well, the rest will have to wait. I'm not ready to face it. Not yet.

The bar is crowded and noisy when we arrive. Chris, Diego, and Fran practically drag me inside, determined to cheer me up. I don't have the heart to tell them that the last thing I want right now is to socialize.

"Hey, look who's here!" exclaims Diego, pointing to a table in the corner.

My stomach tightens when I see Rosie sitting there, surrounded by a group of girls. And next to her, with an arm casually draped over the back of her chair, is him. Mr. Perfect. With his perfectly styled hair—a long wave swept back, held in place by enough hair products to rival a model's—clean-shaven face, white t-shirt, blue blazer, and matching trousers. White sneakers. Who the hell even dresses like that? His city-slicker vibe is obvious even from the neighboring ranch. And, of course, there's his million-dollar watch, shamelessly displayed on the arm draped over Rosie's shoulders.

Of course.

They really do make a perfect pair.

What was I even thinking? Did I seriously believe I had a chance? Clearly, Rosie wasn't flirting with me.

"Let's go say hello," suggests Fran, already heading towards their table.

I want to protest, but I know it would look suspicious. So, with a heavy heart, I follow them.

"Hey guys!" Rosie greets us with a radiant smile. Her eyes meet mine for an instant, and I think I see a flash of... something. Concern? Guilt? But it passes so quickly that I might have imagined it.

"Let me introduce you to my best friend, Ethan," she says, gesturing to the guy beside her. "He came to visit me from Los Angeles."

Best friend.

The words hit me like a punch to the stomach. I don't know whether to feel relieved or even more confused.

Ethan stands up, extending his hand. "Nice to meet you, guys! Rosie has told me a lot about you."

I shake his hand, trying not to appear too hostile. But I can't welcome him as warmly as the others do.

We spend the next few minutes in forced conversation. Ethan recounts anecdotes from

Rosie's life in Los Angeles, and she laughs, adding details and playfully correcting him. They seem so at ease together, so... right.

I can't stand it.

It's obvious that he doesn't want to be just her best friend... Rosie is so perfect, who wouldn't want to have more?

Besides, he's gone to the trouble of following her overseas... just because he's her best friend?

Tell that to someone who believes it.

With the excuse of getting a drink, I move away from the table.

At the bar, I order a double whiskey, hoping the alcohol might dull the ache in my chest.

"Heartache?"

I turn to see the bartender, a middle-aged woman with kind eyes, looking at me with understanding.

I sigh. "Is it that obvious?"

She smiles gently. "I've seen that look many times, honey. Want to talk about it?"

For a moment, I'm tempted. But then I shake my head. "There's not much to say. She's... out of my league."

The bartender passes me my drink and I return to the table.

Rosie gives me a questioning look when I sit down, but I avoid her gaze. The evening continues, and I try not to observe too closely the chemistry between Rosie and Mr. Perfect, try not to notice how at ease she is with him, how she laughs with him...

I order drinks two or three more times, or maybe four or five... I don't know.

From time to time, the guys give me glances, so I try to appear as normal as possible.

The thing is, I'm usually not the one who stays on the sidelines of conversations, I'm not the one who doesn't liven up the evenings.

So... I certainly can't lie to my friends who have already figured out pretty much everything.

Chapter 24

Alex

The evening at the bar drags on, becoming increasingly unbearable as the hours pass. Rosie and Ethan seem to exist in a world of their own, laughing at private jokes and reminiscing about shared moments that none of us can comprehend. Every interaction between them is like a dagger to my heart.

"Remember that time in Malibu?" Ethan says, smiling at Rosie. "When we spent the whole night on the beach, watching the stars?"

Rosie laughs, a sound that once filled me with joy but now only brings pain. "How could I forget? It was one of the best nights of my life."

I can't take it anymore. I stand up abruptly, startling everyone at the table.

"Alex? Everything okay?" Chris asks, concerned.

"Just fine," I reply, my voice sharp. "I just need some fresh air."

I rush out of the bar, ignoring my friends' calls. The night air isn't exactly fresh, as we're in the middle of summer in southern Italy... so it's practically a sauna rather than a breath of fresh air, but at this moment I don't miss the bar's air conditioning one bit.

The anger, jealousy, and pain I've been trying to repress all evening explode within me.

Without thinking, I head towards my pickup. I need to get away, to drive until I can't feel anything anymore.

"Alex! Wait!"

I turn to see Rosie running towards me, her expression worried.

"What is it, princess?" I spit out, my voice laden with bitterness. "Shouldn't you be inside laughing with your Mr. Perfect?"

Rosie stops, struck by my words. "Alex, what are you saying?" She looks confused. Then I see a flash of realization, and she hastily adds, "No, wait, it's not what you think..."

"No?" I say, louder than normal, completely losing control. "Then what is it? Because from where I'm standing, it looks like you and your city boy are planning your happy future together!"

Rosie looks at me, shocked, her eyes filling with tears. "Alex, please, let me explain..."

But I'm too hurt, too angry to listen. "There's nothing to explain, Rosie. I understand perfectly. Go back to your Ethan. You don't owe me an explanation, there's nothing between us and there never will be. I was just having fun."

Without giving her a chance to respond, I jump into my pickup and peel out. The last thing I see in the rearview mirror is Rosie standing in the parking lot, tears streaming down her face.

What was I thinking? Did I seriously believe that Rosie, with her refined little bottom, would have considered me?

Damn it!

I'm a poor fool.

I drive for hours, aimlessly, trying to escape the pain that's consuming me. But no matter how far I go, I can't rid myself of the image of Rosie and Ethan together, happy and perfect.

When I finally return to the ranch at dawn, I'm exhausted and hollow. I know I've ruined everything, destroyed any chance I ever had with Rosie. Maybe it's better this way, I tell myself. Better to hurt now than keep deluding myself.

Did I ever have a chance? No. She wasn't flirting with me—just joking around or being friendly, or something else I'll never understand.

As I step into the house, ready to retreat to my room and lick my wounds, a voice stops me.

"Alex."

I turn to see Rosie sitting on the stairs, her eyes red and puffy. She's been up all night, waiting for me.

We stare at each other in silence, the weight of everything said and unsaid pressing between us. I look away, unable to face her. I don't want her pity.

"Alex, wait!" Her voice carries urgency, but I pretend not to hear, quickening my pace.

"Alex, damn it, stop!"

Her footsteps rush toward me, and she grabs my arm, forcing me to turn. Her eyes burn with anger and pain, and I can't bear to meet them.

"What is it, Rosie? Haven't you said enough?" My voice drips with sarcasm, my usual defense. "Or did you forget some detail about your glamorous life in Los Angeles and come back to fix it?"

I know the words are cruel. I know they'll hurt her. But right now, wounded and angry, I can't stop myself. Sarcasm is the only thing keeping me from breaking in front of her.

Rosie flinches, her eyes shimmering with fresh tears. Guilt stabs through me, but I bury it beneath my pain.

"It's not what you think, Alex," she says, her voice trembling. "If you'd just let me explain…"

"Explain what?" I snap. "How you and your perfect Ethan are meant to be together? How your life in Los Angeles is so incredible you can't wait to go back?"

"Stop putting words in my mouth!" she yells, frustration breaking through her calm facade. "It's not like that!"

"Oh no?" I retort, crossing my arms. "Then enlighten me, princess."

Her nickname comes out like a curse. I see the hurt in her eyes, but I don't stop.

"Ethan is just a friend, Alex," she says, trying to steady her voice. "There's nothing between us."

I laugh bitterly. "Sure. And I'm an idiot. I saw you together, Rosie. I'm not blind."

"What you saw isn't what you think," she insists, stepping closer. "If you'd just listen—"

But I don't want to listen. I can't. If I do, I might believe her, and I can't let myself hope again.

"You know what? It doesn't matter," I say, stepping back. "Go back to Ethan. I have work to do."

I turn to leave, but her next words stop me cold.

"You're an idiot, Alessandro Ricci. A jealous, stubborn idiot who can't see what's right in front of him."

Her words hit me like a slap. I stare at her, stunned. She knows my full name? And damn, it sounds so good coming from her lips.

Damn it, I'm doing it again.

"Ethan has been my best friend forever," she says, her voice rising with emotion. "There's never been anything between us, and there never will be. He's not my type, and I'm definitely not his. He's gay, Alex. And he's engaged. He came here to support me because he knows I'm going through a tough time."

I stand there, silent, her words crashing over me. Relief seeps in, but shame and regret follow close behind.

"A tough time?" I manage, my voice quiet. "Why didn't you talk to me about it?"

Rosie looks at me like I've lost my mind. "Talk to you? Why would I? We're not exactly best friends, Alex."

Her words sting, but I know she's right. What do I really know about her, besides her name and that she's from Los Angeles? I never gave her the chance to open up. I thought about it—wanted to—but I always messed it up.

"Well, I..." I start, but my words trail off. What can I even say?

Rosie crosses her arms. "I've explained the situation with Ethan. I don't owe you anything else—especially after what you said outside the bar."

I flinch, shame prickling at the memory of my words. "You're right. I was an idiot."

"At least we agree on that," she says, a faint smile breaking through her frustration.

I attempt a grin. "What do you say we start over? Hi, I'm Alex—the cowboy who can't keep his mouth shut. Who are you?"

She rolls her eyes but, to my surprise, her expression softens. She studies me for a moment, as if deciding whether to indulge me. Then, with a sigh that's half exasperation, half amusement, she plays along.

"Alright, cowboy," she says, a spark of mischief lighting her eyes. "I'm Rosie—the city girl who apparently doesn't know how to pick her company."

Chapter 25

Rosie

The day of the camping trip has finally arrived. Over the past few days, I've managed to get Ethan and Alex to talk a bit, although Alex is still a little reluctant to be friendly with him. Despite this, Ethan has integrated surprisingly well with the group of guys, and the girls adore him. His presence has brought new energy to the ranch, and seeing how everyone has welcomed him has made me feel more comfortable here.

Despite the initial tensions and misunderstandings, Alex and I decided to go ahead with the camping plan. But as I pack my bag, I feel anxiety growing inside me. I've never camped before. My childhood was marked by the early loss of my mother and a father always immersed in work. No one ever had time to take me outdoors, to teach me the basics of life in nature.

"Breathe, Rosie," I tell myself, trying to calm my nerves. "It's just camping."

But I know it's not "just" camping. It's a leap into the unknown, into a world completely new to me. And I'm doing it with Alex, which adds a whole new level of complexity to the situation.

As I load my bag into Alex's pickup, I feel a strange mix of excitement and nervousness in my stomach. I don't know what to expect from this trip, but I know it could change everything.

"Ready, princess?" Alex asks, appearing by my side with a crooked smile.

I try to hide my anxiety behind a smile. "Ready as I'll ever be," I reply, hoping to sound more confident than I actually feel.

The journey to the campsite is silent at first, both of us lost in our thoughts. But as we get further from the ranch, the atmosphere lightens. Alex turns on the radio and starts humming a country song, making me smile and helping me relax a bit.

"I didn't know you were a singer," I tease him, grateful for the distraction from my anxious thoughts.

He gives me an amused look. "Oh, you haven't seen anything yet. Wait until you hear me sing around the campfire after a few beers."

I laugh, already feeling more at ease. "I can't wait."

As the landscape rolls by outside the window, I find myself thinking about how I got here. From a hectic life in Los Angeles to camping in the middle of nowhere with a cowboy. It's surreal, but somehow, it feels right. Maybe this is the kind of adventure I've always needed without knowing it. And then there's Alex. I steal a glance in his direction, observing his profile focused on the road. These past few days, I've found myself thinking a lot about us. And... even though Alex has an unmatched talent for driving me completely insane, there's something undeniably sweet about him in his own way. It's not the grand gestures—it's the small, quiet things he does when he thinks no one's watching that steal my breath and make all the difference. It's incredible how he always manages to make me feel better, even in the most difficult moments. He has this innate gift of understanding when I'm not comfortable or when I have too many thoughts troubling me.

What I appreciate most is that he doesn't ask too many questions, doesn't open endless and embarrassing conversations trying to dig into my thoughts. Instead, he simply does something to make me smile and lighten the situation. Like now, as he hums this off-key country song, occasionally throwing me amused glances. He knows I'm nervous about this camping trip, but instead of putting pressure on me, he's creating a light and carefree atmosphere.

It's a perfect balance between being present and giving space, between caring and not smothering. With him, I feel seen and understood, but also free to be myself, with all my insecurities and doubts.

As I watch him drumming his fingers on the steering wheel to the rhythm of the music, I feel a wave of gratitude. Maybe this is why, despite all my fears and uncertainties, I'm here on this pickup, heading towards the unknown. Because with Alex, even the unknown seems a little less scary and a bit more like an adventure.

We arrive at the campsite in the afternoon. It's a beautiful place, surrounded by trees and with a breathtaking view of the mountains in the distance. While Alex starts setting up the tent, I stand there, a bit uncertain about what to do.

"Hey, princess," Alex calls out, noticing my hesitation. "How about you take care of the campfire? I'll show you how it's done."

I nod, grateful for the task. Alex patiently guides me through the process of gathering wood and preparing the fire. His hands brush against mine as he shows me how to arrange the twigs, and I feel a shiver that has nothing to do with the evening breeze.

"See? Nothing complicated," he says with an encouraging smile when we're done.

"Thanks," I reply, feeling a bit more confident. "Maybe I'm not a lost cause as a cowgirl after all."

Alex laughs. "Never had any doubts about you, princess."

As he returns to the tent, I look around, trying to absorb the beauty of the place. Suddenly, a movement among the trees catches my attention.

"Hey, look!" I exclaim excitedly, pointing to a spot among the trees. "A deer!"

Alex turns, smiling at my excitement. "Welcome to the wild, princess."

We spend the rest of the afternoon exploring the surroundings, Alex showing me the different plants and telling me stories about the local wildlife. I realize how little I know about this world, and how much I enjoy learning from him. His passion for nature is contagious, and I find myself asking question after question, absorbing every bit of information like a sponge.

As the sun begins to set, we return to the camp. Alex lights the campfire while I take out the food we brought. We sit close, enjoying dinner and the tranquility of the night falling around us.

"So," Alex says after a while, passing me a beer, "what do you think of the camper's life so far?"

I look at him, his face illuminated by the firelight. There's something magical about this moment, something that makes me feel more alive than ever.

"It's... different from anything I've ever done," I admit. "But in an incredibly good way. I feel... I don't know how to explain it. Free, maybe?"

He smiles, and I feel my heart speed up. "I'm glad you like it. Sometimes we need to get away from everything to remember who we really are."

His words strike me deeply. "Yes," I whisper, "I think you're right."

Silence falls between us, but it's not an awkward silence. It's comfortable, charged with something I can't quite define yet, but it makes me feel safe and excited at the same time.

"Alex," I finally say, looking at the stars above us, "thank you for bringing me here. For showing me all this. I don't think I've ever felt so... at peace."

He turns to me, his eyes shining in the firelight. For a moment, he seems about to say something important. Then, with a sweet smile, he simply says: "Thank you for coming, Rosie. For giving all this a chance."

At that moment, sitting next to Alex under a starry sky, with the crackling of the fire and the sound of nature around us, I realize that I'm falling. Falling hard. And the scariest thing is that I'm not sure I want to stop. The silence of the night is broken only by the crackling of the fire and the distant howl. Alex explains that there's nothing to fear, but I can't help but move a little closer to him.

"Are you cold?" he asks, noticing my movement.

"A little," I admit, though I'm not sure if it's really the cold or the emotion of the moment making me shiver. I had gotten used to the heat of the ranch... here the air is more mountainous.

Without hesitation, Alex gets up and goes to get a blanket from the pickup. He returns and wraps it around my shoulders, his arm staying draped over me for a moment longer than necessary.

"Better?" he asks, his voice low and warm.

I nod, unable to find words. His closeness, the warmth of the fire, the intimacy of the moment... everything feels so intense, so real.

"You know," Alex says after a while, looking at the stars, "when I was little, my father always used to take me camping here. He taught me the names of the constellations, told me stories about how cowboys of old used the stars to navigate."

I look at him, surprised by this unexpected openness. "That must have been nice," I say softly.

Alex nods, a nostalgic smile on his face. "It was. I miss him, you know? Even though he was tough on me sometimes, moments like these... they were special."

I feel a lump in my throat. "He... he's not here anymore?" I ask simply. I don't want to bring up sad topics... but I want to know more about him.

Alex seems lost in his thoughts then answers, "Both my parents are gone. My mom died giving birth to me... so I never knew her. My dad... well, he had a horse riding accident."

For a moment, I stop breathing.

Alex... always so cheerful and playful... I can't believe he carries such a sad past. Losing both parents is terrible. And he and his father seemed to be so close.

And that's not all... his father died in a horse riding accident... I can't help but think about how much Alex loves horses and how his greatest passion must remind him every day of what was probably the most tragic moment of his life.

I don't know what to say... but I squeeze his hand. I rest my head on his shoulder with a silent invitation for him to get closer to me. I don't miss how careful he is with physical contact. How he tries not to take more liberties than I grant him and how he gives me time to get used to it and decide how close I want him.

"I'm sorry," I whisper.

"Don't be sorry, princess. And I'm sorry if I saddened the evening," he replies, squeezing my hand back.

"I'm glad to know you better, cowboy."

Alex gives me a small smile. His expression is no longer sad... now he looks tender.

"You've never been camping before, have you?" he asks, trying to lighten the moment... even though I've avoided this conversation as much as possible until now.

But in light of Alex's confession, it seems futile and foolish to keep hiding it.

"I'm sorry I never had experiences like this with my father," I confess. "He was always too busy..."

Alex turns to me, his eyes full of understanding. "Hey," he says gently, "it's never too late to create new memories. Maybe... maybe this can be the beginning of something new for you."

His words strike me deeply. He's right. Maybe I can't change the past, but I can choose how to live the present.

"Thank you, Alex," I whisper. "For all this. For... making me feel at home here."

He smiles, and for a moment he seems about to say something more. Instead, he just holds me a little tighter.

We stay like this, wrapped in the blanket, watching the stars and listening to the sounds of the night. There's no need for more words. At this moment, everything seems perfect.

But as the night progresses and the fire dies down, I can't help but wonder: what will happen tomorrow? And after? This feeling that's growing inside me... is it real? And most importantly, can it last beyond this magical night under the stars?

With these thoughts swirling in my head, I slowly fall asleep, my head resting on Alex's shoulder, his arm still protectively around me.

Chapter 26

Alex

The fire has now reduced to glowing embers, casting a soft light over our small campsite. I don't have the heart to move, not even to revive the flames. Rosie has fallen asleep on my shoulder, her steady breathing mingling with the sounds of the night. Her scent, envelops me, intoxicating me. There's nothing more beautiful in the world than this moment, I think to myself. It's perfect in its simplicity, in its quietness.

Thinking back to earlier today, the memory of Rosie's nervousness at the beginning of the journey strikes me. I had noticed it right away, evident in her eyes, in the way she moved, uncertain and a bit scared. Like a fawn ready to bolt at the slightest noise. It broke my heart to see that vulnerability in her, that fear hidden behind a brave smile.

I never want her to feel that way with me. I want to be her safe harbor, a place where she can be completely herself without fear of judgment or expectations. I want her to feel free, happy, peaceful in my presence. Just as she is now, sleeping peacefully by my side.

I watch her sleep and think about how much I want her to open up to me. I want to tell her that she can trust me completely, that I'll never judge her, whatever she decides to share. That her secrets, her fears, her dreams are safe with me. I want her to understand how much I care for her, even though I've known her for relatively little time.

It's strange how life sometimes surprises you, I think with a smile. If someone had told me a month ago that I would find myself here, in the middle of nowhere, with a "city princess" asleep on my shoulder and my heart beating like a teenager's first love, I would have laughed in their face. Yet here I am, with feelings so strong and deep for Rosie that they sometimes take my breath away.

During the evening, I was on the verge of telling her all this several times. When she laughed at my jokes, the sound of her laughter warming my heart more than any fire could. When her eyes sparkled watching the deer, full of wonder and pure joy. When she thanked me for bringing her here, her voice heavy with emotion. Each time, the words were there, on the tip of my tongue, ready to come out. But each time, I held back.

I don't want to force things. I want everything to happen naturally between us, every step forward to be natural and desired by both of us. If there's one thing I've learned in life, working with animals and nature, it's that the best things can't be rushed. They must grow naturally, like a flower blooming at the right moment, not a second before or after.

I did try to tell her something about myself... even though I didn't want to dampen the mood with my dramas. But I thought I couldn't hope for her to open up to me or start trusting me if I didn't take the first step. I usually don't talk openly about anything from my past... but with her it's different. Everything is different with her.

I sigh softly, enjoying the weight of her head on my shoulder, the warmth of her body against mine. This moment, here and now, is perfect as it is. I only need this: the quietness of the night, the stars above us, and Rosie by my side.

Slowly, with all possible gentleness to avoid waking her, I move Rosie into a more comfortable position. I take off my jacket and put it over her like an extra blanket, smiling when I see her instinctively curl up in its warmth. Then, I lie down beside her, close enough to feel her warmth, but not so close as to invade her space. I respect her boundaries. The universe only knows how much I want to immerse myself in her and never let go... but I want her to be ready. I want every time she comes closer to me and seeks contact to be because she wants to.

And I never want to behave again like I did the other night.

I was an idiot. I saw her cry and I walked away. I left her there... alone. Damn, I even made her cry... I really am an idiot.

Looking at the stars above us, I make a silent promise. Whatever happens, I'll be here for her. As a friend, as a confidant, as whatever she needs me to be. Because Rosie deserves this and much more. She deserves someone who supports her dreams, who comforts her fears, who loves her for who she truly is.

And if that someone should be me... well, I'd be the luckiest man in the world.

With this thought, I close my eyes, letting the sound of her breathing lull me to sleep. Tomorrow is another day, and I can't wait to live it with her. To show her more wonders of nature, to see her smile, to hear her laugh.

I feel more at home than ever.

And home, I realize with a smile, smells like Miss Dior huile de rose and sounds like Rosie's breathing in the night.

Chapter 27

Alex

I wake up slowly, the morning sun filtering through the trees. For a moment, I remain still, enjoying the sensation of peace that surrounds me. I've slept deeply, better than I have in years.

And then I remember the dream. Rosie. She was in a meadow, her bare feet caressing the green grass. Her red hair danced in the wind, brown eyes shining with an intense light. She wore a loose white dress that swayed gently, and wildflowers were woven into her hair. She was... ethereal. Beautiful.

In the dream, I approached her. She laughed, a pure and joyous sound that seemed to merge with the birdsong around us. She took my hand and we began to dance, light as air, happier than I'd ever been.

A smile forms on my lips at the memory. It was such a vivid dream, so real. I can almost still smell the flowers, feel the warmth of her hand in mine...

And then, suddenly, I stop. The smile vanishes from my face as realization hits me like a punch to the stomach.

Last night. My thoughts before falling asleep. I had thought... oh, damn.

I sit up abruptly, panic beginning to grow inside me. No, no, no. It can't be. I couldn't have had all those thoughts...

Damn... this seems like much more than a simple crush, or attraction, or any other damn sentimental thing that was already enough to send my brain into overdrive.

This seems dangerously more like something Chris might think.

And if Chris is in the equation... it all seems dangerously too sentimental, all too similar to love.

I can't have fallen in love. Not with Rosie. Not this quickly.

"Calm down, Alex," I mutter to myself, running a hand through my hair. "They were just passing thoughts. They don't mean anything."

But as much as I try to convince myself, I know I'm lying. The way my heart races every time I see her, the thrill I get from our playful banter, the constant pull to have her near me—none of this is normal. This is unlike anything I've ever felt before.

"Shit," I whisper, suddenly realizing how screwed I am. I'm in deeper than I expected. It's not a passing crush, not just physical attraction. It's something deeper, more dangerous.

I stand up, trying to shake away these thoughts. I can't afford to think like this.

But then I hear movement and turn around. Rosie is still asleep, curled up in my jacket. The morning sun illuminates her face, making her hair shine like molten copper. She's so beautiful it takes my breath away.

And in that moment, looking at her, I know it's too late to protect myself. I've already fallen, and fallen hard.

"You're in trouble, cowboy," I mutter to myself, unable to look away from her. "You're in serious trouble."

With a sigh, I head toward the fire to relight it and prepare breakfast. While I work, I try not to think about how screwed I am, about how difficult it will be to say goodbye to Rosie when the time comes and she won't want me with her.

Why would she want me? What would she do with someone like me?

I focus on the present. I have to, otherwise I'll go even more crazy. I focus on how to give her the best possible experience at this campsite. On how to make her smile, how to make the experience carefree.

Because if these are the only moments I'll have with her, I want them to be perfect. Even if it means suffering afterward.

"Good morning, cowboy," Rosie's sleepy voice makes me jump. I turn to see her stretching, her hair tousled and her eyes still half-closed.

And despite all my doubts and fears, I can't help but smile. "Good morning, princess. Sleep well?"

"Slept wonderfully," Rosie responds with a smile, moving closer to the fire. "I didn't think you could sleep so well outdoors."

I watch her as she sits beside me, wrapped in my jacket. My heart does a somersault in my chest at the sight, but I try to stay calm."It's the fresh mountain air. Works wonders," I respond, trying to keep a light tone.

Rosie nods, looking around with eyes full of wonder. "It's all so quiet and peaceful here."

"Do you miss the city?" I ask cautiously, not wanting to pressure her.

She turns to me, a thoughtful expression on her face. "Actually... not as much as I thought I would. I mean, I miss some things, sure. But here... I don't know, I feel more like myself."

Her words give me a spark of hope, but I try not to get carried away. I know how complicated her situation is.

"Well, you're always welcome here," I say, trying to be supportive without forcing the issue.

Rosie remains silent for a moment, watching the fire. When she speaks again, her voice is low, almost a whisper:

"Thank you, Alex. That means a lot to me."

I wish I could tell her how much I want her to stay, but I know it has to be her decision.

"So, what's on the schedule for today, cowboy?" she asks with a smile, clearly trying to change the subject.

I decide to follow her lead and not push. "I thought I'd take you hiking. There's a special place I want to show you."

Her eyes light up with excitement. "Sounds perfect!"

Chapter 28

Alex

I can't stop thinking. My mind churns with doubts and unspoken desires as we walk among the trees. Rosie is here, her hand in mine, yet she feels so far away. We've been holding hands since I helped her over the log. Has she noticed? Does it mean something to her?

There's so much I want to say, so much I want to ask. But every time I open my mouth, the words fail me. I want to tell her I'm falling for her. That her presence has brought a light into my life I didn't know I needed. That the thought of losing her terrifies me. But how do I say all this without ruining everything?

I glance at her as we walk. Her expression is calm, but there's something in her eyes—a flicker of uncertainty. Is she confused? Hesitant? I wish I could read her mind, understand what she's truly thinking. Would she regret leaving this place for her life in Los Angeles? Or would she regret staying here and changing everything?

The thought that she might be as torn as I am fills me with a strange, protective urgency.

"So cowboy, do you often bring girls to this special place?" Rosie suddenly asks, interrupting my stream of consciousness. I clear my throat... and decide to answer honestly. I can't expect her to be comfortable and open up to me if I don't do it first.

"I've never brought anyone here actually... it was a place my father used to take me." She looks at me, surprised but attentive. Her bright eyes encourage me to continue. "After he died... I only came here alone. To be honest, initially I didn't even come alone. Then I started coming to feel close to him... at some point I stopped completely. I haven't been here in years."

I feel Rosie's hand gently squeeze mine, a silent gesture of comfort that gives me the strength to continue. And it also makes me realize that she too is aware we're still holding hands.

"How old were you when you lost your father?" she asks. She seems a bit hesitant, but I can hear her despite the faint tone.

"Fourteen. But I was lucky... I was adopted by Chris's family. We've been friends forever and when I was left alone, his parents helped me and showered me with love."

"They did a beautiful thing... they must be really good people," she responds with a tender smile while squeezing my hand once again. A gesture that means more to me than a thousand words.

"Yes, they are. And so is Rory. And Chris. I've never known anyone kinder or more pure than him. He's my brother... all the guys are."

We've been walking for a while now. The silence between us has settled into something easy, interrupted only by Rosie's curious questions about the trees or the animals we pass, or by my quiet explanations.

The rhythmic crunch of our footsteps on the soft forest floor mingles with the gentle trills of birdsong. Rosie's hand remains in mine, and with every step, I become more aware of it. There's a warmth there, steady and grounding, that I don't want to let go of.

"The ranch, the animals, the wilderness... being here, surrounded by it all, makes me feel like I'm part of something bigger than myself," I admit.

I look at Rosie, hoping she can understand how deeply rooted this life is within me. I'm not good at opening up, but for her, I want to try. For the first time, I want someone to truly see me.

"I know it might sound strange," I continue, "but here... I feel complete. Every sunrise spilling over the mountains, every creature I care for, every trail I explore—everything reminds me that even with all the pain and loss, life is still beautiful."

The words hang in the air between us. I've never said anything like this to anyone before, and it feels both terrifying and freeing. But with Rosie, it feels... right.

"That's why I brought you here," I admit, turning to meet her gaze. "I wanted you to see this, to understand why I love this life so much, even when it's hard."

Rosie doesn't answer immediately. Her eyes drift across the landscape, her expression thoughtful. Finally, she says, her voice soft, "Alex... I'm sorry for what I said the other day. I didn't mean to..."

I cut her off, sensing where her thoughts are going. This isn't about guilt or apologies—I want us to understand each other better, not dwell on past mistakes.

I shake my head. "No, Rosie, that's not what this is about. I don't want your apologies. Honestly, I deserved it. If anyone needs to apologize, it's me," I confess, my voice low but sincere. I haven't had the chance to say how much I regret everything. "And actually... let me apologize again for it all. I was an idiot."

Her lips curve into a smile, one that's equal parts tender and teasing. "You are an idiot, cowboy," she says, her voice laced with warmth, "but we've already decided to start fresh, haven't we?"

Her words hit me in a way I can't explain, soothing a part of me that's been restless for far too long. And then there's her smile, that mischievous spark that always manages to unnerve me. Every. Single. Time. Like only Rosie can.

We continue walking, the sun filtering through the canopy above, casting playful patterns of light and shadow along the trail. From time to time, I share stories—like the first time I tamed a wild horse and how alive I felt, or nights spent under the stars with the ranch hands, laughing and dreaming about the future.

I glance at Rosie as I speak, hoping to see a spark of her own memories, a story she's ready to share. She listens, smiling and nodding, but something holds her back.

Finally, I can't hold back any longer. The urge to know more about her, to understand the pieces of her life that shaped her, is too strong. I decide to start small, to ease into something personal. It's a simple question, but one that genuinely intrigues me. I want to know if her life has turned out the way she always dreamed. "And you, Rosie? When you were a little girl, what did you dream of becoming?"

A shadow passes over her face, and for a moment, I regret asking. But then, she takes a deep breath and answers.

"When I was little... I wanted to be a writer," she says quietly. "I spent hours filling notebooks with stories and hiding them under my bed."

Her words tug at something inside me. "What happened?" I ask gently.

Rosie looks away, her shoulders dropping slightly. "Life happened, I guess. I chose the practical path. I studied marketing, got a good job, a nice apartment in Los Angeles. On paper, I have it all..."

"But?" I prompt softly, sensing there's more.

"But I'm not happy," she admits. "I'm always stressed, always rushing. I can't even remember the last time I wrote something just for myself."

Her voice trails off, and the vulnerability in her words hits me hard. I feel an overwhelming urge to protect her, to help her find that part of herself again.

"Since coming here," she continues, "I've realized how empty my life in Los Angeles feels. Here... I can breathe again."

The awareness of her pain mixes with a deep sense of empathy, and I can't help but wish with all my heart that I could offer her a safe haven. "What about your family?" I ask gently.

Rosie hesitates, her gaze dropping. "I lost my mom when I was a kid. And my dad... well, he was always too busy for me."

Her words make my chest tighten. Without thinking, I squeeze her hand a little more firmly.

"I'm sorry, Rosie," I say quietly. "That must have been hard."

She meets my gaze, her eyes shimmering with a mix of pain and relief. For a long moment, we simply look at each other, something unspoken passing between us.

As we walk on, the sound of a distant stream reaches us, mingling with the scent of pine and earth. Rosie breaks the silence.

"I didn't realize how much I needed to say all that," she admits, her voice softer now.

"Sometimes, keeping it all inside is the heaviest burden," I reply.

She nods. "In L.A., it felt like I couldn't show any weakness. Like everyone had it all figured out, and I was the only one struggling."

We stop at a clearing overlooking the valley below, bathed in golden sunlight.

"It's different here," I say, gesturing to the view. "Nature doesn't judge. It just... is."

Rosie smiles, her face lighting up with something I can only describe as hope. "I feel that. Like I'm finally allowed to be myself."

I clear my throat, gather my thoughts, and finally say, "You can be whoever you want with me... I'll never judge you."

She gives me a shy smile, her eyes dropping to the ground, but I notice her posture ease. Then, she whispers a quiet thank you, almost too soft to hear. But it's there, and it builds upon the feelings that are slowly becoming my new reality. I can only hope, somehow, that I'll find a way to reach her... even though she seems like the very definition of perfection.

We stand there for a while, hand in hand, the world quiet around us. Then, with a playful glint in her eye, she asks, "So, cowboy, where to next?"

I chuckle, the tension breaking. "Oh, I have a surprise waiting. Trust me."

And as we walk deeper into the forest, I can't help but think this trail is leading us to something far more significant than just a destination.

Chapter 29

Rosie

The trail winds before us, a ribbon of packed earth disappearing among the trees. I'm curious to know where Alex is taking me. He said it's a special place, and I can't wait to get there.

It's strange, I can't even remember why I was so nervous about this camping trip anymore. I'm loving every single moment! The fresh air, the sounds of nature, the peace surrounding me, the more personal conversations with Alex...

I'm surprised at how things are going between us. It's all been so... sweet. I think back to how he lifted my spirits at the beginning of the trip, without asking invasive questions. And last night, when he gave me an extra blanket because he was worried I might be cold.

A smile forms on my lips at the memory. I'm almost certain I fell asleep on his shoulder.

And then... the way he opened up to me, telling me about his family, his feelings. He was so sincere, so vulnerable. And strangely, it was easy for me to do the same. I never thought I'd tell anyone about my childhood dreams, my insecurities, my family. Yet with Alex, the words came naturally.

"Hey, are you okay?" Alex's voice brings me back to the present. I realize I've stopped, lost in my thoughts.

"Yes, sorry," I answer with a smile. "I was just... reflecting."

Alex looks at me with those deep eyes of his, as if he could read inside me. "Positive thoughts, I hope?"

I nod. "Very positive. I was thinking about how happy I am to be here."

His face lights up at these words. "Really? I'm glad to hear you say that."

We resume walking, and I find myself wishing I could stop time. To stay in this moment, on this trail, with Alex by my side.

"So, cowboy," I say, trying to lighten the atmosphere that has suddenly become charged with unspoken emotions. "How much further to this special place?"

Alex laughs, a sound that makes me feel warmth in my chest. "Patience, princess. The best things are worth waiting for."

I roll my eyes playfully, but inside I know he's right. And as we continue walking, I realize it's not just the special place I'm anticipating with excitement. There's something growing between Alex and me, something I can't quite define yet but that fills me with excitement and a bit of fear.

As we walk, I reflect on how my perception of Alex has changed in such a short time. At first, I felt constantly judged by him. His teasing and his confident cowboy attitude made me feel inadequate, as if every move I made was under scrutiny.

But now... now I see things differently. I've understood that's simply his way of being, his sense of humor. There's no malice in his words, just a genuine desire to make me feel comfortable, even if sometimes in a slightly awkward way.

And those eyes of his... at first I found them intimidating, as if they could see through me. Now, every time I meet them, I see only sweetness. They're warm, welcoming eyes that make me feel safe. I'm discovering they're truly as gentle as they seem, perhaps even more so.

This realization makes me want to open up to him even more. There's something about Alex, about his way of being, that makes me feel protected and understood.

I take a deep breath and decide to take another step toward vulnerability.

"Hey cowboy," I begin, my voice a bit uncertain, "I need to confess something." He looks at me with curiosity, slowing his pace to walk beside me.

"I'm all ears, princess."

I smile at the nickname, now familiar. "At first, I was terrified about this camping trip."

Alex raises an eyebrow, surprised. "Really? I never would have guessed," he says with an ironic smile.

I give him a light push on the arm, laughing. "Okay, maybe I was a bit obvious. But it wasn't just about the missing comforts or the insects."

"What was it about then?" he asks gently.

I hesitate for a moment, then confess: "I was afraid of not being good enough. Of looking like the incompetent city girl. And... I was afraid of disappointing you."

Alex stops, turning completely toward me. His eyes are full of a tenderness that takes my breath away.

"Princess," he says softly, "you could never disappoint me. You've been incredible. You've faced every challenge with courage and good humor."

I feel my cheeks flush under his intense gaze. "Thank you," I murmur. "And thank you also for... well, for everything. For how you've encouraged me, for how you've made me feel comfortable. For showing me all this beauty."

Alex smiles, a smile that lights up his whole face. "It's been my pleasure, Rosie. Really. But stop thanking me."

Hearing my name roll off his lips does something to me. He doesn't say it often, but when he does, it's like a spark ignites inside me. There's something about the way he says it—something intimate, magnetic—that makes my pulse quicken.

This entire trip has been undeniably sweet, but the pull I feel toward Alex, the sheer physical attraction, is always there, simmering just beneath the surface. Ignoring it isn't just difficult—it's impossible.

For a moment, we stay like this, looking into each other's eyes. There's something in the air, a palpable tension that makes my heart race.

Then Alex clears his throat, breaking the spell. "Well, better get moving if we want to arrive before sunset."

I nod, a bit disappointed but also excited about what awaits us. Why isn't he making a move? Does he feel the same magnetic pull toward me that I can't seem to escape? Sometimes it feels like he does... so why does he keep holding back? I'm on the verge of losing control, consumed by this desire, while he seems so calm, so in control—like none of this is even affecting him.

And if it's true that he seemed really upset when he thought Ethan was something more to me, I can't be certain what's going through his head.

"Everything okay, princess?" Alex's voice brings me back to reality.

"Yes, yes," I reply quickly, trying to seem casual. "Just a bit tired. How much further?"

"Not much," Alex answers with a smile. "You'll see, it'll be worth it."

I nod, trying to focus on the trail ahead of us instead of the whirlwind of emotions inside me. The woods are getting thicker, the air fresher. I hear the sound of water in the distance.

Suddenly, the trail opens up and I find myself facing a breathtaking sight.

A waterfall pours into a small crystal-clear lake, surrounded by mossy rocks and wildflowers. It's like a secret oasis, hidden in the heart of the forest.

"Oh, Alex," I whisper, breathless. "It's... it's wonderful."

He looks at me, his eyes shining with pride and something else I can't decipher. "Do you like it?"

"Like it? It's incredible!" I exclaim, forgetting all my worries for a moment.

I approach the water's edge, fascinated by how the light plays on the surface. I feel Alex approach behind me.

"This is my special place," he says quietly. "I come here when I need to think, to find myself again. But as I told you before... it's been a while since I've been here."

I turn toward him, struck by the vulnerability in his voice. "Thank you for showing it to me," I say sincerely.

For a moment, we stay like this, looking into each other's eyes. Part of me wants to step forward, close the distance between us. But the other part, the rational part, reminds me not to misinterpret. If he wanted to kiss me, he would have done it already, right?

Maybe he's simply respecting my space to give me room... maybe he doesn't want anything more to happen.

In the end, I'm the one who breaks the moment. "So, what do you say about a swim?"

Alex laughs, and the tension breaks. "It's déjà vu, princess."

I take off my shoes and socks, enjoying the sensation of cool grass under my feet. Alex does the same, then removes his shirt with a fluid movement. I can't help but stare at his perfectly defined muscles, his abs so chiseled they look like they were carved by a sculptor, his broad chest, and those powerful arms. God, just his forearms alone had nearly driven me to madness... damn.

I quickly look away, my body burning with heat. I have to remind myself how to breathe.

"So, princess," says Alex with a grin, "ready for some adventure?"

Before I can answer, he takes a short run-up and dives into the lake with a joyful shout. Water splashes everywhere, making me laugh and step back.

"Come on, Rosie!" Alex calls, emerging and shaking water from his hair. "The water's perfect!"

And now, wet like that, he's even hotter. He moves with such confidence, emerging from the water like a Greek god. Drops of water trail down his hair, his sculpted body glistening, flawless, utterly tantalizing.

I hesitate for a moment. I've never been a great swimmer, and the idea of diving into an unknown lake makes me a bit anxious. Now that I don't have alcohol giving me courage like the other night... I'm a bit more intimidated.

But there's something about Alex's enthusiasm, about the wild beauty of this place, that pushes me to dare.

"Alright," I say, taking a deep breath. "But no tricks, okay?"

Alex raises a hand, making the scout's honor sign. "Scout's honor."

I giggle.

I take off my shirt, staying in my tank top and shorts. Then, before courage abandons me, I run toward the water and dive in.

The cold hits me like a shock, making me hold my breath for a moment. But then, as I swim to the surface, the sensation becomes refreshing, revitalizing.

"You did it!" exclaims Alex, swimming toward me with a wide smile.

"I did it," I respond, smiling back. I feel alive, electrified. "You were right, the water is perfect."

We spend the next few minutes swimming lazily, enjoying the coolness of the water and the beauty of the landscape around us.

"It's incredible," I whisper, more to myself than to him.

"It is," Alex agrees, his voice close. I turn and find him beside me. It's just the two of us, suspended in the water, surrounded by the wild beauty of nature. I feel my heart speed up, and it's not just from swimming.

But before I can say or do anything, before I drive myself crazy with inappropriate thoughts about possible feelings I might have for this infuriating cowboy... Alex dives back in, shattering the spell. When he resurfaces, he's wearing his usual playful grin.

"How about a race to the waterfall?" he proposes.

I laugh, grateful for the distraction. "Haven't you figured out yet that I'm not an expert swimmer like you, cowboy?"

"I'll give you a head start," he says with a wink.

And that's how, ladies and gentlemen, the butterflies in my stomach go crazy.

Chapter 30

Alex

Rosie dives into the water with a natural grace that leaves me breathless. When she resurfaces, wet hair falling across her face, radiant smile, it's a sight I'll never forget. But what truly strikes me is how unaware she is of her beauty. It's as if she doesn't realize how incredibly attractive she is.

When she took off her clothes to get in the water, I had to make an immense effort to stay calm. She wasn't completely naked, and I've definitely seen her in less before—if you count the bikini. But the simple act of watching her undress, even just a little, was enough to make me hard. Everything she does gets to me... always. And even though this trip feels like an emotional crisis of unprecedented proportions with all the things I'm terrified I might feel for her—even though I'm trying to avoid filthy thoughts and keep a respectable attitude because, well, it's just the two of us alone, and I don't want to put her in a position where she'd have to reject me or feel embarrassed—I can't help the overwhelming need I have for her. I can't help the kind of attraction that aches.

She's wearing a white tank top now, no bra from what I can tell, and a pair of tight shorts. Even before she dove in, I already had a clear enough view of her body. But now, soaked through with lake water, everything she's wearing is practically transparent. And I'm losing it. Completely.

This vision of her has me on the edge, and I'm desperately trying not to stare, trying to keep things playful instead. It's the only way I know to keep myself from losing control.

"So, cowboy, are you ready for the race?" she challenges me with a mischievous smile.

I try to focus, to push away the thoughts that distract me. "Always ready, princess," I respond, trying to mask my turmoil with a playful tone.

We swim together, our laughter echoing in the air. Every now and then, I can't help but glance at Rosie. She's so full of life, so spontaneous. She makes me feel alive like I haven't felt in a long time. Every smile, every gesture makes me want to know her even more, to understand every nuance of her being.

When we finally reach the waterfall, I pause for a moment to observe the landscape. The falling water creates a relaxing melody, and the sun filtering through the tree leaves creates patterns of light on the water. But none of this can compete with Rosie's beauty, with her smile that illuminates everything around her.

"It's incredible here," she says, her eyes sparkling with wonder.

"Yes, it is," I respond, but my eyes are fixed on her, not the landscape. She seems to notice, blushing slightly.

"Stop looking at me like that," she says laughing, trying to hide her embarrassment.

"I can't help it," I respond honestly. "You're... you're incredible, Rosie." The words escape my lips before I can stop them. Yet, I can't bring myself to regret it. Someone needs to remind this breathtaking woman just how remarkable she is. Judging by the way her eyes widen, the way she momentarily freezes, it's clear she doesn't hear it nearly as often as she should. The urge to tell her again, to make her see herself the way I do, swells in my chest. I want to say it a thousand more times, to burn the truth of her worth into her soul. But I hold back, not wanting to push too far, not wanting to risk losing this fragile moment.

She looks at me for a moment, surprised by my words. Then she smiles, and that smile hits me like a punch to the stomach. It's a smile full of warmth, of sweetness. It's the smile of someone who is happy, genuinely happy.

"Thank you, Alex," she says softly.

God.

It's enough to drive me wild when she calls me "cowboy" with that playful, teasing edge in her voice—but when she says my name? It's game over. My knees go weak, my pulse pounds, and I'm seconds away from losing it entirely. Hell, I'd willingly drop to my knees for her, surrendering completely. And the things I'd do from that position... things so sinful they'd make the devil blush.

I move closer to her, feeling an ever-stronger connection between us. The urge to kiss her is almost irresistible, but I know I must resist. I can't afford any missteps, I don't want to make mistakes. But perhaps it's time to bring some clarity and talk a bit explicitly with her.

I move even closer. I can feel her quickened breath, see the slight trembling of her lips. The waterfall continues to fall behind us, creating a natural curtain that isolates us from the rest of the world.

"May I..." I whisper, raising a hand to brush her face.

She nods almost imperceptibly, her eyes fixed on mine. I place my hand gently on her face, my fingers brushing against her soft skin, savoring every second of the touch. It's almost too much. God... I'm in deep.

I don't push it further. Maybe I'm a coward, or maybe I'm terrified of what might happen if I cross that line. But here I am, mesmerized by her beauty, lost in the sheer thrill of just holding her face in my hands.

I see her inhale, and for a split second, I consider pulling away, afraid I might be pushing her too far. But then she leans into me, her lips brushing mine in a kiss that sends a jolt through every part of me.

When our lips meet, it's as if everything else vanishes. The kiss is sweet, gentle, almost shy at first. Her lips are soft and have a slight taste of fresh water. I feel her tremble slightly as my hands caress her face, and her body draws closer to mine in the water.

The moment is perfect: the water flowing around us, the sound of the waterfall in the background, and Rosie in my arms, right where she seems to belong.

The sweet kiss slowly transforms. It begins with a deeper caress of my lips on hers, a touch that becomes bolder, more confident. Her breathing becomes faster, and I feel it vibrate against my mouth. My hands slide down, leaving her face to stop at her neck, feeling her heartbeat quicken under my grip. Rosie responds with a sigh that makes me lose all inhibition. Her hands climb up my chest, making me shiver, she clings to me, pulling me closer, as if she wanted to merge our bodies and leave no space for the water that surrounds us. The kiss intensifies, our lips moving with more urgency, exploring without fear.

"Alex..." she whispers my name against my lips, and that sound drives me crazy. I gently bite her lower lip, drawing out a moan that makes me tremble. Her nails lightly scratch my back, sending electric shocks throughout my body.

The world around us completely disappears. There's only Rosie, her body pressed against mine, her lips responding to mine with the same passion. Our tongues brush, seek each other out, dance together in an increasingly intense rhythm.

I gently push her against the rocky wall next to the waterfall. The water continues to flow around us, but we don't even feel it anymore. We're lost in each other, in this moment of pure passion that seems endless.

Her hands wander over my back, my hips, as if she wanted to memorize every inch of my body. I respond by exploring the curve of her neck with my lips, savoring the taste of her skin mixed with fresh water. I feel her gasp when I gently bite her earlobe.

"You drive me crazy," I whisper hoarsely in her ear, making her tremble in my arms.

"Then don't stop," she responds breathlessly, before capturing my lips again in a kiss that takes my breath away.

The heat between us grows, becoming an uncontrollable fire. My hands move, sliding down the line of her body, fingers slipping under the water, following the curve of her hips and gripping her more tightly. Her breathing becomes broken, and each of her moans pushes me to want more... as if I wasn't already completely lost to her.

The feeling of her fingers on my skin is almost too much to bear, and I feel a moan escape my lips.

I lift her up, her legs wrapping around my waist, and carry her to a flat rock near the waterfall. I set her down gently, our lips not parting even for a second. The sound of falling water, the scent of wildflowers, everything blends into a single symphony that tastes of Rosie, of us, and I fix this moment as the most beautiful of my life so far.

Her hands find the edge of my shorts, pulling them down with a hurry that mirrors my own. My hands do the same with hers, feeling her soft skin under my fingers.

When we're finally free of our clothes, the feeling of her bare skin against mine is the most right and intoxicating sensation I've ever experienced.

Rosie arches her back, pressing her chest against mine, her legs slowly wrapping around my hips.

She moans again, and I join her.

My hands slip between her thighs, feeling the tense muscles, ready to give in under the weight of passion. The way she looks at me, eyes half-closed, breath ragged, drives me crazy.

"Is this okay?" I ask, starting to touch her. She nods, writhing and holding onto me even tighter. There's nothing more beautiful in the world than Rosie, naked and all mine.

"You're so beautiful", I whisper against her neck, kissing along her jawline, biting her gently in a way I know will make her tremble.

"Don't stop..." she repeats, her voice almost a moan, suffocated by the desire consuming us. And I don't. I don't stop until I feel her come for the first time.

Chapter 31

Alex

Rosie looks at me, her dark eyes lit with a passion I've never seen before. Her breathing is quick, her cheeks flushed, and I'm completely lost in her gaze, unable to think of anything but how much I want her. How beautiful she is like this, how good it feels to make her feel good, how much I want to think of her as mine.

"Alex," she whispers, her voice warm yet trembling with resolve. "I want you, now."

My heart races as I reach out to touch her cheek, my thumb grazing her velvety skin. "I want you too, Rosie. More than you could ever imagine." My voice comes out rough, loaded with an emotion that grows, strong and unstoppable.

Our lips meet again in a deep kiss, filled with an intensity that leaves no room for hesitation. My hands explore her body, tracing the soft, graceful lines I've come to adore. She answers my kiss with the same fervent passion, pressing her body against mine, seeking closeness, connection, the feeling of belonging we both crave.

My mind is racing, but in a rare moment of clarity, I stop. "Rosie, wait," I murmur against her lips, my breath still ragged as I try to regain control. "I don't have a condom with me." I feel like a complete idiot. "I didn't expect…" I try to explain as she watches me, her eyes intense yet gentle, filled with affectionate understanding. But she interrupts me.

"I'm on the pill," she whispers, her lips brushing against mine as she speaks, her warm breath on my face. "If you trust me, I trust you."

Her words resonate deeply, carrying an intimacy that takes my breath away. I look at her, feeling the meaning of that gesture, of that total trust. "I trust you," I reply softly, my voice reflecting the truth of the words. She smiles, a shy smile that kindles a new warmth within me, a tenderness I feel only for her.

I lift her into my arms and carry her toward the riverbank, laying her gently on the soft grass. I brush her coppery hair away from her face, leaving her beautiful features fully revealed. Resting my forehead against hers, I hold her face in my hands.

"Are you sure?" I ask her once more. I want her more than anything, but I need to know that her decision isn't clouded by the passion of the moment. I don't want her to regret this later.

She gives me a teasing smile. "Hurry up, cowboy... or are you getting performance anxiety?"

I burst out laughing. I love my Rosie.

"Oh, I'm going to make you regret that, princess."

Rosie

I can hardly believe what just happened. I kissed Alex—I made the first move. The thought alone makes my heart race, but I couldn't hold back any longer. I'd reached my breaking point. For one agonizing moment, fear gripped me after my lips met his. What if I'd gone too far? But then, his lips moved against mine, and that fear melted away, replaced by a rush of pure, unrestrained relief and something far deeper. He kissed me back.

I'm not the type of person with much experience in these things... I guess my insecurities about relationships have kept me a little in the dark. But after that kiss... it was like that one kiss snuck through all our defenses and gradually dismantled them completely. Like the solution to an equation that suddenly becomes clear.

And that orgasm Alex gave me? The most intense of my life.

Sure... I've never had an orgasm against a rock at the hands of a cowboy before, so that probably played a part... but something tells me that's far from the whole story. Alex has this mix of sweetness and passion that drives me crazy.

Just like the kiss before. It started as the softest, shyest thing in the world... and then he devoured me, burning me up.

He started out touching me so delicately, seeking my approval... and then he gave me the strongest orgasm of my life.

Now he's laid me gently on the grass. He takes care of my whole body, still looking for my approval, checking in, waiting for my final "yes" before he enters me.

I never thought I'd be so drawn to a guy this sweet.

"Oh, I'm going to make you regret that, princess", he says, laughing at my last playful remark.

And there's my cowboy again.

Which version do I like best? Do I really have to choose?! Alex is perfect in every way.

He bites down on the curve of my shoulder... and a tingling shiver runs all the way down my spine, reaching the tips of my fingers. I can't hold back a moan.

"That's it, princess, I want to hear you when you like it," he whispers, rewarding me with another bite. Meanwhile, he slowly starts to ease himself between my legs, nudging forward to let me get used to him... and I can already tell this will be incredible.

"Oh God, Rosie... you're going to kill me," he says, his voice so husky it doesn't even sound like him. I cling to him, too overwhelmed to say anything, already lost in sensation. I dig my nails in a little too deep, but he doesn't complain.

Then, he slides fully inside, and we start finding our rhythm. His body blends completely with mine, and nothing has ever felt more right. I've never felt more complete, more alive.

Alex is perfectly fitted to me, and he moves with the skill of someone completely aware of his own body, like no one else has done with me before. And combined with the words he whispers in that broken voice, it's enough to drive me crazy.

"Yes, baby, just like that."

"Oh God, you're perfect."

"I'll never get enough of this."

I don't know if he truly believes these things or if it's just the heat of the moment... but it has a profound effect on me.

And he keeps moving, kissing me, touching me everywhere, like I'm the most precious thing in the world.

His skin is warm and solid under my hands, and every touch feels like worship.

Our hands intertwine, and together we reach the end of this dance, overwhelmed by a storm that leaves us still, close, holding each other tight, completely spent.

Chapter 32

Alex

I wake up slowly, feeling a bit dazed at first. The first sensation I register is being entangled with a warm body... the most pleasant feeling ever. I don't open my eyes yet, wanting to savor this moment of pure sensation. Her steady breath tickles my neck, her hair brushes my cheek, her fingers delicately rest on my skin. It's incredible how perfectly she fits against my body, as if we were molded for each other.

Rosie.

Immediately, a foolish smile spreads across my face.

I breathe deeply, and her perfume mingles with the scent of grass and earth beneath us. Only now do I begin to feel the coolness of the evening air on my skin. I focus on every point where our bodies touch: her leg intertwined with mine, her hip pressed against mine, her warm breath caressing my chest. I've never felt so at peace, so complete.

I don't think I've ever slept so deeply in my life... and I don't even know for how long.

Finally, I open my eyes, and the first thing I see is the sky above us beginning to take on the colors of sunset. A moment of pure panic courses through my body like an electric shock. Shit. We fell asleep. We haven't set up the tents yet, we haven't dried off, I haven't started a fire. The panic grows when I feel Rosie's skin under my fingers and try to gauge how she feels. Will Rosie be cold? Yesterday evening she was cold even when completely dry and in front of the fire. I bite my lip, angry with myself. I should have been more responsible, thought about the consequences. Instead, I let myself get carried away by the moment, by desire, by happiness, and now Rosie might get sick because of me. I watch her sleep, so peaceful and trusting in my arms. She put her trust in me, and what did I do? I left her sleeping on damp grass while the sun sets. What kind of idiot am I? I was supposed to protect her, take care of her, especially after what we shared. Instead, I was selfish, lost in my pleasure and happiness. Her hand moves slightly on my chest, and guilt mixes with a wave of tenderness so strong it almost hurts. I can't let her get cold. I have to wake her, even though I hate the idea of interrupting her peaceful sleep. We need to set up camp before it gets completely dark, find a sheltered spot, light a fire. I need to make up for my mistake. "Rosie," I whisper softly, stroking her hair. Her body presses even closer to mine, seeking warmth, and my heart clenches. "Little one, we need to wake up."

The sun continues to sink toward the horizon, and with it, the air temperature. Every passing second increases my anxiety, but at the same time, I can't help but lose myself in the sensation of her body against mine, in the way she clings to me in her sleep, in the total trust she shows. It's a contradiction that drives me crazy: the desire to protect her and the wish to never move from this perfect moment.

But I must be responsible. I must be the man she deserves, one who knows how to take care of her, not just lose himself in passion. I gently caress her back, trying to wake her in the gentlest way possible. "Rosie, love, it's getting dark. We need to set up camp."

Among all these fears... for a moment, I remain still, trying to determine if it was all real or just an incredibly vivid dream.

I stare at Rosie sleeping beside me. Her face is serene, her hair spread across the grass like a copper waterfall. It's real. It's all real.

I still can't believe what happened between us. It was... there are no words to describe it. Wonderful, incredible, magical - none of these do justice to what I felt.

Never in my life have I experienced such a deep, intense connection with someone. It wasn't just physical - though that was extraordinary - it was as if our souls had touched. As if, for a moment, we had become one.

Yet, as I watch her sleep, I feel a pang of worry. Is she okay? Was it good for her too? Will she regret it when she wakes up?

Rosie is so... perfect. Intelligent, beautiful, brave. And me? How can I be worthy of a woman like her? While these thoughts torment me, I feel Rosie stirring slightly beside me.

Then I decide to prioritize problems, and the fact that it's almost night frightens me again.

Concern for her well-being takes precedence over everything else.

"Rosie," I whisper softly, "are you awake?"

She mumbles something incomprehensible, then slowly opens her eyes. "Alex?" she says in a sleepy voice.

"Hey," I respond, trying to keep my voice calm despite the growing anxiety inside me. "How do you feel? Are you cold?"

Rosie stretches slightly, then seems to realize the situation. I see her shiver slightly. "A little," she admits.

Without hesitation, I get up and start gathering our scattered clothes. "We need to get you dressed and I need to set up camp," I say, passing her her clothes. "We can't stay like this all night, you could get sick."

While Rosie dresses, I can't help but voice my concerns. "I'm sorry, Rosie. I shouldn't have let us fall asleep here. It was irresponsible of me."

She looks at me, surprised by my sudden seriousness. "Alex, everything's fine. I was happy to fall asleep here with you."

But I can't calm down. "What if you catch a cold? Or worse? I'm the guide, I should have thought about this."

Rosie comes closer to me, taking my hands. Then she bursts out laughing and stares at me as if I'm the strangest person in the world. "Alex, look at me. I'm fine. Yes, it's a bit cold, but it's nothing serious. And what happened between us... it was worth it, don't you think?"

Her words calm me a little, but not entirely. "Of course it was worth it. It was... incredible. But I want to take care of you, Rosie. I don't want you to suffer because of me."

She smiles sweetly. "And you are. But don't panic... I'm not that fragile."

I nod but immediately make a mental list of everything I need to do to keep her warm. I help her dress, wrap her in a blanket, and start setting up the fire. Between tasks, I return to Rosie to hold her close, trying to protect her from the night's cold. I can't help but think about how everything has changed in such a short time, and how scared and excited I am at the same time about what the future might hold.

But for now, my priority is making sure Rosie is okay. The rest... we'll face the rest together, one step at a time. Despite my worry, I can't help but feel a spark of joy having her so close.

"Are you okay?" I ask again, unable to contain my anxiety.

Rosie nods, pressing herself even closer to me. "I'm fine, Alex. Really."

I reluctantly pull away from her again, and my hands move automatically. Soon, flames begin to dance, casting a warm glow over the clearing.

"Here," I say, guiding Rosie toward the fire. "Sit here, you'll warm up in no time."

She sits, extending her hands toward the warmth. I watch her carefully, looking for signs of discomfort or illness. But all I see is the reflection of flames in her eyes and a slight smile on her lips.

I sit beside her, wrapping an arm around her shoulders. We remain quiet, the crackling fire casting a warm glow around us, lost in the simple, perfect pleasure of being together. No words are needed; just the gentle rhythm of our shared presence is enough.

Chapter 33

Rosie

I wake slowly, sunlight spilling through the tent and warming my face. For a moment, I stay still, the soft hum of the morning surrounding me. Memories from last night flood back—Alex, the waterfall, the way his touch felt like a fire under my skin, and the way our bodies fit together so perfectly. A smile tugs at my lips, unbidden.

But it's more than the passion I remember. It's Alex himself. How he worried about me afterward, his hands gentle as he helped me into my clothes, his voice low and soothing as he wrapped me in a blanket. He held me so close, as though keeping me safe was all that mattered. My chest tightens with an emotion I'm almost afraid to name.

I open my eyes, turning toward his sleeping bag—but it's empty. The small space feels colder without him, and unease begins to creep in. Wrapping the blanket tighter around myself, I slip out of the tent.

The crisp morning air brushes my cheeks, the scent of dew and pine filling my lungs. A soft sound pulls my attention—coffee bubbling over the campfire. Relief washes over me as I spot Alex crouched by the fire, his back to me. When he turns, his smile is like the sunrise, warm and bright and just for me.

"Good morning, princess," he says, his voice teasing yet gentle.

"Good morning, cowboy," I reply, my cheeks heating. How do you act the morning after a night like that? My thoughts race, and for a moment, I feel shy under his gaze.

Alex seems to sense it. He rises slowly, approaching as though not to startle me. "Did you sleep well?" he asks, his tone softer now, full of concern.

I nod. "Yes, very well. And you?"

His smile deepens, crinkling the corners of his eyes. "Never better."

We stand there, the quiet stretching between us. The crackling of the fire and the distant birdsong are the only sounds, yet the air hums with something unspoken. Alex steps closer, his eyes searching mine, and then, as if drawn by some invisible pull, he wraps his arms around me.

The blanket falls away, but I hardly notice. His embrace is warm and steady, his chest solid against my cheek. I close my eyes, breathing him in, the familiar scent of pine and leather grounding me.

He leans back slightly, just enough to meet my gaze, his expression soft. Slowly, his lips brush mine in a kiss that's gentle, tender, and achingly sweet. It's different from last night's fiery passion. This kiss is slower, deeper, like a promise neither of us is ready to put into words.

When we part, his mischievous smile returns, lighting his face. "How about breakfast? I make a mean pancake."

I laugh, grateful for the ease he brings to the moment, for the way he always knows when to break the tension. "Oh really? Is that a challenge, cowboy?" I say, mustering a playful tone to match his.

He winks. "You'll just have to taste and see."

Chapter 34

Alex

I move closer to the campfire, where the pancake batter is already waiting. Rosie follows me, still wrapped in her blanket, her hair delightfully messy, her cheeks flushed—perhaps from the morning chill, or maybe from something else entirely. As I pour the batter onto the sizzling pan, I can feel her gaze on me, curious and mischievous, tugging a small smile to my lips.

"You know," she says, her tone light, her head tilted just slightly, "there's something ironic about watching a rugged cowboy so focused on making fluffy pancakes."

I glance over my shoulder, pretending to be offended, though the grin that curves my mouth betrays me. "Hey, princess, you already know about my golden hands." My voice is playful, and I raise my eyebrows for effect, emphasizing the double meaning.

Her blush is immediate, and God, there's nothing I adore more than the soft pink coloring her cheeks. She takes a step closer, her smile coy yet daring. "Maybe," she murmurs, her voice barely above a whisper, "I need a little reminder."

Her words ignite something deep inside me—or maybe that fire never really went out. If it were up to me, we wouldn't have slept at all last night. She'd have woken up in my arms, my body still claiming hers, leaving no doubt that she's mine.

But I hesitate, uncertain of how much she wants, how much of me she's ready for.

Still, one thing is clear: for me, this isn't temporary. I don't want it to be just one night. I don't want it to end with this camping trip, or with the summer.

But Rosie doesn't know that yet.

And maybe I'm not sure if she even wants it to last as much as I do.

What I *am* sure of is that, right now, she wants me.

And who am I to deny my princess?

"Well then," I say, a teasing smile tugging at my lips, "I guess these pancakes will have to wait."

I lunge for her, and she takes a quick step back, pretending to run, but there's no escaping me. I catch her in seconds, my hands firm yet gentle as I pull her close. Her playful laughter fades into a soft gasp as I lift her effortlessly and lay her down on the blanket beside the fire.

The morning sun filters through the trees, casting golden reflections across her skin. I kneel beside her, letting my hands glide slowly along the edge of the blanket, uncovering her body inch by inch. Her eyes meet mine—dark and heavy with desire—as my fingers find their way to her warm, pulsating skin.

Her hands clutch at my shoulders as I begin to explore her. When pleasure overtakes her, her back arches, and the sunlight spills over her face, illuminating her features in a glow that takes my breath away. The sound of her moan—soft yet intense—is a melody I could listen to forever.

My fingers keep moving, a slow, deliberate rhythm that pushes her beyond the edge, carrying her further as my heart beats in perfect unison with hers.

I serve the pancakes on two plates, adding a generous drizzle of maple syrup. I sit down next to Rosie, passing her plate to her. She's wearing nothing but my flannel shirt, with the most satisfied expression I've ever seen. I feel a surge of pride at that, and seeing her wrapped in my shirt, I feel something else too... but I try to ignore it. I can't think about that right now.
"I'm absolutely starving!" Rosie says, taking a bite of her pancake. Her eyes light up... Then she lets out a sound of pleasure that shatters all the walls I was trying to build and reignites all my desire for her.
"Oh my God, Alex! These are absolutely incredible!" I smile, satisfied. "Looks like you lost the bet, princess." She smiles and pushes me, but I move closer and wrap her in an embrace, positioning myself to have breakfast while holding her. "Is this okay?" I whisper to her, seeking reassurance that she's comfortable having me close even in moments like this—simple, everyday moments when her mind isn't clouded by pleasure or lost in the throes of ecstasy. She nods with a smile and leans into me more. We continue breakfast in comfortable silence, enjoying each

other's company and the beauty of nature around us. Occasionally, our eyes meet and we smile, sharing a moment of intimacy without needing words. As we finish eating, I realize that despite all my fears and insecurities, I'm happy. Happy in a way I haven't been in a very, very long time. And it's all thanks to this extraordinary woman sitting beside me. When Rosie finishes two plates of pancakes, I look at her with the most satisfied expression I can muster – which doesn't take much effort, considering I truly am satisfied. Then I stand up, gesturing for her to wait there.

Chapter 35

Rosie

I watch Alex as he returns to me, his steps confident, a satisfied smile on his face. I can hardly believe how good I feel with him, how well we fit together, and how much I still want him. I'm pulled from my thoughts when I realize he's up to something... he has that look, his classic "Alex the cowboy" expression.

In his hands, there's a dark blue notebook, worn at the corners, and a pen. He sits down behind me, his legs framing mine, and wraps me in his arms. The warmth of his chest against my back gives me a sense of security that still surprises me. I can't believe he practically asked for permission to hold me like this. That, beneath all that bravado, there's so much uncertainty. That after everything we've shared, he'd still ask for permission to do something so simple... it's endearing, making the moment feel even more intimate.

"Princess... how about we write something?" he says, using that gentle tone he always adopts when he knows I'm about to panic. That tone that tries to ease even the most intense situations.

A lump forms in my throat. Has he really been mulling this over all this time? I'd told him about my childhood dream, about the hours I used to spend creating stories in my notebooks, about how I'd chosen the "safe" path instead of following the desire that burned inside me. But then... caught up in the moment, I'd let it slip from my mind.

"Alex..." I whisper, my hands trembling slightly. "I haven't written in years. I was never even good at it."

He hugs me a little tighter, as if he's trying to lend me his courage through that embrace.

"I'm right here with you, princess. You don't have to do it alone. Just start by having fun with it. Write something about this magical place, about what's around you... about how you feel. I think it might be a great starting point for a beautiful story. Don't you think?"

I stare at the notebook he's holding out to me. It's a simple dark blue book, but it suddenly feels like the most intimidating object in the world. That part of me—the little girl who dreamed of telling stories—I had locked her away long ago. I'd done it carefully, like folding away winter clothes at the arrival of summer, convincing myself it was the right thing to do.

"Alex... I..." My voice comes out smaller than I'd like, and I'm not even sure what to say.

Great, Rosie, that's definitely proof you're not cut out to be a writer.

"Let's make it a game, princess. You start writing, and for every page you fill, I'll reward you," he says, with a playful grin.

"It doesn't work like that... I can't just write on command," I reply, my voice slightly shaky.

"Then I think you might need a little encouragement."

Without another word, he leans down and starts planting small, maddeningly slow kisses along my neck, and within half a second, I'm covered in goosebumps.

He trails his way down my spine and then back up, grazing my skin with gentle bites until he reaches my ear. In his rough, thrilling whisper, he says, "Now start by describing what it's like to be in a cowboy's arms. There's an orgasm waiting for you for every page."

Chapter 36

Alex

I'm between Rosie's legs, and damn, I can't get enough of this. I'd been waiting to taste her... but I left that for dessert. Meanwhile, my little princess is holding up her end of the deal. She's filled five pages in the last few hours, and I've rewarded her with the promised orgasms.

Good thing I have a vivid imagination!

"Well done, my girl. You've earned every one of them," I tell her... because I like it, because I noticed she likes it when I talk to her, and because in moments like these, I can call her "my girl" without thinking about what we haven't yet discussed—about what she wants us to become.

Despite Rosie claiming she wasn't any good... she's incredibly good. This woman needs to be a writer, and I'll make sure it happens. The rewards definitely helped break the ice... and it's an activity I absolutely love. Did I mention I can never get enough of her?

I taste her, savoring every inch, and she's the sweetest thing I've ever known. And there she goes again.

I adore her. She needs to be mine. But more than anything, I need to make her dreams come true.

"Cowboy... I don't think I can take another one. I need a break," she says, wearing that blissful "I'm on cloud nine" expression.

"That depends, princess... have we established that you're the best at writing?"

I watch a mix of emotions flash across her face: excitement, nervousness, gratitude.

It's damn beautiful to watch her come undone, but it's just as captivating to see her immersed in her writing. I've watched her over the last few hours... the focus on her face, the way her eyes light up as words flow onto the page. There's something magical about watching her pour herself into her writing, as if she's rediscovering a part of herself she had forgotten.

And then, the thousand other expressions that cross her face: the slight furrow of concentration in her brow, her lips moving silently as she forms words only she can hear, her eyes dancing across the page, following her thoughts as they take shape. And then there are those moments she pauses, gazing off into the wild landscape around us, searching for inspiration, only to dive back in with renewed passion.

"Alex... all this scares me," she replies, her honesty carrying a vulnerability she hadn't shown before.

I lift myself from her intimacy and lean up close to her face. I shift, pressing my body to hers as I lay her back more comfortably. I rest my forehead against hers, framing her face with my hands to hold her full attention and, because I want to be as close to her as possible, to feel her with every part of me.

"Princess, I'm here, so you don't have to be scared. We'll take this journey together, I want this for you. I want to help you make your dreams come true... and we both know that your life until now wasn't your dream. You can always change course, go back, or find a way to have it all. I'll support you in whatever you choose, but I don't want you to run from happiness."

Our eyes meet, and my heart tightens. Her gaze shimmers, tears unshed, catching the sunlight. In that moment, it feels like I'm seeing right into her soul.

I know those tears hold a range of emotions. There's happiness, the pure joy of rediscovering a forgotten passion. But I also see pain, a deep pain from years of compromise, from choices made for security rather than passion. Years spent following a path that perhaps wasn't truly hers, chasing a life that didn't entirely reflect who she is.

My heart aches for her, for everything she's left behind, for all the dreams she's put aside. I wish I could erase all that pain, turn back time and give her the chance to follow her true desires from the start. But I know I can't change the past.

What I can do, though, is be here for her now. We haven't talked about us, about our future, about what all this means. But right now, it doesn't matter. What matters is that I'm here, by her side, ready to support her in whatever direction she wants to go.

Then I see a small smile forming on her lips despite the tears. And there's no need for words. In this moment, in this place, it's just the two of us, surrounded by the wild beauty of nature, sharing a moment of vulnerability and connection that goes beyond words. We stay like that for a while, close, entwined, letting the silence speak for us. I feel Rosie's breathing gradually steady, her fingers relaxing their grip on my side. When she finally looks up, her eyes are still glistening, but there's a new light in them, a spark of determination I hadn't seen before.

"Alex," she says at last, her voice low but resolute, "thank you. I... I don't think I've ever felt so much like myself as I do right now."

I smile at her gently, caressing the back of her hand with my thumb.

Rosie takes a deep breath. "You know, for years I've kept this part of me locked away. The writing, the dreams, everything. I thought I had to be practical, follow a safe path. But now..."

Her voice falters, and I squeeze her hand, urging her on.

"And now?" I prompt softly.

"Now I realize how much I've missed all this. How much I've missed... myself." She lifts her gaze to meet mine, her eyes filled with emotion. "And you... you're helping me find her again."

My heart pounds in my chest. I want to tell her how much she means to me, how much she's changed my life in such a short time. But instead, I choose simple honesty.

"Rosie, you're extraordinary. All I did was give you space to be yourself."

She shakes her head, a trembling smile on her lips. "No, Alex. You did so much more. You showed me a different world; you made me see possibilities I'd forgotten existed, ones I was always too afraid to even consider."

There's a pause, laden with emotion and unspoken words. Then, with an unexpected movement, Rosie hugs me tighter. I feel her body tremble slightly against mine, and I hold her close, trying to convey all my affection and support.

"I don't know what comes next," she murmurs against my chest, "I don't know how I'll balance all this or what I'll do. But I know I don't want to lose this part of me anymore."

I stroke her hair softly, breathing in her scent. "You don't have to decide now," I tell her gently. "We have time. And whatever you decide, I'll be here to support you."

Rosie pulls back slightly, looking into my eyes. There's a question in her gaze, a vulnerability that tugs at my heart.

"Promise?" she asks, her voice barely a whisper.

Without hesitation, I nod. "I promise, Rosie. Whatever happens, whatever you choose, I'll be there."

And as I say these words, I realize just how true they are. There's no ambiguity... I've told her I'll be there, wherever and however... if she'll have me. I don't know what the future holds, whether Rosie will choose to stay or return to her life in Los Angeles. But I know that, one way or another, I want to be part of her life, to help her realize her dreams, to help her reclaim the part of herself she's hidden for so long.

Rosie smiles, a radiant smile that warms my heart. Then, slowly, she leans in and kisses me. It's a sweet, tender kiss, filled with gratitude and unspoken promises. And as I return the kiss, surrounded by the wild beauty of nature, I feel that, whatever happens, this moment, this connection, will always be a part of us.

As the kiss ends, I keep my eyes closed for a moment, savoring the sweetness of it. When I open them again, I see Rosie looking at me with a mix of tenderness and gratitude that makes my heart tremble.

She asked me to promise I'd be here. She made me promise I'd stand by her. This request echoes in my mind, raising a thousand questions. For a moment, I'm tempted to ask her openly how she feels, to lay everything out and understand where we're heading. But I hold back. I look into her eyes, still glistening with the emotions we just shared, and realize this isn't the time.

Rosie is going through a period of profound change. Her whole reality, everything she thought she knew about herself, is shifting. She's rediscovering parts of herself she'd forgotten, rethinking the choices she's made so far. The last thing she needs now is an insecure cowboy digging into her feelings.

No, I decide. I won't ask her anything. She asked me to be here, and that's what I'll do.

Chapter 37

Rosie

The warmth of the fire caresses my face, but it's nothing compared to the heat I feel inside me as Alex holds me close. He's fallen asleep with me in his arms. It seems trivial since we've known each other for such a short time, filled with firsts... but the fact that he's dozed off before me feels special. I love seeing him like this. He's always in motion, full of energy, but I've never seen him so tender, so vulnerable.

The Alex I'm getting to know is... unbelievable. In the best possible way. He's completely surprised and disarmed me. It's not just his knowledge of nature, his strength, or his courage. It's his kindness, his attentiveness, the way he looks at me as if I'm the most precious thing in the world.

When he gave me that notebook to write in... it was the sweetest thing anyone has ever done for me. It awakened a part of me I thought I'd lost forever. The words started flowing, and with them, a piece of me came back to life.

And can we talk about his hot encouragement? I blush just thinking about it... but it's another thing about him that I'm adoring. I've never felt so comfortable with anyone that I can do the things he makes me do... and it's liberating.

He's revealed another side of me.

And then he even promised he'd be there for me no matter what I decide... Does this mean he wants more for us? Would he be willing to move? The thought spins my head. Can I really ask him to move across the ocean, to a place so different from this paradise, just for me?

This is his life. I can see the passion he has for everything around him. I could never ask him to relocate with me... it would be like chaining him down. He wouldn't be Alex anymore.

But then... do I really want to go back to Los Angeles? The more time passes, the more I realize I just want to stay here, at the ranch. This thought is frightening. Terrifying, to be honest. It means leaving everything I know, my career, my life. And yet, as I sit here, in Alex's arms, surrounded by this wild and beautiful nature, everything feels possible.

It's right here, surrounded by everything I desire, that for the first time in years, I allow myself to daydream, to imagine a future different from the one I had planned.

What if I really became a writer? The idea makes my heart race with excitement. I can see myself sitting on the ranch porch, a laptop on my knees, my fingers flying over the keyboard as I write stories inspired by this magical place.

I envision my days: waking up at dawn, making breakfast for Alex before he heads out to take care of the horses. Then, hours of writing interrupted only by the birds singing and the rustling of the wind through the trees. In the afternoon, long walks with Alex, exploring new corners of this earthly paradise, gathering ideas and inspiration for my books. I could even ask him for riding lessons.

And Alex... I see him coming home from work, his smile lighting up the room as soon as he sees me. My sexy cowboy, always ready to share his day's adventures, to inspire me with his knowledge of nature and his passion.

The evenings would be filled with laughter, deep conversations, moments of sweet intimacy. I could read him the chapters I wrote during the day, and he would give me honest feedback, always encouraging me to be my best.

And this place... this fairytale setting would become my muse. Every corner of the ranch, every path in the woods, every breathtaking sunset would be an endless source of inspiration. I could write novels set here, love stories and adventures that capture the magic of this place and the people who inhabit it.

I see myself growing as a writer, publishing my first book, then the second, the third... And Alex would be there, by my side, every step of the way.

It's such a vivid dream, so real that it almost takes my breath away. For a moment, I let myself fully believe in it, to imagine that this could be my reality.

But something pulls me from my daydreams.

Something very tender and real.

I feel Alex's lips giving me a sweet kiss on the cheek.

"Hey, you okay?" His voice is soft, laced with sleep and maybe a bit of concern.

I look at him, a smile on my lips. "I was dreaming," I admit.

He chuckles. "And what were you dreaming about?" he asks, curious.

I hesitate for a moment, then decide to be honest. "I was dreaming of a life here. With you. Me writing, you taking care of the ranch... a simple life, but full of love and adventure."

Alex looks at me, his eyes shining in the firelight. "You know, princess? That sounds like a wonderful dream."

And as he pulls me closer, I think that maybe, just maybe, this dream could become a reality.

"But..." he adds with a mischievous smile, "you didn't mention my skills." He tightens his embrace, and I can feel him already hard.

"I have a bad memory, cowboy; I think I need a refresher," I reply, smiling back. I've never felt this cheeky. I like it!

"Oh, princess... if you keep this up, you'll get a nice little punishment."

And that's how we end up naked, making love under the stars.

How could I ever want to go back to my old life?!

Chapter 38

Rosie

The pickup truck shudders to a halt in front of the ranch, the engine's rumble fading into silence. I sit frozen, hands pressed against my knees, struggling to process the finality of this moment. The absence of Alex's off-key country singing and our playful banter leaves an emptiness that seems to echo through the cab.

The camping trip is over. The thought crashes into me with physical force, stealing my breath. It's over. This magical, wild, life-changing adventure has run its course.

I hear Alex's door creak open, followed by the soft crunch of his boots hitting gravel, but I remain still. While my body sits anchored in his pickup, my mind wanders back to our campsite – to pine-scented air, diamond-scattered skies, and the hypnotic dance of flames that witnessed our whispered confessions.

"Rosie?" Alex's voice, gentle with concern, pulls me back. "You alright, darlin'?" I manage a mechanical nod and finally force myself to move. As my feet touch the familiar ranch soil, something feels shifted, altered. Or perhaps I'm the one who's changed.

While Alex busies himself with our bags, I stand rooted, taking in the scene. The ranch sprawls before me, exactly as we left it mere days ago, yet it seems transformed – or maybe it's my perspective that's been irreversibly altered.

Emotions surge through me in relentless waves: the ache of endings, the sweet pull of nostalgia, the electric thrill of fresh memories, and the trembling uncertainty of what comes next. And underneath it all, something else stirs – something I can't quite name.

"Hey," Alex murmurs, suddenly close. "Talk to me." I meet his gaze and attempt a smile, knowing it doesn't reach my eyes. "I'm just... I don't even know how to describe what I'm feeling."

Alex nods, understanding etched in the soft lines around his eyes. "Been some pretty intense days," he says, then hesitates, as if wrestling with unspoken words. Something flickers across his face – worry? Fear? – before he catches himself.

Intense. Yes. Intense. Overwhelming. Soul-shaking.

Somehow, in the span of a few short days, I've lived what feels like a lifetime. I've unearthed parts of myself I thought were lost to time, dusted off dreams I'd carefully packed away. And I've discovered Alex – the real Alex – in ways I never imagined possible.

But now what? Now that we're back in the "real world," what becomes of us? Do promises whispered under starlight survive in harsh daylight?

"Ready to head inside?" Alex gestures toward the house. I hesitate. Crossing that threshold feels like officially closing a chapter I'm not ready to end. Like facing questions I've been carefully avoiding.

"Could we... maybe stay out here a little longer?" My voice wavers slightly. His smile is tender as he laces his fingers through mine. "We've got all the time in the world, princess."

We stand in companionable silence, letting the ranch's familiar landscape embrace us. The setting sun paints the sky in a masterpiece of amber and rose, bleeding into deep purple at the edges. I've watched this same sunset countless times since arriving here, but tonight it feels weighted with meaning, as if nature itself is marking this moment of transition.

"Walk with me?" Alex's question breaks gently through my reverie. I nod, grateful for the suggestion. Movement has always helped clear my head, and right now my thoughts are a tangled mess needing to be sorted.

We amble along the well-worn path beside the paddocks, our footsteps falling into an easy rhythm. The horses raise their heads as we pass, some offering soft whickers of recognition. The air is rich with the earthy perfume of hay and soil, stirring memories of my first anxious days here. That feels like another lifetime now, another version of myself – before Alex, before everything changed.

"Share those thoughts with me?" His voice is soft, patient. I release a shaky breath, trying to organize the chaos in my mind. "Everything," I admit. "These past days, how different I feel, how different everything feels. I'm thinking about..." I swallow hard. "What comes next."

Alex stops walking, turning to face me. In the fading light, his eyes search mine, filled with a depth of understanding that makes my heart ache. "Rosie," he says, my name like a prayer on his lips, "what happened out there – what's happening between us – it's real. You know that, right?"

His words wrap around my heart like a warm blanket, but they also unleash the fears I've been trying to contain. "But what if..." My voice cracks slightly. "What if all those things I said under the stars were just... temporary insanity? What if I go back to Los Angeles and realize I can't just abandon my whole life there?"

Alex's hands find mine in the growing darkness, his calloused fingers intertwining with my own. His touch is gentle but grounding, like an anchor in a storm. "Then we'll figure it out together," he says, his voice steady and sure. "I'm not asking you to blow up your whole life tonight, Rosie. I'm just asking you to give yourself permission to want what you want. To dream what you dream. Without letting fear make the choice for you."

Something releases in my chest at his words, like a knot slowly unraveling. He's right – I don't have to have all the answers right now. I can take time to explore these new feelings, these reawakened dreams, this version of myself I'm just beginning to know.

We resume our walk, the silence between us now comfortable, filled with possibility rather than dread. As darkness settles over the ranch like a soft blanket, the first stars begin to peek through the purple twilight. A strange peace washes over me, not erasing my uncertainty but making it feel more manageable somehow.

The ranch spreads out around us, solid and unchanging, yet somehow different through my new eyes. Maybe that's what transformation feels like – not a sudden shift, but a gradual awakening to new possibilities in familiar places. And maybe, just maybe, that's exactly what I need right now: not answers, but the courage to keep asking questions.

In the growing darkness, Alex's hand remains steady in mine, a silent promise that whatever comes next, I don't have to face it alone.

Chapter 39

Alex

[Cowboy Stallions 🐎🌵]

Chris: 📣 HEADS UP! Our wandering cowboy has returned from his "camping trip"! Bet he mastered some new tent-pitching techniques! 😏⛺

Diego: The prodigal son returns! So Alex, did you show Rosie the true meaning of Western riding? 🐎😏

Fran: Ten bucks says they explored more than just the trails! 💰🖤

Me: You're all depraved. It was just camping.

Diego: Sure it was... 😂

Chris: Alex "Romeo of the Range" rides again! 🤠💫

Fran: All hail the Prairie Charmer! 🤠😎

Me: Nothing happened. Period.

Diego: And I'm a virgin! 🙄

Chris: Was it your campfire skills that sealed the deal? 🔥😏

Me: You're insufferable. It was a simple trip.

Fran: Coming soon: "The Art of Ranch Romance" by Alex - Chapter One: Starlight Seduction ✨

Me: I'm disowning all of you. Permanently. ✌️

Chris: Not getting off that easy, cowboy! Spill the juicy details!

Diego: Or should we say... the wild details? 💭😏

Fran: A-L-E-X and R-O-S-I-E sitting in a tree...

Me: I need new friends. Immediately. 😑

The floorboards creak beneath my boots as I enter my room in the main house, my backpack landing with a weary thud that seems to echo my exhaustion. The air hangs still and heavy, like a forgotten memory waiting to be disturbed. Everything looks exactly as I left it, yet somehow different – as if the room itself has become a stranger during my absence. Or perhaps I'm the one who's changed.

The thought of my neglected cabin suddenly strikes me with unexpected clarity. Before the camping trip, I'd dismissed it as an unnecessary project, content with my comfortable corner in the main house's B&B. But now... now the idea of creating my own sanctuary feels less like a whim and more like a necessity. And maybe, in some secret corner of my heart, I'm already imagining it as a place where Rosie might someday feel at home...

The drive back had revealed subtle shifts in her demeanor – changes she tried to conceal but couldn't quite hide from someone who's learned to read the subtle language of her expressions. I'd done my best to keep things light, filling the air with terrible renditions of country classics and ranch stories, but beneath our laughter lay a current of unspoken words and unanswered questions.

The moment we pulled into the ranch still haunts me – the way she sat frozen in the pickup, her gaze fixed on some distant point only she could see, looking so lost it physically ached to witness. Every fiber of my being wanted to reach out, to pull her close and promise that whatever storm was brewing in her mind, we'd weather it together. But I held back, afraid that pushing too hard might only make her retreat further.

Sinking onto the edge of my bed, I run my fingers through my hair, trying to sort through the tangle of thoughts in my head. I understand the weight of what Rosie's facing – her established life in Los Angeles, her rekindled passion for writing, the crossroads she's found herself at. The last thing I want is to become another pressure point in her already complicated equation.

Yet I can't bear the thought of her tormenting herself over me, over us. I need her to know that my presence in her life isn't conditional, that whatever path she chooses, I'll be standing firmly in her corner. I tried to convey this during our meandering conversations under the stars, but words have never been my strong suit, and some messages are too important to leave to interpretation.

When I think back to our time together – the way her eyes would soften when they met mine, those precious moments of vulnerability we shared – I know in my bones that what's growing between us is real. The depth and nature of her feelings might be a mystery, but their existence is as certain as the sun rising over the ranch each morning.

Rising from the bed, I move to the window, where the ranch sprawls out before me, bathed in silvery moonlight. Everything looks exactly the same as it always has, yet somehow the familiar landscape seems filled with new possibility. I feel different, as if the past few days have shifted something fundamental within me.

A decision crystallizes in my mind. Tomorrow, I'll begin work on the cabin. I'll create a space that's truly mine, a place for reflection and dreams, and perhaps... perhaps someday, a home to share. For now, though, I'll practice the hardest kind of love – the kind that gives space while remaining steadfast, that speaks through actions rather than words, that waits patiently while hearts find their way home.

[Cowboy Stallions 🐎]

Chris: Alert the media! Our wilderness explorer has emerged from the wild! 🤠 Rusty Spur celebration is NON-NEGOTIABLE!

Diego: @Alex don't even think about weaseling out... 🐴

Fran: Ready for all the steamy ranch tales! 😏

Staring at the screen, I release a heavy sigh. Every muscle in my body screams for rest, but my friends are nothing if not persistent...

Me: Just got back, guys...
Chris: Absolutely not! Your presence is required... plus, the ladies will be gracing us
Diego: so you won't pine for your cowgirl
Me: you're all impossible...
Chris: but now that you know SHE'LL be there, we'll see you at eight, right?!

Me: @Chris real rich coming from you????!
Diego has added Ethan to the group

My stomach twists at Ethan's name, an involuntary reaction I immediately feel guilty about. This irrational antipathy towards him goes against everything I stand for, yet I can't seem to shake it.

Ethan: Hey everyone! Thanks for including me – looking forward to the festivities!

Perfect... Guilt gnaws at me as I think about Rosie's friendship with Ethan. I know I should be better than this... There's no logical foundation for my hostility.

Closing the chat with more force than necessary, I wrestle with my frustration. The rational part of my brain knows I need to extend an olive branch to Ethan, if not for my sake, then for Rosie's. I make a silent promise to approach tonight with an open mind, though the prospect feels about as comfortable as breaking in a new saddle. Maybe, if I give it an honest chance, I'll discover there's more to him than my prejudiced mind has allowed. For now, though, all I can do is brace myself for what promises to be an emotionally taxing evening.

The situation with Ethan continues to prey on my mind as I prepare for the night ahead. The thought of maintaining a façade of normalcy through hours of forced interaction sets my teeth on edge.

Perhaps it's time to lance this boil before it festers any further.

Making an impulsive decision, I set out to find him before we're all thrust together at the Rusty Spur. The ranch spreads out vast before me, offering countless hiding places. As I exit the main house, I consciously push away the hope that I won't find him with Rosie. Their friendship, however much it niggling at my insecurities, is something I need to accept. Still, I take comfort in knowing she's likely preparing for the evening ahead.

After checking the obvious locations – kitchen, living room, even the stables – I finally spot him by the horse corrals. He's gentle with Tornado, the young colt we welcomed just weeks ago, and something about seeing him so natural in my domain creates an unexpected knot of emotion in my chest. For a moment, I consider retreating, but I force myself forward. Some things need doing, comfortable or not.

Drawing in a steadying breath, I approach with measured steps.

"Ethan," I call out, working to keep my voice level despite the tension coiling in my gut. He turns, surprise flickering across his features.

"Alex," he returns, hand still resting on Tornado's velvet nose. He's dressed entirely in linen—khaki pants paired with a crisp white shirt. He wears Italian loafers with an ease I can't comprehend; to me, they're nothing short of torture devices. His perfectly styled hair and impeccably groomed appearance are hard to ignore. My stomach tightens again at the thought of how effortlessly Rosie would look beside someone like him.

The silence that follows feels heavy enough to sink into. The air between us crackles with unspoken words, with assumptions and misunderstandings that have grown too large to ignore. Ethan waits, patient as a seasoned ranch hand with a spooked horse, while I struggle to wrangle my thoughts into something resembling coherence.

Finally, drawing on reserves of courage I usually save for breaking wild horses, I decide to face this head-on. I've never been one for pretty words or elegant expressions, but some things need saying, however inelegantly.

"Listen, Ethan..." My voice comes out rougher than intended, thick with the weight of what I'm trying to convey. "I owe you an apology. My behavior since your arrival... it hasn't been what it should be. I let assumptions and prejudices color my judgment, and that wasn't fair to you."

Surprise blooms in his eyes, followed by something warmer, more understanding. A smile tugs at the corners of his mouth, genuine and disarming. "I appreciate that, Alex," he says, sincerity evident in every word. "Really. I get it – it's not exactly comfortable having your girl's best friend show up, especially when we have the history we do."

His frankness catches me off guard, leaving me momentarily floundering. "Yeah, well..." I stumble over the words, wrong-footed by his directness, "Rosie explained that you're just friends, but..." Ethan's smile widens with understanding. "But we seem to fit together so naturally that it's hard to believe there isn't more to the story?" I nod, shame coloring my cheeks at having my insecurities laid so bare. I move closer to Tornado, running my hands along his coat and showering him with affection... God, how I've missed being around horses! But then, something unexpected happens —Ethan and I keep talking. Our conversation flows effortlessly, weaving from one topic to the next, and to my surprise... I find myself enjoying it more than I ever thought I would.

Chapter 40

Rosie

I sit on the porch of the main house, hands empty, eyes locked on the horizon. The sun is just starting to rise, painting the sky in soft pinks and golds that stretch endlessly over the ranch. It's a sight I'll never grow tired of.

Three days have passed since we returned from the camping trip, yet my mind is still caught in a storm of conflicting emotions. On one hand, there's a growing sense of belonging, a feeling I haven't experienced in years, like I've finally found a place I can call home. But on the other, fear lingers—fear of change, of leaving behind the life I built in Los Angeles, even if that life feels like it's slipping further out of reach with every passing day.

And then there's Alex.

I sigh, my thoughts drifting back to him. These past few days, he's been nothing but patient, giving me space without ever making me feel guilty or pressured. But I can see it in his eyes—he's wrestling with his own feelings, just as I am.

"Hey," a familiar voice startles me. I turn to see Ethan approaching, two mugs of coffee in hand. "Hey," I respond with a weary smile. "You're up early." He settles beside me, handing me one of the mugs. "Couldn't sleep, huh?" I nod, grateful for the caffeine. "Too much on my mind."

We lapse into silence for a while, enjoying the view of the sunrise. It's one of the things I love about Ethan - he never feels the need to fill every quiet moment with chatter.

"You know," he finally says, "I spoke with Alex the other day."

This piques my interest. "Really? About what?"

Ethan smiles faintly. "He apologized for how he's been acting. Said he let some 'wrong impressions' influence his behavior."

I feel a swell of pride for Alex. Not only has he admitted his mistakes, but he's also apologized openly. And he didn't even tell me - he just did it because he knows I care about my best friend.

"And what did you say to him?" I ask, curious. "I told him I understood, and that I appreciated his apology." Ethan pauses, holding my gaze. "And I told him that you're my best friend, and that all I want is to see you happy. And that it seems like he makes you happy."

I feel my eyes fill with tears. "Oh, Ethan..." He pulls me into a hug, and for a moment, I allow myself to let go, to cry all the tears I've been holding back these past few days.

"Rosie," he says gently as I calm down, "I know you're scared. Change is always scary. But I've known you for a lifetime, and I've never seen you as...alive as you've been these past few weeks."

I pull back, wiping my eyes. "I know. It's just that...what if I'm making a huge mistake? What if I leave everything behind to come here and then..."

"And then what?" he interrupts softly. "Rosie, life is full of 'what ifs'. You can't let the fear of what could go wrong paralyze you. You have to think about what could go right."

His words strike a deep chord within me. He's right, I know that. But there's still a part of me that hesitates.

"What about my marketing job?" I ask, voicing one of my concerns. "I can't just abandon that."

Ethan smiles. "Do you really care about your marketing job, Rosie? You've always dreamed of being a writer. Alex has pushed you to reclaim that dream, remember? And frankly, I think this place inspires you more than Los Angeles ever did."

I reflect on his words.

"Maybe you're right," I admit slowly. "In Los Angeles, I felt trapped in a stressful routine. Spending my days creating marketing campaigns for products I didn't care about..." "Exactly," Ethan says. "But here, you've rediscovered your passion for writing. I've seen you happier and more fulfilled in these weeks than in all the years you spent in Los Angeles."

I laugh, feeling lighter than I have in days. "Thank you, Ethan," I say sincerely. "I don't know what I'd do without you."

"Probably still be stressing about deadlines and presentations in LA," he teases.

I give him a playful nudge, but I know he's right. Without his encouragement, I would never have come here. And now... Now, I watch as the sun fully rises over the horizon, bathing the ranch in its golden light.

"So, when are you moving in too?" I joke... even though a part of me really wishes he would.

"You know, that's not a bad idea," he muses. "Italy, fashion, getting away from Theo..."

I freeze. "I'm sorry, what?"

"We broke up," he says bluntly. "I was going to tell you soon, but I wanted to be less angry about it, you know? Turned out he was cheating on me. And you know what? I think starting a new life here might not be such a bad idea."

"Oh my god, Ethan, I'm such a terrible friend..." I trail off, guilt flooding me.

"No, you're not, piccola," he reassures me. "You're my best friend. And you brought me to Italy - that's always been my dream. Screw the ex. I'll launch my first fashion line right here. If you can be brave, so can I."

I can't contain myself any longer. I burst into tears again. For myself.

For Alex. For Ethan.

This is the cycle I'm stuck in when it comes to my feelings: one moment, I'm unsure. Then, I convince myself I've made my decision, only for fear to creep back in and leave me questioning everything all over again.

I know I can't play with people's emotions—and I swear, that's not my intention. The last thing I want is to hurt anyone, especially Alex.

But the truth is, I'm terrified.

Chapter 41

Alex

I can't sleep. Again. I toss and turn in bed, staring at the ceiling of my room in the main house. It's been three days since we returned from the camping trip, and I feel like I'm coming apart at the seams.

I promised Rosie I'd give her space, but the distance between us is killing me. She said she needed time to think about her future—about us—and I nodded like a fool, pretending I could handle it. But now I can't help wondering: if I can't be the one to help her through the hard times, what's my place in her life?

With a frustrated groan, I swing my legs over the edge of the bed and sit up, staring at the darkened room. There's no point in pretending I can sleep. I get dressed and head to the veranda, hoping the cool night air will calm me.

I look toward the cabin. I started working on it, hoping it could become our love nest if Rosie decided to stay here.

But now? Now I don't even know if she still wants me in her life.

The thought feels like a punch to the gut. What if she's realized I can't give her the life she deserves? What if I'm nothing compared to the opportunities waiting for her in Los Angeles?

I rake a hand through my hair and try to banish the thought, but it won't leave. Every time I see her walk by without even looking at me, the fear grows.

I can't sit here anymore. The ranch feels suffocating, the silence too loud.

Without thinking, I head to the stables. Horses have always been my escape, my way of finding clarity when everything else feels impossible. Saddling Storm is muscle memory, my hands working automatically in the dark.

"C'mon, boy," I whisper, mounting him. "Let's go."

The moment Storm takes off, the wind hits my face, cool and sharp, cutting through the haze in my mind. I let him run, his hooves pounding against the earth as the ranch disappears behind us. Usually, this is all I need to steady myself—to remember who I am.

But tonight, even the familiar rhythm of the gallop doesn't quiet the storm inside me. No matter how far we ride, my thoughts keep circling back to Rosie: her silence, her distance, the pain in her eyes that I can't seem to reach.

The hours pass in a blur of moonlit meadows and shadowed streams. When the first light of dawn begins to creep over the horizon, I finally turn Storm back toward home.

As we near the main house, I spot them on the porch: Rosie and Ethan.

She's leaning into him, her head on his shoulder, her body trembling with silent sobs.

My heart seizes in my chest. For a moment, I freeze in the saddle, unable to think or move.

Then, slowly, I dismount, my boots hitting the ground with a dull thud.

What is he saying to her? What is she telling him?

The instinct to rush to her, to take her in my arms, burns through me. But I don't move. I don't know if she wants me there—if I still have the right to be the one she leans on.

Instead, I stand there, rooted to the spot, the ache in my chest growing with every passing second.

And then Ethan sees me. His gaze meets mine, calm but full of meaning.

"Alex," he says quietly, "maybe you should..."

"No." My voice is firm, louder than I intend. "I'm not leaving."

Rosie lifts her head at the sound of my voice. Her eyes, red and swollen, lock with mine. For a moment, I think I see relief flicker there. But then she buries her face against Ethan's shoulder again, and my heart shatters.

I take a slow step forward. Then another. "Princess," I say softly, "what's wrong?"

She doesn't answer.

Ethan looks at her, then back at me. "Alex, I think she—"

"I said I'm not leaving." My voice is quieter this time, but the resolve in it is unshakable. I step onto the porch, kneeling in front of her.

"Rosie," I say gently, my voice barely above a whisper, "I'm here. Whatever it is, we'll face it together. Just... talk to me."

Her body trembles as she lifts her head again, her tear-streaked face breaking me all over again. For a long moment, she just looks at me, as if searching for something.

Finally, she takes a deep breath, her voice shaking as she speaks. "Alex... I'm afraid."

My heart tightens at her words. "What are you afraid of, princess?"

She hesitates, her hands twisting in her lap.

Then, slowly, the words begin to tumble out. "Everything. Leaving. Staying. Messing up. Messing *us* up." Her voice cracks on the last word, and she looks away, her shoulders slumping.

I reach out, hesitating for only a moment before resting my hand lightly on hers. "Rosie, look at me."

She does, her eyes glassy with unshed tears.

"You won't mess us up," I say, my voice firm but full of emotion. "I don't care where you want to be —here, in L.A., or anywhere else. I just want to be with you. If you want to stay, I'll be the happiest man alive. And if you want to go back to Los Angeles..." I swallow hard. "Then I'll find a way to make it work. I'll follow you."

Her breath catches, her lips parting slightly in shock. "You'd... you'd do that?"

"I would. Wherever you are, that's where I want to be."

She stares at me, her tears finally spilling over. Slowly, tentatively, she leans forward, resting her head against my shoulder.

For a moment, I just hold her, my hand lightly stroking her back.

"You're not alone in this," I murmur. "Whatever you're afraid of, we'll face it together. I promise."

Out of the corner of my eye, I catch Ethan wiping away a tear. Then, without a word, he slowly gets up and walks away, leaving us wrapped in our intimacy, as if he knows this is a moment meant only for us.

Her voice is muffled against my shirt, but I hear her whisper, "I'm sorry I pushed you away."

I pull back just enough to look at her. "It doesn't matter. What matters is that we're here now."

She nods, her lips trembling into a small, tentative smile.

The sun rises behind us, painting the sky in shades of gold and pink. For the first time in days, I feel hope. Rosie is in my arms, and for now, that's enough.

Chapter 42

Rosie

Alex's words echo in my ears, making my heart tremble. I can't believe what I've just heard. This stubborn, annoying, incredibly sexy and sweet cowboy... he's just laid his heart bare before me. And I? I'm simply stunned, disbelieving, yet suffused with a happiness I never thought possible.

His hands on my face are warm, reassuring. His eyes, so sincere and full of love... I'm not sure I even deserve it, damn it! This thought makes me feel dizzy.

I mentally retrace the last few days, after the camping trip, after that magical night under the stars. I've behaved horribly toward him, I know that. Fear paralyzed me, pushing me to shut myself away like a hedgehog. That evening at the Rusty Spur, when he asked me to dance with that irresistible smile of his, I felt panic overwhelm me. I asked him for time, stammering an excuse, and then I began avoiding him like a coward.

And him? He's been simply wonderful, far more than I deserved. He's given me all the space I needed, without questions, without pressure. Even now, looking into his eyes, I can see how much my behavior must have hurt him. The guilt twists in my stomach.

He told me he'd follow me to Los Angeles if necessary. Los Angeles! Him, who loves this ranch more than anything in the world. Him, who would suffer in a big city like a bird in a cage. Yet he was willing to do it. For me. This thought takes my breath away.

And this awareness, this act of love so great and selfless, has given me the strength to open up, to confide in him my true thoughts. To admit that I want to stay here, with him.

"Alex," I whisper, my voice trembling with emotion, "I don't know what to say. You're... you're incredible."

Okay... well, very eloquent, Rosie, well done! Now Alex will really know how you feel. My inner voice scolds me, making me realize I'm not doing a very good job.

His words continue to echo in my mind like a sweet melody. *You can trust me completely, Rosie. You can entrust me with your heart, your dreams, your fears.* And damn it, I want to. I want to trust him with every fiber of my being, even though the idea terrifies me.

I take a deep breath, trying to find the right words to express the whirlwind of emotions I feel inside. "I've never been good at relationships. I've always kept people at a distance, out of fear of suffering, out of fear of losing myself. I've never had a real relationship. But you... you've torn down every one of my defenses. You've barged into my life like a hurricane, upending every certainty I had. And this terrifies me and exhilarates me at the same time..." I start to panic. Oh god, I'm so bad at this.

"Shhh" Alex saves me, silencing me.

Alex pulls me into his embrace, and I let myself melt into it, finally feeling safe. His scent, a mix of leather, pine, and something uniquely Alex, envelops me, calming my nerves.

Suddenly, I feel his arms tighten around me even more. I look up at him, and before I can say anything, his lips are on mine. The kiss is sweet and passionate at the same time, charged with all the emotions we've held back these past few days. I lose myself in that kiss, feeling my heart race and the world around us disappear.

When he finally pulls away after what feels like an eternity, I'm slightly dazed but also more at peace.

But before I can catch my breath, I see that familiar, cocky smile spread across his lips.

Oh no, I know that look.

"Princess..." he says, his tone a mix of amusement and tenderness, "you said you're not good at relationships. Does that mean we have one?"

The question catches me off guard. I feel the heat rise to my cheeks as I realize what I've said. The words came out without thinking... I didn't mean to say too much, to go too far. But now that I think about it, it's exactly what I want.

For a moment, I feel the familiar panic start to grow within me. Is it too soon? Am I moving too fast? But then I look at Alex, see his smile, his eyes full of hope and love. I remember his words, his offer to follow me to Los Angeles if necessary.

I take a deep breath, trying to calm the frantic beating of my heart. "I... I suppose so," I finally respond, my voice a bit uncertain but with a smile starting to form on my lips. "I mean, if that's what you want too."

Alex's smile widens even more, if possible.

"If that's what I want?" He repeats, shaking his head slightly as if he can't believe my question. "Princess, it's all I've wanted since the moment I laid eyes on you."

His words fill me with a joy I never thought possible. I laugh lightly, feeling suddenly lighthearted.

"Well, then I guess we officially have a relationship, cowboy," I say, leaning in slightly to give him a quick kiss on the lips.

Chapter 43

Alex

The world around us seems to pause as I look at Rosie, her face aglow with the first rays of dawn. Without hesitation, I stand and sweep her into my arms in one fluid motion. She lets out a soft gasp, instinctively wrapping her legs around my waist. My heart races at the feel of her body pressed so intimately against mine.

"Alex!" she exclaims, surprise laced with laughter that melts me from the inside out.

I hold her close, savoring the warmth and weight of her in my arms. There's no space between us—just the heat of our bodies and the shared rhythm of our hearts. Slowly, I turn so she can see the view unfurling before us. The sky is a breathtaking canvas, painted with streaks of pink, orange, and gold, each hue brighter than the last. It's a masterpiece that takes my breath away—almost as much as she does.

"Look," I whisper, tilting my head toward the horizon. "Isn't it beautiful?"

Rosie nods, her gaze fixed on the sunrise. "It's incredible," she murmurs, her warm breath brushing against my neck.

But I can't take my eyes off her. In the golden light, her profile glows, her eyes shining with wonder. She's beautiful in every way—not just in how she looks, but in the way she moves, laughs, and loves. Her strength, her vulnerability, her fire... every part of her pulls me closer.

My heart feels so full I think it might burst. I know it's too soon. I should probably wait, hold back. But right now, with her in my arms and the world waking around us, I can't stop the words from spilling out.

"I love you," I say softly, my voice rough with emotion.

Her head snaps toward me, her eyes wide with surprise. For a moment, I panic—but then her lips curve into a radiant smile, one that rivals the sun rising behind her.

"I... I love you too, Alex," she whispers, her voice trembling but sure.

The world freezes. Those three words I'd only dared to hope for are now a reality. A wave of emotion crashes over me: joy, relief, desire. I feel weightless and anchored all at once, and I can't stop the incredulous grin that spreads across my face.

Our lips meet again, this time with an intensity born of shared love. My hands tighten around her hips as the kiss deepens. Her fingers weave into my hair, pulling me closer, until there's nothing between us but heat and need.

Still holding her, I turn and walk toward the cabin, each step purposeful. The door swings open easily, and I carry her straight to the bedroom. The room is bathed in the soft glow of morning light, warm and inviting, just like her. I lay her gently on the bed, her arms still looped around my neck. For a moment, I just look at her: hair tousled, eyes dark with desire, lips swollen from our kisses. She's perfect.

I lower myself beside her, and our lips find each other again. Each kiss is electric, igniting a fire deep inside me. My hands move over her body with a hunger I can't contain, tracing the curves that have haunted my dreams. Her skin is warm, impossibly soft, and she responds to every touch with a shiver that drives me wild.

"Alex," she breathes, her voice thick with longing. "I want you."

I lean down, my lips tracing a path of kisses along her neck, down to her collarbone.

"You have no idea all the things I want to do to you, *princess*," I murmur against her lips, my breath hot and uneven. Even with my mind hazy, I place a special emphasis on the word *princess*. I love teasing her.

Rosie smiles, her eyes sparkling with passion and affection.

"If you don't follow through, *cowboy*, you're going to lose credibility," she says, with the same emphasis on *cowboy*.

I let out a low growl.

Her hands trail down my back, leaving fiery paths on my skin. The tenderness, the passion, the mischievous glint in her eyes, she makes me lose control.

I tear away the last remnants of her clothing.

Hell, I'll buy her all the clothes she wants... if it means I can tear them off every time.

I shed the last of my clothes, leaving us both completely bare, our bodies melting into one another as we revel in the warmth and intimacy of our skin touching, unguarded and alive.

I feel my body responding to hers in ways I've never experienced; I'm harder than ever, and she's already so ready. Rosie lets out a sweet laugh as I cover her with little bites; the sound is like music to my ears.

Rosie's skin against mine feels like silk, warm and inviting, and her breath mingles with mine, filling the air with unspoken promises.

"Alex," she whispers, her fingers tracing delicate patterns on my back. "Don't stop."

"Never," I reply, my voice thick with emotion. "I never could."

As our bodies move in unison, each touch, each kiss building in intensity, I feel our connection deepen. Every breath, every caress is a tangible expression of our love.

With slow, deliberate tenderness, I slide inside her. The warmth of her breath on my neck, her touch—steady and sure—make me feel whole, at home.

"I was always here, Rosie," I whisper, my voice barely a breath, heavy with emotion. "Even when I was far away, my heart was always with you."

I hold her close, feeling every fiber of my being respond to her presence. "I missed you so much," I say, my voice breaking from the intensity of the moment.

Our lips find each other again in a kiss that's both sweet and passionate. I'm ready to give her every thrill she wants if it means we get to make love like this before or after.

Each movement is an explosion of sensations that bind us closer. We come together, overtaken by a powerful wave, and then lie still, trembling but connected, for I don't know how long.

"Rosie," I murmur, my gaze locked on hers, "I never want to be away from you again. This is our beginning, our future."

Then, finding the strength to move, I rise... not bothering to clean myself or her.

We're not done yet.

I place my cowboy hat on her head.

"Now, princess, get ready, because this cowboy is going to fuck you good."

And then we start fucking for hours in every possible way in that bedroom.

Chapter 44

Rosie

I wake slowly, wrapped in a comforting and familiar warmth. It takes a second to place where I am, but then it all comes into focus: I'm in Alex's arms, the best place in the world. A sweet ache lingers between my thighs, a wicked reminder of the way my cowboy claimed me with his rough hands, tongue and cock, leaving me trembling and craving more of his untamed heat. I should probably blush... but it felt too good to feel embarrassed.

He was so sweet at first. I don't think I'd ever really made love before, but now I understand what it means. Then, just as only Alex can, after we reached that perfect peak together—after we held each other as close as humanly possible for who knows how long, after he whispered his vulnerable words, after his tender and reverent touches—he placed his hat on my head and let "Cowboy Alex" take over.

I don't think I'll ever be able to choose between the two sides of him... I love them both.

And I still can't believe that in less than five minutes, Alex made it clear that we're in this together and that he loves me. I've never been this happy or this comfortable with anyone else.

I have no idea what time it is. The light filtering through the curtains suggests it's mid-morning, maybe even early afternoon. A fleeting thought crosses my mind—Alex is probably supposed to be at work—but I push it aside. I don't want to ruin this perfect moment with worries.

I know how seriously he takes his work, and lately, he's been a little off-balance because of me... but selfishly, I want him here just a little longer.

I look up at his sleeping face. His lips are curved into a slight smile, like he's dreaming something pleasant. His hair is adorably messy, and I have to resist the urge to run my fingers through it so I don't wake him.

I snuggle closer, savoring the rise and fall of his chest with each breath. There's something incredibly intimate about this, maybe more than anything we've shared so far. Just lying here, naked and vulnerable, just existing together like this... it's perfect.

A deep peace settles over me, so complete that it almost scares me. But with Alex, all my fears and insecurities seem to melt away. I feel safe, protected, loved.

A smile spreads across my lips as I remember his words:

I've always been here, Rosie.

And he was right. Even when we were apart, even when I tried to deny how I felt, some part of me knew I belonged to him.

I feel Alex shift a little, his arm tightening around me. I'm not sure if he's awake or still dreaming, but I don't care. I could stay right here forever, if I could.

I look up just as his eyes slowly open, still soft and sleepy.

"Hi, princess," he murmurs, his voice low and rough.

My heart flips. How is he this perfect first thing in the morning?

"Hi, cowboy," I reply, unable to hold back my smile.

He pulls me in even closer, and I feel his lips brush against my forehead. "How long did we sleep?" he asks, his voice still warm with sleep.

I shrug lightly. "I have no idea. And honestly, I don't care."

Alex chuckles softly, the sound vibrating through his chest. "I should probably be at work…"

"Probably," I agree, but neither of us makes a move to get up. Instead, I just hold him tighter.

Chapter 45

Rosie

Alex gently pulls me closer, his lips finding mine in a sweet, slow kiss, and I can't help but lose myself in him once again. Our hands move languidly, caressing skin, exploring with a familiarity and tenderness that warms my heart.

I suddenly realize that I'm in Alex's arms, in a bed... but I have no idea where we are.

"Hey, cowboy," I say, pausing him, "what is this place? I mean... we're not in the main house. I thought you slept there."

Something incredible happens: I see Alex, the confident cowboy, blush and seem embarrassed. He scratches his head and gives a half-smile.

"Ah, right," he says, and then it seems he's searching for the right words. "This is our home," he says suddenly, without beating around the bush.

What? Our home?

"And when did I miss that part, cowboy?"

"Uh... I've always had this cabin. Since Chris asked me to work with him at the ranch. It was supposed to be my home... but I never bothered to fix it up. Then a beautiful princess stole her way into my heart... and I thought we might want to live somewhere together someday," as he continues speaking, I can see his initial bravado fade. He becomes more uncertain, more insecure. "I've been working on it since we got back from the camping trip," a veil of sadness crosses his face, "I needed something to believe in... a distraction."

I don't let him continue. I've abandoned him for a few days, and I can see how much pain I've caused him. And what he's done with the cabin... damn, it's such a sweet gesture. *A gesture so typical of Alex.*

"Alex..." Damn it, I'm at a loss for words. I see the panic in his eyes increase even more.

"Rosie, I know I should have talked to you about it. Consider it a refuge... we can make a home wherever you want, however you want it... I mean... do you want to make a home with me?"

"Hold on, hold on, cowboy. I'm just surprised, amazed, speechless. This place is magnificent, I mean, your gesture is magnificent. I adore all of this and can't wait to see the cabin properly."

Alex visibly relaxes and buries his face in the crook of my neck. "I love you, princess," he whispers.

"I love you too, cowboy."

And we spend an eternity cuddling. Yes, we are definitely the cuddling type.

Somewhere between Alex's fingers idly combing through my hair and the way he peppers my face with endless kisses, it hits me. The realization settles deep in my chest, as sure and steady as his heartbeat against mine: I'm not going back to Los Angeles.

There's no doubt anymore—maybe there never truly was. I've only been too afraid to admit it until now.

"Cowboy," I say, my voice barely above a whisper, stopping him as he nuzzles his forehead into the crook of my neck.

He lifts his head, his eyes meeting mine. They're impossibly soft, full of a tenderness that makes my breath catch.

"This is where I want to be," I say, the words simple but heavy with meaning.

I don't need to explain. He already knows. I can see it in the way his expression changes, his smile deepening into something breathtaking, something that feels like home. He leans in, capturing my lips in a kiss that's as sweet and certain as only he knows how to give.

"Do we really need to get up?" asks Alex, his voice a mix of laziness and desire.

"Yes, unfortunately we do," I chuckle, starting to search for the scattered clothes in the room. "I have no idea what time it is."

Between one kiss and the next, we start to gather our clothes. Every so often, Alex pulls me to him for another series of kisses, and each time I let myself go, savoring every moment of this intimacy. Suddenly, I feel my phone vibrating incessantly amidst the pile of clothes. Sighing, I grab it and see a series of messages from Val and Lexy.

"What's happening?" murmurs Alex.

"I have no idea," I reply, unlocking the screen. "But judging from the number of notifications, it must be important."
As soon as I open the messaging app, I'm inundated by a flood of texts.

Val (8:30): "Rosie, wake up! Important day today!"
Val (8:45): "Don't tell me you've forgotten about Mum's wedding dress!"
Val (11:00): "ROSIE THORME, where are you?"
Lexy (12:00): "Hey, sleeping beauty, don't forget we have an appointment at the boutique at 5 p.m.!"

"Oh crap," my heart leaps into my throat, "I completely forgot! We're supposed to go wedding dress shopping for Maria today!"
I keep dressing frantically, trying to type out a reply at the same time.

Me (4:16): "Girls, I'm alive! Sorry, I just woke up. I'll be ready in 20 minutes, I promise!"

Almost instantly, my phone explodes again with responses.

Val (4:16): "FINALLY! Move that beautiful butt of yours, we have a dress to find!"
Lexy (4:16): Did a certain cowboy keep you up too late?
Val (4:17): Don't even try to deny it... we even tried calling him.
Lexy (4:17): Ethan confirms!!! P.S. Get ready and hurry up, you can't miss it... Aurora is already missing!

Me (4:18): What? Why? And of course I won't miss it!
Val (4:19): Rory is at university. Move your sweet ass!

I smile, shaking my head. This day is shaping up to be interesting. With one last glance at Alex, I rush out, ready to face my friends and the hunt for the perfect dress for my future mother.

Chapter 46

Rosie

I arrive at the bridal shop out of breath, just in time to avoid the wrath of Val. The girls welcome me with a mix of relief and curiosity in their eyes. I'm happy to see that Ethan is also there, knowing him, he wouldn't have missed a wedding dress shopping day and I'm glad he's integrated well with everyone.

"Finally!" exclaims Val, hugging me. "We were about to send out a search party."

"Sorry again," I murmur, trying to tidy my hair. "I had... an eventful morning."

Lexy raises an eyebrow, a mischievous smile on her lips. "Eventful, huh? This story deserves more details."

"Ah, so that's how it's said now? Piccola, you won't get away with it that easily," says Ethan, gesturing and emphasizing the nickname "piccola" that he's given me since the day I announced I would be leaving for Italy.

Before I can respond, Maria comes out of the dressing room, her face radiant.

The store is a true paradise for brides. White and ivory dresses fill every corner, a butler in livery approaches with a tray of fizzing champagne flutes.

"Oh, this is definitely the right way to start," laughs Val, grabbing a glass.

Meanwhile, my best friend, who is also the best in fashion, hands Maria a load of dresses he has chosen for the fitting.

My chest tightens when I think that he will also stay here... and that he will finally devote himself to his first collection.

As Maria begins to try on the first dresses, we settle on the velvet sofas, sipping champagne and commenting on each dress.

"So," begins Val, turning to me with an inquisitive look. "Are you going to tell us what happened with the sexy cowboy?"

I feel my cheeks flush. "Nothing much," I try to divert, but my smile betrays me.

"Oh, come on!" exclaims Lexy. "That smile says otherwise. Spit it out!"

I take another sip of champagne, already feeling more relaxed. "Okay, okay. Alex and I... well, let's just say we've cleared things up."

The girls burst into excited squeals, attracting the attention of some sales assistants.

"Details, we want details!" insists Lexy, refilling our glasses.

"Clearing things up... does that mean you just had sex like the world was going to end tomorrow, or that you're now together?" Ethan asks with his usual boldness.

I turn ten shades of purple and red... and try to hide behind my flute.

But everyone has their eyes on me and it doesn't seem they'll let me go any further without an answer.

I take a sip and whisper "both."
And that's how everyone erupts in laughter, applause, and shouts of "thank goodness."
Luckily, another round of champagne arrives.
Maria continues to try on dresses, but our attention is divided between her and my increasingly detailed account.
"So," says Val with a grin, "does the cowboy know how to use his... lasso?"
I burst out laughing, almost choking on the champagne. "Val! You're terrible!"
"Oh, come on!" Lexy interjects. "I bet he rides very well."
At this point, we're laughing so hard that some customers look at us scandalized. Maria comes out of the dressing room with another dress, but we're too caught up in our hysteria to notice her right away.
"Girls?" Maria calls, trying to get our attention. "What do you think of this one?"
We all turn to her, trying to compose ourselves. Maria looks stunning in a mermaid dress that perfectly accentuates her figure.
"Wow," Lexy manages to say between sniffles of laughter. "You're... hic... gorgeous!"
"Yes," I agree, wiping away tears of laughter. "Dad will be left breathless."
But we all turn to Ethan. He has the final word. Our tacit agreement is that we trust his good taste and opinion.
He's already crying and runs to hug Maria.
No words are needed at this point.

Val gets up, with her classic contagious smile. "We have to toast to this!" she exclaims, grabbing a new bottle of champagne.

The sales assistant looks at us with a mix of amusement and concern as we refill the glasses.

"To the perfect dress!" shouts Lexy.

"And to cowboys who know how to use the lasso!" adds Val with a mischievous wink.

We all burst out laughing again, including Maria, who, despite not having drunk, seems to be infected by our euphoria... and amused by our conversations. She's fantastic, and I don't have a hard time imagining where the girls get their temperament. I know nothing about Val and Lexy's father... but they definitely have Maria's spirit.

In that moment, despite the champagne and raucous laughter, I feel a deep wave of affection for these women. For Maria, who is about to become part of my family. For my friends, who are always by my side. And for myself, for finally opening my heart to love.

Obviously for Ethan as well. My very first friend. The one who's had my back for years and continues to do so. The brother I never had.

"One last toast," I propose, raising my almost-empty glass. "To family, in all its forms."

"To family," they all repeat, and in that moment, surrounded by laughter and affection, I truly feel at home.

After finally finding the perfect dress for Maria, we leave the bridal shop, still laughing and slightly swaying.

"Okay," says Val, clinging to my arm to keep her balance, "we can't end the day here. It's too early!"

"I agree!" exclaims Lexy. "How about we go for an aperitif? I know a great place nearby."

As soon as we sit down, a waiter approaches with the menus. "Can I get you something to drink?"

Before Maria can suggest something non-alcoholic, Lexy intervenes: "A bottle of your finest prosecco, please!"

The aperitif quickly turns into another session of laughter and banter. The prosecco flows freely, and with it our inhibitions continue to lower. And the food... it's delicious. I've never eaten such a large quantity of olives, mini pizzas, meatballs, and rustici (or as I've learned, as a perfect local resident: olive, pizzette, polpette e rustici). This is my first Italian aperitif since I've been here... and I'm already obsessed.

"So, Rosie," says Lexy, leaning on the table with a mischievous smile, "have you already thought about what your wedding to the cowboy will be like?"

I almost choke on the bite I was eating. "Lexy! Alex and I are just starting to..."

"Oh, come on!" Ethan interjects. "It's clear from a mile away that you two are made for each other. I bet you'll be at the altar within a year!"

I feel my cheeks flush, but I can't deny that the idea makes me smile. "You guys are getting ahead of yourselves. For now, I'm just happy as I am."

Maria smiles at me sweetly. "Love has its own timing. Let Rosie and Alex enjoy this moment."

"Right!" exclaims Val, raising her glass. "A toast to Rosie and her sexy cowboy! May they ride happily into the sunset!"

We all burst out laughing, once again attracting the attention of other customers.

As the evening progresses, the conversation moves from one topic to another, and with every glass of prosecco, we become more sentimental.

"You know something?" says Ethan, his eyes glistening. "I'm so happy to have you all in my life. You girls are my family." Typical of my sentimental best friend.

I adore him, and it's impossible not to love him - he's a pure and spontaneous soul.

"Aww, Ethan!" exclaims Lexy, hugging him. "You're our family too!"

Soon we find ourselves in a group hug, laughing and crying at the same time.

Suddenly, I feel the need to share with my friends and Maria the decisions I've made.

"Girls," I say, addressing the girls since Ethan already knows, "there's something I need to tell you."

Everyone turns to me, their eyes a little hazy from the alcohol but attentive. I take a deep breath.

"I've decided to move here... I'd love to stay at the ranch" I announce, feeling a smile form on my lips as I say those words out loud.

For a moment, there's silence at the table. Then, suddenly, they burst into shouts of joy.

"Oh, Rosie!" exclaims Val, almost spilling her drink in an attempt to hug me. "This is wonderful!"

Lexy and Maria join in the hug, creating a tangle of arms and laughter.

Maria, with glistening eyes, takes my hand. "Rosie, darling, you have no idea how happy I am to hear you say that. Robert will be thrilled."

I feel tears in my eyes. "Really?"

Maria nods, squeezing my hand. "Your father loves you so much, Rosie. Knowing that you'll be staying close to him... well, it will be the most wonderful gift you could give him."

"There's more," I add, feeling emboldened by their reaction. "I've decided to change careers. I want... I want to become a writer."

The girls remain silent for a moment, then burst into another wave of enthusiasm.

"It's always been my dream," I admit, suddenly feeling vulnerable. "But I never had the courage to truly pursue it. Until..."

"Until the sexy cowboy came along," Ethan finishes with a grin.

I laugh, nodding. "Yes, until Alex came. He... he made me realize that I can do it. He's encouraged me to follow my dreams."

Maria smiles at me sweetly. "Love does that, darling. It gives us the strength to be the best version of ourselves."

"A toast!" exclaims Lexy, raising her glass. "To Rosie, her new life at the ranch, and her writing career!"

We all raise our glasses, toasting with laughter and a few tears of joy.

"So," says Val with a mischievous smile, "your first book will be a love story set on a ranch, right? With a sexy cowboy as the protagonist?"

I burst out laughing, feeling light and happy. "Who knows? Maybe. I certainly won't be lacking in inspiration."

"Oh, I'm sure of that," says Ethan with a wink. "Especially for the steamy scenes!"

We all laugh, the atmosphere charged with joy and affection.

Suddenly, I miss Aurora. It would have been nice to have her here with us today.

"I'm sorry Aurora couldn't be here," I let slip.

"Oh, we can fix that! We absolutely have to update her!" yells Val with her usual energy... and she starts a video call. The call that will be the longest of my life because our little friend is the most curious and grudging person in the world.

In that moment, surrounded by my friends and Maria, with my heart full of love for Alex and excitement for my future, I feel truly complete. I've found my place in the world, and I'm ready to embrace this new adventure with all my heart.

In the end, Ethan admits he wants to move here and surprises everyone by announcing his plan to launch his first clothing brand. The girls couldn't be happier, and Val doesn't waste a moment before offering him a job. The ranch's athletes need uniforms, and there's no one better than Ethan to design them. Still, not wanting to turn the evening into a work meeting, they all agree to discuss it properly tomorrow. Aurora is, of course, over the moon, but she can't hide her frustration at having missed the "juicy moments," as she calls them.

Three hundred questions and a bit of pouting later, we're ready to go home.

Home...

"Thank you," I say, feeling emotional. "For your support, for your friendship. I don't know what I'd do without you."

"Oh, Rosie," says Maria, her eyes glistening. "We're the ones who are lucky to have you. And I'm so happy to be a part of this family."

We hug again, laughing and crying at the same time. The future is bright, full of possibilities, and I can't wait to live it, with Alex by my side and these wonderful people as my extended family.

Chapter 47

Alex

As we head towards the small gym at the ranch, the guys continue to tease me mercilessly.
"Hey, Alex," says Fran with a grin, "I bet you now spend more time lifting Rosie than weights."
"Very funny," I respond, rolling my eyes. "For your information, I still know how to lift a barbell."
"Oh, yeah?" chimes in Diego, opening the gym door. "Prove it, Romeo."
I enter the gym, the familiar scent of sweat and metal welcoming me. "What do you guys have in mind?"
The guys exchange conspiratorial looks. "A challenge," announces Chris. "Who can do the most push-ups in a minute."
"Easy," I say confidently. Perhaps too confidently.
"Oh, not so fast," Ethan smiles mischievously. "One-handed push-ups."
I feel the smile faltering on my face... thinking of all the sleepless nights I've had since Rosie had asked me for space and the energy I don't have. "You're joking, right?"
"Scared, love-struck cowboy?" taunts Chris.
"Never... and you're not authorized to make jokes, Mr. Perfect Couple," I reply, even though I know I'll probably regret it.
Chris doesn't retort... he just flashes his smile that we've nicknamed the "Val smile."

We get into position, ready to start. Ethan keeps the time.

"Ready... go!"

We start the push-ups, and immediately I feel my muscles protest. It's harder than I thought.

"So, Alex," pants Diego next to me, "give us some juicy details about Rosie."

"Don't... even... think... about it," I respond between push-ups.

"Oh, come on," insists Fran, who's counting. "At least tell us how your first time went."

I almost lose my balance at that question. "Guys!" I exclaim, trying to maintain focus.

"Look how he's blushing!" laughs Diego. "It must have been really special."

"I bet he took her on a romantic picnic under the stars," suggests Chris.

"Nah," interjects Diego. "Knowing Alex, he probably took her for a sunset horseback ride."

"I hate all of you," I grunt, feeling the muscles burn from the effort.

"Time!" Ethan finally shouts.

I collapse to the ground, panting heavily. "So? Who won?"

Chris sits next to me, equally exhausted. "Hate to admit it, but I think you won, Romeo... tied with the other tender-hearted cowboy," says Diego, huffing.

"Ha!" I exclaim triumphantly, weakly raising a fist in the air. "I told you I still know how to train."

"Yeah, yeah," says Fran, helping me up. "But you still haven't answered our questions about Rosie."

I sigh, knowing they won't leave me alone until I say something. "Alright, what do you want to know?"

"How did your first time really go?" asks the relentless Diego, his eyes shining with curiosity.

I feel a smile form on my lips at the memory. "It was... perfect," I admit. "We were at the lake, I've never felt anything like it in my life."

"Aww," the guys coo in chorus, pretending to be moved.

"Shut up, idiots," I say, but I can't help but smile.

"And now?" asks Ethan. "What do you have in mind for the future?"

The question catches me off guard. "I... I don't know," I admit. "I just know I want to spend the rest of my life with her."

Silence falls in the gym. The guys look at me, for once without a trace of mockery in their eyes.

"Wow," says Chris finally. "This is serious."

I nod, feeling suddenly vulnerable. "It is."

Fran puts a hand on my shoulder. "We're happy for you, man. Really."

Diego seems unusually pensive. Lately, he's been a bit... strange. He's been quite distracted. Then he seemed manic... now he seems a bit tense, a bit down, a bit thoughtful. Ethan's pat on my back distracts me before I can ask him for an explanation. Even though lately when we've asked, he hasn't given many.

"I'm happy for you," Ethan tells me. He seems moved. I really appreciate that he doesn't hold a grudge against me. I've been a real jerk to him. I'll have the rest of my life to make amends and I intend to do so. I return the pat and send him a grateful smile.

"Thank you, guys," I say, feeling grateful for their friendship.

The moment of seriousness doesn't last long, though.

"Alright," says Chris with a grin, "now that we've established that you're completely, irrevocably in love, how about a leg press challenge?"

I burst out laughing, grateful for the return to normalcy. "I'm in. Get ready to lose, cowboy."

Chapter 48

Alex

I wake up slowly, my mind still hazy from sleep. It's pitch black, it must be the middle of the night. The first thing I notice is the comforting weight of Rosie in my arms. I'm about to close my eyes again when I realize she's awake, her gaze curiously wandering around the room.

I suddenly realize I've never really shown her the cabin properly. Yet, I've already asked her to live here with me. Typical of us, I think with an inward smile. We always go straight to the point, burning through the steps as if we're in a hurry to live every moment together.

I love her so much that the idea of waiting even one more day to start our life together seems unbearable. But Rosie deserves better. She deserves everything.

In fact, we didn't have much time for the house tour... yesterday we spent the whole time here, distracted by ourselves. Then when she came back late in the evening, she was so tipsy and happy that I didn't think much about it... I helped her in a playful struggle with a particularly stubborn boot, braided her hair, undressed her and put her to sleep in my arms. My heart swells with tenderness when I think about it... she was so sweet, all wobbly and smiley.

Then this morning I went to work very early but she left the house at the same time as me. She told me enthusiastically that she was going with Val and Lexy to the station to pick up Rory... and then she spent the whole day with those crazies because Aurora wanted to be updated on everything in person.

We came back here... and after a quick snack we crashed. Apparently Rosie hasn't gotten used to waking up early yet... and I was exhausted from the lack of sleep of the last few days and the gym challenges.

"Hey, princess," I whisper sweetly, letting her know I'm awake.

Rosie turns towards me, a sweet smile on her lips. "Hey, cowboy," she responds softly.

"I'm sorry," I say, feeling a bit guilty. "I haven't shown you the cabin properly yet."

Rosie giggles softly. "Well, the first time I was here I was a bit... distracted."

The memory of that morning makes me smile. "Yeah, I was pretty distracted too."

I rise slightly, looking into her eyes. "What do you say to a guided tour now? I know it's the middle of the night, but..."

"Oh, come on, cowboy, get your ass up!" Rosie responds, all energetic and enthusiastic.

How nice it is to see her so...?

I get up from the couch, holding out my hand to her. "So, my princess, will you honor me by letting me show you our potential love nest?"

Rosie laughs, taking my hand. "The honor is all mine, Mr. Cowboy."

I turn on some soft lights as I lead Rosie through the cabin. The dim light creates an intimate and warm atmosphere, perfect for this impromptu tour in the middle of the night.

"Well," I begin, gesturing towards the living room, "this is obviously the living room. I know it's not huge, but I've always thought it was cozy."

Rosie nods, her eyes wandering over the bookshelves. "I really like it," she says softly. "It's... warm. Inviting."

Her appreciation fills me with joy. I lead her to the small kitchen, separated from the living room by a rustic wooden counter.

"The kitchen's not great," I admit, "but I thought we could expand it a bit. Maybe add a central island?"

Rosie smiles, running her hand along the counter. "I like the idea. We could cook together."

The image of us preparing dinner, laughing and joking in this kitchen, warms my heart.

I then guide her towards the hallway. "Here's the bathroom," I say, pointing to a door. "And this is the main bedroom."

I open the door, letting Rosie enter first. The room is dominated by a large wooden bed, with a handmade quilt that my grandmother gave me years ago. There's a window overlooking the pasture, and a built-in wardrobe that takes up an entire wall.

"It's beautiful, Alex," Rosie whispers, looking around the room in wonder.

"There's an extra room, too," I add, leading her to the last door. "I thought it could be perfect as your writing studio. It has a nice view of the ranch."

I open the door and Rosie steps in, stopping in the center of the room. It's smaller than the bedroom, but has a large window overlooking the green of the ranch and the distant mountains. There's an old desk that I inherited from my grandfather, perfectly positioned to enjoy the view.

Rosie turns to me, her eyes shining. "Alex, it's... it's perfect."

Her enthusiasm fills me with relief and joy. "Do you really like it? I tried to work on it quickly... the idea was to make it livable. Of course, we'll find a style you like and furnish and decorate everything as you dream."

She nods vigorously. "I love everything. The cabin, the view, the atmosphere. It's exactly what I was dreaming of without even knowing it."

I pull her into my arms, hugging her tightly. "I'm so glad you like it," I murmur into her hair. "But remember, if you want to change anything, or if you'd prefer to look for another place..."

Rosie steps back slightly, putting a finger on my lips to silence me. "Alex, listen to me. This cabin is perfect. It's our place. I don't want to live anywhere else."

Her determined tone makes me smile. "Are you sure? I don't want you to feel obligated..."

"The only thing I feel obligated to do," Rosie says with a mischievous smile, "is to kiss you right now."

And before I can respond, her lips are on mine, in a sweet and passionate kiss that takes my breath away.

When we separate, both breathless, I can't help but laugh softly. "So," I say, "welcome home, princess."

Rosie smiles, resting her head on my chest. "Home," she repeats softly. "I like the sound of that."

Chapter 49

Rosie

The sun's golden rays dance across the sky, painting it in shades of pink and orange that reflect off the distant mountains. I sit nestled on the porch's enchanting wooden swing, a steaming cup of coffee cradled in my hands. I can't tell if it's truly the most delectable brew I've ever tasted, or if it's simply divine because Alex made it for me, but in this moment, it's absolute perfection.

The rooster's cheerful crow echoes through the crisp morning air. That sound that used to irritate me so much now makes me smile. It has become part of the soundtrack of my new life, a daily reminder of how much my world has changed in so little time.

Alex just left, not before making sure I was comfortably settled on the swing and that my breakfast was ready. He had some backlogged work to do and rushed off to tend to his beloved horses, to feed them and for his morning equestrian training session. His enthusiasm was contagious, and I couldn't help but smile as I watched him hurry away.

Now I'm here, enjoying the breathtaking view while I write on my laptop.

This is my new routine. My new life. And I couldn't be happier.

I'm savoring every moment, every second of this new adventure.

The words flow easily, inspired by this environment and all the emotions I'm experiencing. Occasionally I look up, letting my eyes wander over the green pastures and majestic mountains, feeling incredibly grateful to be here.

A sudden idea makes me smile: I could surprise Alex by preparing a picnic. The image of the two of us sitting on a blanket, surrounded by nature, as we share a meal I've prepared with my own hands, fills me with joy. I could join him when he's finished with his workday.

My phone vibrates, interrupting my thoughts. It's a message from my father:

Dad: Booked for a walk at 10. Since you've been here, that quirky cowboy has seen you more than your dear old dad.

I can't help but smile reading the message, but at the same time I feel a pang of guilt. He's right, I've been so caught up in Alex and this new life that I've neglected my father a bit. And there's more: I still haven't told him about my latest choices. He doesn't know that I've decided to stay here, to change careers, to live with Alex.

I sigh, taking another sip of coffee. I know I need to talk to him, and soon. My father deserves to know how happy I am, how complete I finally feel. But part of me fears his reaction. What if he doesn't understand? What if he thinks I'm making a mistake?

I shake my head, trying to push away these negative thoughts. My father loves me, and I know he just wants my happiness. I just need to find the right way to explain it all to him. Besides, I've always sensed that my father wished for me to move closer to him... but he's never explicitly asked me to make such a big change. Maria, in part, has confirmed these perceptions when I revealed what I wanted to do.
I respond to the message:

Me: I'll be there, dad. Can't wait to see you.

I close my eyes for a moment, letting the warmth of the sun caress my face. This walk will be the perfect opportunity to open up to him.

Chapter 50

Rosie

The sun shines high in the sky as I meet Dad at the trailhead. His face lights up the moment he sees me, and he pulls me into a warm embrace.

"Rosie, sweetheart! Finally, I get to see you," he exclaims, holding me tight.

"Hi Dad," I respond, feeling a twinge of guilt for neglecting him lately. "I'm sorry I haven't been in touch much..."

He waves away my apologies with a dismissive gesture. "Don't worry about it. What matters is that you're here now."

We begin walking along the trail, surrounded by lush nature. For a while, we chat about trivial things - the weather, his work, how I'm settling in at the ranch.

"So," Dad says with a knowing smile, "how are things with Alex? I saw him the other day when I stopped by to check on that foal. He seemed happier than usual."

I smile, feeling my heart warm at the thought of Alex. "It's... it's really wonderful, Dad. Alex is... he's amazing."

Dad nods, looking satisfied. "I know he's a good man. Always thought so. Someone who loves animals that much can't be bad. And I've seen how deeply he cares about his horses' well-being."

I hadn't considered that my father and Alex might have developed a connection. Of course, with Dad being the ranch veterinarian, they must have spent considerable time together. It warms my heart to know that Dad holds Alex in such high regard.

Taking a deep breath, I know it's time to open up. "Dad, there's something I'd like to talk to you about."

He looks at me attentively. "I'm listening, sweetheart."

"Well... these past few weeks have given me a chance to reflect on my life," I begin, carefully choosing my words. "About my work, about what I truly want..."

Dad nods, encouraging me to continue.

"I've realized that... I'm not happy with my marketing job. Haven't been for a while, actually." I pause, meeting my father's eyes. "And being here, in this magical place, has reminded me how much I loved writing as a child."

I see a flash of understanding in Dad's eyes, but he remains silent, letting me continue.

"I'm thinking of... making a big change, Dad," I finally say. "I want to leave my job in Los Angeles and pursue my dream of becoming a writer."

Dad stays quiet for a moment, then squeezes my hand. "Oh, Rosie. You don't know how happy I am to hear those words."

"Really?" I ask, surprised yet not entirely shocked by his reaction. But my insecurity is a fierce beast, and the last thing I want is to disappoint my father.

He nods. "You know, when you first arrived here, you seemed a bit out of place. So different from my little girl who dreamed of writing stories. But then I saw how your eyes lit up looking at this place. I hoped you'd make this decision, but I didn't want to pressure you."

His words touch me deeply. "There's... there's more, Dad," I add, my heart pounding. "I've decided to stay here. Permanently. With Alex."

For a moment, Dad remains silent. Then, to my surprise, he smiles tenderly. "Well, I can't say I'm completely surprised. The way you look at that boy... it's unmistakable."

I feel tears welling up in my eyes. "I was afraid you wouldn't approve, that you'd think I was making a mistake leaving my career..."

"Sweetheart," Dad says, taking my hands in his, "all I've ever wanted is your happiness. And if your happiness is here, with Alex, chasing your childhood dream, then I couldn't be more thrilled."

I can no longer hold back my tears. "Thank you, Dad. You don't know how much it means to hear you say that."

He hugs me tight. "Besides," he adds with a smile in his voice, "now I'll have you closer. I couldn't ask for anything better."

We laugh together, both misty-eyed, as we continue our walk hand in hand, the morning sun casting a golden glow over the trail ahead.

Chapter 51

Rosie

The early afternoon heat is in full force as I approach the horse paddock, the picnic basket swinging gently from my arm. I've never felt so comfortable—or so happy—wearing casual clothes. I've never been so content in a pair of denim shorts and a simple top. And then, of course, I added cowboy boots, the ones I know Alex loves. I'll admit, it's a bit too hot for boots, but these are lightweight and barely come up my calves. And if it gets too warm, I can always kick them off and walk barefoot. That last thought really makes me smile, especially when I think back to the barbecue night and how much effort it took to let myself walk barefoot.

I feel like a completely different woman now.

Completely different, yet more myself than I've ever been.

I also feel light, as if a massive weight has been lifted off my shoulders after my conversation with Dad. A weight I hadn't even realized I was carrying. His support and understanding have given me a renewed energy, a newfound determination.

As I get closer, I see him.

Alex is there, magnificent as always, riding one of his favorite stallions. His long chestnut hair flows in the breeze, his muscular, sun-kissed arms holding the reins with confident ease. It's a sight that steals my breath every time.

I stop for a moment, captivated by the scene in front of me. Alex is in his element, wild and free, just like the horses he loves so much. His green tank top clings to his impossibly defined frame and bronzed skin. His snug jeans hug his powerful legs, and his cowboy boots complete the perfect image of a rugged, sexy rancher.

My heart races as I watch him guide the horse with such assurance, his deep voice murmuring words of encouragement to the animal. There's something incredibly alluring about the way he moves, the way he connects with the horses. It's as if he's a part of this wild landscape, as natural here as the mountains on the horizon.

I can't hold back any longer.

I drop the basket to the ground and run toward the paddock, calling his name.

"Alex!"

I see him turn his head in my direction, a smile spreading across his face the moment he spots me. He slows the horse and steers it toward me, dismounting gracefully when he gets close enough.

"Princess," he says, his raspy voice sending a shiver through me. "What a beautiful surprise."

I run into his arms, ignoring the dust and sweat. Alex pulls me against him, his body warm and solid against mine.

"I brought you lunch," I say, looking up at him. "I thought we could have a picnic."

His smile widens even more. "You read my mind, princess. I was just thinking about how hungry I was."

He lifts me into his arms, spinning me around, and I can't help but laugh. When he sets me down, he kisses me softly, his warm, familiar lips pressing against mine.

"Beautiful," he breathes against my mouth, one calloused hand cupping my cheek.

Heat blooms across my face, but it's not from the afternoon sun. "Says the man who looks like a romance novel cover on horseback," I tease, delighting in the way his eyes darken at my words.

His rich laughter rolls across the paddock.

"If that's what you like, I might have to put on a show more often." His large hand finds mine, fingers intertwining with practiced familiarity. "But first, let's see what treasures you've brought in that basket."

As he leads me toward our impromptu feast, I catch the contentment in his profile, the easy set of his shoulders. Here, in this moment, with the mountains standing sentinel and the summer breeze carrying the scent of sage and wildflowers, I know with bone-deep certainty that I've found my place in the world—right beside this man who moves like he's part of the wild itself.

Chapter 52

Alex

"You're beautiful," I murmur again, unable to hold back the words even though I've already said them. I could repeat it endlessly while admiring the freckles that dust her nose and cheeks. I adore those freckles. And her copper hair gleaming in the sunlight.

We head toward the picnic basket, hand in hand. I sit on the grass and pull Rosie close, unwilling to lose contact even for a second. As we eat the delicious food she prepared, I can't stop touching her. I'm only vaguely aware of what I'm eating because my attention is completely captured by this stunning woman. I caress her arm, tuck a strand of hair behind her ear, kiss her shoulder. Between bites, I can't resist kissing her again, deeper this time.

Before I know it, we're lying in the grass, Rosie on top of me, her hair surrounding us like a copper curtain. We laugh together, happy and carefree.

"My girl," I whisper, stroking her face. "My wonderful girl." It sounds so right. Rosie is my girl, my partner, my future. I've never felt anything like this for anyone else. With her, everything feels perfectly aligned.

I've never been particularly good at forming bonds. Probably because I've always felt somewhat alone. I went through dark times after being truly alone following my father's death... but Chris and his family showered me with love. I'll never be grateful enough for that. Chris welcomed me as a younger brother and always took care of me. He made sure I was okay and didn't lose my way.

He gave me a family and friends. But that's where my connections ended. I struggled to consider his family as my own. His parents always treated me like their son, but it took me a while to adjust. It took me time to consider Rory as a sister. It took me time to consider the other guys as my friends too. I never had trouble considering Chris my brother... because he always was. But I never sought out a girl who could be my girl. I don't know if it was fear or because I didn't know how to connect... but Rosie got to me immediately.

Now I can say with absolute certainty that love at first sight exists... because that's what this was. That's exactly why I felt so confused. Looking at her now, her eyes shining with happiness, I know with certainty that I'll never let this woman go. This is where she belongs, in my arms, on this ranch, in my life. And I belong to her, completely and irrevocably.

Rosie catches my gaze, and I can pinpoint the exact moment something exciting crosses her mind.

"Alex, if you don't have much work left to do... could we continue my riding lessons?" Her suggestion makes me smile, taking me back to our first ride together. It had started as a joke, a way to tease her, but it had transformed into something much deeper.

"Of course, princess," I respond, gently caressing her cheek. "I'd love that."

As we get up and head toward the stables, memories of that day flood my mind. I remember how the scent of her hair had intoxicated me, how her body had fit perfectly against mine as we rode together. It had been a magical moment, one of those times when I was completely enchanted by her. Riding with Rosie had been enjoyable. Perhaps a bit too enjoyable. The sensation of her body pressed against mine, her hands gripping me... it had awakened rather strong feelings. Feelings that return just thinking about it. Well, fortunately now I can satisfy them.

But first, I should focus on her lessons. Now I should try to let her ride a bit on her own. So she can better understand how to handle herself. As I saddle the horse for Rosie, I feel a twinge of worry. The idea of her riding alone terrifies me. The memories of my father's accident are still vivid in my mind, a wound that's never fully healed.

But I look at Rosie, see the excitement in her eyes, the determination in her smile, and I know I can't let my fears limit her. I can't clip this wonderful woman's wings because of my past traumas.

"Ready?" I ask, offering my hand to help her mount. Rosie nods enthusiastically, taking my hand. I lift her gently, admiring how she settles into the saddle with increasing grace.

"Remember," I tell her, my voice a mix of affection and concern, "keep a firm grip on the reins, but not too tight. Let the horse feel your confidence." Rosie nods, focusing on my words. I see the determination in her eyes, the desire to learn, to be part of my world. My heart swells with love for her. As I guide her through the basic steps, I can't help thinking how fortunate I am. Rosie is a wonderful dream that seems too good to be true.

"You're doing great," I encourage her, watching her move with increasing confidence. I try to suppress part of what I'm feeling because I'm currently overwhelmed by a mixture of pride and concern growing inside me. Her confidence increases with every step, and I can't help but admire her. She's determined, brave, and making remarkable progress. But it scares me.

Stop it, Alex. I mentally scold myself. This is a beautiful moment between us, and I can't let panic take over.

And I can't be so hypocritical as to ruin Rosie's experience. Not when I'm in the saddle every day, enjoying every moment with my beloved horses. She doesn't need to know anything about this new anxiety. She should just enjoy the journey and love every single moment. "Want to try going a bit faster?" I ask, trying to mask my apprehension with an encouraging smile. Rosie nods enthusiastically. "Yes, please!"

I give her some instructions on how to gently urge the horse into a light trot. As I watch her increase the pace, my heart beats faster. Part of me wants to run alongside her, ready to catch her if she falls. But I know I have to let her do this on her own. Rosie is a strong woman and has always been independent, and I don't want to be an overbearing boyfriend.

Rosie laughs with joy as the horse speeds up, her hair waving in the wind like a copper flag. She's beautiful, free, radiant. In that moment, I realize I'm witnessing something special: Rosie falling in love with this world just as much as I'm in love with her. "You're doing amazing, princess!" I shout, unable to contain my enthusiasm.

After a few laps, Rosie slows the horse and approaches me, her face flushed with excitement and effort.

"That was incredible, Alex!" she exclaims, her eyes sparkling. "I feel... alive!" Her words strike me deeply. I understand exactly what she means. It's the same feeling I get every time I mount up, the same freedom, the same sense of connection with nature.

"I'm so proud of you, Rosie," I tell her, helping her dismount. As soon as her feet touch the ground, I wrap her in my arms, lifting her and spinning her around. Her laughter fills the air, the sweetest sound I've ever heard. When I set her down, our eyes meet. There's a new light in hers, a spark of understanding and sharing that wasn't there before. In that moment, I feel we've grown even closer, that we've shared something deep and meaningful.

We kiss sweetly, the taste of joy and love on our lips. When we part, Rosie turns to the horse, affectionately stroking its muzzle. "Do you think one day I could have a horse of my own?" she asks, looking at me hopefully. The question catches me by surprise, but it also fills me with joy.

"Of course, my love," I respond, feeling my heart swell with love.

Chapter 53

Rosie

Life at the ranch has settled into a gentle rhythm. Each morning, I rise with the sun and find myself drawn either to the desk Alex thoughtfully positioned by the picture window, or to the old wooden rocker on the porch. In both spots, my fingers find their way across the keyboard as if guided by an unseen hand, weaving tales of endless prairies, snow-capped peaks, and sunsets that paint the sky in impossible colors. My romance unfolds like a love letter to this place that has become my home, to this untamed landscape that has embraced me, and most of all, to the cowboy who has stolen my heart.

The characters on the page come to life, reflecting fragments of the people I've met here. Above all, though, the male protagonist is a clear tribute to Alex—strong, gentle, and big-hearted. Inspiration seems to flow effortlessly, whether I'm gazing at the mountains on the horizon through the window or breathing in the fresh morning air on the porch.Our afternoons belong to us alone. Together, Alex and I breathe life into the cabin, transforming it day by day into a haven that speaks of both our souls - his rugged charm mingling with my contemporary touches until every corner tells our story.

Between these cherished moments, we throw ourselves into the joyful chaos of Dad and Maria's wedding preparations. My heart swells watching them pore over every detail, their eyes bright with anticipation. Seeing Dad radiate such happiness, and finding a true friend in Maria, feels like an unexpected gift.

Then there are my riding lessons, each one bringing me closer to this wild, beautiful world I'm learning to call my own.

Yet beneath this tapestry of contentment, an undercurrent of disquiet tugs at me. I still haven't submitted my resignation. Each time I contemplate it, anxiety creeps in like morning frost. Something feels off-kilter, as though I'm overlooking a crucial detail. This nameless fear troubles me more than I care to admit.

Today finds me at the window before dawn, watching nature's daily masterpiece unfold as the sun crests the mountains, setting the sky ablaze with coral and gold. It's a sight that usually fills me with wonder, but today my thoughts cast long shadows.

I hear Alex's familiar tread behind me, then feel the warm strength of his arms encircling my waist. His presence wraps around me like a favorite blanket, steady and sure.

"Morning, princess," he whispers, sleep still roughening his voice.

His lips find my skin - feather-light kisses trailing from shoulder to neck to cheek. Each kiss is like a caress, sweet and loving. I melt into his embrace, feeling my worries begin to loosen their hold.

But Alex knows me too well. He senses something's wrong. "Rosie," he says softly, turning me in his arms to look into my eyes. "What's wrong? You've seemed worried for days." He furrows his brows and studies me with those eyes capable of seeing into my soul, then adds worriedly, "Did I do something wrong?"

My heart constricts at his words. This man, who has shown me nothing but unwavering devotion, somehow still doubts his worth.

I shake my head emphatically and burrow deeper into his embrace.

His hand traces soothing circles on my back until finally, the words I've been holding back spill forth.

I press my forehead against his chest, drawing strength from his steady heartbeat.

"It's the job," I confess quietly. "I still haven't resigned, and I can't explain why, but whenever I think about it, this wave of anxiety washes over me. Like I'm standing on the edge of something, and I can't quite see what's below."

His arms tighten around me as he strokes my hair. "Change is scary, sweetheart. What you're feeling is perfectly natural."

"I know," I murmur. "But it's more than that. There's something... something just beyond my grasp. I can't put my finger on it."

Alex draws back slightly, cradling my face in his weathered hands. His eyes hold mine, brimming with such tenderness it nearly undoes me. "Listen to me, Rosie. Whatever comes, we face it together. If you need more time before resigning, take it. If you're ready to leap, I'll catch you. All that matters is your peace of mind."

Tears prick at my eyes. "How did I get so lucky?"

He answers with a soft kiss. "I'm the lucky one, princess. Together, there's nothing we can't handle."

I nod, feeling the weight on my shoulders lighten. His quiet confidence lends me strength I didn't know I possessed.

"You're right," I say, meeting his steady gaze. "It's time to face this. I want to resign, Alex. And I want you beside me when I do."

He squeezes my hands, his eyes shining with pride and support. "Every step of the way, love."

I draw a deep breath. "I'm still uncertain about the novel - if it will sell, if I can make it as a writer. But I know in my heart this is what I need to do."

"Rosie," he says softly, "your talent shines through every word you write. But even if your first novel doesn't top the bestseller lists, it doesn't matter. What matters is you're following your dreams, giving life to your passion. And I'll be here, supporting you, always."

His words fill me with courage. Yes, uncertainties remain. The book might not sell, I might face rejection and disappointment. I try not to dwell on potential readers' reactions - the thought alone sends anxiety spiraling through me. Yet I can't entirely banish such thoughts; they creep in unbidden.

But I counter them with a beautiful truth: for the first time in my life, I'm pursuing what truly sets my soul alight, surrounded by all the love and support I could ever need.

"Okay," I say with newfound determination. "Let's do this. Let's write that resignation letter."

Alex's smile radiates pride. "That's my girl. Come on, I'll make your favorite coffee while you work on it."

Chapter 54

Rosie

With a mix of relief and excitement, I click "Send." The resignation letter is officially gone, marking the beginning of a new chapter in my life. I stare at the screen for a few seconds, almost expecting something dramatic to happen. But, of course, nothing does. The world keeps turning, the sun keeps shining outside the window.

"You did it," Alex says softly from behind me. I turn to see him, his eyes gleaming with pride and love.

"I did it," I echo, feeling a smile stretch across my face. "It's done, Alex. I'm officially a full-time writer."

Alex sweeps me into his arms, lifting me from the chair and spinning me around. I laugh, holding onto his strong shoulders.

"I'm so proud of you, Rosie," he murmurs against my hair when he finally sets me down. "You followed your heart. You were brave enough to take this big leap."

I pull back slightly to look into his eyes. "I couldn't have done it without you," I say honestly. "You gave me the strength, the courage, and the support I needed."

Alex smiles, gently brushing his fingers along my cheek. "You already had it in you, princess. I just... lit the match."

I chuckle at his choice of words, feeling light and happier than I have in years. "Well, Mr. Matchmaker," I tease, "how about we celebrate this moment properly?"

Alex's eyes spark with mischief. "Hmm, and what do you have in mind, Miss Writer?"

Instead of answering, I pull him close for a passionate kiss. Alex responds instantly, his hands sliding down my back, drawing me closer. The kiss deepens, charged with love, desire, and promises.

When we finally part, we're both breathless. "You know something? I think you should read me a passage from your novel," he murmurs, his eyes gleaming with a hint of playfulness.

My face immediately heats up because I know exactly which passages he's hinting at. And I also know that once Alex gets that look in his eye, he won't back down. I try to glance away, but he won't let me; he holds my gaze, determined not to let me escape.

With one fluid motion, he slips off my shorts, guiding me to sit on the edge of the couch. He places the laptop beside me, his hands warm and steady.

"Pick a chapter," he whispers, his voice a blend of authority and desire. "Read it out loud... I'm at your command, princess."

His confidence, his tone, awakens every nerve in my body. I want to resist, my heart pounding, but the thought of reading the most passionate parts of my novel – just for him – is as thrilling as it is embarrassing. I take a moment and, with fingers trembling slightly, I open the right chapter.

I take a breath and start to read, but my voice shakes, broken by little gasps I can't hold back. Alex doesn't move, but his eyes are fixed on me, following every word I utter. Then he leans in, slowly, and I feel the warmth of his breath on my skin. His fingers trace a gentle line along my cheek, encouraging me, before he kneels in front of me, his hands gliding down my legs, softly parting them.

He begins with slow, hungry kisses, punctuated by gentle bites along my inner thighs. My voice grows even shakier, unable to keep up with the rhythm of the words.

When his mouth finally reaches my center, I freeze completely, unable to continue. A shiver runs through me, and he lifts his gaze, provoking me. My eyes meet his, full of desire and a hint of challenge.

"All done, princess? Already finished reading?" he whispers, his tone deep and intense, sending a tremor through me.

"Alex... I... I can't..." I barely manage to reply, but he insists, not moving an inch.

"Keep reading," he commands, his voice low and sure. "If you want to come."

I try to steady myself, to find my voice again, but each word is a struggle against the rising desire. I manage to get out a few lines before he resumes, his movements as intense as before.

I feel the heat of his breath on my most sensitive skin, as he plants a kiss, savoring his interpretation of the words, driving my excitement even higher. A thrill runs through me, and I try to press on with the reading. His tongue begins tracing slow, calculated movements, following every line I utter. He lightly nibbles my clit, his touch gentle but utterly consuming, before beginning to suckle, his pace maddeningly deliberate. I break again, my voice catching for what seems like the hundredth time, and he stops, lifting his gaze with an intensity that leaves me feeling exposed in every possible way. Without pulling back, he gives me a look, one that says everything.

"Keep going," he orders, his tone brooking no argument.

I have no choice but to obey, as though it's impossible to break free from his spell. I try to pick up where I left off, but my voice trembles, barely a whisper. Alex watches every move, every hesitation, and continues with precise intent. The tension mounts, nearly unbearable, and every touch brings me closer to that point of no return.

Then he releases me, just before I can lose control, his gaze capturing mine again. "You're not finished yet, princess," he murmurs, a dangerous smile on his face.

His mouth returns to me, and at that moment, all resistance dissolves. I keep reading, but now the words mix with my gasps, completely unable to hold back everything he's making me feel.

We're caught in a game of control and surrender, where every word, every breath, and every movement forges a connection that goes beyond simple desire. And as I finally let go, giving myself to him with no reservations, I know that this moment will stay with me, like a chapter in the book we've just written together.

Chapter 55

Rosie

I wake with a knot of anxiety twisting in my stomach. I immediately check my phone, my heart pounding as I see a new email in my inbox. It's from the marketing firm in Los Angeles.
With trembling hands, I begin to read:

Dear Ms. Rosalie Thorne,
Regarding your letter of resignation, we regret to inform you that we cannot accept such short notice.
As stipulated in your contract, a minimum 60-day notice period is required for the termination of your employment. Your proposal to conclude your duties within two weeks does not comply with this clause.
We urge you to reconsider your decision or, alternatively, to honor the contractual notice period.

Sincerely, Jennifer Patel
Human Resources Director
Anchor Media Group

I drop the phone onto the bed, feeling the air leave my lungs. It's as if the world is crumbling around me. I hadn't considered this possibility, and now I'm completely blindsided.
Without a second thought, I hurry out of the room and rush downstairs, searching for Alex. I find him in the kitchen, focused on preparing breakfast.
"Alex!" I cry, my voice thick with emotion.

He whirls around, alarm etching his features at the tone of my voice. No further words are needed. He opens his arms, and I fall into them, finally letting the tears I'd been holding back flow freely.

"Shh, I'm here," he murmurs, stroking my hair. "What happened?"

Through my sobs, I explain the email from the marketing firm. Alex listens in silence, continuing to hold me close.

"I don't know what to do," I whisper finally. "This changes everything."

Alex gently eases me back, cupping my face in his calloused hands and meeting my gaze. His expression is pensive yet calm. Somehow, this soothes me in return - because he seems collected, as if he's already considering a solution. Surely a solution must exist.

"Rosie, listen to me. This is just a temporary obstacle. We'll find a way through this." His voice is unwavering.

I nod weakly, clinging to his words like a lifeline.

"Now," he continues, his tone firm yet tender, "let's have breakfast. Then, calmly, we'll explore all our options. Okay?"

"Okay," I reply, feeling a glimmer of hope reignite within me. We sit at the kitchen table, the aroma of freshly brewed coffee drifting through the air. Alex pours me a cup and takes the seat opposite, his eyes filled with affection and determination. I didn't expect this reaction from him. He's always told me we'd face challenges together, but I anticipated him feeling just as discouraged as I do.

I mean, my whole world just came crashing down. Yet he seems unfazed. Resolute. In control.

"Alright," he says after a moment of silence. "Let's think through this situation. What are our options?"

I sigh, trying to organize my thoughts. "Well, I could honor the 60-day notice period," I say slowly. "But that would mean delaying my plans by two full months. Going back to Los Angeles..."

Alex nods, pensive. "That's an option. What else?"

The mere thought terrifies me. How can he not be troubled by this?

"No, Alex, I can't..." He scoots his chair closer and tenderly caresses my cheek.

"It's the worst-case option, but it's not a disaster. Just two months. I could take a vacation and come with you if you don't want to go alone. It's not a problem... but let's see if we can find another solution first. If not, we'll do it. Just two months."

I look at him, overwhelmed with love. Who would have thought a person, a man, could make me feel this secure?

The idea of returning to Los Angeles, even for two months, fills me with unease. I lived there my entire life, but the prospect fills me with anxiety and dread.

"We could try to negotiate," suggests Alex, having clearly read my distress. He always understands. "You could offer to work part-time and remotely during the final month, for example."

I nod, a glimmer of hope stirring. "There's also the option of paying a penalty to leave early," I add, recalling a clause in my contract. "But I'm not sure I can afford that."

Alex takes my hand, squeezing it gently. "Don't worry about the money right now. If that's the best option, we'll find a way."

His unconditional support warms my heart. "Thank you, Alex," I whisper.

"There's one more thing to consider," Alex says thoughtfully after a moment. "In the meantime, try sending a follow-up email to your boss. Explain the situation again and see if you can find a mutually agreeable solution."

"I could try..." I say, feeling slightly more optimistic but still doubtful.

"See?" Alex smiles. "We have several options. This isn't a hopeless situation."

I nod, feeling much better than I did just minutes ago. "You're right. I think the first step is to talk to my boss. If that doesn't work, we can always look at the other options."

"Agreed," says Alex. "Would you like me to help you prepare what to say?"

"Yes, please," I reply, grateful for his support.

Chapter 56

Alex

I'm finishing up the last preparations for the garden party, occasionally glancing over at Rosie as she helps Maria set up the tables. Still no response from her boss, but I know we'll find a solution. I've promised Rosie, and I'll do whatever it takes to make it happen. No matter the cost. I have some savings set aside, and if necessary, I'll use them to pay the penalty. I want Rosie to be free to start her new life, to pursue her dreams without obstacles. I would have happily gone with her for two months, even though it would have been difficult to leave my work here. They would have had to find a replacement for the lessons... the ranch has a business of horse competitions and lodging among other things. But we're all a big family, and I know we would have found a solution together for my replacement. I hate causing problems for my brothers, but I know they'd be ready to help me. However, I've seen in Rosie's reaction that even having my company wouldn't be helpful to her. I've seen that the idea of packing up and leaving again... even for a period of just two months, troubles and anxious her. She's surely accumulated more than we thought over the years... if she can't even bear the idea of going back there. And I have no intention of making her feel bad. I'll find a solution. At any cost, she won't set foot in that city again.

Tonight the atmosphere is charged with excitement. The occasion is the arrival of Maria's sister, the famous Aunt Tina. She's the superstar of our big family. I can't wait to see Rosie's reaction when she meets her. Rosie hasn't had the chance to get to know her yet, and I know there'll be plenty of laughs. Aunt Tina is... well, unique. In a good way, of course. Everyone loves her, but it's undeniable that she's a bit eccentric. Her personality is a unique mix of traits that make her unforgettable.

First of all, she's a first-class hypochondriac. There's not a day that goes by without her self-diagnosing at least three rare diseases. The last time she was here, she was convinced she had contracted malaria... in the middle of southern Italy. It took hours to convince her that her "tropical fever" was just a heat stroke, which hits these parts very hard.

Then there's her driving. Oh, her driving. Aunt Tina drives as if time doesn't exist, at a snail's pace, stopping at every intersection to check three times in every direction. The last time she came to visit us, it took her three hours to do a half-hour trip. She justified the delay by saying she had avoided at least twelve potential accidents and saved the life of a squirrel that couldn't decide whether to cross or not. Going on a car trip with her... it's a mystical experience.

But her most peculiar trait is her obsession with horror movies. Aunt Tina devours them like others eat popcorn. She knows by heart every jump scare, every unsettling soundtrack, every genre cliché.

The last time she came to the ranch, she organized a three-day horror movie marathon. We saw everything, from classics like "The Exorcist" to obscure B-movies that probably only she knew existed. Though she prefers the old ones. Things like the Halloween movies (the Michael Myers ones), for example. For her, Halloween is a national holiday. She comes here to the ranch and organizes a big celebration. Of course, we all happily participate and dress up.

The funny thing is that despite her passion for horror, Aunt Tina is easily frightened. During the horror movie marathon, we've seen her jump on the couch, hide behind the cushions, and scream at the top of her lungs more times than I could count. Yet, as soon as a movie was over, she was ready for the next one, with contagious enthusiasm.

And let's not forget the time she convinced all of us to do a nighttime "ghost tour" of the old barn. She showed up with a homemade Ghostbuster-like outfit, made up mainly of pots, forks, and a modified old hair dryer. Needless to say, the only "supernatural" thing we encountered that night was a particularly noisy owl, but Aunt Tina was convinced it was the spirit of a cowboy from the last century.

"Hey, cowboy," Rosie's voice pulls me from my thoughts. "What are you smiling about?" I turn to her, pulling her into an embrace. "I was thinking about Aunt Tina," I admit. "I can't wait for you to meet her." Rosie raises an eyebrow, curious. "Is she that special?" I chuckle. "Oh, darling, you have no idea. Let's just say with Aunt Tina, you're never bored."

At that moment, we hear the sound of a car approaching... very slowly. "That must be her," I say, taking Rosie's hand. "Come on, let's go welcome our guest of honor."

We approach the ranch entrance just as a shocking pink Fiat 500 stops with exasperating slowness. The door opens, and a woman in her sixties emerges, with bleached, puffy, and frizzy hair like a cloud, and a bright lime green dress that hurts the eyes. "Family!" Aunt Tina exclaims, opening her arms. "I survived the trip! You know, I thought I was going to have at least three heart attacks during the journey."

Maria runs to hug her sister, followed by Val and Lexy, who laugh with joy. Rosie and I hang back, observing the scene.

"Alex, my dear!" Aunt Tina notices me and comes over for a hug. "Oh, and who do we have here?" she asks, spotting Rosie.

"Aunt Tina, this is Rosie," I introduce her, unable to hold back a smile. "My girl."

Aunt Tina's eyes light up. "Oh, how wonderful!" she exclaims, enveloping Rosie in a tight hug. "Welcome to the family, dear. I hope you're not allergic to my new pistachio perfume, I read about a terrible case online the other day."

Rosie seems a bit overwhelmed, but she smiles. "Thank you, it's a pleasure to meet you. And no, no allergies to perfumes." I exchange an amused look with Rosie. Oh yes, with Aunt Tina here until the wedding, there's sure to be plenty of entertainment.

The evening is in full swing, and as always, Aunt Tina is the center of attention. After dinner, she makes herself comfortable on the garden sofa, surrounded by young people eager to hear about her latest adventures.

"Well," she begins, with a conspiratorial air, "I must tell you about my recent medical visits."

Val raises an eyebrow. "Really, Auntie? What happened this time?"

"Well," Aunt Tina continues, "my doctor prescribed me activated charcoal. He says I'm bloated from flatulence... and here I was thinking I'd gained weight!"

Everyone laughs, and Lexy asks, "And how did it go at the dentist?"

Aunt Tina's eyes light up. Dental visits are always her favorite, and she goes several times a week. "Oh, kids, it was a fantastic experience! I stocked up on all the free gadgets they had. Do you know how many mini strawberry-flavored toothpaste tubes you can hide in a purse?!"

Chris bursts out laughing. "Auntie, don't tell me you stole them all!"

"Stolen? Of course not!" exclaims Aunt Tina, pretending to be offended. "They were free gadgets!"

Meanwhile, Fran, who had been fiddling with the cables, has finally finished setting up the karaoke station... and naturally, Aunt Tina jumps to her feet.

"Karaoke!" she exclaims. "It's my time to shine!"

She heads toward the microphone with a determination that makes everyone smile. She starts singing a very personal version of "I Will Survive," complete with theatrical gestures and sudden changes in tone.

Ethan, fascinated by this performance, approaches. "Aunt Tina, that was fantastic! Can I join you for a duet?"

"Of course, darling!" responds Aunt Tina, enthusiastically. "How about 'Don't Go Breaking My Heart'?"

From that moment on, Aunt Tina and Ethan become inseparable, monopolizing the karaoke with an endless series of duets. They move from classics to more recent hits, with Aunt Tina adding her personal touch to every song.

I observe Rosie, who has remained cuddled up to me for most of the evening, and I'm very happy to see her smile. She seems happy... she's been more anxious lately, and I'm glad to see her more relaxed. And it's wonderful to see her so affectionate toward me. I continue caressing her, pausing only to give her kisses on her cheek. Then her forehead. Then the tip of her nose. Finally, she's the one who kisses me on the lips, unable to hold back.

"Kids!" exclaims Aunt Tina between songs. "We absolutely must make some videos to post on Facebook. My followers will go crazy!"

Rosie bursts out laughing in my face while she was about to give me another kiss, then amused, takes out her phone and starts filming. "Aunt Tina, I didn't know you were so social!"

I feel inexplicably happy hearing Rosie call Aunt Tina "aunt"... she had specified from the start that Rosie should call her that, but seeing that Rosie feels part of my whole world... it warms my heart.

"Oh, dear," responds Aunt Tina with a wink, "at a certain age, you have to keep up with the times. Besides, how else could I share my pearls of wisdom with the world?"

After yet another duet, Aunt Tina pulls Ethan aside, though they're still within earshot of everyone.

"Ethan, darling," she says conspiratorially, "since you're a fashionable young man, give me some advice on how to make new conquests."

Ethan, surprised but amused, responds, "Well, Aunt Tina, being yourself is always the best approach. Have you tried any group courses or activities?"

Aunt Tina sighs theatrically. "Oh, Ethan, if you only knew. I tried a group dance class last week."

"And how did it go?" asks Ethan, curious.

"A disaster!" exclaims Aunt Tina, shaking her head. "I thought I'd find a young, energetic group ready to let loose, and instead..."

Chapter 57

Rosie

I can hardly remember why the decision to move to the ranch seemed so difficult. Immersed in this fantastic family atmosphere, with laughter filling the air and surrounded by warmth and affection, I feel cherished and happy in a way I've never experienced before.

Alex is by my side, his arm wrapped protectively around my waist. Even though I occasionally catch him throwing amused glances at Aunt Tina, trying to tease her with provocative questions, he doesn't let go of me for a moment. And I haven't moved away from him for even a second. Being cuddled up against him is the most wonderful feeling in the world. His touch is reassuring, a constant reminder that this is where I belong.

And then there's Aunt Tina. Why has no one ever told me about her before? She's absolutely fantastic! I watch her as she tells yet another improbable story, gesturing animatedly and making everyone laugh hysterically. Her energy is contagious, her spirit indomitable.

"I swear!" Aunt Tina is saying, "I was so startled that my tooth fell out... and it was the front one... I had to rush to the dentist!"

I burst out laughing with the others, imagining the scene. Aunt Tina has a gift for turning every anecdote into a hilarious adventure.

I snuggle closer to Alex, feeling grateful and happy. This is the family I've always wanted, the sense of belonging I've searched for my entire life.

"Hey," Alex whispers in my ear, "what are you thinking about? You look so peaceful."

I smile at him, my heart swelling with love. "I think this evening is perfect," I whisper back. "And I'm lucky to be here, with you, with all of you."

Alex pulls me closer and places a gentle kiss on my temple. "We're the lucky ones to have you here," he murmurs.

At that moment, Aunt Tina stands up, raising her glass. "A toast!" she exclaims. "To family, old and new. And to Rosie, my new niece-by-choice. Welcome, dear. Prepare yourself for a life of madness and love!"

Everyone raises their glasses, and I feel enveloped by a wave of affection. *Yes*, I think to myself while returning Aunt Tina's smile, *I'm ready for this life of madness and love*. I couldn't wish for anything better.

While we hold our glasses up for the toast, my heart is full of gratitude. I can't stop thinking about how fortunate I am to be here, surrounded by people I already consider family.

But just then, a sound catches my attention. The roar of a powerful engine makes its way up the ranch's driveway. Turning, I see a white Porsche approaching slowly, its headlights cutting through the evening darkness.

The car stops a few steps away from us, the engine dies, and a sudden silence falls over the party. It's Lexy's reaction that immediately catches my eye.

In an instant, I see her transform before my eyes. The smile vanishes from her face, replaced by an expression I've never seen before. Her eyes, usually warm and welcoming, harden, fixing on the car with a mixture of shock and... is that fear I see? Her shoulders visibly stiffen, as if preparing for a blow. Her hands, which until a moment ago were holding her glass lightly, are now clenched into fists so tight that her knuckles are white.

I instinctively press closer to Alex, seeking comfort and protection. I feel his body tense beside me, his arm holding me a bit tighter. "Who is it?" I whisper to Alex, confused by this sudden change in atmosphere.

Before Alex can answer, the car door opens. My heart pounds in my chest, a strange tension in the air that I can't fully comprehend.

I watch as a figure emerges from the car. It's a man, tall and well-dressed. Even in the dim light, I can notice an air of confidence, almost arrogance, in the way he moves.

"I hope I'm not interrupting anything important," the man says, his deep, captivating voice breaking the silence.

I look at Lexy, trying to understand what's happening.

Lexy seems almost petrified. Her face is pale, every trace of color gone. Her lips are pressed into a thin line, and I can see a slight tremor in her chin, as if she's fighting to maintain control. Her eyes, however, never leave the man's figure, following his every movement like prey watching a predator.

A thousand questions crowd my mind. Who is this man? Why is Lexy reacting this way? What's the history between them? And why has no one ever mentioned him to me? The festive atmosphere from just minutes ago seems like a distant memory, replaced by tension so thick you could cut it with a knife.

The man steps forward, entering the garden lanterns' light. Now I can see him clearly: he's attractive, in his mid-thirties, with dark hair and penetrating eyes. His smile, however, doesn't reach his eyes.

"What are you doing here?" Lexy's voice breaks the silence. It's cold, distant, laden with emotions I can't fully decipher. Anger? Pain? Fear? Perhaps a mixture of all these things.

The man takes a step forward. "Can't I make a surprise visit?" he asks, his tone light but with a note of challenge.

The tension in the air is palpable, and I continue to watch Lexy, trying to understand what's happening. But just when I think the situation couldn't get more surreal, the unthinkable happens.

Suddenly, Chris, Fran, and Diego rise from their seats. To my great surprise, they run toward the man, their faces lighting up with smiles. In an instant, they surround him and greet him with masculine pats on the back. Their voices overlap in a chorus of "Welcome back!" and "What a surprise!"

I stand open-mouthed, unable to reconcile their warm reaction with the tension still emanating from Lexy. How can they welcome him so warmly when Lexy seems to want to strike him dead with her gaze?

Then, to my further surprise, I feel Alex move beside me. He gives me a quick kiss on the cheek and whispers: "I'll be right back." I watch him walk away and join the group, shaking hands with the man with a smile. The man returns the greetings with apparent warmth, but there's something in his demeanor that makes me uneasy. His smile never quite reaches his eyes, and there's an air of... what? Arrogance? Self-satisfaction? I can't define it precisely, but it's unsettling.

While everyone seems happy to see him, I can't help but notice that Lexy hasn't moved an inch. Her body is still tense, fists still clenched. Her eyes have never left the man, and the hostility in her gaze is almost tangible. If looks could kill, I'm certain this man would have already fallen to the ground.

I feel completely disoriented. How can there be such a discrepancy in reactions? Who is this man really? And why does Lexy seem to hate him so deeply while others welcome him with open arms?

I remain motionless, observing the surreal scene unfolding before my eyes. After Chris, Fran, and Diego, even Val, Aurora, Maria, and her father approach the man, greeting him warmly in turn. Their smiles and cheerful voices contrast sharply with the tension still emanating from Lexy.

The guys continue giving him shoulder pats and friendly pushes, but he remains impassive. He doesn't move an inch, as if made of stone. There's something unsettling about his immobility, almost... inhuman.

"You're a bastard, you never answer messages!" Chris exclaims, laughing.

Diego adds: "You always disappear! Where the hell were you this time?"

The others continue with similar comments, mixing playful reproaches with genuine expressions of joy at seeing him again. The familiarity in their tones confuses me even more.

Suddenly, Alex turns to me. His smile is warm, but there's something in his eyes I can't decipher. "Rosie, darling, come here," he tells me, gesturing for me to approach. "I want you to meet a dear friend."

With legs that feel like jelly, I slowly approach the group. The man fixes me with a penetrating gaze that makes me shiver.

"Rosie," says Alex, putting an arm around my shoulders, "this is Maximilian. Max, this is Rosie, my girlfriend."

Maximilian. The name resonates in my mind as I try to process this new information.

"Nice to meet you Miss Rosalie," says Maximilian, his voice deep and controlled. The way he pronounces my name makes my blood run cold. No one ever calls me Rosalie... except on formal occasions. And I don't even know how he knows my full name. I decide to ignore it because it's easy to guess that Rosie is short for Rosalie... so maybe I'm overreacting.

He extends his hand and, hesitating for a moment, I shake it. His grip is firm, almost too much so, and his hand is strangely cold.

"The pleasure is mine," I respond automatically, trying to keep my voice steady.

While exchanging these pleasantries with Maximilian, I can't help but glance at Lexy. She's still motionless, her gaze fixed on us. The hostility in her eyes hasn't diminished one bit.

Chapter 58

Rosie

The party continues, but I'm still very confused. I observe everything with new eyes, trying to catch every detail, every nuance in the interactions.

Lexy hasn't stopped staring at Max with a look that could kill. Max, on the other hand, seems completely at ease, ignoring Lexy's hostility as if it doesn't exist.

The guys are gathered around Max, hanging on his every word. They bombard him with questions about his travels, his work, his adventures. Max barely responds or does so enigmatically, leaving more questions than answers. I can't understand why the guys seem to adore him so much or even why they're friends... they have nothing in common.

Max is... unsettling. There's something about the way he moves, talks, even breathes, that seems not quite human. His eyes are too intense, his smile too perfect. He gives me chills. At one point, I even saw Alex step away with him for a while.

Finally, after what feels like an eternity, the party comes to an end. I say goodbye to everyone, trying to maintain a normal appearance, but I can't wait to return to the cabin with Alex. I have too many questions burning inside me. As soon as we close the door behind us, Alex, still happy and carefree, starts covering me with kisses. His lips trace a path from my neck to my cheek, but I stop him, placing a hand on his chest.

"Alex, wait," I say, moving slightly away.

His face changes immediately. A shadow of fear crosses his eyes and his voice trembles slightly when he asks: "What's wrong? What's happening?"

I quickly reassure him, caressing his face. "Nothing serious, love. It's just that... I need to understand some things."

Alex seems to relax a bit, but I can still see the worry in his eyes. "What things?"

"Who is Maximilian, really?" I ask directly. "Why is he so... unsettling? And why does Lexy seem to hate him so much?"

Alex sighs, running a hand through his hair. "I noticed you were worried," he admits. "But really, there's nothing to worry about. Max is a good guy."

"A good guy?" I repeat, incredulous. "Alex, there's something about him that gives me the chills."

Alex smiles. "I know, he can seem a bit strange at first. But you get used to it, trust me. He's like a brother to me, just like the other guys."

I look at him carefully, trying to determine if he's hiding something from me. "And Lexy? Why do she and Max hate each other so much?"

Alex shakes his head, seeming genuinely perplexed. "Honestly? It's a mystery to all of us. There's always been this tension between them, but nobody knows exactly why. We've learned not to ask questions."

I remain silent for a moment, trying to process all this information. Something doesn't add up, but I can't figure out what.

"Rosie," Alex says softly, taking my hands. "I promise there's nothing to worry about. Max might seem a bit peculiar, but he's part of the family. You'll see, with time you'll understand too."

I nod slowly. Alex seems genuinely convinced and has assured me that Max is like a brother to him. I trust him... I know he would become very protective if there was something to worry about... I know how he takes care of me even in moments that don't require it. If Maximilian were the shady character I thought he was... Alex would surely be freaking out. Yet a small voice keeps repeating to me: what if there's something he doesn't know?

I'm surely being paranoid and influenced by Lexy's reaction...

Chapter 59

Alex

The sun burns on my skin as I work in the horse paddock. My hands move automatically, performing familiar tasks, but my mind is elsewhere.

I think back to last night and this morning, how I held Rosie close to me, cuddling her more than usual. I can't shake off that feeling of panic I experienced last evening, when I noticed her change in mood and how she pushed me away as soon as we entered the house. I was really scared.

I've never been such an insecure guy, but with Rosie... it's different. I'm too afraid. I keep thinking that at any moment she might realize she's too good for me, that I don't deserve her. It's a thought that torments me more than I'd like to admit.

Fortunately, she was just worried about Max.

Max... who, speaking of which, snaps me out of my thoughts.

I look up and see him, standing beyond the fence. He's wearing an elegant suit, as if it were the most natural thing in the world to be dressed like that in the middle of summer, on a ranch. Only he could pull it off with such ease.

I observe him for a moment. Max always seems so unbeatable, invincible. He appears cold on the surface, but he's always been a good friend, a brother. He's always been there for all of us, even if he's not exactly the sentimental type. He always knows how to get out of any situation.

That's why I wrote to him about Rosie's resignation problem. I wanted advice on how to handle it. Max never responds to our joking messages in the group chat... I don't even know if he really reads them. Sometimes I wonder why he's still part of it, considering he's never replied to a single message.

He didn't even respond to my personal message... but I asked for help, and he showed up the next day. I know it's not a coincidence. That's how Max is: he never explicitly says he'll help you, he simply does it.

"Hey, Max," I greet him, approaching the fence.

Max doesn't return the greeting. Small talk isn't his thing. He looks at me with his penetrating eyes and simply says: "It's all taken care of."

His words completely throw me off guard. As always. I stare at him for a few seconds, trying to process the information.

"What... what do you mean by 'all taken care of'?" I finally ask, confusion evident in my voice.

Max slightly raises an eyebrow, as if surprised by my question. "The problem with Rosie's resignation," he responds flatly. "I made some calls. The company will accept her resignation without issues and without a notice period."

I feel my jaw drop. "But... how did you do it? I mean, thank you, but..."

Max waves his hand, as if to dismiss my questions. "It doesn't matter how. It's done."

I look at him, a mixture of gratitude and unease stirring inside me. Max has always had this effect on me: on one hand, I'm grateful for his help; on the other, his way of doing things, so efficient and mysterious, makes me uncomfortable.

"Thank you," I finally say, not knowing what else to add.

Max nods briefly, as if he had just performed the most mundane of actions.

I'm not surprised that he doesn't ask questions or make jokes about me being in love. His silence is simply his quiet approval. If he had had any problems with Rosie, he would have pointed them out without hesitation.

He turns to leave, but something compels me to stop him.

"Max," I call out. He stops, turning slightly toward me. "Will you stay until the wedding?"

As always, Max responds enigmatically. "Maybe," he says, his flat tone betraying no emotion.

Yet, despite his vague response, I already know how it will end. Maria will ask him to stay, and he won't be able to say no to her. He never has. There's always been something special about the bond between Max and Maria, something none of us has ever fully understood.

"Maria will want you to stay," I say, more as a statement than a question.

For a moment, I think I see a flash of... something in his eyes. Affection? Resignation? It's hard to tell with Max.

"Probably," he responds, and for an instant, his mask of indifference seems to crack slightly.

I nod, knowing this is the closest thing to confirmation I'll get from him.

Max has just left, leaving me with a strange mixture of gratitude and perplexity. I'm still trying to process everything that happened when I hear quick footsteps approaching. I turn to see Rosie running towards me, her face lit up with a radiant smile.

Before I can say anything, she throws herself into my arms, holding me tight. "Alex! Alex!" she exclaims, her voice vibrating with joy. "You won't believe it!"

I hold her back, savoring the warmth of her body against mine. "What is it, princess?" I ask, though I already have an idea of what it might be.

Rosie pulls back slightly, looking into my eyes with an expression of pure happiness. "My boss accepted my resignation!" she says, almost jumping with excitement. "They found a qualified replacement who can take my position immediately. They don't need any training, so... they simply accepted! I can leave right away!"

I try to look surprised, but I know I'm not a good actor. My smile is genuine - I'm truly happy for her - but my eyes probably betray the fact that this isn't entirely unexpected news for me.

"That's fantastic news, Rosie!" I say, hugging her again.

Rosie pauses for a moment, studying my face. "Alex," she says slowly, "you don't seem very surprised."

I sigh, knowing I can't hide the truth from her. "Well..." I begin, searching for the right words. "I asked Max for some help with the situation. He just stopped by and told me he had taken care of everything."

Rosie's eyes widen. "Max?"

I sigh, knowing I need to explain better. "Yes, I had asked him for advice on how to handle this situation. I didn't expect him to resolve everything himself..."

As I speak, I notice a change in Rosie's expression. Her radiant smile vanishes, replaced by a mixture of emotions I can't fully decipher. She seems angry, hurt, perhaps even disappointed.

"Wait," she says, taking a step back. "You asked Max for help?"

My heart sinks. I absolutely didn't want to make her angry or upset. "Rosie, I..."

"Why didn't you tell me?" she interrupts, her voice tense. "Why Max?"

I shake my head quickly, realizing that perhaps I've made a huge mistake. "I... I wanted to help you, resolve the situation. I couldn't stand seeing you so worried."

Rosie crosses her arms, her body language clearly defensive. "But why ask Max? Why not talk to me first?"

I run a hand through my hair, frustrated with myself for handling the situation poorly. "I don't know, Rosie. I thought... I thought I was doing the right thing. I didn't want to make you angry or hurt you. I just wanted to help."

Rosie remains stone-faced. Her eyes are wide, and I'm seriously starting to panic.

"Hey baby, tell me what's going through your mind," I plead.

She stares at me for another long moment that feels like an eternity.

Finally, she speaks. "A lot of things are going through my mind, but above all, I still don't trust Max. I don't understand what magic he worked to make all this possible, and most importantly, I don't understand why you took over my problem and decided to solve it on your own out of nowhere."

Suddenly, fear grips me. I look at Rosie, studying her face. Her eyes, usually warm and welcoming, are now distant, clouded by a veil of disappointment and confusion. Her lips are pressed into a thin line, as if holding back a flood of words.

"It was our problem. And I tried to solve it. I told you I would find a way," I say sincerely.

Rosie seems even angrier.

"I thought you would support me and that we would figure something out together, not that you'd outsource everything to some random creepy guy!" she says, raising her voice.

"I..." I try to find the words, to reorganize my thoughts and fix this mess. "Max... he's like a brother to me... I just asked for advice. I didn't tell you because I hadn't received a response from him yet."

Rosie shakes her head, a mixture of frustration and sadness in her eyes.

"You assured me he wasn't shady..."

I feel a pang of pain at her tone. "He's not! I know you don't trust him..."

"Then tell me: how did he solve the problem?" she interrupts.

"I... I have no idea... I asked for advice, and he showed up here telling me everything was resolved."

"Seriously, Alex? And you expect me to believe there's nothing strange about his methods?"

She looks at me for a while... I shake my head. I know Max isn't an angel from heaven, but he's never gotten me into trouble... in fact, he's always gotten us out of trouble.

"And then it didn't occur to you that I might be perfectly capable of solving my own problems without asking for help around?"

She adds, even more indignant.

"Listen, Rosie... I don't know how Max did it, but he's not a bad person. I'm sure he found a legitimate way. I trust him. And I didn't mean to imply that you can't solve your own problems. You're an incredibly strong woman, and I'm sure you can handle anything... I just wanted to be there for you."

Rosie's eyes are glistening. I watch her take a small step backward, and here my world is about to crumble even more.

People fight... and this is just our first fight. I should stay calm, right?

"Ros," I try to say, but she interrupts me.

"I need to take a walk. I'll see you later," she says, continuing to shake her head.

Chapter 60

Rosie

I look at Alex, standing in front of me, his eyes truly full of fear. Part of me wants to throw myself into his arms, tell him everything is okay, that I understand. But I can't. Not yet.

"I need to take a walk. I'll see you later," I say, my voice calmer than I expected. I don't want to hurt him... but I need to breathe and reorganize my thoughts. I've always made impulsive decisions in life and jumped in headfirst. I don't want to repeat what I did in Los Angeles.

I know I love Alex, and I know I love this place, and that this is the right choice for me... but in moments like this, panic overwhelms me.

I know couples fight and misunderstandings happen, but I'm not used to this, and I want to learn how to handle everything in the best way possible.

I see the pain in Alex's eyes, but he nods understandingly. "I understand, Rosie. Take all the time you need."

His way of reacting and giving me space... it already makes me feel better. I don't know why I expected an even bigger fight... but he's Alex, and somehow he always puts me at ease.

As I walk away, I feel a tangle of emotions inside me. I feel... I don't know, confused perhaps. Maybe more than I should be. After all, I know Alex meant well. He didn't want to hurt me; he just wanted to help me.

I feel my anxiety rising but also subsiding... because Alex is a wonderful man, and his way of doing things helps me so much. I know he trusts Max, but I don't. I know he was acting in good faith... but I reacted a bit exaggeratedly to all this. I don't really understand why.

Perhaps it's simply that I'm not used to relationships. The fact that I've fallen in love and am doing so well here scares me a little... I feel like something is about to happen, like this bubble of perfection could shatter at any moment.

This morning, I was so happy, so proud of myself. I thought I had solved everything on my own, that I had finally taken control of my life. And instead... I discover that everything was resolved by someone else.

I'm glad Alex has my back... but I wish he would consult me when making decisions about me. And the fact that he asked for help from someone who is still a mystery to me and whom I find unsettling... makes everything worse.

Why him of all people? I still can't understand why Alex is so attached to such a... shady type. There's something about Maximilian that makes me uncomfortable, a coldness, a detachment I can't decipher.

I stop for a moment, looking at the ranch around me. This place that has become my home in such a short time. Alex, who has become my world almost overnight. It's all so intense, so overwhelming.

I take a deep breath. I know we'll need to talk more, Alex and I. Clarify many things. But for now, I need to be alone, to reorganize my thoughts and feelings.

I'm not sure how long I've been wandering around the ranch, lost in my thoughts, when a shrill voice suddenly makes me jump.

"Rosie, darling! Just the person I was looking for!"

I turn and see Aunt Tina approaching, wearing a multicolored polka dot apron over a floral dress that would make a spring field pale in comparison.

"Hi, Aunt Tina," I respond, trying to force a smile.

"Oh, don't make that face! Come with me, and I'll tell you about the time I almost married an Aztec prince during a trip to Mexico. Or was he a Japanese sumo wrestler? Well, the details are a bit fuzzy, but he was definitely real!"

Before I can protest, Aunt Tina grabs my arm and drags me toward the main house. "Anyway, we're making a strawberry tart with pastry cream. You absolutely must join us!"

We enter the kitchen, and I'm greeted by a chaotic but cheerful scene. Maria, Lexy, Val, and Aurora are all working, laughing and chatting. The kitchen looks like it's been hit by a flour explosion.

"Look who I found!" Aunt Tina announces triumphantly.

"Rosie!" Maria exclaims, smiling. "Finally! We thought you'd forgotten about us."

"Yeah, you didn't even respond to our invitation today," Lexy adds, pretending to be offended.

"I'm sorry," I mumble, feeling guilty. "I've had... an intense day."

The girls exchange a glance. Aurora approaches, her forehead furrowed with concern. "Rosie, are you okay? You seem a bit down."

I try to smile, but I know it's not convincing. "I'm fine. Just a bit tired."

"Nonsense!" Aunt Tina interjects. "Nothing that a bit of sugar and good company can't cure. Now, do you want to know what happened to me this morning? A disaster! I met an owl, and it was staring at me... do you know what that means?! It's an omen of death!"

Aunt Tina starts, and everyone bursts out laughing. The cheerful atmosphere and the affection of these women slowly begin to melt the knot in my stomach.

Val hands me a rolling pin. "Come on, help us with the shortcrust pastry. It'll do you good to get distracted a bit."

Just as I start rolling out the dough, the kitchen door swings open with a theatrical bang.

Ethan makes his triumphant entrance, wearing a shocking pink apron with the words "Sexy Cook" (complete with a spice level meter).

"Sorry I'm late, ladies!" he exclaims with an exaggerated bow.

Aunt Tina claps her hands enthusiastically. "Ethan, darling! Have you heard about my encounter with the owl?"

Ethan laughs while listening to the story. "Aunt, I think you're watching too many horror movies."
"No, no, dear!" Aunt Tina responds, laughing. "There's no such thing as too many. Shall we watch one together tonight?"
"Only if we stuff ourselves with popcorn!"
"Oh, Ethan," says Aunt Tina, her eyes heart-shaped, "you certainly know how to have fun!"
As the two continue their absurd conversation, I find myself smiling genuinely for the first time in hours. The absurdity of this pair, combined with the affection and warmth of these people, is slowly melting the tension I've been carrying inside.
Maria comes closer and puts an arm around my shoulders. "See?" she whispers with a conspiratorial smile. "Sometimes all we need is a bit of madness to forget our problems."
I nod, grateful for this moment of lightness. Perhaps, I tell myself, not everything is as complicated as it seems. And maybe, with the help of this crazy but loving family, I'll find the clarity I need and shake off this feeling of impending catastrophe.

Chapter 61

Rosie

It's sunset when I leave the main house with a lighter heart and a strong desire to see Alex and clear things up once and for all. The day spent with Aunt Tina and the others has done me an incredible amount of good, temporarily pushing away the dark thoughts that had been plaguing me.

Suddenly, I realize I haven't checked my phone for hours. I pull it out of my pocket, and my heart races when I see a series of messages from Alex.

The first ones are casual, attempts at light conversation:

Alex 🖤: Tempest is being particularly stubborn today... reminds me of you

Alex 🖤: Hope you're enjoying your day.

But as I scroll down, I notice a change in tone.

Alex 🖤: I miss you, hope we can talk soon.

Alex 🖤: I'm really sorry about how things turned out.

Alex 🖤: I'm afraid I've ruined everything between us, please tell me we can fix things.

A wave of conflicting emotions overwhelms me. Guilt mingles with tenderness as I realize how much my reaction has shaken Alex. I'm sorry for overreacting. His concern is palpable through those messages, and I know all too well his kind and caring heart.

I bite my lip, thinking about how he's always been there for me, how hard he's tried to help and protect me. Yes, perhaps his approach wasn't the best, but his intentions were pure. I can't leave him in uncertainty for another minute.

I start walking toward the cabin, sure to find him there after his day of work and training. But as I advance, something catches my attention: a horse, outside the fence, trotting away. I don't know if it's the only one, and I can't recognize which horse it is from this distance.

"What's going on?" I mutter to myself, changing direction. How did it escape? I approach quickly, but the horse is already too far to reach on foot. I know many horses are in athletic preparation for upcoming competitions. Alex recently told me about all the extra work he's been doing. And I also know that at this hour, all horses should be in their enclosure.

I don't know what's happening, but something's wrong.

Without thinking twice, I run to the nearest stable. Remembering my riding lessons, I quickly saddle a horse and mount, trying to put everything I've learned into practice.

While spurring the horse in pursuit, I pull out my phone and dial Alex's number with trembling fingers. "Come on, answer," I whisper, keeping my eyes fixed on the runaway ahead of me.

The phone rings once, twice, three times. No answer. I leave a hurried voice message: "Alex, it's me. I'm fine, but there's a horse outside the fence. I'm trying to catch it. If you hear this, come help me. I'm heading toward the woods east of the ranch."

I end the call and focus on the chase. The wind whips my face as I gallop, my heart racing with adrenaline and worry.

Chapter 62

Alex

Sweat drips down my back as I hit the punching bag with all my strength. But it's not enough. No matter how hard I train, I can't shake off the anxiety gripping my stomach.

I've sent Rosie countless messages. At first, I tried to keep a light tone, hoping not to pressure her. But as the hours passed and her silence lingered, I couldn't hide my growing concern.

"You're a fucking idiot, Alex," I mutter to myself, hitting the bag even harder.

Chris, who's holding the bag steady, gives me a questioning look. "You good, man?"

I ignore the question, focusing on my punches. Left, right, left, right. The familiar rhythm should calm me, but today it's not working.

Fran and Diego, training nearby, exchange a meaningful look. They're realizing something's wrong, but for now, they have the sensitivity not to ask questions.

Max, as usual, hasn't joined us. "I prefer solitary training," he said in that detached tone of his before disappearing. Right now, I almost envy him.

"Come on, let's take a break," Chris suggests, stepping away from the bag.

I stop, panting. Not from physical fatigue, but from the weight I feel on my heart.

"Alex," Fran intervenes, approaching. "It's obvious something's wrong. Want to talk about it?"

I hesitate. Part of me wants to scream, confess everything. Another part just wants to run away, find Rosie, and beg for her forgiveness.

"I screwed up," I finally admit, my voice hoarse. "With Rosie. And if I've ruined everything... if I've lost the best thing that's ever happened to me..." My voice breaks.

The guys exchange worried glances, but no one ventures easy reassurances. They don't know how serious the situation is, and I appreciate their caution.

Diego breaks the silence: "Hey, man. I don't know what happened, but if you want to talk about it, we're here."

I nod, grateful for their support, but the knot in my stomach doesn't loosen.

"Thanks, guys," I mumble. "I think... I think I'll go take a shower. I need to clear my head."

I head toward the locker room, feeling their concerned gazes on my back. The silence that follows me is heavy, loaded with unasked questions and palpable worry.

I step into the shower and turn the hot water on full blast, hoping the steam might somehow blur my tormented thoughts. The drops run down my body, sliding along my tense, aching muscles from the intense workout.

I rest my forehead against the cold tiles, seeking some kind of relief. The water flows, flows, flows, but the weight on my chest doesn't diminish. If anything, it seems to increase with each breath.

I close my eyes, and Rosie's image appears vivid in my mind. Her smile, her eyes full of trust... and then the hurt and disappointed expression when she discovered the truth. A shiver runs through me, despite the scalding water.

I punch the shower wall in frustration. The physical pain is almost a relief compared to the emotional torment I'm experiencing.

"Stupid, stupid, stupid," I mutter, rhythmically banging my head against the tiles.

The water keeps flowing, but it can't wash away the guilt that grips me. It can't turn back time and make me make the right choices. I had no idea it would bother her... I just wanted to resolve the situation and see her happy. How serious is what I did?

Fear coils in my stomach like a living thing. Fear of losing her. Fear of shattering our carefully built trust. Fear of returning to the emptiness of life without her.

I stay under the water stream longer than necessary, hoping for some epiphany, some magical solution that could fix everything. But when I finally turn off the tap, I feel exactly the same as before: lost, guilty, and terrified.

When I leave the shower, wrapped in a towel, I notice my phone flashing. My heart leaps into my throat as I grab it.

There's a notification from the ranch's security app: some horses are out of the main enclosure. But what immediately catches my attention are Rosie's notifications. A missed call and a message.

With trembling hands, I open the chat. There's a voice message. Her voice, anxious but alive, fills the locker room: "Alex, it's me. I'm fine, but there's a horse outside the fence. I'm trying to catch it. If you hear this, come help me. I'm heading toward the woods east of the ranch."

Relief mingles with concern. Rosie has responded to me. But now she's out there, alone, chasing after a horse.

"Guys!" I shout, already frantically getting dressed. "We have an emergency!"

Chapter 63

Rosie

The wind strikes my face like liquid steel, each gust a sharp reminder of my precarious pursuit. The escaped horse remains ahead, a dark silhouette dancing just beyond reach, mocking my desperate chase. My heart thunders, a raw symphony of adrenaline and fear. "Come on, you can do this," I whisper, the words as much for myself as for the powerful creature beneath me. The handful of riding lessons I've taken suddenly feel woefully inadequate against the urgency of this moment.

The terrain shifts, growing treacherous as we approach the forest's edge. The horse accelerates, and I'm struck by our velocity, a sudden, stomach-dropping realization of our speed. Panic begins to bloom like a dark flower in my chest.

"Whoa, slow down," I stammer, pulling tentatively on the reins. But the horse, intoxicated by the chase, seems deaf to my pleas.

Trees blur into a green-brown smear along the path. My breath comes in ragged gasps, sweaty hands sliding desperately on leather reins. "Too fast," my mind screams, terror rising like a tide. Without warning, a rabbit darts from the undergrowth, crossing our path. Startled, my horse rears up violently—a sudden, terrible vertical motion.

Everything happens in a heartbeat. I lose my grip, my body flung backward. For one suspended moment, I'm airborne, weightless, disconnected. Then, impact.

A searing pain explodes in my head as I strike the ground. The world spins in dizzying, nauseating circles. I try to move, to cry out, but my body lies unresponsive, a broken marionette.

The last thing I see before darkness claims me is the sunset sky above, achingly beautiful, utterly indifferent.

Then silence. Then darkness.

Chapter 64

Alex

My heart pounds in my chest as I run breathlessly toward the woods east of the ranch. Rosie's message echoes in my head, mixing with my worst fears.

From the device connected to our app, we can see that all the horses are out of the enclosure. Consequently, we don't even waste time going to saddle one to be faster. The mini quads are on the other side of the ranch, so we'd lose just as much time. In silent agreement, we all run on foot, hoping to make it in time. I don't understand what happened; I was the last one to enter the stables. Horse training is my responsibility. Diego was at his training on the other side with the bulls. Fran had the day off. Chris was in the office reviewing the season's scheduled competitions. Ergo, I was the one who locked up the horses, and despite my mind being crowded with thoughts of Rosie, I'm one hundred percent certain I locked them in.

The only other staff members who have access are the veterinarians and sports managers. But right now, that doesn't matter. The only thing that matters is that Rosie is riding a horse chasing another one, and she doesn't have the expertise to do it. And all the horses are out.

"Let's split up!" I shout to Chris, Fran, and Diego. "Cover more ground!" I see their nods of agreement before they head in different directions.

In an instant, I'm alone with my fear.

"Faster, damn it!" I mentally scream at myself, pushing my body to its limit. The cool evening air burns my lungs, but I don't slow down. I can't. Trees whiz by in my peripheral vision as I enter the woods. "Rosie!" I shout, my voice broken from running and terror. Only silence answers me, amplifying the anguish that grips me.

I stumble on a root, falling hard. The sharp pain in my knee is immediately overshadowed by desperation.

I get up in an instant, ignoring the blood trickling down my leg. "Rosie! Where are you?" My voice echoes among the trees, desperate and trembling.

Every passing second is agony. My mind produces increasingly terrible scenarios.

Rosie hurt, Rosie in danger, Rosie needing me and I'm not there.

"Please, please, let her be okay," I whisper, a desperate prayer to whoever might be listening.

I try to force my mind not to remember past traumas.

I try to file away the memory of my father lying lifeless on the ground.

I try not to think about the fact that if Rosie had the brilliant idea to saddle a horse, it's because I taught her how to do it.

I try not to think about our last conversation.

I try not to think that the love of my life is terribly and frighteningly in danger.

I try to focus on finding her.

Then, in the distance, I glimpse something. A flash of color among the green undergrowth. My heart skips a beat. I rush in that direction, pushing myself beyond every limit. When I finally reach the spot, the world seems to stop.

Rosie is lying on the ground, motionless. A trickle of blood runs from her temple.

"No, no, no, no," I repeat like a mantra, falling to my knees beside her. My hands shake violently as I try to check her pulse.

It can't be.

Not again.

Not her.

"Rosie, princess, please, open your eyes," I beg, tears blurring my vision. "You can't leave me, not like this. We promised each other forever."

Panic threatens to overwhelm me as I wait, in endless agony, for any sign of life. At this moment, I would give anything to see her open her eyes, to hear her voice.

"I love you, Rosie," I whisper, my voice broken by sobs. "Please, stay with me. I can't lose you. I can't."

With trembling hands, I pull out my phone to call for help, praying it's not too late. Time seems to stretch while I wait for an answer, each second an eternity of terror and desperate hope.

"Hello, emergency," finally answers a voice on the other end of the line. The words come out in a chaotic torrent, my voice broken with anguish. "I need an ambulance, now! My girlfriend... she fell from a horse. She's not responding, there's blood... oh God, please hurry!"

While giving the coordinates, I don't take my eyes off Rosie. Her face, so pale and still, breaks my heart. I gently caress her cheek, as if my touch could bring her back to me. The voice on the other end assures me they'll send someone soon but meanwhile bombards me with useless questions.

"She's showing no signs of life, her birthday doesn't matter, just send someone now!" I shout desperately. After an eternity, I end the conversation with the assurance they'll arrive with a red code.

"They're coming, my love," I whisper, my voice trembling. "Hold on, please." The minutes drag like hours. Each of Rosie's breaths, weak but present, is both a relief and torture. I hold her tight, trying to protect her, to transmit my strength to her.

"You can't leave me," I murmur against her hair. "We still have so much to live together, Rosie. Please, fight. Fight to live... I only care that you live."

Tears stream down my face, falling silently onto her motionless face. Remorse grips me, mixing with fear. What if these were our last hours together? What if I never had the chance to make up for my mistakes, to tell her how deeply I love her?

"I'm sorry," I sob, holding her tighter. "I'm sorry for everything. I promise if you wake up, if you stay with me, I'll spend the rest of my life making you happy. Just... don't leave me. I can't live in a world without you, Rosie."

In the distance, finally, I hear sirens. Relief washes over me like a wave, but fear doesn't loosen its grip. "Did you hear that, princess? They're coming," I say, my voice broken with emotion. "Just a little longer, hold on just a little longer."

As the ambulance lights illuminate the woods, I pray like I've never prayed in my life. I pray for a miracle, for a second chance, for the life of the woman I love more than myself. I even pray to give my life in exchange if there's no other way. I pray without knowing who I'm praying to... because I'm not actually religious. I pray to the universe, to nature... I don't even know.

"I love you, Rosie," I whisper one last time before the paramedics reach us. "Please, come back to me."

The sound of sirens tears through the silence of the woods, growing louder and louder. Blue and red lights begin to filter through the trees, illuminating Rosie's pale face with spectral glows. "Over here!" I shout with all the strength I have left. "We're here!"

In moments, the paramedics emerge from the undergrowth, followed by Chris, Fran, and Diego. Their faces are masks of worry and shock when they see the scene before them. "Please," I beg the paramedics as they quickly approach. "Save her. Please, save her."

I reluctantly move away from Rosie, allowing them to work. My legs give way and I fall to my knees, unable to take my eyes off the motionless body of the woman I love.

Chris reaches me, putting a hand on my shoulder. "Hey bro," he says softly, "let them do their job."

But I can't move. I can't even breathe as I watch the medics check Rosie's vital signs, apply a cervical collar, prepare her for transport. "Weak pulse but present," I hear one of them say. "Possible head trauma. We need to move fast."

Those words hit me like a punch to the stomach. Head trauma. Images of Rosie, smiling and full of life, violently clash with the reality before me.

"I'm coming with her," I ask, my voice barely a whisper. The paramedic makes a negative sign. "No accompaniers. You can follow us separately."

As they lift Rosie onto the stretcher, I stand up with Chris's help. My legs are shaking, and not just from the earlier fall.

"No way," I say, gathering all my remaining energy.

"Bro, look at me," Fran says. "We'll follow them by car, if you protest we'll only lose time."

I nod mechanically, unable to formulate a response.

I follow the stretcher out of the woods, eyes fixed on Rosie, afraid she might disappear if I look away even for a second.

The sirens scream into the night as we race toward the hospital, taking Rosie away from me. And meanwhile, my heart breaks completely.

The guys guide me to the nearest car. I follow them as if in an out-of-body experience.

Every second feels like an eternity. Every kilometer, an infinite distance.
Tears flow desperately down my face.
At this moment, I would give anything to see her eyes open, to hear her voice.

Chapter 65

Alex

The ambulance lights slice through the darkness of the woods like blue and red blades, creating dancing shadows that seem to chase us. The sound of the siren pierces the night, a constant scream that reflects the anguish gripping my heart.

Diego is driving, and we've broken every possible speed limit to catch up with the ambulance and allow me to be as close as possible to Rosie. I vaguely hear my brothers occasionally trying to say something to keep me anchored to planet earth, but they're shaken too. The tragedy of my father is still alive and present within each of us. Chris is squeezing my shoulder tightly. He, more than anyone, remembers well. He was with me that day. He's always been with me. I keep my hands clenched into fists, I'm a bundle of nerves.

Finally, we arrive at the hospital, and I catch a glimpse of Rosie as they wheel her out of the ambulance. I rush as close as I can. Her pale face is intermittently illuminated by the flashing lights, giving her an almost spectral appearance.

"Pressure dropping," I hear a paramedic say, the voice muffled as if coming from far away.

Those words mix with the whirlwind of thoughts in my mind. Images of smiling Rosie alternate with the sight of her motionless body. The memory of our first kiss clashes with the fear of never being able to kiss her again.

Someone bumps into me, making me startle. For a moment, I think I see Rosie's eyes moving under her eyelids.

"Rosie?" I whisper, full of hope. But there's no response.

Everyone begins a desperate run. We follow them. The constant beep of machines, the urgent voices of paramedics - everything merges into a single background noise to my silent mantra: "Please live. Please live. Please live." Remorse mixes with fear, creating a toxic cocktail of emotions that threatens to overwhelm me. But I can't break down. Not now. Rosie needs me to be strong.

And then in a whirlwind of movement and urgent voices, Rosie is taken away from me. The hospital doors slide open with a hiss. Rosie is surrounded by a swarm of doctors and nurses.

"Female, 29 years old, head trauma..." The paramedic's words are lost in the chaos. "Rosie!" I shout, trying to make my way through the medical staff.

Strong hands grab me, holding me back. "Bro, stop!" Chris's voice penetrates the fog of my mind, but I can't process it completely. "Let me go! I need to be with her!" I struggle, trying to break free from my friends' grip. "You can't follow her now," says Fran, his voice a distant rumble. "Let the doctors do their job."

The world around me becomes blurry, as if I'm looking through a fogged glass. I see Rosie's stretcher moving further and further away, swallowed by the sliding doors of the emergency room. "Rosie!" I shout again, my voice broken with desperation. The voices around me blend into an indistinct buzz. Fragments of sentences reach me, but I can't make sense of them.

"... in good hands..."

"... we have to wait..."

"... Alex, can you hear me?"

My legs give way and I find myself on my knees on the cold hospital floor. My breath breaks into uncontrollable sobs.

"I lost her," I mumble, more to myself than to others. "I lost her again."

The world continues to move around me, but I'm paralyzed. The ambulance lights continue to flash in my short-term memories, creating dancing shadows that seem to mock my pain. I vaguely feel Chris and Diego helping me up, guiding me toward the entrance of the waiting room. Their voices are a constant buzz, words of comfort that fail to penetrate the bubble of desperation I'm trapped in.

As we enter the room, I take one last look at the emergency room doors, now closed. Rosie is in there somewhere, fighting for her life. And I'm here, helpless, with nothing but regrets and prayers. "Please, Rosie," I whisper, as I let myself be guided and pushed toward a chair. "Don't leave me. Not like this."

Chapter 66

Alex

The clock on the waiting room wall ticks like a hammer striking my skull. Each passing second is agony, a constant reminder that Rosie is in there, fighting for her life, while I remain here, powerless.

The hours drag on in a blur of coffee, uncomfortable chairs, and oppressive silence. Chris, Fran, and Diego are still here with me, silent presences offering comfort I can't feel. Occasionally they try to speak, but their words of encouragement slide off me like water on glass.

The sound of hurried footsteps breaks the waiting room's silence. I look up to see Robert, Rosie's father, enter with eyes full of fear and concern. Behind him, Maria and Aunt Tina, their faces pale and drawn. Ethan, Rosie's best friend, follows closely, looking lost and frightened.

"Alex," Robert's voice is hoarse, "what happened? How's my daughter?" I stand up, my legs trembling from exhaustion and anxiety. "We... we don't know yet," I answer, my voice barely a whisper. "The doctors haven't told us anything definitive."

Robert runs a hand over his face, anguish evident in every gesture. Maria places a hand on his shoulder, trying to offer comfort. Aunt Tina, for once, is silent, her usual humor swept away by the gravity of the situation. Ethan approaches me, his eyes glistening.

Val, Lexy, and Aurora arrive shortly after, joining the group in silence. Their faces are masks of worry and fear.

Max... I don't know where he is.

Aurora runs to embrace me the moment she sees me. I can see her concern as she squeezes me tight with her slender arms. She was only four when I became part of her family, and she welcomed me with the carefree joy that only children possess. Now she's grown. She's 24... but to Chris and me, she'll always be our little girl.

Despite us being ten years older, she's always been good at lifting our spirits and solving our problems. Unfortunately, there's not much she can do this time, but I appreciate her embrace.

"Big brother... Rosie will pull through. She's strong," she tells me, trying to hold me tighter. I let out a sob and lean on her shoulder. Chris joins us and wraps both of us in his strong, large arms. We stay like that for a while, silent and holding each other close, just like when we were children. Then Val joins us too.

Gradually, we all gather together, a family united by fear and hope. The silence is broken only by the ticking clock and occasional muffled sobs.

The hours pass, slow and painful. Every time the door opens, we all look up, hoping for news, for anything that might ease this terrible wait. But the silence persists.

My gaze wanders around the waiting room, but I can't really focus on anything. The faces around me are blurred, indistinct. I hear hushed voices, fragments of conversations I can't fully comprehend.

My world has narrowed to this: the waiting, the terror, and the constant thought of Rosie. I can't process anything else. The people around me might as well be ghosts for all I can interact with them. I'm trapped in a bubble of fear and anxiety, unable to reach or be reached.

I feel like I'm drowning. Each breath is a struggle. Every second without news is torture. The weight of guilt and fear threatens to crush me.

Rosie, I think, closing my eyes to hold back tears, *please hold on. We all need you. I need you.*

But the silence continues, relentless and cruel, as we wait for news that could change everything.

In my confused state, a movement catches my attention. It's Lexy. For a moment, her face hardens with an expression I can't fully decipher. Then, just as quickly, she catches herself and turns away.

I unconsciously follow her earlier line of sight and, across the waiting room, I see him. Max. He's leaning against the wall, arms crossed over his chest, expression impassive. I hadn't noticed him before, lost as I was in my thoughts.

Max has never been one to offer comfort or openly show his emotions. He's always been more of a man of action, ready to step in when needed. Yet, as I watch him, I see something change in his gaze. For a brief moment, his mask of imperturbability seems to crack.

To my surprise, he pushes off from the wall and walks toward me. His stride is purposeful, his posture rigid. Max stops right in front of me. His eyes meet mine for a brief instant before dropping.

"Everything will be fine," he murmurs so quietly that only I can hear. "I contacted the best specialists. Had them flown here as quickly as possible."

His words hit me like a punch to the stomach. Not for their content, but for the simple fact that Max spoke them. Max isn't the type to solve situations and then let you know about it. He's never been like that.

I realize he's telling me this only to try to reassure me. It's a surprisingly kind gesture from him, so out of character that for a moment I don't know how to react.

"Thank you," I finally manage to whisper, my voice hoarse from hours of silence.

Max nods briefly, then moves to leave. Before turning completely, though, I notice his eyes dart quickly to a point behind me. I follow his gaze and see Lexy, now sitting with the other girls. It's such a quick, imperceptible movement that if I hadn't been paying attention, I would have surely missed it.

Chapter 67

Alex

The oppressive silence of the waiting room is suddenly and finally broken by the sound of opening doors.

We all look up abruptly, our hearts beating in unison with a mixture of hope and terror. A doctor in a white coat emerges, his expression serious but not grim.

"Family of Rosalie Thorne?" he asks, looking around.

Robert stands up immediately, followed by Maria and Aunt Tina. I remain paralyzed in my chair, unable to move, fearing what we might hear.

"I'm her father," Robert says, his voice trembling. "How is my daughter?"

The doctor takes a deep breath before speaking.

"Miss Thorne is stable at the moment. She suffered a head trauma, but we managed to reduce the intracranial pressure. She's now in a medically induced coma to allow her brain to recover."

A collective sigh of relief fills the room, but the tension doesn't completely dissipate.

"When will she wake up?" I ask, finally finding the strength to stand and approach. The doctor looks at me with understanding eyes.

"It's difficult to say with certainty. It could be a matter of days or... it might take longer. Every case is different."

His words fall heavily upon us.

Rosie is alive, but not out of danger. Relief mingles with a new wave of concern.

"Can we see her?" Maria asks, squeezing Robert's hand.

The doctor nods. "Yes, but only two people at a time and for brief periods. It's important that she remains in a calm environment." Robert and Maria exchange a meaningful look. Then Robert turns to me, his eyes tired but kind.

"Alex," he says softly, "would you like to go in with me?"

The lump in my throat prevents me from speaking. I look at Maria, feeling guilty for taking her place, but she nods encouragingly. "Go," she whispers, "Rosie would want you to be there."

I nod, grateful for their understanding, and follow Robert and the doctor through the hospital corridors. Each step seems to weigh a ton. My heart pounds in my chest, a mix of anxiety and hope. I feel Robert putting an arm around my shoulders and pulling me closer to him. I've always had an excellent professional relationship with him, and sometimes we've even had drinks together.

Lately, however, I've been consumed by my feelings for Rosie and then by the wave of work leading up to the competitions. I suddenly feel guilty for not telling Robert that I intended to get serious with his daughter.

The doctor stops in front of a door and turns to us. "Please remember that the appearance might be shocking at first. There are many machines and tubes, but they're all necessary for her recovery."

With a final encouraging look, he opens the door. The constant beep of the heart monitor fills the room. Rosie lies motionless on the bed, surrounded by machines. A breathing tube extends from her mouth, and various cables are connected to her body. Her skin is pale, almost transparent under the fluorescent lights. I slowly approach the bed, my legs trembling. Robert stays back for a moment, giving me space.

"Rosie," I whisper, gently taking her hand. It's cold to the touch, but I can feel the faint pulse of her heartbeat. "I'm here, princess. We're here for you."

The tears I've been holding back for hours finally begin to flow. I cry silently, holding Rosie's hand as if it were a lifeline.

"Please come back to us," I murmur. "You have so many people who love you, who are waiting for you. I... I'm waiting for you."

I feel a hand on my shoulder. It's Robert, his eyes glistening but determined.

"She's strong," he says hoarsely. "Our Rosie is a fighter. She'll make it."

I nod, unable to speak.

For several minutes, we remain like this: united in silence, in pain, and in hope. The constant beep of the heart monitor is the only sound in the room, a reminder that, despite everything, Rosie is fighting.

Chapter 68

Alex

Twenty-four hours have passed.

Twenty-four endless hours since Rosie entered this room, and still she hasn't awakened.

The constant beep of the heart monitor has become the backdrop of my existence, a rhythm that marks the seconds, minutes, hours of this unbearable wait.

I've obtained permission to keep vigil here, by her side. I couldn't bear the thought of leaving her alone, not even for a moment.

The hospital staff has tried to convince me to take a break, to eat something, to rest, but how could I? How could I move away from her when any breath could be the one that wakes her?

Time dissolves into itself, hours bleeding into one endless vigil. The sun sets and rises again, but in here, in this hospital room, time seems to have stopped.

A hand finds my shoulder, warm and steady. I turn, my vision swimming into focus. Chris stands there, concern etched deep in the lines of his face.

"Alex," he says gently, "you need to rest a bit. You can't go on like this."

I shake my head, turning back to look at Rosie. "I can't leave her," I murmur.

Chris sighs. "I know, bro. But you won't be any help to her if you collapse. Go home, take a shower, eat something. I'll stay here with her."

I hesitate. The thought of moving away even for a moment terrifies me.

"I promise I'll call you immediately if there are any changes," Chris insists.

Finally, yielding more to exhaustion than reason, I nod. I stand up slowly, my legs numb from hours of sitting.

I lean over Rosie, brushing her forehead with a light kiss. "I'll be back soon, princess," I whisper.

The journey home is a confused blur.

When I push open my apartment door, her presence hits me with physical force. She's everywhere - in the throw pillow askew on the couch where she last sat, in the coffee mug she left on the counter, in the very air that still seems to hold molecules of her perfume.

The shower's heat penetrates my muscle but can't touch the cold core of fear inside me. Water streams down my face, mixing with tears I thought I'd exhausted. Afterward, as I pull on fresh clothes, my eyes catch on a photograph perched on the bedroom shelf. It's us, caught in a moment of perfect joy during our camping trip. The self-timer captured more truth than any professional photographer could have - Rosie seated between my legs, my arms wrapped around her like I could keep her safe forever, both of us laughing against a backdrop of mountains. Her smile in the photo is incandescent, her eyes holding all the light in the world.

"Please," I murmur to her image, "don't leave me."

I eat something without even realizing what it is. The food has no taste, it's just fuel for a body that wants nothing more than to return to her.

As I'm about to leave, my phone vibrates.

My heart leaps into my throat.

It's a message from Chris:

Chris:Come quickly. Rosie moved.

The journey to the hospital exists only in fragments of memory. The corridors stretch endlessly before me as I run toward her room, my heart a wild drum in my chest.

I burst in, breathless. Chris stands beside the bed, his face painted with cautious hope.

"What happened?" I demand, rushing to Rosie's side.

"She moved her fingers," Chris says. "The doctor says it might be a good sign."

I take Rosie's hand in mine, holding it with the delicacy one might afford a butterfly's wing.

"Rosie? Rosie, can you hear me? It's me, princess. It's Alex."

For a moment that stretches like eternity, there is nothing. Then, so faint I might have dreamed it, I feel a whisper of pressure against my fingers.

My heart forgets how to beat. "Rosie?" I breathe her name like a prayer, my voice trembling with raw emotion. Slowly, so slowly I fear my mind is conjuring phantoms of hope, her eyelids begin to flutter.

"I'll get the doctor," Chris says, slipping quickly from the room.

I remain anchored to her hand, my eyes fixed on her face as if looking away might break this fragile spell.

"Don't worry, my love," I murmur. "I'm here. I've got you. Take all the time you need."

And then, finally, her eyes open.

Confused, disoriented, but open.

My heart explodes with joy and relief, a supernova of emotion in my chest.

"Hi," I whisper, tears streaming freely down my face. "Welcome back, princess."

Chapter 69

Rosie

The hospital seems like a distant dream now, days after my awakening. The doctors have declared me fully recovered, though it appears someone hasn't quite received that particular memo.

"Alex," I say, watching him dart to my side with a glass of water, trying to mask my fond exasperation, "I can actually manage to pour my own water."

"I know, I know," he says, yet still extends the glass toward me with those worried eyes. "It's just —"

"That you need to take care of me," I finish, letting warmth seep into my smile. "And I love you for it. But I'm okay now. Really."

He nods, but I see it there—the shadow that flickers across his face, the echo of fear that hasn't quite released its grip.

The girls told me everything: how he maintained his vigil by my bedside, how he refused food and sleep, how he spoke to me endlessly while I lay unconscious.

The thought of his devotion makes my heart ache with a bittersweet mix of love and regret.

"Hey," I murmur, reaching for his hand. The contact grounds us both. "I'm right here. Solid and real and not going anywhere."

His fingers intertwine with mine, seeking anchor. "I know," he whispers, voice rough with memory. "But when I thought I'd lost you—"

"But you didn't," I cut in gently. "I'm here, and what I need most is for us to find our way back to normal. Can you help me with that?"

Finally, a real smile breaks across his face, reaching all the way to his eyes. "Okay."

My mind wanders to all I've missed: the final touches for Dad and Maria's wedding, the apparently legendary bachelorette party that the girls are dying to tell me about.

Yet I'm grateful to be here at all, present for the wedding itself.

"Two days," I muse aloud. "I can hardly believe Dad's getting married this Friday. And there's still so much—"

"That's completely handled," Alex interrupts smoothly. "The girls have managed everything. Your only job is to show up and celebrate."

The mention of recent events brings to mind something that's been nagging at me.

"You know," I begin carefully, watching his reaction, "I'm still processing what you told me about Maximilian."

Alex stiffens slightly at the mention of his friend, but nods. Thinking about the fact that Max had specialists flown in for me makes me feel... confused.

"It's strange," I say thoughtfully. "I can't figure him out. One moment he seems so... cold, and the next he does something like this."

Alex sighs. "Max is... complicated. But in his own way, he cares about us. Even if he'd never admit it."

I nod slowly. "And then there's this whole thing with Lexy. I don't understand why he hates her so much."

"That's one of the universe's greatest mysteries," Alex admits.

I notice the subtle shift in his demeanor, the way his shoulders tighten, how his eyes grow distant.

He's working himself up to something, and I think I know what it is. Before I can speak, he finds his voice.

"Rosie... about what happened with Max, with the whole Los Angeles situation..." he pauses, wrestling with the words. "I'm truly sorry. I never meant—"

"Hey," I interrupt, squeezing his hand.

We talk it through, acknowledging that arguments are part of any relationship. We're both navigating these waters for the first time, learning to sail together.

After all, love doesn't come with an instruction manual. We're writing our own as we go along.

We're lying on the couch, cocooned in the soothing silence of the house. Alex holds me close, his steady, warm breath brushing against my hair. This recovery period has been all about moments like these, me being pampered beyond belief and Alex tending to my every need with infinite care.

But I crave more. He hasn't touched me intimately yet, and his restraint is wearing thin on my patience. I want my Alex back—the cowboy version, the one who doesn't hesitate to take what he wants.

It's time to act. I shift slowly in his arms, letting my hands drift along the hard lines of his chest. He watches me, his brows furrowing in mild confusion, but he stays silent. Smiling coyly, I lean in and press a soft kiss to his lips.

He kisses me back, hesitant at first, but I'm not stopping there. Emboldened, I deepen the kiss, teasing his lips apart and slipping my tongue into his mouth. He doesn't stop me, but I can feel the tension radiating from his body.

I move closer, tangling my legs with his as the heat between us intensifies. My body presses against his, and I can feel the unmistakable hardness of his arousal. Still, he holds back.

His hands find my hips, gripping them as if to steady me—or stop me. But I have no intention of stopping. Straddling his lap, I settle my weight against him and start to move, slow and deliberate. The friction sends a shiver through me, and I hear the rough hitch of his breath.

"Rosie..." he murmurs, his voice hoarse, yet laced with resistance.

I tilt my head, giving him a mischievous smile.

"Come on, cowboy. Aren't you my part-time doctor? Shouldn't you be taking better care of your patient?"

He shakes his head, but the darkness in his eyes betrays him, smoldering with unspoken desire. "Rosie, it's too soon. I don't want to hurt you."

This man, he makes me feel cherished, desired, and utterly exasperated all at once. Leaning in, my nose brushing his, I lower my voice to a whisper.

"I'm fine." I sigh dramatically, rolling my eyes. "And you know what else? I'm yours. I want you to touch me, Alex. I need to feel alive. I need *you*."

He swallows hard, his gaze fixed on mine, a storm of emotions swirling within. I know he's fighting a losing battle with himself, and I don't plan to make it easy.

My hands slip beneath his shirt, trailing over the taut muscles of his abdomen. I tug the fabric upward, pulling it over his head to reveal his warm, bare skin.

"Rosie..." he tries again, but his voice trembles, his resolve crumbling.

"Shh," I hush him, capturing his lips once more, this time pouring everything I have into the kiss. My hands roam over his chest, while my hips move rhythmically against him, igniting sparks that make us both gasp.

At last, his hands surrender, gripping my hips with a possessive force that sends my pulse racing. He guides my movements, pressing me harder against him, and his control begins to slip. His hands slide lower, gripping my ass firmly, his touch branding me.

His fingers tighten, his breathing deepens, and I see it in his eyes—the dam is about to break. A thrill of anticipation rushes through me as I lean forward, grazing his earlobe with my teeth.

"So, doctor," I murmur, my voice a sultry purr, "don't you think your patient needs a more... *thorough* treatment?"

Alex groans softly, the sound sending a delicious shiver down my spine. His hands trail over my body, slow and deliberate, igniting a fire beneath my skin.

"Rosie," he whispers, his voice gravelly with need.

I bite my lip, meeting his gaze as I press harder against him, the friction drawing a low moan from both of us.

He closes his eyes, breathing deeply as if summoning the last vestiges of control. When he opens them again, I see the change—a spark of surrender that sets my heart racing.

"Alright," he says, his voice low and edged with hunger. "If you want to play, I guess I'll have to show you just how good of a doctor I can be."

A jolt of excitement courses through me as Alex effortlessly lifts me into his arms, carrying me to the bedroom. He sets me down on the bed with a tenderness that contrasts with the fierce intensity in his eyes. Kneeling above me, his hands skim my sides, his body radiating heat.

"So, Miss Rosie," he begins, his tone teasing but laced with authority. "How long have you been experiencing this... *problem*?"

I smile, my heart pounding as I run a hand through my hair, locking my gaze with his.

"Oh, doctor, it's been building for a while. A heat so intense I just can't cool it. Do you think you can help me?"

Alex leans in close, his lips hovering just above mine. "And where exactly do you feel this... *heat*?"

"Everywhere," I breathe, my voice thick with desire. "But especially here." I take his hand, guiding it down my body to rest just below the waistband of my silk shorts.

He exhales sharply, his resolve visibly faltering. His hand moves slowly, tracing lines over my bare skin, making me tremble under his touch. "This seems... serious," he murmurs, his warm breath caressing my neck.

"It is," I whisper, letting out a soft moan as his lips graze my collarbone.

"I think we'll need to remove these shorts for a... better examination," he says, his tone low, dangerously seductive.

Both his hands slide beneath the waistband of my shorts, and my breath hitches. With a single, deliberate motion, he pulls them off, his lips curving into a knowing smile as he watches my reaction.

"Doctor," I manage to say, my voice trembling, "I think we need to take this treatment... deeper."

Alex chuckles, the sound low and intoxicating, reverberating through me. His fingers trail over my thighs, slipping inside me with slow, deliberate precision.

"Oh, Rosie," he murmurs, his voice dark and full of promise. "We're going to go as deep as it takes."

And with that, Alex surrenders completely, unleashing the raw intensity he's been holding back.

Chapter 70

Alex

Rosie is still asleep beside me, curled against my chest. Her cascade of copper hair covers me. Her breathing is slow, regular, and her warmth envelops me like a blanket.

I never thought I could be grateful for such seemingly ordinary things as the warmth of a body or slow, regular breaths... but since I touched Rosie's ice-cold skin when she was fighting between life and death, since I spent hours trying to ensure she was breathing... all of this is more than special now. I am more than grateful.

It had been a while since we'd spent such a passionate night together. It was spectacular, though I must admit I was terrified it was too soon.

I've been so scared lately that sex was the last thing on my mind.

I was just frightened for my Rosie.

My phone vibrates on the nightstand, breaking the spell. I move slowly so as not to wake her, trying not to interrupt that perfect peace. I pick up the phone and glance at the screen:

an email from Chris. **Come to the office. We need to talk.**

I stiffen. I know that when Chris is this direct, it's never just a casual conversation. I rise carefully, arranging the blankets around her body. She barely moves, her face relaxed in the abandonment of sleep. I can't help myself: I lean down to brush her forehead with a light kiss.

"See you later, princess," I whisper before leaving the room.

Chris's office is as always a mix of practicality and controlled chaos. The desk is covered with stacks of files, charts, and empty coffee mugs, but everything is arranged with a precision that reflects his way of working. He sits behind the desk, his cowboy hat resting on a nearby chair, reading a document with a serious expression.

"Morning, bro," he says, looking up. He gestures for me to enter.

"Hey," I respond, settling into the chair facing him. "What's going on? I got your email."

He leans back in his chair and interlaces his fingers.

"So..." he says thoughtfully, searching through some files. "So far, Fran and I have covered for you... now I expect you to come back to work. The competition season is demanding, and we can't afford distractions. We have too many expectations on the ranch, and too many people counting on us."

He pushes a folder towards me. "Here are the details of the colts racing this year. Take a look, study them, and start working on them immediately. We have little time to prepare them."

I open the folder, quickly scanning the pages. Names, statistics, training sheets—a world I missed more than I thought.

I nod, clenching my jaw. Only now do I realize how tired Chris is. He has deep shadows under his eyes, and I can see his exhaustion even though he tries to remain focused and invincible.

I immediately feel guilty.

"Bro... I'm sorry if I..." he doesn't let me finish.

He waves his hand, interrupting me immediately. "Don't even think about it. I can only imagine how I would have felt if something like this had happened to Val. We covered for you well anyway," he says with a half-joking smirk. Then he sighs and adds, "In any case, that's not why I called you here."

I see him stiffen and become more serious.

Okay, something's wrong. He sighs, leaning on the desk. "It's about the horses that got out the night of Rosie's accident."

I stiffen. That thought has been tormenting me for days. I know all the horses were brought back and are fine. Chris immediately raised the alarm to other staff members while we were rushing to the hospital.

"What did you discover?"

"It wasn't an accident," he says gravely. "Someone tampered with the gates."

His statement hits me like a punch in the stomach. "Impossible. I checked those fences myself."

"I know," he responds, understanding and determination in his eyes. "That's why I asked Max to investigate. We discovered the responsible party is Diego's sports manager. The one who managed his bull riding competitions."

I'm stunned. "Diego's manager? What the hell does he have to do with our horses?"

Chris purses his lips. "He was an infiltrator. He wanted to sabotage our equestrian sector. Max found evidence he was planning to target the bulls in the next competition. He probably hit the horse sector first to avoid suspicion..."

My blood boils. "And Diego? Does he know?"

"He's been informed," Chris responds. "He's devastated. He trusted him, Alex. He was his right-hand man and a vital figure in his career. But at least we stopped him in time. Max has sorted everything out and alerted the authorities. He's out of the game. Obviously, we'll proceed legally."

I exhale slowly, trying to calm down. "But we're still in a mess."

Chris nods. "No need to tell you how... we're examining every employee, we don't know who we can trust anymore. We're without a sports coordinator that we desperately need..." another sigh, then a half-smile "don't worry, we'll find a way".

Chris has always been a force of nature. But he's not alone in this. He's my brother, and I and everyone else will do everything to help.

I look him straight in the eyes. "You're not alone, bro. I'm a hundred percent in."

A tired smile spreads across his face. "I know, Alex. I trust you. You're my brother, and I don't forget that."

I stand up with the folder in hand, ready to go home and immerse myself in work. But before I leave, Chris calls me back. "Alex?"
"Yes?"
"Give my regards to Rosie."
I can't help but smile. "I will."

Chapter 71

Rosie

I wake up with a smile on my lips, aware that today is the big day: Dad's wedding to Maria.

I've always loved weddings.

I've never had a large family or many friends, so I haven't attended many weddings in my life. The only time I went to one, I was a child and accompanied my father to a colleague's wedding. At that time, my father was still living in America with me. This upcoming wedding will be Italian-style, and I'm beyond excited about the idea.

Obviously, the fact that it's my father's wedding makes it even more special. I'm truly happy to know that he has finally found peace. I saw him sad, defeated, and apathetic for far too long after my mother's death. Moreover... if I now have a large family, many friends, and have found the love of my life, it's because of him.

I get out of bed, feeling excitement grow inside me. Through the window, I see the ranch's meadow transformed into a floral paradise. Sunflowers, Maria's favorites, tower everywhere, their yellow corollas seeming to capture and reflect the sunlight. Among them, patches of lavender and wild daisies create a colorful carpet that stretches as far as the eye can see.

After giving a quick kiss to Alex, still half-asleep, I head towards the main house. It took me an eternity to free myself from his strong, heavy embrace.

And... have you ever seen Alex when he's half-awake?

He holds me tight, it's like talking to someone drunk, and the more I try to move, the more he curls up even closer.

I adore him.

I love him.

The fresh morning air caresses my face, bringing with it the sweet scent of flowers and the more pungent aroma of freshly cut grass.

Entering the house, I'm welcomed by a jubilation of laughter and excited chatter. Val, Lexy, and Aurora are already at work, surrounded by an organized chaos of clothes, accessories, and beauty products.

"Here she is, finally!" exclaims Val, running to meet me and embrace me.

"Hey, it's not my fault Alex didn't want to let me go," I respond, laughing, returning the embrace.

"Oh, poor thing," Lexy jokes, pouring me a glass of champagne. "It must be terrible to have such a devoted boyfriend."

I accept the glass with gratitude, feeling my heart swell with love thinking of Alex.

Maria emerges from the bedroom, wrapped in a silk bathrobe, her hair still damp from the shower. Her face glows with happiness and anticipation.

Just then, the door opens, and Aunt Tina makes her entrance, dragging an enormous bag that seems about to explode.

"Girls, I'm here!" she announces, breathless from the effort. "I've brought everything necessary to survive an outdoor wedding!"

Curious, I approach to take a look at the bag's contents. Aunt Tina begins to extract an impressive number of bottles and boxes.

"Look, dear," she explains to me, "here are the antihistamines for pollen, here's the cortisone in case of bee stings, here are the refreshing wipes in case it gets too hot..."

I can't help but laugh. "Aunt Tina, do you really think you need all this?"

"You never know, darling!" she responds with conviction. "Better to prevent than to cure!"

At that moment, Ethan makes his triumphant entrance, loaded with makeup cases and accessories. "Good morning, beauties! Who's ready for a red carpet transformation?"

Maria smiles nervously. "I think I definitely need one, Ethan."

While Ethan begins to set up his makeup station, Aunt Tina looks at him with admiration. "Oh, Ethan! I saw your latest tutorial on how to hide dark circles. A masterpiece!"

Ethan takes a theatrical bow.

"Thank you, dear. The art of makeup has no secrets for me."

Suddenly, a lively music starts playing from Aunt Tina's bag. She jumps, then smiles.

"Oh, it's the ringtone I set to remind me to take my pills!"

Instead of taking the pills, however, Aunt Tina starts moving to the rhythm. Ethan, infected by the enthusiasm, joins her.

"Come on, girls!" Aunt Tina exclaims, cheerfully wiggling. "A little movement will do us all good!"

Before I know it, the room transforms into an impromptu dance floor. Aunt Tina and Ethan lead the dance, with exaggerated movements and contagious laughter.

I adore them!

Even Maria, despite her nervousness, gets swept up in the dancing.

Meanwhile, Aunt Tina continues to list the remedies she's brought, all while continuing to dance. "I even have mineral salts, in case someone feels faint from emotion!"

I can't help but smile, watching this surreal scene. Aunt Tina with her bag full of "remedies", Ethan alternating makeup tips with dance moves, and all of us getting caught up in this sudden joy.

In the midst of this joyful chaos, I realize how fortunate I am to have these people in my life. Each of them, with their own eccentricities and talents, is making this day even more special and unforgettable.

While the impromptu dance settles, I feel the excitement for my surprise to Alex growing inside me. I bite my lip, trying to hold back a smile.

"Guys," I say, lowering my voice as if about to reveal a state secret, "I need your help."

Val, Lexy, and Aurora approach, curious. Even Aunt Tina pauses her dancing to listen.

"I want to surprise Alex before the ceremony," I explain, feeling butterflies in my stomach at the mere thought. "But I need a way to get him to the meadow behind our cabin without arousing suspicion."

Lexy's eyes light up. "Oh, I love surprises! What do you have in mind?"

While Ethan starts working on my hair, I explain my idea.

After some discussion, we decide the best approach is for me to send him a message myself. Something simple and natural that won't raise any suspicions.

With slightly trembling hands from excitement, I take my phone and start typing:

Rosie: Can you meet me in the meadow behind our cabin? I need your help with something. Thanks!

I show the message to the girls for their approval. Lexy nods. "It's perfect, Rosie. It sounds like a completely normal request."

I press "Send" and feel my heart racing. Now there's no turning back.

As Ethan continues to prepare me, agitation grows inside me. What if Alex doesn't appreciate the surprise? What if he'd prefer to focus on the wedding preparations?

As if reading my thoughts, Val squeezes my hand.
"It'll go wonderfully, Rosie. Alex adores you." Then she adds with a sweet smile: "What you're doing is such a tender and romantic gesture. Alex will appreciate it enormously, I'm certain."
Her words calm me a bit, but my heart continues to pound in my chest.
Finally, I'm ready. I look in the mirror and barely recognize myself. Ethan has done an extraordinary job, enhancing my natural features without exaggerating.
"It's time," Lexy announces, looking at the clock. "Alex should already be on his way."
I take a deep breath, trying to gather all my courage.
"Go," Aurora encourages me with a smile. "We'll keep everything under control here. You go and drive your man crazy."
Rory has spoken little today. I've noticed that sometimes she seems a bit more absent. Sometimes she seems more uncomfortable... but it's probably just some anxiety about the upcoming graduation. She has the exam next week... but she still came for the wedding. She's adorable, and I make a mental note to pamper her more. I was incredibly nervous before my graduation, so I want to make her feel a bit better.
We'll all go with her for the big day, even though the ranch is going through tough times. The guys are drowning in extra work, and Alex has told me about the delicate situation.
But Rory is the baby of the family, and we'll be there for her.

With a final look of gratitude to my friends, I leave the main house and head towards the meadow behind our cabin. My heart is beating so hard I fear the entire ranch might hear it.

I hide behind a large tree, waiting with trepidation. Every second seems to last an eternity. Then, finally, I hear footsteps approaching and Alex's familiar voice calling my name.

It's the moment. I close my eyes, take a deep breath, and prepare to make my entrance.

Chapter 72

Alex

Rosie's message caught me off guard. *"I need your help with something."* Those words quicken my pace as I head toward the meadow behind our cabin. My heart pounds, a mix of worry and anticipation tightening my stomach.

Ever since Rosie's accident, I can't help but fear the worst whenever something unexpected happens. I know it's probably nothing, but the thought of losing her terrifies me more than anything else in the world.

I reach the meadow, my eyes scanning the area frantically. "Rosie?" I call, my voice betraying a hint of apprehension. "Rosie, where are you?"

And then I see her.

Time seems to stop. Rosie is running toward me, a radiant smile lighting up her face. Her red hair streams behind her in the wind, interwoven with tiny wildflowers. She's wearing a long white dress, flowing and airy, swirling around her like a cloud. Her bare feet barely touch the grass as she moves.

My breath catches in my throat. She looks exactly as she did in a dream I had long ago, back when I already loved her but hadn't realized it yet. That dream I've told her about so many times, confessing how much I adored it and how often it still lingers in my mind.

I can't believe my Rosie made that dream a reality. Emotion washes over me like a wave, leaving my heart trembling.

When she reaches me, I sweep her into my arms, lifting her off the ground. I spin her around, her crystalline laughter filling the air. Her scent, a blend of wildflowers and something uniquely *Rosie,* overwhelms me.

"Alex!" she exclaims through her laughter, clutching at my shoulders. "Put me down!"

But I don't want to let her go. I hold her tightly, feeling the steady beat of her heart against my chest. Then, slowly, we sink into the soft grass of the meadow.

I can't stop looking at her, touching her, as if to confirm she's real and not just another dream. My hands roam through her hair, over her face, along her arms.

"You're... you're stunning," I whisper, my voice hoarse with emotion. "I can't believe you did this for me."

Rosie smiles, her eyes shining with happiness. "I wanted to surprise you. I wanted us to have a moment just for ourselves before the madness of the day begins."

I can't hold back anymore. I kiss her, pouring every ounce of love, gratitude, and awe I feel into that kiss. My lips brush her cheeks, her forehead, her nose, always finding their way back to her soft, sweet mouth.

Rolling in the grass, I pull her close, laughing and kissing her alternately. Rosie's dress fans out around us like a white cloud, the flowers in her hair mingling with the grass.

"I love you," I murmur between kisses. "I love you so much, Rosie. You're my dream come true."

In this moment, with Rosie in my arms, surrounded by the beauty of the ranch and the promise of our future together, I feel like the luckiest man in the world.

But maybe… we can make this moment even more special. We still have a bit of time.

I glance around to ensure we're alone before ducking my head beneath the flowing fabric of her dress, ready to show my woman that her mischievous cowboy is truly back.

Rosie laughs at first, but those giggles soon give way to excitement and breathless moans.

A quick romp before the wedding? I'd say it's the perfect idea!

Chapter 73

Rosie

My heart still beats strongly as I adjust my dress, reflecting on the hour just spent with Alex. His reaction to my surprise was more than I had dared to hope. The way he looked at me, as if I were the embodiment of a dream... I will never forget it.

But now it's time to focus on the ceremony. The air vibrates with excitement as we gather at the garden entrance. Sunflowers, Maria's favorite flowers, are everywhere, creating a golden sea that sways gently in the breeze.

I look around, observing my friends in their bridesmaid dresses. We chose the same color for everyone - a warm gold that perfectly matches the sunflowers - but each dress is unique, designed to highlight each of our individual beauty.

Val looks like a forest fairy in her dress, fitted at the waist and wide on the skirt. Her petite figure is enhanced by the light fabric that waves with every movement, making her seem almost ethereal.

Aurora is stunning in her short pants outfit, enriched with golden and transparent veils that fall softly, giving the illusion of a floating, long skirt. The fluid fabric moves like liquid gold with every step, capturing light enchantingly. Her choice is as elegant as it is practical, allowing her to move freely in preparation for her performance. She's an excellent ballerina, and her show will be wonderful.

Lexy, always bold, chose a form-fitting dress that highlights her slender figure. The golden fabric shines on her skin, making her look like a living statue.

My dress, with its heart-shaped neckline that made me fall in love at first sight, makes me feel like a modern princess. The soft skirt moves gently around my legs, while the two side slits add a touch of sensuality and allow freedom of movement.

The guys all look splendid in their elegant suits, with details subtly echoing the golden color of our dresses. I can't help but notice Alex, his eyes shining as he looks at me with an intensity that makes my heart tremble. His gaze seems to tell me a thousand things without uttering a word.

Not far away, Chris can't take his eyes off Val. He looks at her as if she were the most precious thing in the world, covering her with his infinite love with every glance, every gesture. Val blushes slightly under his attention, but her radiant smile reveals how happy she is.

Ethan moves frenetically among the guests, his camera constantly shooting. He captures every detail, every emotion, creating a visual narrative of this special day.

In stark contrast to Ethan's energy, Max stands apart, his face as impassive as always. Fran and Diego try to involve him, telling jokes and amusing anecdotes, but their attempts seem to break against a wall of indifference. They can't even draw a smile from him. Diego glances towards the girls, but I'm not sure who the glances are directed at. They seem like furtive looks.

Lexy, beautiful in her golden dress, seems serene while chatting with other guests. But I can't help but notice how her gaze hardens every time it falls on Max, throwing glances loaded with resentment.

At the improvised altar, adorned with sunflowers and golden ribbons, my father Robert waits nervously. His hands move restlessly, adjusting and readjusting his tie. By his side, his best friend, who is also Chris and Rory's father and Alex's adoptive father, ready to officiate the ceremony, whispers words of encouragement. There's something incredibly sweet in this scene, in seeing the love and support surrounding my father at this important moment.

I've recently met Alex's adoptive parents, and they are wonderful people, just as they were described to me. I can't wait to get to know them better, but they have already made me feel loved and welcomed.

Suddenly, the music changes and everyone turns towards the garden entrance. Maria makes her entrance, splendid in her form-fitting lace dress. The fabric seems to merge with her skin, creating a timeless elegance effect. Her eyes shine with happiness as she slowly advances along the flower-lined corridor.

I look at my father and see his nervousness instantly dissolve. His eyes light up and a radiant smile opens on his face. In that moment, I see all the love he feels for Maria, and I feel my eyes fill with tears of joy.

As Maria approaches the altar, I feel that this is truly the beginning of a new chapter for our family. And I couldn't be happier.

Chapter 74

Alex

The ceremony has started.

I'm glad Marco and Paola, my adoptive parents, arrived last night. It's always nice to have them around - they're wonderful people I'm genuinely attached to.

I was thrilled to introduce Rosie as my girlfriend. I felt exactly like a son presenting his girlfriend to the family, and having Chris and Rory beside me when I did it helped me feel less nervous and more at ease.

I've always been grateful, and always will be, for this second chance I've been given.

Rosie likes them, and they obviously like her - no need to say how much this makes me happy.

They would have come earlier, but they also manage a ranch and have been busy. Their ranch is smaller and fortunately hasn't been in as much trouble as ours lately, but they've been quite occupied with the births of new foals.

Everything went smoothly... and I can't wait to see them. I'm always excited about new foals - seems I've developed quite the paternal instinct.

Marco is officiating with a charisma and elegance I'm familiar with. His warm voice fills the air, telling the story of how he brought Robert to Italy and how, thanks to him, Robert and Maria met.

His words are touching, full of emotion and meaning.

But as moving as Marco's speech is, I can't fully concentrate on it. My eyes keep returning to Rosie. She's simply breathtaking. The golden dress suits her incredibly, making her red hair and fair skin glow. But it's not just her external beauty that captivates me. It's her smile, the way her eyes shine with happiness for her father. It's the grace of her movements, the sweetness of her gaze. It's everything about her.

While Marco speaks of the love that united Robert and Maria, of how they found each other despite distance and cultural differences, I can't help but think about me and Rosie. How much I would want such a happy ending for us. How much I would love to stand here, in front of everyone, promising my eternal love to Rosie.

But I know it's too early. We've known each other for just over three months, though it feels like a lifetime. Rosie has already made enormous changes for me: she left her country, her job, everything she knew. I can't ask her to take another such significant step now. I need to give her time to settle in, to be sure of her feelings, to be happy here.

Yet, watching Rosie wipe away a joyful tear as her father and Maria exchange vows, I can't help but imagine a future where we are the ones standing there, promising eternal love to each other. It seems I was born just for her, as if every moment of my life had led me to this, to her.

I know Rosie is too good for me. She's so intelligent, so strong, so wonderful. Sometimes I wonder how I got so lucky to have her in my life. And precisely because of this, I don't want to risk ruining everything with a premature proposal. I would never want her to wake up one day thinking she made a mistake by marrying me.

Marco is concluding the ceremony, his words full of hope for Robert and Maria's future. I look at Rosie once more, and my heart fills with love and hope. Perhaps I can't ask her to marry me now, but I can promise myself to love her every day, to make her happy, to be the man she deserves.

As applause erupts for the newlyweds, I take Rosie's hand in mine. She turns towards me, her smile as bright as the sun. And I fully realize that no matter how long it takes, I will wait. I'll wait until she's ready, until she's sure. Because I know Rosie is my future, and I'm not in a hurry to get there. I want to enjoy every single moment of our journey together.

Chapter 75

Alex

After the ceremony, it's time for speeches. Rosie stands up, slightly nervous but with eyes sparkling with emotion. Her speech for her father and Maria is incredibly sweet, brimming with love and hope for their future together. Her words touch everyone's hearts, and I catch Robert discreetly wiping away a tear.

Then comes Aunt Tina's turn. As she rises with an endless-looking rolled-up scroll in her hand, I notice Maria's eyes widening almost imperceptibly. Aunt Tina begins to unroll the parchment, and continues... and continues... and continues. For a moment, I fear her speech might last until tomorrow. But when she starts speaking, all worry vanishes, replaced by growing hilarity.

A few more speeches follow, and then the reception kicks into gear. It's an outdoor event with a country-chic style. The garden is filled with white-clothed tables and golden chairs, perfectly complemented by sunflowers. The food is endless and exquisite—and don't even get me started on the wine. I hover close to Rosie, filling her plate with delicacies. I'm delighted to see her enjoying herself and curious about which of our traditional dishes she loves most.

While we're standing and sipping yet another glass of wine, it's time for Rory's performance. She's a magnificent dancer and captures everyone's attention. I even notice Diego—who I don't think is typically interested in classical dance—watching her intently. Fran whistles and applauds. Lexy films the performance. Val and Chris are lost in their own world of kisses. Max, as always, is... well, Max—with his apathetic expression, standing apart. Yet I notice he's always within eyesight, keeping Lexy in his peripheral vision. Rosie is right—there's something brewing between those two that goes beyond mere dislike.

The performance ends, and it's time for everyone to hit the dance floor. Of course, I waste no time in asking my Rosie to dance. We sway closely together, and I can't help but repeatedly kiss her temple and whisper how much I love her.

Epilogue

Rosie

A year has passed since I decided to move permanently to Sunrise Ranch, and I can barely remember my life before this. I've been living with Alex for twelve months now, and our life together is a sweet flow of days filled with love, tenderness, and passion.

Every morning, Alex rises early but never forgets to prepare my coffee. I've become an early riser too, and the rooster's crow—which I've affectionately named Giliberto—no longer disturbs me. Instead, it's become an integral part of our dawn's soundtrack.

Alex prepares breakfast before heading to work, and I follow him to the porch. We shower each other with kisses, barely able to part, until we reluctantly must. He goes to work with his beloved horses, while I remain on the porch, sipping what I now consider the world's best coffee and writing.

My first book has been published and became a bestseller. I still can't believe how fortunate I've been. I've received excellent reviews, and it particularly impressed Read_with_Amelie, a trending bookstagrammer who continues to talk about it and has sent me the sweetest messages.

Now I'm continuing the series, with endless ideas for creating new stories.

My horseback riding lessons with Alex continue. It makes me smile that my first lesson, which seems like a lifetime ago, was at dawn, whereas now we've agreed to have them at sunset. It's a more convenient hour because Alex goes to work early... but I'll never forget how I felt that first day on the horse, those first brushes with Alex, and the magnificent colors of the dawn sky—which, honestly, I had never truly seen before.

Our lessons have become the most anticipated moments of my days, an opportunity to be together, learn, and enjoy the breathtaking beauty of ranch sunsets.

Life is perfect. Sometimes I wonder if it's all a dream, but then Alex smiles at me, and I know it's real, tangible, wonderful.

The sun begins its daily descent as I make my way to the paddock for our riding lesson. The air is saturated with scents: freshly cut grass, leather saddles, the sweet hint of wild flowers dotting the fields. Alex awaits me, leaning against the fence with a smile that still makes my heart flutter like the first time.

We mount our horses and set off along the trail beside the stream. The sound of hooves on packed earth blends with the gurgling water and the chirping of birds preparing for the night. The sky above is a living painting: streaks of orange, pink, and gold merge into a masterpiece no artist could ever replicate.

Sunset light caresses everything, softening contours and giving an almost magical glow to the landscape. Alex's figure stands out against the fiery sunset sky, his body's outline made even more defined by the golden light. He rides his favorite horse, a powerful black stallion, and together they form an image straight out of a western film.

The muscles of his arms and shoulders flex as he firmly holds the reins, his body moving in perfect synchrony with the horse's. His plaid shirt, sleeves rolled to the elbows, reveals tanned, toned forearms sculpted by ranch work.

His chiseled, masculine face is partially hidden by a cowboy hat, but I can see the determined line of his jaw and the intense gaze of his eyes scanning the horizon. There's a pride in his bearing, a quiet strength emanating from every movement.

I can't help but think how lucky I am.

Suddenly, Alex pulls his horse's reins, stopping. There's something different about him, a tension I've never seen before. He dismounts with a fluid motion, but his eyes betray an emotion I can't quite decipher.

I watch, curious about what he might do next.

Time seems to slow down, each second stretching into infinity. Alex helps me dismount and then kneels before me. Tall grass caresses his legs, and the sun behind him surrounds him with a golden halo, like an angel descended to earth.

With trembling hands, Alex takes my hands.

After placing a tender kiss on each of my hands, he breaks our contact. He looks up at me, and in his eyes, I see an ocean of emotions: love, hope, a hint of fear.

He takes a small box from his pocket and opens it.

Oh my god... I can't believe it.

I don't know whether to jump for joy or cry.

He hasn't spoken yet, but that beautiful, delicate, sparkling ring leaves little to the imagination.

When he speaks, his voice is low and husky, charged with emotion: "Rosie, my love..." He pauses, as if gathering courage. "Would you like to become my wife?"

The world around me seems to stop. The birds' chirping, the stream's murmur, even the wind's breath among the trees—all falls silent. The entire universe reduces to this moment, to this man kneeling before me.

The sun appears to have halted its descent, suspended on the horizon as if it too were holding its breath, waiting for my response. The golden sunset light envelops Alex, making him seem even more beautiful, if possible.

I look into his eyes, deep wells of hope and love, and feel something bloom inside me. It's as if every moment of my life has led me here, to this perfect instant. And in that moment, I know with absolute certainty what my answer will be.

Tears blur my vision, momentarily obscuring Alex. But I don't need to see him to know he's the man with whom I want to spend the rest of my life. My heart overflows with a love so intense it takes my breath away.

And I throw myself into his arms.

The ring falls onto the grass because I'm not the most graceful person in the world... but it doesn't matter. We'll find it.

For now, we'll enjoy an endless embrace and a breathtaking kiss.

Thank you for reading the first romance of the *Sunrise Ranch* series. The story continues with the second book, *Unmasked*. While you wait for its release, enjoy this exclusive sneak peek!

Unmasked

Prologue

The air in the hallway hangs heavy, dense and unmoving, as if suspended between reality and the inevitable. Here, far from the buzz of the floors below, every sound is a hushed whisper. Each step I take on the plush velvet feels deliberate, an unspoken call, a note in the prelude of something unknown. My breathing is steady, controlled, but my heart pounds wildly, like the frantic wings of a caged swan, desperate and relentless, echoing off the shadowed walls.

The corset around my waist is a vice, not just shaping me but whispering who I am tonight—or perhaps who I wish to be.

The mask I wear is my answer. Black as onyx, adorned with sleek feathers fanning out like delicate wings, it clings to my face, leaving only my lips bare, a crimson flame in the sea of dark.

It hides me, yet it frees me.

My dress moves with me, as alive as I feel tonight. Soft feathers skim over my chest and meld into a sheer interplay of fabric that stretches down my arms and waist, a second skin. The short, flirty skirt sways with each step, scandalously daring, far too bold.

A black swan, poised between seduction and destruction, woven into every thread of the fabric clinging to my body.

The corridor's dim light pulses faintly ahead, a crimson glow, like the heartbeat of something dark and alive. It guides me, leading me closer to what waits beyond. Every step feels fated, every turn preordained, as though I'm dancing to a script I've never read but somehow already know. My breaths deepen, a tremor sneaking in as I near the door left slightly ajar.

I push it open gently. The room inside is cloaked in shadow, its walls wrapped in velvet that swallows all sound. The red light is a slow, deliberate pulse, stretching across the floor like liquid fire, casting long, flickering shadows.

And there he is, standing.

His suit is ink-black, swallowing the light, turning it to rippling darkness that clings to him. The silver mask obscures his face, fractured in geometric edges that distort what little I can see. His eyes remain hidden, but I feel his gaze as if it's carved into me—sharp and penetrating, like the blade of a knife.

We do not speak. That is the rule. The unspoken pact.

The silence becomes a third presence, amplifying everything our bodies scream without words.

I take a step closer, my heels breaking the silence with rhythmic defiance. Each sound echoes against the velvet stillness, matching the steady pull between us. I stop just steps away, and for a moment, the world halts. The only sounds are our breaths, slow, deep, synchronized.

Then he moves.

It's slow, almost predatory. His hands rise to meet my shoulders, fingers brushing the edges of the feathers there. They trail down my arms, firm yet unhurried, pausing where my corset grips my waist. A shiver runs through me, impossible to hide.

He feels it; I can tell.

Like Odette surrendering to Rothbart's spell, I yield.

His hands tighten, drawing me closer. The scent of his skin, warm and rich, invades my senses. For a moment, our masks graze, a fleeting touch of cold metal against metal, sending a shock through me. The tension we've built shatters, replaced by something consuming and undeniable.

His lips find my neck, warm and soft, leaving a kiss that lingers just long enough to make me ache. Then he bites enough to send a sharp pulse of sensation racing down my spine, a wave of sensation that melds pain and pleasure into a perfect dance.

His hands glide down my back, loosening the corset just enough. The feathers quiver as my body tightens in response.

With practiced ease, he shifts the corset lower, freeing my small breasts. I let go, my thoughts dissolving into the heat of his presence.

He traces my nipples with his fingertips, cupping my left breast with a reverence that feels like worship.

Tonight, I am beauty incarnate, perfection embodied.

A black swan.

He explores my body with a quiet intensity, his hands mapping every curve as though learning me by heart. Each touch sets fire to my skin, every motion deliberate, a slow crescendo that builds to something I can't contain.

When his lips finally claim my breast, they leave trails of heat, drawing an invisible path only he knows. The room fades away; there is only us, our bodies entangled in the soft, flickering crimson light. The world beyond is forgotten, and this moment becomes our stage.

His hands grip my hips, his breath mingling with mine as my dress falls away, piece by piece, leaving nothing but scattered feathers on the floor and my bare body pressed to his.

Every touch is measured, every move agonizingly slow, almost cruel in its restraint. Our masks brush again as his lips claim mine, but the cold metal cannot temper the fire consuming us. My hands find the edges of his suit, pushing it aside to reveal the warmth beneath. Every layer I strip away feels like another step away from control.

Our bodies meet in the semi-darkness, where every sound is absorbed by velvet and crimson light.

He guides me and gently lays me down on the soft, plush bed.

The faint rustle of a condom is the only reminder of reality before he presses against me. He teases, retreats, then enters with a single, forceful thrust, reigniting the shivers and sparks of his bite, but magnified.

I thought tonight might be my rebirth, but it feels more like the swan's final act, a death so blissful, so perfect, I know nothing else will ever compare.

Every movement is a crescendo, every breath a fragment of passion spilling over. With each motion, I surrender a piece of my soul to this stranger. Time vanishes; the outside world ceases to exist.

Then, as we collapse, breathless and entwined, his hand lifts toward my mask. He pauses, giving me a choice.

This is not part of the pact.

I hesitate. My eyes seek his, but they remain hidden in shadow. I take a deep breath, then nod.

His fingers move slowly, lifting the onyx mask from my face. Cold air rushes in, and with it, the truth.

He freezes. He looks at me as if he's seen a ghost.

In turn, my hands reach for his silver mask. My fingers tremble as I remove it, deliberate and final. When his features emerge in the crimson glow, my heart skips a beat.

It's not a stranger. It's him.

His name forms on my lips, but I don't say it. The eyes staring back at me are filled with shock, confusion and guilt.

We've gone too far. The feathers scattered on the floor can never be gathered again. The dance is over, and the lake is deep.

I don't wait for him to speak. Grabbing my clothes with shaking hands, I flee.

Acknowledgments

I want to extend a heartfelt thank you to my first readers.

A special thanks to my Bookstagram friends who have continuously encouraged me and asked for updates. Your support, advice, and enthusiasm have meant the world to me. None of this would have been possible without you.

Thank you to my partner; I never believed in love until I met you.And to my family, thank you for always believing in me and supporting every project I undertake. Your unwavering faith in me has been my anchor.

II

II

Made in the USA
Las Vegas, NV
31 March 2025